Hatchet Women

by

Nick Sconce

Hatchet Women by Nick Sconce
Copyright © 2016 by Nick Sconce

ISBN 13: 978-0-88100-164-8
ISBN10: 0-88100-164-3
Library of Congress Number: 2016946336

Cover Design by NZ Graphics

Cover Illustration by Natasha Alterici

Published by National Writers Press, Inc.

Library of Congress Cataloging-in-Publication Data

Sconce, Nick
Hatchet Women by Nick Sconce
International Standard Book Number 10: 0-88100-164-3
International Standard Book Number 13: 978-0-88100-164-8

1. Fiction/Contemporary Women
2. Fiction/ Mystery & Detective/Amateur Sleuth
3. Fiction/General
I. Title   2016946336

For N and E

Equality is always worth fighting for. Don't let anyone convince you otherwise.

Chapter One

Mona didn't recognize the shade of lipstick encircling her cigarette butt. She took the next drag anyway and blew the smoke above her head. The embellished cloud in the fall air drifted away from her, downwind, toward the copse of trees that shielded her townhome from forty-three others.

Mona turned and her reflection in the storm door startled her. Her ash blonde hair still looked like a wig or a black ski cap that had accidentally been bleached. *It could have been worse*, she told herself. *It could have turned out peroxide orange.*

She took another drag and sighed more than exhaled. Even with her massive Bono shades, she didn't look anywhere near as awesome as she did before the new assignment. Edie owed her more than the recent salary bump with relocating from Colorado Springs to this forgettable, Twin City burb. Mona still couldn't understand why the hair color change had been such an unflinching requirement for the position. Who cared if there was even one brunette in the event planning division?

Not just any brunette, Mona told herself, a jet-black, head turning hottie with olive skin.

Scratching her eyebrow, she peered closer into the storm door. These damn eyebrows. "Blondes don't usually have as thick of eyebrows as brunettes," she said, mimicking Austin's sensible however shrill voice. The plucking, the redness, the bleaching out and then the coloring. For her flipping eyebrows.

Her beautiful, powerful eyebrows that could disarm any bloke at the bar with the slightest raise, could win any coworker argument with a cocked hint of violence. Now, they were practically white, devoid of strength, and worst yet, full of flirtiness.

Flirters should be shot dead and left where they're found.

Mona took a second to last drag, right above the word Marlboro. Then she rushed herself through the last drag. She couldn't bear the thought of that final dose dwindling to smelly air without first spreading through her lungs. Again, she exhaled upward and turned to face her car and her neighbors' townhomes.

Mona had lucked out with her living situation. On the other side of her quad, where she shared a central wall rather than the circular driveway she now faced, a new cast of Sesame Street child actors were being pruned. They were the color of the human rainbow and, as near as Mona could tell, had corresponding parents on some rotation. No two individuals were ever together in one setting. *And forget about actually supervising your viral, fungal, rat-befriending offspring,* Mona thought.

That was enough to convince her of a second cigarette. Edie and the termination review board could wait. Mona knew the case in totality. She would serve as the sword in that meeting, much like she had in Colorado Springs. If she were ten minutes late, that would give the terminated agent more time to ogle at Austin.

Austin was the calming presence. That was the established dynamic. Edie was the presider, Mona, the executioner, Austin, the comforter and elicitor of confessions. And of course, Becca, the quiet and persistent researcher who was incapable of rendering judgment.

Mona had always been the knife wielder. She loved it. *Never make a move unless you have a clear advantage,* she thought. *And then only if the advantage was clear to you and not your opponent.* Her eyes drifted pensively to her neighbor's window as she rubbed the red lightsaber tattooed on her right shoulder, and from there, as was her habit, she massaged the dark elf brandishing twin scimitars just over her shoulder blade.

The lightsaber had been the obvious selection in Deep Elem, Dallas during a drunken bet with a girlfriend Mona couldn't now name. It had been a tribute to her successful love life. Since junior high, Mona had been an unashamed *Star Wars* freak, not only for the purity of its inherent theology, a perfect marriage and total rip off of transcendentalism, but also for the expansion of her boyfriend marketplace.

By high school, her type had been set. Sure, she'd dated all strands of geeks, nerds, and social misfits. But for Mona, the girls with high standards pining for the quarterback or incessantly writing the point guard's name in flowery diary lettering left them worse than alone. It left them stranded in an underdeveloped sense of what traits made for a suitable companion.

Not so with Mona. For her, the choice had always been clear. You could prowl with the other sharks and never get so much as a smile, or you could set reasonable expectations and have a never-ending supply of boys to date, to make out with, to engage in meaningful conversation, and ultimately to have decent sex with. The nerds and geeks tried harder. Hot man flesh always considered their looks to be the sum total of required foreplay. Swap that out for glasses, freckles, the occasional and unfortunate sprinkle of acne, and a hidden creative streak, and you'd get an acceptable rub-down. Besides, Mona had never met a woman who made out with her eyes open.

Mona stared at the sky. The sun never shone here either. Mona thought of her first day in the Home Office building when she'd overheard someone joke that Minnesota only had twelve good days a year.

Yes, Edie could wait.

Taking another pull from her smoke, she squinted into her neighbor's window. Something had caught her eye. Something wasn't right. The elderly lady across the way had busted her smoking with a shaking finger countless times. Only now as Mona peered into that open window, something was off, much like a black and white photo tilting slightly up and to the left. There was an unmistakable sense of falling out of composition.

The lamp and night stand were in the right places. The fan blades were spinning in their usual lazy pattern. But something was pressing against the curtains. Pressing up and backing off in no discernable rhythm. As though something were dangling and crashing into them.

Did the old lady have a cat? Most old ladies had at least one cat, and this one was a classic shut-in. Other than the pear-shaped woman who picked her up once a week, the lady never went outside. Still, there was plenty of evidence of her living there. The grocery delivery truck pulled up every Thursday evening precisely when Mona would back out of her garage to meet up with some online gamer who just couldn't believe she was as hot as she really was. The oxygen van then came before dawn on Monday mornings. The van's reverse gear alarm always woke Mona. This would infuriate her until she'd remembered she'd bagged the gamer from Thursday but hadn't devised a suitable escape route. Loud, obnoxious BM's usually did the trick, and most would depart, leaving a post-it note with a mobile number, email address, and echoes of intellectual pillow talk from the evening before.

Wait. This is Tuesday, Mona told herself. *The trashcan wasn't there.* On Tuesdays, the old lady's trashcan would appear before her garage without footprints or tracks in the snow. Mona assumed one of her other neighbors pulled it to and from the curb. She scanned the driveway for the neighbors' footsteps in the snowpack. They weren't there either.

Mona squinted past the glare in the window. Whatever was brushing up against the curtain hadn't stopped, but the random frequency had slowed. Then she saw a hand shuffle out beyond the curtain. Mona stepped back and cast her eyes to the ground, not prepared for the judgment from those deep-set, ancient eyes. Then she held her breath and listened for the wrapping at the window telling her the lady had spotted her and would wait well past noon for Mona to show herself. What else did she have to do, watch all four hours of the *Today Show*, waiting for her stories to come on?

But the knock never came. At least not within the twenty seconds Mona could hold her breath before wheezing and bringing on brutal self-judgment. Mona opened her eyes and stepped forward. What was one more shameful finger-wagging? The old lady wasn't standing there, looking down at her. Even in the glare, Mona knew that the wrinkled upon wrinkled face wasn't there. A hand was though. It was the back of a hand, and then a bare arm up to the elbow. Then it disappeared behind the curtain.

Is she hiding from me, too?

Then the hand and arm scooted out with more force than before, weak but identifiable. Something was batting the arm, that freckled, moley, brown-blotched arm.

Mona cleared her steps in one second and slid across the icy asphalt in two others. *Damn these shoes!* Another ridiculous job requirement. She was up the old lady's steps and banging on her screen door. After the clattering echoed off her own townhome, there was silence. A pause where Mona waited to hear thumping footfalls. Nothing.

Mona ripped open the screen door and pounded on the thick front door. "Hey, hey, lady! I'm sorry I don't know your name, but it's Mona from across the way. I'm just checking on you."

The responding silence grew heavier, injecting a stillness, the stillness of vacancy. Mona couldn't feel the old lady inside the house. She couldn't hear the white noise people ignore unless not present: the electricity, the refrigerator, the ice machine, the dish washer, the washer and dryer, the central heat and air. Nothing seemed to be running.

Was she dead then? Had Mona not noticed her passing? Could she be knocking at an empty townhome?

No, the hand and arm belonged to someone, and something was moving them.

Then it came to Mona. She shook off her wedge and backed up to the porch's edge. Propping the screen door open, she aimed her foot just above the door's lock and threw her entire weight behind her leg. Her foot slammed against the door, and as the shock and pain coursed her nerves, Mona felt the door give, a sadistic assurance that if she tried again, it just might burst open.

She lifted her foot again, the pain now exploding hot, searing tears in her eyes. The air kicked up to freeze her foot, making the next attempt that much more excruciating. Mona growled and projected herself forward, focusing all thought and force onto the door. This time it creaked upon impact. Mona screamed in a pairing of frustration and unforgiving nerve response. She could feel her body asking her just what she was doing and why was she doing it.

But Mona knew. To her core, she knew. Shaking her head, she drove out the dead people memories, centralizing her mind on one last kick.

This time, something gummy bent in her foot as it connected with the door. The dead lock broke through the inside molding, and without sound, the door creaked open. Mona fell through the doorway, clinching her teeth and pulling her foot close to her body. What was that? What was in her foot that felt gummy and stretchy and now torn?

She didn't have time. "Hey, lady! Are you okay?"

But the silence still had no answer. And in not answering, it told Mona what she already knew. It was possible to become sick of being right, the torturous treasure reserved only for cynics and the condemned.

Still, she had to make sure. "Hey, lady! I still don't know your name, but it's Mona from across the way. You know, the smoking woman. Do you need to call the cops or something? I'm not trying to break in or steal anything. I'm just worried about you."

Mona pulled herself along the banister leading to the split level's upstairs. The old lady's townhome was the mirror image of Mona's, the floor plan reversed. Even more disorienting when coupled with the dangling arm transfixed in Mona's mind. She steadied herself on her good foot and then distributed her weight between both feet. Her left buckled like her kid sister's baby before bedtime.

Mona hopped up the next step, counting them down to ward off the pain. There must be seven steps up and six down, just like her place. She kicked up her now gimpy foot and leaned on the banister to propel forward.

"Can you hear me?" she screamed. "Have you lost your hearing aids?" Anything would be better than what Mona knew she'd find in the bedroom. Grasping for closet and bathroom doorknobs, she skipped along the wall until she reached the room. The door was ajar.

Inside, the old lady was hanging from a blue tether strap tied to a ceiling stud. She'd cut a hole into the ceiling to find the board.

Mona cussed under her breath, more angry than panicked, horrified, or empathetic. She guided herself along the dresser and then leaned onto the bed and scooted across it to reach the dead woman.

A cat was clawing at the old lady's bare leg. Dark blood seeped out of deep gashes. The cat dove under the bed when it saw Mona, but she'd seen red coating its whiskered face.

"The only good cat is a dead cat," Mona growled.

Mona looked up at the woman. Under the pressure of the trapped blood in her head, her eyes were about to burst from her eyelids. Her swollen tongue had flopped out, turning colorless against the blanching of her face.

"Why tether straps?" Mona asked her, although she knew the answer. The old lady had meant to die. The straps were unforgiving, unflinching. It was a final and complete success.

Mona lifted her left pant leg to examine her now swelling ankle and also to pry her jack-knife from its case velcroed around her lower calf. She'd made a habit of carrying the knife in college when she fantasized about defending herself against some bar idiot who took himself or her half hearted advances too seriously. Mace on a keychain was impractical. By the time a woman fished her keys from her purse, fiddled with the canister lid and aimed the acidic spray, her assailant would have already thrown her in the back of a windowless van bound for some underground human traffic outlet.

Mona's eyes drifted to the other puddles on the floor where the old lady had released her living hold of bladder and bowels.

She shook her head. *Besides,* she thought, *it's much more fun to wield a knife.* Most men cower at the emasculating visual, and stabbing a perp would be far more rewarding than blasting him with pepper spray and listening to him howl. There was a dignified silence in penetrating a man's gut with a blade, a resolved *take-that*. Mona had practiced the maneuver at the bathroom mirror without end, and over time, wearing the knife had become a comfort similar to wearing a bra. It just felt right.

Now came the task of sawing at the strap without losing balance. On her knees now, Mona reached for the ceiling fan to pull herself onto her good foot. The bed wobbled underneath her as she knocked loose dust clumps along the fan's motor. She clinched the blade in her teeth and with her free hand, locked it open along the handle's edge.

This wasn't Mona's first encounter with death. There had been the thirteen-year old neighbor girl when Mona was five, who decided to hang herself in the garage rather than testify against her molesting step-father. The woman who'd spiraled off the highway, losing control of her car, landing in a ditch and having her femoral artery punctured by the broken shards of her rearview mirror. The two teenage boys who'd also lost control of their cars racing along the highway and careening up an embankment in front of Mona's college clunker. She could see them all in stark contrast: swinging arhythmically, face full of resigned despair: breathing in a fit of fury and panic before realizing that as the blood rushed out of her face and through her open leg that she would never catch her breath; a neck so broken that the boy's head sat squarely on his left shoulder.

Now, Mona had another face to add to her accursed collection. This one, though wrinkled, full of that same resolve, despair, and yet pride in accomplishment. If the old lady could open her eyes, Mona knew she'd see her own *take that* facial expression.

The knife was half way through the strap, and Mona realized that she would have to sharpen the blade if she were to have any hope of living out her fantasy. The old woman's weight overpowered the frayed ends, and she plummeted to the floor, landing in her various puddles and creating an ill-gotten mélange of final humanity.

Mona shrugged it off. Her memory would be of the *take that* face, not the bio spatter now caking the inevitable livor mortis.

She felt her pockets for her cell phone, debating on whom she should call first: the cops or Edie. *Let Edie sweat a little,* Mona told herself. *I need to get to a doctor. My foot is still alive.*

She dialed 911 first, gave her location and situation and instructed the dispatcher to be sure to send the ambulance as she needed her ankle looked at.

Ten minutes later, smoking on the dead woman's mirror image porch and imagining just what judgment must have looked like from this angle, Mona phoned Edie and left her a purposely sketchy and warbled message with no apology.

Chapter Two

Seeing Mona's call on her mobile, Edie winced and glanced at her watch. She was seated in the windowless executive conference room with Austin and Becca, waiting for the terminated agent, his attorney, his district manager, and the Minnesota state executive director to enter. All had been planned, and their collective entrance would be coordinated as a subversive tactic, an attempt at intimidation.

The state executive was spineless, far too pro agent, but preferred to look like he could urinate abreast with any man. The district manager was an unfortunate chuckle head who loved to rant about the old days when office politics amounted to women and men cheating on their spouses to celebrate the closing of a big case or simply to relax and orgasm guilt-free after a harrowing day of happy hours. The attorney was there for the billable hours. Sure, he'd put up the occasional objection, but he was really only scouting Edie's credibility. The agent would be an Impressionist's palette of emotions, just under the surface, giving the women a clear idea of what he was feeling but still clinging to his manliness enough not to erupt with confessional details.

This would be Edie's sixty-sixth termination review board. They all reeked the same foul stench of men behaving badly.

Tucking strands of her now dishwater blonde hair behind her ear, Edie internally recited a favorite passage from *Lost Boys*, much like when she pitched high school softball to annihilate background noise. *No two vampires go out the same way. Some scream, some go quietly. Some implode, some explode. But all will try to take you with them.*

Her eyes met Becca's, and she shook her head. No, Mona was not coming.

It didn't matter much. Mona excelled in her actual job so her presence wasn't required. Mona had served the agent the letter notifying him of his immediate company termination. She'd contributed to the minutes and notes in the file and helped Becca coordinate all the evidence and research into the various company systems that had allowed the agent to commit his particular flavor of fraud.

But Edie also knew Becca took comfort in Mona's presence. Becca would never need utter a syllable as long as Mona was in the room.

Austin looked as though she'd been up since four this morning. Scrimping and primping on each hair, plucking nose hairs, sculpting eyebrows, layering makeup, and combining fragrances for her wrists, armpits, neck, cleavage and breath before trying on dozens of tops that when necessary would reveal the right amount.

No, Mona will not be needed, Edie told herself. She'd served her purpose and supported her team. Edie had the proceeding memorized, her opening statement prepped to perfection. Her presentation and review of the evidence would be flawless, her closing arguments and clarification of the company's position executed with surgical precision.

She glanced at her watch again after making sure Becca and Austin were occupied and not looking at her for further guidance. The men's entrance was past due, drifting beyond the customary jock talk at the urinals and now in danger of colliding with disrespect and chauvinism. Edie thought of Mona's favorite sci-fi movie quote for just such times.

—*Your pride will be your downfall.*
—*Your faith in your friends will be yours.*

So maybe Mona's presence was needed. Edie would need to determine what had thrown her schedule into conflict.

Edie had worked with Geoff Siemens forty-eight times in their six months in Minnesota, and knew what to expect from the executive director. This was, however, the first time her team had terminated an agent under this particular district manager, but Edie had read the personnel file on him as well as the file Becca had created. The attorney, well, he was just another attorney. And the agent; he was terminated.

With gusto, chuckles, and a nervous guffaw, the four men entered, the only one choosing to remain silent being the lawyer. It was his performance that mattered most. Siemens was first into the room. He was not entirely unattractive as Edie had acknowledged some time ago, with a basketball player's build, sharp, Greco-Roman facial features and the decision to Bic down his receding hairline. His was one of the few Caucasian heads that justified the decision. Geoff had left his dreams of playing professional ball twenty years ago, having settled for slapping others away from the corporate backboard and trash talking on peasant agents, none of whom came within four inches of matching his height. To Edie's unadmitted disappointment, Geoff had chosen to wear a two-decade-old teal, double-breasted suit with a tie that had no chance to match his ensemble. The suit fitted a stouter, younger man, one who hadn't yet become addicted to running and its side effects, incessantly shaving arms and legs and looking down upon the other ninety-nine percent of Americans who became winded after the first flight of stairs. Just the opposite of his outward projection of glory day revelry, it almost made him the Frosted Mini-wheat version of his former self. *But the old man in me can't even fill in the chest and shoulders of this coat.*

Second onto the scene was Ralph Tomczyk, St. Paul's district manager. Ralph was a bull dog with bowed knees, a gut that defied physical explanation, and jowls that chameleoned with the slightest uptick in blood pressure. His face reminded Edie of the enormous squids on the Discovery channel. His outfit was beyond reproach, especially if he had been an extra on *The Untouchables* with Kevin Costner, and he was fond of showing it off. His suit was monochromed with his shirt. His cuff links were the complimentary bull and bear of the free markets, which might as well have been the dramatic facades of comedy and tragedy. Making his voluminous belly appear gutted, his tie was a blood red. Ralph still abided by the old fashion rules of keeping your silver and gold on separate hands, but he certainly ached for additional fingers, a gold nugget riding one full, hairy knuckle, a lion's head protruding off another, even his two pinky rings were bedazzled with gems rumored to be the birthstones of his children and grandchildren.

Ralph had been a district manager for nearly thirty years and practiced a J. Edgar Hoover form of politics. His past time in the '80s wasn't for the ladies of the Aurora Service Center, or those of Home Office, but rather to acquire photography of them and their satyrs. This made him an Untouchable. This allowed him to finance his lavish needs from greater commissions and sales overrides, starving off his agents without Home Office getting wise.

Walking so closely next to Tomczyk, he could have passed as a servant, came Thomas "Tommy" Illikanien, the terminated agent. With a dress shirt buttoned incorrectly and barely tucked into an unflattering pair of khakis that caused central bulges that would have commanded greater appreciation from Edie and Austin had they been attached to another specimen, Illikanien was a sad stereotype to countless degrees. First, while his build, a galloping six-foot-five-inches accompanied by monstrous shoulders and arms, and his facial features, blond and blue, were consistent with the local Finnish custom of not breeding with mud bloods, he was otherwise the byproduct of a stagnant gene pool where it seemed even scars imprinted onto the genome. His nose and jaw were hideous: large, disproportionate and only lovable through arranged marriage in Michigan's Upper Peninsula. His hair, kinky curly and receding, gave way to a sun-burnt scalp. His diet hadn't slowed with his football playing metabolism, and so his gut would one day rival his district manager's if this termination were somehow impossibly rescinded.

Illikanien's loafers broke wind as he huffed into the room. He threw his eyes toward Edie and then downward until he noticed Austin, who smiled and nodded, concerned for how he was feeling, exactly as she'd been instructed.

Illikanien's attorney lagged four feet behind his client, his body language aloof and disinterested: from his hands in his pants to his dry, sniffling nose, to his tax court lawyer, George

Carlin late '90s ponytail. It was all Illikanien could afford, particular without the policy renewal commissions from his former customer base.

All too easy, Edie thought and cleared her throat. She rose to greet Siemens and Tomczyk, waiting for them to approach her, reversing the typical custom of men rising from their seats to meet ladies. District Manager Tomczyk's fourth chin enlivened with radiant pink flesh, unnerved by the show of feminine dominance. *Very apropos,* Edie thought. The greed monger wasn't turned on by the display.

"Good morning, Mr. Siemens," Edie said. She gripped his hand until his fingertips had whitened.

"Morning, Edie," he said. Siemens had vocal chords that were polished with a cheese grater, the effect of his "between these four walls" tirades with his underlings.

"District Manager Tomczyk, I'm Edie Firebaugh. Good to see you again." She reached for his hand, which softened and surrendered under her squeeze as though his ample palms would blemish from contact with her permanent calluses.

"Wish it were under different circumstances," Tomczyk said at a volume Edie had expected.

District managers preferred slow agent deaths with Hallmark moments: flashbacks to favorite Thanksgiving meals, kids winning spelling bees and little league championships, falling back in love with the wife on a cruise meant for much younger passengers. The district's agents encircling the deathbed, ridiculous heirlooms in hand to be left in the casket: a softball bat from when the agent hit the winning run at the district picnic, the agent's green vase trophy from when he wrote his first six life insurance policies, the pinnacle plaque awarded annually for reaching the highest of multiline sales channel mediocrity.

All managers invariably proposed this scheme, a ninety-day termination for the agent to get his affairs in order and prepare to relinquish those precious renewals he'd built up. Edie and her team, although newly transplanted in totality from Colorado Springs, were seasoned. Compassion and understanding were now *their* tools, not those of the district managers, and were used only when agent suicide was a concern.

When Edie had used compassion in Colorado Springs, it had cost the company thousands and nearly cost her any hope of promotion out of a blacklisted service center. There, she had terminated her first agent, agreeing to the ninety-day version rather than the immediate termination upheld in the agent appointment agreement. While her boss at the time, the Colorado state executive director, supported her decision and approach, over the following three months, the agent's book of business, ghastly unprofitable and labeled deteriorating, vanished to a competitor in a flood of replacement notices.

Becca's quick analysis, although never documented, had saved the team's careers. The business's level of unprofitability had no parallel in the state. Garage addresses and mailing addresses on auto policies were different sixty percent of the time. Rate classes on auto policies were at eighty percent leisure class while the average age of the insured was thirty-five. Half the homeowners' policies had mismatched zip codes and addresses placing them in counties with better experience and cheaper rates. Becca had argued that by allowing the agent to replace the business with other carriers and by avoiding all the pending risk of the agent's misrepresentations, the company had managed to save money.

The result of compassion was the further annuitization of renewals and churned replacements paid out as new business commissions while the district manager schemed to have his agents bid for the policy reassignments. Edie suspected in Tomczyk's case, had she agreed to the ninety-day termination, at his policy assignment auction the bidding would have started at two percent less renewal commissions, kicked back to the district for the assigned policies.

"Wish you could have listened to reason, Edie," Tomczyk said, now finding courage when Siemens hadn't barked at him.

Edie cleared her throat. "Let's get started." She took her seat and left an empty chair between her and Austin. Protocol dictated that Becca sit at the far end of the conference table, isolated from the proceeding to provide an objective write-up for Siemens to approve and submit to Home Office.

As presider of the non-arbitration hearing, Siemens took his seat at the head of the table. Tomczyk, Illikanien, and the attorney took seats in ranking order of importance. Illikanien was surrounded by support.

Siemens leaned forward and began the review. "Ladies and gentleman, we're here today to review the circumstances that preceded the events of Edie Firebaugh's recommendation for Mr. Illikanien's immediate termination from the company and the company's decision to proceed with that recommendation. Now, it's important for all to realize that while Mr. Illikanien has chosen to be represented today, this is in no way a hearing of the court in the state of Minnesota or Hennepin County. The resulting decision of the review board carries no binding arbitration, and that the board's subsequent decision will be either to recommend a rescission of the termination or recommend to continue to support the termination in its entirety…"

Siemens leveled his gaze at Tomczyk. "We are not here to renegotiate the terms of the termination or champion any causes. Does everyone understand?"

Everyone muttered their agreement.

Siemens continued. "Edie Firebaugh will present the review of the company's findings and then Mr. Illikanien will be able to present his understanding of the events surrounding his termination." He motioned to Edie. "Please begin."

Edie checked her team. Leaning forward, Austin had her hands folded in a pleading manner. The look on her face made it apparent to any man that all she wanted was to get up and hug Illikanien. Becca busied herself with her invented short hand, locked in her mind where she received and translated data without personal slant.

"Thank you, Mr. Siemens," Edie began. "I am Edie Firebaugh. I work for the company's internal auditing and special investigations unit. I work closely with our portfolio underwriters, who, as everyone here knows, monitor systemic anomalies on all the agents' technology systems, from commissions, to new business submissions, to pending business and renewals, to folio payment and debit and credit activity.

21

"On September 12th, one of our portfolio underwriters alerted me to such a systemic anomaly involving Mr. Illikanien's three personal auto policies. All three of which had been reinstated after having lapsed for non-payment of premiums for the last five years.

"My team and I then ran a report on which user name, login and password had been used to reinstate these policies and determined that it was in fact Mr. Illikanien's user name, login, and password."

Illikanien bristled and turned red. Tomczyk patted his shoulder and then his hand. Austin looked as though she were about to cry. The heartlight twinkle in the attorney's eyes settled to a burnt ember and then to dead ash. He had no case, just billable hours bundled into a few harassing letters to nameless, faceless company minions.

"On September 28th, I accompanied District Manager Ralph Tomczyk to Mr. Illikanien's office to discuss this matter with him," Edie continued. "Mr. Illikanien postulated several theories as to how this might have happened. First, he proposed that his office manager, knowing the financial strain Mr. Illikanien was under, began reinstating the policies as soon as the lapse notices were sent to her. He suggested that she feared for her job, even his ability to pay her. The agency hadn't grown in ten years since the company had decided to price itself out of the auto and homeowners markets, all to cover the billions of dollars in losses incurred during the black mold housing crisis in Texas. Mr. Illikanien's second postulation was that perhaps someone at the district office, having access to his folios and knowing that he was being driven out of business by the company's decision might have taken pity on him and ensured that he remain insured. Third, and finally, Mr. Illikanien admitted to reinstating his personal policies, claiming that his wife's competitive skiing outings were starting to consume their lives and drain their finances."

Siemens cleared his throat, a clear warning for Edie not to mention the losses in Texas again and to quicken the pace of her review.

"I then asked if Mr. Illkanien had ever reinstated other customers' policies after notice of lapse for non-payment of premiums. He said that he had not reinstated any other policies. I then produced the report that made it apparent that under his user name, login, and password, every auto policy with the last name Illikanien as the head of household had been reinstated after notice of lapse for non-payment of premiums for four years and four months, the most recent coinciding with his own last reinstatement."

The agent's nostrils were at full flare. Tomczyk kept his hands off his agent. The attorney was counting his money in his head, and Austin's eyelids were puffy and pink.

Only Siemens and Becca were unmoved.

Edie pressed forward. "I then asked Mr. Illikanien if he believed this to be fraud. He said that he did not believe that. I asked him if he believed this to be embezzlement. He said he did not believe that. I then assured Mr. Illikanien and District Manager Tomczyk that the company, however, did in fact regard this practice as both fraud and embezzlement, which called for Mr. Illikanien's immediate termination. I then notified Mr. Illikanien that I had pursued the recommendation for such immediate termination, and that a member of my team was waiting to deliver his letter of termination, which she then did."

"Was District Manager Tomczyk aware of this, that your team was there to hand the agent his termination letter?" Siemens asked.

"Not to my knowledge," Edie said.

"So you did not notify him of this when you scheduled the meeting at Mr. Illikanien's office?" he continued.

"No, I did not."

"Why did you decide not to inform District Manager Tomczyk of your intentions and how you were going to represent the company that day?" Siemens's voice had been rising with every question, but Edie had played this role with him. His motive was to beat up Home Office first to show the field, through Tomczyk, that he still favored agents over bureaucracy. He would then invite her to place him into a winless situation where there was no alternative but to uphold the termination. It reeked of amateur politics.

"I decided not to inform the district manager because this district manager has a history of pleading for his agents and attempting to negotiate resignations or longer terminations when the agent appointment agreement clearly spells out the terms and conditions of agent termination as well as the nature and scope of certain breaches of contract," Edie said.

"And did District Manager Tomczyk attempt to negotiate a longer termination or a resignation in this instance?" Siemens fired back.

"Yes, he did," Edie replied. "He informed me that he had already accepted the agent's letter of resignation and willful termination on ninety-day notice on behalf of the company."

"Did you accept this resignation on behalf of the company?" Siemens asked Edie.

"No, I did not," she said. "The agent appointment agreement specifically states that in cases of embezzlement, under no circumstances, shall an agent be allowed to resign. Further, the company is obligated to report the matter to all pertinent legal authorities including the Division of Commerce in Minnesota, which houses the state's Division of Insurance."

"But the district manager had already accepted the agent's letter of resignation," Siemens said.

"Under the district manager appointment agreement, the district manager is expressly denied the authority to accept the letter of resignation on behalf of the company. While he may be required to obtain the physical letter as circumstance permits, he has no expressed or implied authority to officially accept the resignation of his agents," she explained.

"So District Manager Tomczyk is also in violation of his appointment agreement for having accepted this agent's resignation?" Siemens asked.

Edie shook her head. "He acted outside of his authority. He did not actually accept the resignation of this agent. I corrected his misunderstanding of his own appointment agreement shortly after our meeting at Mr. Illikanien's office."

Aside from his deli tablecloth checkered neck, Tomczyk looked ten pounds lighter from having received his absolution.

"And so as the district manager had no authority to accept the resignation and ninety-day termination of Mr. Illikanien's agent appointment agreement, it was not binding in this situation?" Siemens asked.

"That's correct. The binding documentation here is the termination letter, exhibit six, that called for the agent's immediate termination on September 28th," Edie said.

"Do you have any more to add to your review, Ms. Firebaugh?" Siemens asked.

Edie smiled at him and shook her head. "No, that concludes my review."

Siemens turned to Illikanien and his attorney. "You are now free to present your understanding of the circumstances surrounding your termination."

As the lawyer rose from his seat, the agent's eyes crumpled, his shoulders heaved, and spittle erupted from his mouth. His weeping scared Edie. She hated seeing huge men cry.

"If it was so wrong, why did the company build it into the system for the agents to reinstate their own policies?" he bellowed. "I'm not the only one who does this. This is just a witch hunt. I'm suing all of you because you owe me three months' commissions and renewals because my district manager accepted my resignation and because he told me he could do that for me."

Chapter Three

A ustin stared into Thomas Illikanien's reddened face. She wanted to speak to him, to tell him to keep breathing. But she knew she couldn't. She'd already gotten too many warning looks as they left the conference room. Edie had given her the scheduled glance, attempting comfort and understanding. Siemens, when he did make eye contact, had thrown her a distasteful if not threatening glare as though she were a bona fide agent advocate. It was the look senators and congressmen gave each other when someone brought up the altruistic reason to insure someone's life: widows and orphans. Mr. Tomczyk and the attorney never brought their gazes above her breasts, so she'd accomplished her wardrobe mission with them. Thomas Illikanien would not look at her, and Austin knew why.

She reminded him of his wife, which made him think about his children. Austin had never met the woman, had no idea as to whether she looked like the agent's bride, but she could read the hazy, distant gaze well enough. A faithful man's eyes drifted into a sea of memory as soon as he'd given her the once-over. Sure, she was pretty, bright, big-eyed, curvy. Of course, she had recognizable flaws like the babyish double chin that refused to melt away no matter how much time she spent at the gym. Or the scar above her left eyebrow. Or the pinkish hue that sprinkled her forehead and chest, a thunder cloud of ever-present acne buds that three soaps and two crèmes had no effect on.

Thomas Illikanien had started where most men start and cascaded downward: face, boobs, butt. It was as automated and natural as breathing: face, boobs, butt, breathe, face, boobs, butt, blink, face, boobs, butt, swallow. This meant nothing, this was looking for a favorite menu item at a restaurant. This was ignoring the specialty the server mentioned. This was not cheating.

Thomas Illikanien, unlike most men, thought of his wife, made the immediate comparisons to her form from Austin's in his mind, and that is where his fidelity kicked in. His mind, as simple and as beautiful as it was, jumped from this animalistic appraisal of scarce resources to memories of their most recent love making, the last time he told her he loved her, the last bottle of wine they shared. Austin didn't need to know if she looked like his wife. She probably didn't have any common features beyond their golden blonde hair.

From there, he would think of his children, most likely daughters, given the almost shameful furrow of his brow and glint when he thought of them so closely after his eyes had plummeted the contours of Austin's form.

Now, Thomas would not look at her, though it wasn't due to guilt. His shame was heading in the right direction, down the predictions of the short-term future. Thomas Illikanien was thinking of how he'd tell his wife he'd been terminated from the company after having devoted ten plus years of service. Most terminated agents waited until after their termination review boards to admit to their wives that their careers with the company were over.

Thomas was no different. He lacked the coating of resolved steel a woman could lacquer her husband with, a fresh layer of justified anger that empowered him to fight for his family. It was not in his shoulders, hanging formlessly from his broad chest. It was not in his back, which had once arched with athletic pride as much to mitigate his expanding mid-section. It was not in his stance as he rose from his chair and walked, alone, out of the conference room, leaving his former district manager and state executive to their whispered discussions, refusing to pay his attorney the respect of a sideward snarl. No, Thomas Illikanien had not told his wife and kids that he was unemployed, out of business, with nothing left but his licenses, which might now be in jeopardy because of his actions.

Another thought stung Austin, her ears reddening, as she walked out of the conference room, falling in line behind Edie and allowing Becca to take up the rear. Embezzlement had been the grounds for this termination. Thomas would not be entitled to any of his contract value. An agency of his size with over a thousand policies combined with his years of service was the value of his career contract with the company. This allowed the company to buy back the business after normal termination or retirement. The contract value would be in excess of two hundred and fifty thousand dollars.

Austin shook her head. The agent could have easily taken out loans on his contract through the company's credit union to pay for his policy premiums during times of hardship. The interest would have been half a regular bank's unsecured loan.

Instead, Thomas Illikanien had chosen to reinstate his policies and those of his extended family for several years without processing any payment of premium. Even if he decided to pursue the balance of his contract value against the repayment of these premiums, Austin knew how the company worked. It was more important for the company to keep the two hundred and fifty thousand than to prevent the agent from ever working in the industry again.

Austin wanted to tell Thomas Illikanien this, to tell him to tell his wife that they needed to walk away from the lump sum unless they were prepared to suffer a long battle. Taking the chance that the Division of Insurance would not pursue criminal charges against him was too great. But that was not her place. It could cost her her job. Thomas Illikanien was too far down the basement level corridor.

Ahead of her, Edie slowed her pace. Austin knew her boss didn't want to share the elevator with Siemens, who expected her to accompany him in showing the district manager and former agent out of the building.

Siemens and Tomczyk were struggling to keep up with Illkanien's giant, Finnish strides. Even his attorney was scampering between the other three.

As Siemens stepped into the elevator, he was surprised that Edie and her team weren't directly behind him. With a head shake and a downcast look, he let the doors shut.

Edie cleared her throat, something Austin thought she did too often.

"Are you okay?"

Austin squeezed Edie's forearm. "You don't have to ask that every time. I'm fine."

"It's just that I know you, well, feel for them," Edie explained.

Austin found herself torn with Edie's attempt at maternal concern. It was fake, fake in her shifting eyes that wanted so desperately to roll at having to descend to such a level of weakness, fake in her clinched jaw and stammering, fake in her crossed arms and cocked hip, exuding argumentative readiness. But Edie *had* recognized the need to ask, the need to seem compassionate and sensitive, the need to displace her motivational anger that enabled her relentless pursuit of the bad guys.

"I'm fine, Edie. Really," Austin said.

"But you were thinking about how Illikanien would tell his wife that he's terminated," Edie said.

"You know me too well," Austin said with a smile.

Becca approached, hugging her portfolio to her chest, her natural reaction around Austin. She'd seen the diminutive woman hug her collar as though they were in Victorian England and Becca were a House of Lords member's wife suffering a glance at the prostitution the industrial revolution brought to her fair city. Austin never failed to appreciate the varied and disparate emotional responses her appearance evoked in both men and women.

"Whatever money he saved them stealing from the company was surely spent within his family to maintain their lifestyle," Becca said.

"With all the rate hikes over the last few years, what if he were simply trying to keep up appearances?" Austin said.

"Rate increases are a good thing," Becca retorted. "They drive off unwanted business and increase the agents' and district managers' renewal commission, sometimes doubly compensating them for the loss of policies in force."

"We've been over this, Austin," Edie said.

"I know, but you two never realize that agents like to sell, they love to sell. It's what they do, it's how they measure themselves. They can't respect themselves or the company even though they're getting larger folio statements, if they can't find a way to sell something," Austin explained.

"So fraud and embezzlement are clear alternatives?" Becca asked.

Austin shook her head. "I never said that. These guys have a relationship with the company. Sometimes it's a paternal bond, like with the old guys who think they helped build the company and make it what it is, sometimes it's more maternal like when they refer to it as Mother Company."

"I don't see your point," Becca said.

Edie squinted at Austin. "Are you suggesting they're punishing their mothers by behaving so badly, stealing, lying, cheating?"

"In a certain way, yes," Austin said.

"And we're supposed to be accountable to this twisted, neurotic tendency?" Edie asked.

"Not accountable, mindful, aware," Austin said.

"Would that make the job any easier?" Becca asked. Her tone was genuine. Becca remained clueless about the stress and considerable emotional strain it took to terminate agents.

Edie turned to Becca. "No, it would not."

"Thomas Illkanien has a wife and children to support," Austin said.

"Which is why he should have made better choices," Edie countered.

"It's not his family's fault that he's terminated," Austin said.

"All the honest agents have spouses and kids, too," Becca said. "And when someone frauds the company, it impacts our profitability, which restricts our ability to maintain a competitive position in the marketplace, which in turn, makes it harder and harder for the agents to sell products."

"Becca is spot on," Edie said. "We're defending the honest, ethical agents, and their ability to continue to be successful, which helps them better provide for *their* families."

"I sympathize with how difficult it will be for this agent to go home and admit his failures, his bad decisions, and his ruined career," Austin said. "Good people are still capable of making horrible choices."

"Good people don't steal money from the company they work for," Edie said.

Turning from Edie and Becca, Austin pushed on the heavy door to the staircase, which made her wrist ache a little.

She wasn't growing frustrated with her boss. Austin knew that they were playing out the melodrama for Becca's benefit. This was core to the group dynamic that had in part evolved and in part been decided upon when Austin joined the team.

When Austin was introduced to the other three now bottle blondes, Edie, Becca, and Mona were already sealing their relationships. Edie had taken on assignments as the hatchetwoman, Becca was in portfolio underwriting, and Mona worked in the internal marketing department with Austin. While Mona worked in policy reassignment, Austin was an information management systems rep. She'd supported the multiline channel's antiquated proprietary technology platform.

Austin was no computer geek, and she never needed to be. In her team within a team, she was evaluated on how many passive marketing systems they persuaded agents to use. All of these systems were Home Office creations, and some were actually quite beneficial from a cross-selling perspective.

The stairway to the next elevator bank was windowless. Austin missed the sun, which made her think of her yellow file folder. When she needed a boost from the flood of negative emotions, she'd review her sunshine file. John Taylor, Edie's boss, had suggested the sunshine file to the entire regional office at the last annual justify your job conference in Colorado Springs.

During that hellacious week, managers and supervisors from personal lines to commercial to life and annuity would undergo the torturous grilling on why goals weren't achieved followed by a scalpel precision analysis of what exactly made each individual his or her own unique brand of failure.

Internal marketing played double duty, planning the entire event down to the meals, hotel and travel accommodations, as well as individual gift baskets for each berating senior VP that ranged from the finest wine Colorado offered to vegetarian snack packs to diet sodas kept at exactly thirty-six degrees Fahrenheit to an assortment of Ramen noodle packets, including the elusive barbecue shrimp.

Bob Neubeck, the senior IMS rep on Austin's team, a man who'd been exposed to so much Agent Orange in the Vietnam War he was literally rotting from the inside out and suffered horrible bodily stenches unrivaled by the natural however unpleasant odors of humanity, was always assigned the grueling task of finding separate, paid in cash hotel rooms so that certain executives could continue their infidelities with their not so anonymous mistresses, married regional office lifers who were assured job security and spot bonuses for their services.

Austin always felt sorry for Neubeck, not only for having to facilitate such debauchery, (he had been the most faithful man in the entire regional office even before his afflictions took him out of contention for affairs), but also for the way the two other IMS reps treated him. Of course, he was untouchable now that he knew exactly who was putting it in whom. Sure, he was the most unreliable co-worker in the history of unreliability. But Austin thought of him as belonging to the most elite of American heroes. Instead of dying on the battle field or in the jungle or even a week later from complications, Bob had been dying a little bit each day for the last forty years.

Janey and Patricia, the other two IMS reps, were simply jealous that he was above termination. They were also jealous that he knew who was illegally fornicating with senior management.

Austin had relocated at just the right time. She had been out-performing the other two lady IMS reps in small part due to her dedication and ability to travel to the farthest outreaches of the region's territory (Jackson Hole, Wyoming, Fargo, North Dakota, and Sioux Falls, South Dakota) and in large part to, breast sizes being eerily equal, Austin hadn't yet caked on years of office cafeteria comfort food.

Her sunshine file was living proof of her success and had been the one positive take away from John Taylor's infamous speech where he had attempted to inspire the regional staff to make daily deposits into the agency force's emotional accounts to balance the major withdrawals the years of bad Home Office decisions had taken.

Smirking at the memory, Austin zipped past the other cubicles on their floor, noticing more from smell than sight that Mona still hadn't made it in. She avoided smiling at Phil, the chop licking buffoon who routinely asked her out, but patted Jerome's shoulder as he made his mail delivery rounds. At the last turn, she hoisted her chest outward as she passed the other bottle blondes in the event planning department. Each of the three actual event planners had dyed their hair four years ago in a sign of solidarity and team building. Austin hadn't cared much about the change. She'd experimented with several hair colors since high school, having been a brunette, a redhead, a pinkhead, a jet black, a comic book purple, and most recently auburn.

Mona had had the most beautiful naturally dark brown, nearly black hair. Becca had had a forgettable light brown, but it had never been dyed. Edie had been a pale-skinned, freckly, piggish nosed Irish girl, so the dishwater shade had little impact on her inability to attract man.

The dye had burned Austin for different reasons though. She'd struggled with getting men to look her in the eye. Sure, have your ogle, but then take her seriously. Now, with golden blonde hair, well, men became even more predictable.

She threw herself into her chair and ripped open her file drawer. Yanking out the obnoxiously yellow plastic file folder, she thumbed through her collection of successes and accolades. She would have loved a cigarette, or to read through the congrats emails and thank you notes while soaking in her tub when the things that went bump in the night fell into their own deep sleeps. Instead, she had to settle for reading at work.

Storming back to her desk had triggered an anger she'd denied for the last six months. They weren't taking her seriously.

They'd forgotten she hadn't been a blonde all along. They were playing her as the bimbo instead of valuing her perspective, which might soon be sorely needed if one of these agents busted out a wrongful termination law suit. All a defense attorney had to do was portray the evil insurance company jumping to a rash, profit protecting decision and make closing arguments portraying the crying faces of the agent's kids to win a judgment of hundreds of thousands of dollars.

But Austin could play the game. One day, they would remember her contributions. One day, when Becca wasn't able to save them from a misinterpreted technicality, Austin would bail them out with a quiet settlement rather than a bloody lawsuit because she'd shown the agent a smattering of compassion.

Someone knocked at her cubicle wall.

Austin glanced up and saw Edie's forehead.

"Yes?" she asked.

Edie stepped into view. "Are you really mad?"

Austin covered the sunshine file with crossed forearms. "What do you think?"

Edie took a deep breath, which accentuated her small frame. "I think they're still intimidated by you, Austin."

"Who?"

"You know who," Edie replied.

"They need to get over it," Austin huffed. "We're on the same team."

"I know, but you're so overwhelming with how much you have to offer. It's easy to become jealous."

"Not my problem," Austin said. "Look, Edie. We agreed to the dynamic before we left the Springs. I know I don't have the experience you three do terminating agents and conducting investigations, but you assured me that the humanistic perspective would be valuable."

"It will always be," Edie said.

"Then why do I feel like they don't respect me? And why do I feel stupid for asking that?" Austin said.

"Give it time," Edie said.

Austin rolled her eyes. "And play the bimbo until they come around?"

"I didn't say that," Edie said.

"You didn't have to, Edie. In the meantime, I still have to play inferior to their experience," Austin said. "It makes me feel so tragically Shakespearian."

Chapter Four

Mona's townhome wasn't far from Edie's church. Stopping by could be an excuse for being in the neighborhood dropping off a donation to Feed All God's Children, or when pressed for the truth, going to confession, which Edie valued as central to her sanity, especially when the confessional schedule coincided with a termination review board proceeding.

Edie parked her Rav 4 in Mona's driveway. There was no indication that Mona was home, but given the series of voicemails, Edie knew her executioner was in no condition to hit the bars. No, she would be holed up in darkness, enshrouded in psychedelic 60s music or its annoying resurgence in late 90s house trance.

Edie only hoped Mona was on her first bottle of red wine and not her second or the dreaded third.

Tucking errant strands of this foreign hair behind her ears, Edie steeled herself. Mona would expect a lashing, licks from the corporate belt (or taken from Edie's childhood, switches from the weeping willow in her grandparents' front yard).

The trees canopying Mona's front yard were already losing leaves. Edie remembered their summer white flower petals. An unnerving thought caressed Edie's mind, one that aided and abetted her subconscious unwillingness to deal with her colleague's new yet fatally recurring experience.

She welcomed the stream of consciousness that brought her mind closer to Mona's. Plants relied on surrogates for their reproduction, if not love making. Budding flowers opened in Shakespearian poetic bloom (to steal a phrase that had resonated, no, cavorted in her mind since Austin had bombed eloquence on her earlier this morning) to lure insects, the most pragmatic of all evolutionists. The bugs were looking for food, yet became sullied when fed the flower's pollen, which was then deposited into a neighboring tree's blossoms to prevent incest.

Would humans ever devolve to this outsourced mating ritual? Edie wondered. She needed a cigarette but had sworn off them since relocation, not that the northern Mid-west culture supported such health. Would humans eventually rely on sexy drones to perform the act of love making to a voyeuristic couple of sedentarily paralytic breeders before accepting the saucy Petree dish of biological goo necessary to bring a new life into the world?

It was a question Edie could ask of Mona.

Mona was a Star Wars fanatic and a closet Trekkie.

Edie knew she could be empathic, one who could chameleon her frame of mind to that of her team members.

Austin and Becca weren't much of a challenge. One wanted to love than be loved, to understand than be understood, to console than to be consoled. The other appreciated logical, computer language direction, a friend for basic input and output.

Mona, on the other hand, was a cynic. She was able to put the proverbial bullet in anyone's head, relying on her commitment to obedience, to following orders, to fill in moral gaps for the social impact of murder. But there was more to Mona. Every cynic was a wounded idealist.

She shut her eyes and prepared herself. She would knock on Mona's door, reach out to the cynic, and when things got thick, bum a cigarette from her enigmatic friend. Though she would be met with ridicule and scorn, Edie knew Mona would lonesomely appreciate her visit. It would prevent Mona from sliding into a cavernous despair detrimental to the team.

What was it about confession that exuded the limits of Edie's mental vocabulary? Was the sponge of her absolved soul paired with the intrinsic need to dispel such fantastic diction?

She needed a drink. She needed a cigarette. She needed to forget how freaking smart she was for a moment or two.

Edie needed to be a friend. More than that, she needed to be a listening friend, which she was ill-equipped to be. Maybe the first tool was presence, the willingness to be there, however ignorant and unable to comfort she really was.

Get out of the car, Edie. Grow a pair.

She slammed her car door harder than necessary to warn Mona and her ankle-biting death mutt of the impending doorbell ring.

As she stomped up the steps, Edie realized that she had to transform herself, to divorce herself of her corporate sheath and to become a woman once again. *If only for the sake of her friend. If only.*

She rang the doorbell. The ancient toy dog flew into a fit of desperate protection, which must have sounded magnanimous to canine ears but was wincing, contrived, and pathetic to humans.

Drop the big words, Edie. You don't need to alienate the woman. Drop the defense. You aren't here to protect yourself. You are here to... to just be here.

"Go away, Edie!" Mona hollered from deep within the townhome. "I know it's you!"

"Just came from the church. Thought I'd check in," Edie replied to the shut door.

"Isn't that special?" Mona said, mimicking the Church Lady from *Saturday Night Live.* "Did you visit with the priest, or as I call him... SATAN?"

"Very funny," Edie said. "Let me in, will you?"

"Why? You're just doing your managerial job," Mona slurred.

Edie surmised that Mona was into her second bottle of wine. "I would have come over even if we didn't work together."

Sharp silence persisted.

"Even if I'd fired you for being so one dimensional," Edie added.

That motivated a decrease in stereo volume, a clomping down the split-level stairs, and a few choice curse words.

Mona tore open the door.

Edie was taken aback, having the wind sucked out of her with the violent greeting. She felt her arms rise to brace herself.

"Yes," Mona demanded. "You've seen me. Now what?"

"Can I come in?"

Mona sighed and gripped the door handle to steady herself. "You're here, aren't you?" Turning, she left the door open. It was the only invitation Edie would get. "Don't mind the smell. I've been ripping them all day. Doc says it could be a side effect of the pain meds."

"You're on pain meds and drinking?" Edie asked as she entered the foyer leading upstairs. She also entered a cloud of noxious fumes and coughed. "I thought painkillers were supposed to back you up. You know, get your hopes up and not deliver."

"Hence the gas," Mona said. She plopped down on her recliner and covered herself in a throw blanket. "It promises something more substantial. Almost like really buff, masculine acting gay men. They flirt for the systems check and aren't remotely interested in delivering the package. It's the same with painkiller gas. Oh, yeah, it spells relief, but results in malnourished product, throwing back to elementary school stalls." She covered her mouth. "Oh, wait. Were you Catholic girls more regular or less? I can't remember if constipation was considered suffering for Christ, or a testament of chastity."

Edie took a seat on the couch opposite Mona's recliner.

"You know I wasn't cradle Catholic, Mona."

"That's right," Mona said with a huff. "You were hoodwinked by a boy who never committed."

Edie shook her head. "It's a commitment to God, not to another person."

Mona rolled her eyes. "Whatever. I'd offer you a drink, but I only have this bottle and one more unopened."

Edie looked at Mona's foot, carefully camouflaged under her blanket "Should you be drinking on painkillers?"

Mona flipped her off. "The pain is minimal. The pain killers are responsive. But they don't account for the emotions. They don't deaden *that* pain. That's where the wine comes in. Prescription drugs deaden the biology. Wine deadens the soul. Isn't that why you call it the blood of Christ?"

"Do you want to talk about it?" Edie asked. She wasn't here to be the senseless Voodoo doll Mona could butcher.

"'Do you want to talk about it?'" Mona mimicked, impersonating Edie's voice with insulting precision.

"Do you?" Edie replied.

"I'd rather converse with merlot," Mona replied.

"It looks like you've already had a very long conversation with it," Edie said and gestured to Mona's wrap. "How's your ankle?"

"Torn ligaments," Mona said.

"How did that happen?"

"When I was kicking in her door." Mona studied her glass, dipping a finger into the red wine and rubbing it around the rim, all to avoid looking at Edie. The ash blonde strands of Mona's hair tickled her glass. Her dark complexion was at odds with the color just as her deep feelings for her dead neighbor warred against her need to remain aloof, brittle to the point of cracking.

"No one should have to go through what you did, Mona," Edie said.

"But people still need to kill themselves," Mona growled. "They still need to be found. Even after they die."

Edie leaned forward. "Are you doing alright?"

Mona winced then snickered. "What do you think, Edie? I've messed up my foot, I'm on painkillers that I'm chasing with wine, and my neighbor of six months is dead."

"Is there anything I can do?" Edie asked. "Is there anything you need?"

Mona huffed and took a long swig from her glass. "I suppose I need you to sit there and take up space, and steal the air in my townhome, and remain uninvited."

"So you want me to go?" Edie asked.

"I didn't say that," Mona said. "I said I need you to sit there, uninvited, take up space, and suck up all my air."

"How many pills did you take before you started drinking?" Edie asked.

Mona rolled her eyes. "Don't worry. I waited for them to wear off before I opened the bottle. I took one at the hospital and then one when I got home. That was early this afternoon."

"Just making sure," Edie said.

"I know," Mona muttered.

Outside the sun was sinking behind the trees that shielded Mona's house from the others in the area. Its vanishing light bled into the burgundy curtains in Mona's living room and kitchen, painting their faces the color of beets before darkening them to a color closer to the merlot.

In the silence of creeping night, Edie noticed that she'd been off her prediction. Mona wasn't listening to house trance. Trickling from her basement's stereo, The Moody Blues' *Nights in White Satin* had been on repeat for as long as she'd been there.

Mona propped up her injured foot on her recliner's leg rest. "The wine is in the kitchen. The glasses are in the hutch downstairs, but there are also tumblers in the cabinets if you don't feel like having Nala attack you."

"Nala?"

"My dog," Mona said and motioned to the floor.

"Oh, that's right," Edie said. "Nala."

"She's losing her hearing, and her eyes aren't so good," Mona said. "About all that's still strong is her sense of smell."

"How long have you had her?" Edie asked.

"Since high school. My dad gave her to me right after I saw those two idiots get thrown from their Mustang racing another moron in a Camero," Mona explained.

"Was that the last time you were around dead people?" Edie asked.

It was an easy secret to keep for her friend. Mona, during a drunken tirade after they had completed four termination review boards in the same week, had admitted to Edie that she'd been around too much death, especially people who weren't related to her.

It was like she was a cop, Mona had said. Then she'd made Edie swear secrecy, not wanting the women in the office to think

she was some Goth freak and not wanting to scare away men
with rumors about curses.

"Do you need another glass?" Edie asked.

"Thought you'd never ask, boss," Mona said and handed her
the empty glass as Edie rose, stepped over the elderly dog, and
headed for the kitchen.

Mona had spent some money on the kitchen and bathrooms.
She'd replaced the orange, particle board cabinets with a warm
mahogany, retiled the floor in varying shades of gray stonework
and thrown granite on the counters. With the black appliances,
the kitchen soaked up most light but reflected a dull glow from
lighting under the cabinets.

Edie once asked her where she'd gotten the money for the
updates. Mona had said that her father liked to waste his money
on his daughters, the guilt fed manifestation of a lapse in
judgment that led to him cheat on Mona's mother. According to
Mona, she still didn't know her father, but his money was a good
substitute for twenty-minute phone calls every other week, and
vague hints that he was coming to see her soon. Edie didn't
know where the man lived.

She found the tumbler easily enough. Edie was no wine snob
but didn't intend to have more than two drinks. She filled
Mona's glass to the brim though, finishing this second bottle and
knowing she'd be expected to open the third.

"Did the police ever get in contact with her family?" Edie
asked, returning to the living room.

Mona reached out her hand for her glass and shook her head.
"I'm not sure. They certainly kept me well past my time, asking
me questions as if I knew anything about her."

"What was her name?" Edie asked.

Mona's face folded into itself and she wiped away tears as
soon as they formed in her eyes. "I don't know. The ambulance
driver told me. They had records of coming to her house a year
ago when she'd fallen in her shower. But I can't remember. It's
like I'm blocking it out. I have no memory of it."

"There's probably a good explanation for that," Edie said.
"Psychological trauma."

"I just don't understand why this keeps happening to me," Mona said. "The girl in the rent house up the road from where we lived killed herself the night before she was scheduled to testify against her molesting step-dad. I found her first. I was friends with her little sister, who thank God, the animal hadn't touched yet.

"And that woman when I was commuting back from college who just lost control of her car. You know, the one who's rearview mirror shattered and freakishly severed her femoral artery? I was the first one there, too. I was right behind her when she spun into the ditch.

"Then the two idiots who had their necks broken when their car flipped on that highway race, I was the last car they passed before they lost control," she continued. "They were a mile ahead of me by the time I caught up with them and saw them dead. I was the first then, too. I was just on my way back from a friend's house. She lived out in the boonies. I wasn't five miles from home.

"And now, the old woman suicide," Mona said. "I was the first there again. I had to cut her down. Her cat had scratched gashes in her leg and was licking up the stream of blood when I got there." She shook her head in disgust. "There is no good cat alive."

"You're asking why me," Edie said.

Mona nodded. "I've been asking myself that for two decades."

"I don't know, Mona, and I won't hazard a guess," Edie said.

Mona wagged a finger at her. "See, that's what I like about you, Edie. Deep down, you're not so goal-oriented. Under the corporate ego, you know when to shut up. You know when not to offer advice that makes you sound like an idiot or a bit character in a Hallmark movie."

Edie nodded. "I just know what I'm not good at."

"Exactly." Mona downed her wine in two gulps and made circles in the air with her empty glass. "Open the final bottle, my captain."

Edie rose again, having only sampled her drink. "I'm not your captain."

"Sure you are," Mona said. "You're here, aren't you? I don't see Austin, and I sure don't see Becca."

"I was worried about you," Edie said from the kitchen. The waiter's corkscrew was next to the final bottle. Soon, it would be open and breathing.

"You're supposed to worry about me," Mona said. "You're my boss. You're all about strategy, guidance, and leadership. I just like shooting bad guys. You help me prioritize the ranking of bad guys and the number of bullets."

"You're being very generous, Mona," Edie said as she returned to the living room with Mona's refill. "You're sure you don't need anything else?"

"Not unless you can invent time travel and give me five minutes with the old lady," Mona said. She gulped down half the glass and winced again.

"You think you could have saved her life?"

"Not at all," Mona said. "In some ways... well, let's just say I respect the look on her face when I found her. There was a pride of accomplishment I could relate to. No, I just wish I would have cared more. Just enough time to say hi, to say who I was, to ask her who she was, how long she'd lived there."

"Wasn't this the same old lady who'd give you looks when you smoked on your porch?" Edie asked.

Mona finished her glass. "Yes, but now she's dead, so there's no telling yourself you'll go back tomorrow and do all the things you know you should have done before. Just invent time travel, Edie. Let me go back in time and introduce myself. Maybe then I could remember her name."

Chapter Five

A s Austin helped the actual event planners finalize the decorations, lighting, and music for the costume party, she didn't feel guilty. She was disappointed though that her offer to help arrange the strands of orange and purple lights didn't even win her a glare from Edie, Mona, or Becca.

Despite the ridiculousness of camouflaging the four hatchetwomen within the event planning department, Austin liked planning soirées. The looks from agents, district managers, and their spouses as they entered the Nicollet Island Pavilion satiated her willingness to help the planners.

The location was bald. Once a loading dock and warehouse for southbound Mississippi barges, the facility had been renovated for elegant see and be seens, and down-to-earth bashes brimming with kegs of Michelob Golden Light beer, a Minnesota must. The pavilion proper overlooked a series of tiered platforms cascading down to the river's ever-present rumble where it first flexed the muscles that finally bulged in New Orleans. The platforms had been tented to protect guests from the unforgiving gusts known to push surface waters into a fine but bitter spray. The tents were adorned with white lighting, disguising them as spacious gazeboes. Portable overhead heaters also had been installed.

Inside, the expanse's only visuals were four pillars supporting the structure's open ceiling and rafters. The walls boasted a restored brick façade with one wall showcasing an elongated stage for live bands and DJs.

The pavilion's Gestalt was unapologetically romantic without the foreboding sense that turned men off. While quaint, warm, and inviting, its ambiance remained huge, open, even utilitarian, perhaps reminding men of the work garage of their fantasies, where massive diesel engines had to be airdropped from military helicopters. Thus unthreatening, the pavilion allowed men to relax in its subtle embrace.

While Austin wasn't necessarily looking for the obligatory and all too easy hook-up, she did feel a certain rush knowing that sex would be enjoyed in dozens of pairings and exponentially in approvable pleasure, much like a wedding, where, without mention, the thought of consecration was on everyone's mind.

Yes, Austin easily could have been a full-fledged event planner had she not cast her lot with the Colorado Springs axe women.

Finished with the last light strand, she turned to locate the three other blades. If trying to find them after three years of looking for Edie's fiery red hair, Mona's devastating jet black locks, and Becca's lackluster auburn proved a formidable task, adding the outfits of Bat Girl, an obscure dark Jedi, and a woman playing a doctor on TV made the challenge doubly difficult.

Austin stepped down from her ladder and crossed to the kitchen, where other blondes were assisting the caterers.

She felt a pinch on her elbow and realized Bat Girl had flanked her.

"You finished pretending you're one of them?" Edie asked Austin.

Without slowing her pace, Austin glanced up at her boss. "I was merely exuding esprit de corps. Aren't we all supposed to be pretending to be something we're not, or are you in fact the Dark Knight's kid sister?"

"This costume looked better when my hair was its natural color," Edie admitted.

"I didn't know Bat Girl was a red-head," Austin said.

"Depends on the depiction," Edie explained. "Sometimes she's red-headed, sometimes it looks more like Becca's hair."

They'd reached the kitchen, which threw out the only surgical and inappropriate light. Mona was hovering along the wall between the kitchen and the restrooms. Edie and Austin joined her, Austin shaking her head in amusement.

"Explain to me who you're supposed to be again," she asked Mona.

With a flick of her wrist, Mona ignited and extended her double-ended red lightsaber. "I am Aleema, Sith Sorceress." She waved the lightsaber in front of her to evoke its built-in sound effects.

"I didn't think there were any evil Jedi women," Edie murmured.

"Not in the movies," Mona explained. "She's in a fifteen-year old graphic novel series. It was set several hundred years before Luke Skywalker's time." She straightened her maroon, crushed velvet tube dress that pinched her knees together while ripping a slit nearly to her hip bone.

So they dressed that trashy, even in a galaxy far, far away? Austin thought. She immediately glanced down at her own costume.

The death angel thing is old and tired, she told herself.

Disapproval sprawled across Mona's face as Becca joined them. "So you decided not to dress up, Becca?"

Becca, nodding slightly, spread her arms in mock pride. "You remember that woman from the late 80's who did the Tylenol commercials?"

The other bottle blondes looked dumbfounded.

Becca sighed. "She started doing their commercials right after the bottle tampering scare and recall. She practically saved the company with how reliably boring she was. I count her as a modern day hero."

"Then what's her name?" Mona asked.

"I'll google it and let you know," Becca snapped.

Austin fretted with the white ruffles under her short skirt. Static either bunched them together and billowed out the black skirt or clung to her legs and drew the skirt back to her rear, the largest of the four.

"Nice one, Becca. So you decided not to dress up and are claiming to be a TV model," Mona said.

"Keep quiet, evil Jedi witch nobody knows about," Austin said. "These aren't the droids you're looking for, and tonight, no one's going to boldly go where no man's gone before."

Mona popped her knuckles. "I hate it when you mix up Star Trek and Star Wars."

"Then leave Becca alone," Austin said.

Edie cleared her throat. "Let's remember we're the only friends we have here. The real event planners roll their eyes when we're around, and the agents and district managers are getting more suspicious with every termination we deliver."

As though cued, the pavilion's far garage door opened, and guests streamed into the hall. Most headed straight for the food and open bar. The Mankato office district manager and his stripper girlfriend badgered the DJ until he dimmed the lights, brought up the disco ball, and unleashed a solid wall of hip hop and R&B. Clearly, the couple intended to be the evening's entertainment, granting men semi-erect members, and permitting women to roll their eyes in disgust. Everyone enjoyed seeing bodies writhe to the rhythm of solid, unrelenting beats.

Austin surveyed the crowd. She didn't recognize specific agents or other home office employees. The employees would be well disguised. The agents were simply unfamiliar to her.

Here was a *Casablanca* couple.

Near the champagne glass pyramid stood Don Corleone.

Mona had ensnared a Darth Vader and a Darth Maul, the weird, demon looking bad guy from the crappiest Star Wars movie. Austin was embarrassed for Mona; the two men were literally rubbing the tips of their lightsabers against the ends of hers. Mona, for her part, seemed to be encouraging the debacle.

The first man to notice Austin was a tall, slender Dracula, who looked like he played basketball in his earlier days. He sported a painted on black hairdo, complete with a widow's peak and a face so made up she couldn't distinguish his facial features. They spoke little but admired each other's costumes and the bodies underneath before she excused herself and made for the bar.

Now, Austin wasn't feeling so self-conscious under Mona's judgmental glare.

Becca was carrying on with the anti-costume league: women who went home and changed one shoe to make a mismatch, and men who merely fashioned their ties into 80's style headbands. One woman was daring enough to wear a large, unflattering, old ladies' bra over her work clothes, but she was accompanied by a man who sported a banana hammock on top of his khakis. Neither outfit incited compliments to their creativity or forms.

Over time, other super heroes banded together with Edie. Spider Girl arm-wrestled with Venom, or black costume Spider Man. Wonder Woman had put on some weight, but looked as though she were ready to pounce on fine young criminals. Superman was indeed dreamy in a purely Finnish gene pool way, and Cat Woman made sure to arch her back and bend at the waist enough to stay in character.

Within the first hour, more than two hundred of the state's five hundred and eighteen agents poured into the Nicollet Pavilion, bringing their significant or apparently not so significant others along for the festivities.

As Austin worked the room, she overheard several comments reflecting that this was a return to the company of old, where no one really needed a reason to celebrate. The eavesdropping devolved into the lamentable whispers of the affairs, office politics, and wife swaping antics that led to the inevitable demise of such company-sponsored debauchery. The key bowl partiers now had to leave early and dish themselves out under a new sense of privacy. Members of home office senior management arrived solo and left when the drinks started overflowing. Only the women agents remained stalwart in their need to massage every man's shoulder, neck, and bicep.

Someone was drawing a large crowd. Guzzling her whiskey sour, Austin squinted to see past the throng of applauding agents and their wives. Soon, she gave up on observing from afar, and, setting down her empty glass, she approached the mass of people.

"Excuse me," she muttered as she brushed against people, collecting elbows and startled looks. "Who is everyone crowding around?"

"Denis Laurent," a pirate said.

"Seriously?" she asked and immediately regretted saying anything out loud.

Eighteen months ago, Denis Laurent, a third-generation district manager, had suffered a debilitating stroke. He'd first lost use of the left side of his body, but had regained functionality in his limbs six months later. His speech and gait were still affected, but he'd held his position and rallied support from his agents over his recovery.

It now made complete sense that he would make an appearance.

As Austin slithered her way to the front, she couldn't contain her laughter and admiration for Laurent's outfit. Wearing a kitchen appliance box and a lamp shade as a hat, Denis kept one arm locked inside his daughter's and high fived the agents around him with his good hand. The box he wore had been painted to look like a cheap hotel end table. Whoever designed the costume had taken great lengths to make the furniture look old and dirty.

"He's a one-night stand!" an agent bellowed behind Austin. She then felt an arm rest on her shoulders.

"Isn't he awesome?" the agent muttered closer to her ear.

"It's very creative," Austin admitted.

The grip on her shoulder grew firmer. The man now pressed his hip against her side. "I'm Kyle Olsen. I'm an agent in Denis's district."

Austin snuck a glance. Even though he was sloshing a Long Island tea and his breath reeked of old cigars, Austin decided he wasn't a bad looking man. He had a strong, square jaw, muscular arms and chest. But he looked fifteen years older and married, given the ring clinking against his glass.

"Wanna dance?" he asked.

She wrenched his hand from her shoulder and scooted away. "I'm Austin. I work with the event planning department."

The smile ran away from his face. "Nice to meet you," he said in quick recovery while forgetting to offer her his hand. "Can you believe they want to force Laurent to retire?"

Austin realized Kyle was desperate to change the subject, but she was surprised that he would bring up such a sensitive topic, particularly at the volume he'd chosen.

"Really?" she asked. Scanning the horizon at face level, Austin swore to herself and sought out Edie. They needed to marginalize the situation before it erupted further.

"You got it, sister," Kyle continued. "Sure, he had a stroke, but he's been running things just fine. Heck, he built the company's biggest Minnesotan district. There's fifty of us agents. And it's not like he hasn't appointed reserve district managers to take over when he's ready to pass on the torch, including his daughter, Alyssa." He nodded and beckoned for Laurent's daughter to join their conversation.

Austin could feel the set up prickle along her skin. This Kyle knew exactly who she was and where she really worked. The Laurent disguise was a ruse to lure one of the four bottle blondes into a trap, get them to commit to something they shouldn't like swearing they wouldn't target the district manager for termination or forced resignation.

Alyssa was a sad, poignant reminder of the hollow persona her father had become. A daughter clearly showered with riches and lavish adornments to compensate for her rather lacking genetic endowments. Alyssa Laurent was broad-shouldered, broad-hipped, and slack-jawed. She carried the weight her father once did, both in spirit and physique. Her hair, stick straight and tired from bi-weekly dying appointments, had black roots bleeding through the top yellow strands. Her eyes were ringed with red veins although the lighting and the atmosphere could have explained that rather than the sinister desperation that oozed from her pupils.

Trusting her father's bad arm to another agent, Alyssa was upon Austin and Kyle in a speed not easily achieved in a crowd under such physical limitations.

Finding new confidence, Kyle side stepped toward Austin and threw his arm around her again. But now he meant her to feel uncomfortable perhaps even intimidated. At first, she acquiesced. Then Austin's empathic bent came to her calling. Kyle and Alyssa were both afraid. Kyle feared losing his leader, his mentor, most likely the man who'd brought him into the business and helped him become successful. Alyssa was terrified to see her father humiliated by the company to which he'd devoted over thirty years of service. Peeling back another layer in her mind, Austin uncovered the deeper fear, the one that perpetuated the social fears she'd just discovered. There was also the proverbial gravy train. No one could afford to lose out on the superfluous district office overrides the company paid Denis.

"Hello, I'm Alyssa Laurent." Alyssa offered her hand to Austin.

With his grip on her shoulder, Kyle thrust Austin forward. "This is Austin. She works in the event planning department."

The tone of disbelief was lost on neither Austin nor Alyssa.

"Nice to meet you, Austin," Alyssa said. "Your team puts on great events. I'm just glad the company finally stopped ignoring the peon multiline channel. Where did they have the brokerage channel incentive trip this year? Prague?"

Austin cleared her throat, which had dried out. "That's right. Although my team and I weren't a part of that project."

"So you didn't get to go to Prague and sit in the lap of luxury, making sure the hotel was just right and the meal plans were spot-on?" Kyle asked.

Austin pulled his hand from her shoulder again and threw it to his side with decisive assertiveness.

Alyssa read the smear of anger and embarrassment on Kyle's face. She placed her hand on his arm and gave him a pat. "Why don't you get the three of us another round, Mr. Olsen?" Turning to Austin, she asked. "What are you drinking?"

"A whiskey sour," Austin said.

"One whiskey sour and a pinot grigio," Alyssa told Kyle. "And sit this one out, Mr. Olsen. You've already had two teas."

Kyle left with a huff and stagger.

Towering over Austin in what looked like the judge in the *The Wall*'s final animated sequence, Alyssa pushed her hair away from her shoulders. "So where exactly do you work in the event department?"

Austin matched her smiled and breathed deeply before answering. "We've been specifically assigned to the multiline channel. They're regionalizing event planning for you guys, so we cover Minnesota, Wisconsin, and Iowa, and the Aurora Service Center covers Illinois, Michigan, and Indiana."

Alyssa made a move to roll her eyes, then checked her cynicism and nodded. "Are there really that many events to keep everyone busy?"

Austin again matched Alyssa's body language without the skeptic sneer. "When you add up all the town hall meetings, usually ten a year by state, the holiday parties, the Life and Commercial Masters meetings, the Summit Club meetings, and the President's Table qualification reporting, there's plenty to do."

"What about retirement parties?" Alyssa asked. "You plan those as well?" There wasn't smiling now.

Austin kept hers, and cocked her head to the side to indicate she was trying to understand and remain engaged in the conversation. "When asked to plan them, yes."

"And who asks you to plan them?"

"Usually Geoff Siemens for Minnesota," Austin answered. "John Taylor has a hand in the other states."

"So the Minnesota State Executive Director tells you when to plan retirement parties for say, district managers the company wants to resign?" Alyssa asked.

Austin laughed and shook her head. "I think you're misunderstanding me. We don't have an event schedule around agents and district managers leaving the company."

Alyssa furrowed her brow. "I find that hard to believe. Everyone knows as soon as your team arrived, all from the Colorado Springs Service Center internal marketing department, the number of agent terminations and resignations sky rocketed. I think we're nearing ten percent of the agency force gone in the last six months."

Alyssa reached for her chain necklace and twisted it around a large, tan mole at the base of her neck. Then she stepped forward, causing Austin to take a step back.

In her periphery, Austin saw a billowing black cape overpower a moose of a man. Austin glanced at the spectacle. Bat Girl, as played by Edie Firebaugh, had negotiated the two drinks from the returning Kyle Olsen and was now swooping in to join Alyssa's and Austin's conversation.

"Alyssa," Edie breathed. "Here's your wine. Austin, your cocktail." Drinks delivered, Edie offered her hand to Alyssa. "I don't believe we've met. I'm Edie Firebaugh. I head up the multiline event planner division."

Alyssa's glare now attempted omnipotence but only managed how dare she awe. "So Austin reports to you?"

Edie nodded. "How's your Series 26 exam going, Alyssa? It's quite the subject in the state office. Geoff Siemens and John Taylor are eagerly awaiting your passing results."

Alyssa took a step back. "Still studying as usual." She turned to Austin with a condescending grin. "It's an extremely difficult exam to pass."

"And one necessary to be an acceptable candidate for the district manager position," Edie explained and leveled her challenging gaze to Alyssa. "I'm sure fourth time's a charm."

"Four?" Austin asked.

Edie giggled her worst fake laugh. "I guess it would have to be the charm. Otherwise, you're barred from the exam for life, right? And you wouldn't be acceptable to the company as a replacement district manager candidate for your father's district."

Alyssa's skin blotched around her neck. The chain had twisted around her mole enough to pop it off. "I'd better check on Kyle. He looked hurt not being able to rejoin our conversation."

"Thanks, Alyssa," Edie called after her. "Tell him that's what happens when you drink to get hurt."

Austin cast her eyes to the floor. "Thanks, boss. I owe you one."

Edie took Austin's drink and sipped it. "You don't owe me anything. They're sniffing us out. They've pegged you as their advocate, just as we planned. They'll tell you anything if they think you'll save them. That's why you're vital to the team."

"I know, but I got cornered," Austin said.

"Get used to it," Edie replied. "Speaking of getting cornered, I think we need to save Mona from that Howdy Doody looking imbecile near the bar. He's pawing at her pretty vigorously."

Chapter Six

The church was sparsely decorated with minimalist architecture, a welcomed change from where Edie had converted to Catholicism for a man who'd ultimately chosen to move to Georgia with his military consulting business, rather than marry her in his chosen church. The white cement brick walls were at least forty feet tall. Green linens streamed from above the altar, emulating rays of light, to the far ends of the sanctuary. A red light shone from the lantern in the tabernacle, showing that Jesus was present for the Mass. Despite the church's pragmatic charm, the stations of the cross adorned the back wall, three giant projection screens cradled the altar, and there were pews enough to seat a thousand parishioners.

The laity reminded Edie of Chicago's Lakefront Liberals. The people here, despite their mass affluence, were very welcoming, not just in their smiles, greetings, and offerings of peace, but also in their ability to resist judging others. One of the twin sister greeters, who made Edie think of a fifty-five year old Mona, was fond of bringing her African-American boyfriend to services. Edie along with everyone else had shaken his hand warmly, genuinely, and not out of post-90's white guilt. Edie had also spotted three lesbian couples who had adopted foster children. Both moms took the Eucharist without flinching. One couple had Edie's deep respect, having a penchant for adopting special needs children, one in a wheelchair, the clear product of shaken baby syndrome, another with years of prior abuse stenciled into her dark eye sockets.

Here the Liturgy of the Word was concise, easy to apply to daily struggles, and tied succinctly to the homily. The senior priest had an astounding gift for speaking to hundreds and sounding as though he were speaking directly to Edie and what she had experienced in the week leading up to Sunday. There was no questioning its rarity, given from Christ, which further proved his existence and benevolence, not that Edie needed any more faith.

Even the associate priest, with his proclivity toward the theatrical in song and dance encouraged people to find the beauty in simple things and to let go of the obstacles that drove one away from a relationship with God.

Here they prayed for the least among us, those marginalized by the pursuit of corporate profit and the illusion of trickle down economics.

Here they prayed for God to grant understanding to politicians that the needs of constituents outweighed the fears of shortened terms in office and the lost opportunities to continue political careers lobbying for those with the loudest voices.

Here they prayed for guidance to ensure that the planet could continue to provide for all species, and for the wisdom of the stewardship humans had been granted.

Here they prayed for the disenfranchised. They prayed that the poverty of spirit be bestowed on all Americans infected with the sickness of greed and consumerism. They prayed to remind those in attendance that the second (and third) coats in the closest belonged to those who had none.

Finally, here they prayed for the bishop, with his eyes fixed on becoming a cardinal, they prayed for the pope, with his trail of letters urging the relocation of pedophiliac priests to other parishes with equivalent child populations. They prayed for the church, to remind it that Jesus said take this often in remembrance of me, whether you regard it as the actual chewy, taut flesh of a carpenter and the iron filled blood of the working class or not.

Edie's new parish was exactly seventeen miles from the archdiocese of St. Paul, much too close to be so compassionate, too far away to be perceived as a threat. The battle between

Martin Luther and the church waged onward in farming communities, which only hoped for consistent crops regardless of the man-made fine print.

Edie felt at home.

The church in Colorado Springs was militant. It tended to pay homage, if not elevate to the status of worship that Catholics reserved for sainthood, and of which Protestants were preternaturally suspicious, to those who gave their lives to advancing the self-interests of the nation over what real Christians should aspire to.

Edie's former fiancé disagreed with her. His paycheck governed his decision, as many do.

Just before the end of the relationship, they'd watched a World War II movie detailing the plight of Russian Jews, who, alerted to the intent of their neighbors to turn them over to the Germans, fled to a remote forest for refugee survival that evolved into the need for a true community. At the climax, the charismatic leader faced the choice of allowing the fragile community to fall victim to a martial law state, the militia dictating where rations were apportioned (ultimately to their favor), or to preserve the culture under attack. The hero of the film made the split second choice of ending the coup's rise with a well aimed bullet to the militia leader's forehead.

Edie had applauded at the explosive entry wound.

Her boyfriend had remained stoic, silent, at odds with the value proposition of laying down one's life for those who are too weak to appreciate your sacrifice.

It led to their break up.

Sure, his certainty of direction, his determination of purpose, had attracted her from the start. Name one woman who isn't attracted to this forthrightness, to that confidence no matter what the slant, she told herself. It led to a base need to ensure her children would be fed, would be clothed, would be sheltered.

That was the apex of their fight. Yes, he could, through the U.S. military, provide for their offspring, but could he support raising them to have sympathy for the plight he'd fought so hard to defend?

It had depended on whether Dick and Jane were still white in first and second grade readers. It had depended on who was elected to enforce border control and the interests of the nation's addiction to foreign oil. It had depended on a president who promised to be against abortion but did absolutely nothing to curtail its use. It had depended on the military industrial complex, against which Dwight D. Eisenhower had warned the entire nation.

So Edie found herself single, attending Catholic services in Apple Valley, Minnesota.

The choir entered through the tabernacle, crossing beyond the confessional rooms, no bigger than janitorial closets, and under the tabernacle lantern. Jesus was here first, the choir entered second, the priest, after some house keeping announcements, entered third, and began the Mass. Edie wondered if this had any symbolism to it, and quickly decided that after centuries of creating traditions on which Jesus himself had been silent, some priest or saint had appended spiritual symbolism to the procession, more than likely citing seraphim or cherubim being a higher order of angels than lowly humans. *If only the Middle Ages had comic books*, Edie thought. *Then Dante could have combined the hellacious artwork of his time with his demented depiction of the godless vacuum.*

The congregation rose with the opening song. Edie cast sideward glances at the deacon, the priest and the altar servers, both girls. The deacon carried the church's crucifix which was planted into a slot just before the cross, giving heraldry to the service. The priest raised his arms and sang atonally along with the choir. He blessed the crowd. They blessed him back, and the Mass was underway.

Edie lost herself in the Liturgy of the Word. There was a dissonance between the suffering or the killing in Old Testament God's name and the reading from blathering St. Paul. In any other Mass, Edie would try to predict the loose dots connecting the Word of the Lord through homily. Today, she found herself embittered all over again with thoughts of her ex-fiancé.

She still had trouble remembering how or why she was attracted to him. She'd been drawn to the muscles on the sides of his arms, those ill-formed or neglected by most men. She also had a liking to shoulders that gently sloped from the neck rather than dropping to the bare collarbone. But she had not been a big fan of the jarhead look. *Men shouldn't be afraid of their hair,* she thought. They should wear it proudly, not fretting about a few strands over the ears or out of place along the bangs. But sadly, men wore their hair for other men, just as women did for other women. At least, women had some inkling of attractive hairstyles. With men, it was as though the bald rose to corporate prowess with the sole intention to encourage other men with beautiful, healthy heads of hair to shave so closely they brandished razor burns along their moley, ill-formed scalps.

John Taylor, her boss, influenced his minions accordingly. You could always spot a junior Taylor stomping down the halls of Home Office.

Her ex's pigheadedness had been difficult to bear. He loved to bring down the final word, especially when Edie argued him into an unmaneuverable position. He was a Republican for God sake! Proverbially born on third and convinced he'd hit a triple, he'd completely forgotten that, prior to being the largest European-American contributors to World War I and II, most of his Italian ancestors had entered the country illegally, having had the letters W O P painted on their jackets because they had left the mother country without securing proper documentation. But here was the same idiot who would just as soon kill a Hispanic American striving for a better life under similar circumstances.

The head priest rose, delivered the Gospel reading, the chapter in Matthew where Jesus described heaven as a huge wheat field under deep blue skies, and left the podium to deliver his homily.

"We have a special message today," he said as he descended the steps from the altar. Edie marked the intent of the motion. The priest always did this so that he became one with the congregation, one speaker, one leader, of the people, not hiding behind the pulpit.

"Many of you know Easton Frost," he continued. "Easton is a relatively new member to this parish although he is a cradle

Catholic, being raised in the faith from birth. His company recently relocated him here from Oklahoma.

"A few weeks ago, Easton contacted me with an amazing experience that he wanted to share. It has been said that our young men will have visions and our old men will have dreams. This is certainly true within the stories of the Old Testament, and God has validated this once again. As always, I invite us all to reflect on Easton's experience and to find encouragement and strength in its faith affirming meaning."

The priest waved his arm and gestured to a man who had been seated near the choir.

Easton Frost rose and switched on his wireless lapel mic. "Thanks, Father Tim. Good morning, everyone."

"Good morning," Edie and the congregation said in unison.

"I give a great deal of presentations at work," Easton said. "Just like Father Tim, I don't like standing behind a podium. I'm more comfortable with a stage. That said, I'll try not to move around too much. Feel free to tell me to stay still if I start bouncing off the walls."

The gratuitous laughter was underscored with a bass line murmur.

"He must go to the seven o'clock."

"He's too young to be at the seven o'clock."

"I think I've seen him at the eleven."

"Does he work with the youth?"

"I don't think so."

"He's too young to have teenagers."

"He's not married."

"Well, then, maybe he goes to the Saturday evening."

"I've never seen him there. I go every other week on Saturday."

"He's from the South. Maybe he speaks Spanish and goes to the Latino Mass on Saturday afternoon."

"He does look a little dark to be all white. Especially here where the sun don't shine."

"Father said he was from Oklahoma. He doesn't sound like he has an accent though."

Edie agreed. He was well tanned for Minnesota. This place was a wretched magnet for slow, brooding, vindictive clouds. He didn't have much of an accent. She liked his hair though. He wore it longer than most, and it made her think of the hairstyles from the '20's and 30's, that Pomade wet look. It also had a rambunctious curl in the back and along the sides, especially over his ears. This Easton had a high forehead, but his hairline stood fast with no trace of retreat. He had that sharp, pointed nose which made men look smart. His appearance was immaculate. His black pinstripe suit and red silk tie created a sense of power and confidence without oozing arrogance or unnecessary compensation.

Edie couldn't tell his eye color from where she sat, but she wanted to find out.

"About a month ago, I was standing on my front porch, smoking," Easton was saying.

The congregation murmured again. There were children present.

She'd tuned out his introduction and background, which somewhat unnerved her.

"Now don't hold that against me, people," Easton said with a raised hand. "I know we celebrate Pentecost when Peter and the apostles were able to speak in languages they'd never learned, burning with the fire of the Holy Spirit, but just consider how you'd feel if Jesus had added a pipe at the Last Supper saying 'Take this, all of you, and smoke it. This is my spirit, which shall never leave you.'"

Several die hard smokers emitted cackles, gasps, coughs, and indignant applause.

"Thank you, thank you," Easton said. "Seriously, though. It's an important detail in my story. Those who know me know that I was in a serious relationship with a woman in Oklahoma, and that I personally wanted more than what Vatican II said I needed. I wanted my girlfriend to convert to Catholicism from Episcopalian before we got married. But it wasn't to be. So here I am a Catholic single in a strange, bitterly cold land, but filling myself with the fire of the Holy Spirit."

Easton stepped to Edie's section of the pews.

"So there I was, looking at the tree in my front yard. It grows like most trees here, really aggressively in the short spring and summer before turning bright orange and shedding its leaves for a long winter death," he said. "I've fought with this tree a time or two. Its branches like to reach out and take swipes at my truck when I park."

He placed his hand over his heart. "I've cut branches from this tree. But after what happened to me, I don't think I'll cut the thick ones back any more. Live and let grow. That's what God told me that night. Live and let grow. I was thinking about how Jesus had said that he is the vine and we are the branches. While I was looking at this tree I realized that there was no human sense I could apply to the way the branches had grown. Sure, science will tell us that the branches grow to optimize their leaves' exposure to sunlight and rain, but have you ever seen a perfectly straight branch or even a stick, for that matter?"

He paused and checked the crowd for nods.

"I haven't either. I tell you. I grew up in Oklahoma where we have impressive pecan trees, but they have the most scary, scraggly looking branches in the winter.

"I got to thinking about the trunk of this tree being the Word of God, being Jesus Christ, as John the Gospel writer describes him. Then I saw the thickest branches as the sacraments that we hold so dear: Baptism, First Communion, Confirmation, Marriage, Holy Orders, Confession, and Anointing the Sick. Along the branch of Anointing the Sick, some of the smaller branches were still dying, some had been trimmed back prematurely." Again, he placed his hand over his heart.

"Along the branch of marriage, there were several branches that split off. Some grew stronger and had smaller limbs growing off them, others stopped growing but were somehow able to stay alive.

"All of these limbs and branches were still a part of the same tree, the same living and growing tree. And I realized that I had been wrong to try to force my now ex-girlfriend into converting to Catholicism. I realized I was afraid that what we'd heard of the Episcopalians were true. That they were Diet Catholics, all the worship and promises of heaven with only half the guilt."

People laughed again. Some clapped.

"I realized I was afraid that if she hadn't converted, she wouldn't take the sacrament of marriage as seriously as I do. So I pushed her away for a certain future rather than face the risk of a possible future. Can you think of ways you've done that?" He raised his hand to encourage others to follow.

"As soon as I'd completed this borrowed metaphor of the tree in my front yard, I felt a presence in my mind, something that wasn't my own voice, the one everyone has in his or her head. It was saying, yes. Yes. Yes!

"And then something felt like it was downloading into my mind, something was being poured into the top of my head. It was encouraging, inspiring, but it was also too much."

Even the infants and toddlers were silent.

"I remember clinching my fists to my temples," Easton said. He recreated the scene, bringing his fists to his head and squeezing his eyes tight. "Without knowing or even hearing the words come out of my mouth, I was telling the presence to stop, to slow down. It was overwhelming me. Then it relented a little and I felt a distinct voice urging me to go back inside and sit down. It was telling me to rest."

He raised his head, opened his eyes, and let his hands fall to his sides again. "So I did what I was told. I went inside, and went downstairs to sit on the couch.

"And that's when it happened. I saw a vision in the center of my mind. Of a wheat field with a windless breeze, a coolness that seemed to pass through me without pushing me. I could see my ancestors in the distance. Have you ever seen a picture of a person who was so out of focus that they were thin, nothing more really that a head shape and a body shape with only thin lines for arms and legs that just vanished underneath them? That's how it was. There were thousands of grey figures."

"The mood was calm. It was a shared mood, a shared feeling, like being able to actually feel someone else's sense of humor, but it wasn't a sense of humor like you and I know it, always looking for a laugh or searching for a witty remark or the retelling of a joke. It was more a sense of humor and understanding and… joy. It was a fearless joy."

Easton then turned his back to Edie's section of pews and strode to the other side of the church. Everyone in her pew leaned forward to hear him. They were as close to the edge of their seats as they could get without kneeling.

Edie could hear sniffles punctuated with sobs. Who was this mystic? Who was this Easton Frost?

"The grey figures stayed in the distance, but I felt an acute connection to each of them. And the presence entered my mind again. I felt it telling me not to worry so much about all the little things I let get in my way. It also filled me with a sensation of amazing appreciation for faith, not my little or troubled faith, but any shred of faith. As though it is truly wondrous that humans could persist and maintain any faith at all. And that any amount of faith proved our love for God, our love for Jesus. As though, as long as we strive to hear the still small voice that this effort was magnified, heard very clearly in heaven and was welcomed.

"I felt then as the very least," Easton said. "I have a very good life. I've never gone hungry. I've never worried about money. I was raised in a privileged household. But in this place, I was the least, and there were hundreds of thousands of others who were closer than I was. And I was overjoyed by this notion. There was no jealousy or questioning. There was only this constant, never ending feeling that all it takes is a base belief in God, in Christ, in the forgiveness of sins for those who are truly sorry, even for the sins I've committed over and over again.

"None of that mattered in this place," he continued. "None of that was even mentioned, brought up, scolded against. I was being invited to a party that both I was crashing but had always been invited to attend."

Easton Frost fell silent and his pause became pregnant, pensive, reflective.

"I realized that good deeds are a sign of faith, of showing what I believe. I realized there was no credit and debit system in place. There are no angelic bookies keeping tabs on my actions. Doing good was simply showing God my love for Him, and committing sins was only a temporary rejection of God's love, much like when a small child pushes you away and wants to doing something all by himself. As though God knows that I will

fail, fall down, in my desire to live alone without Him, left to my
own tiny sense of power. And I realized that God knew I had to
fall so that He could pick me back up and remind me that He is
always there, even when I am not."

Easton Frost bowed his head and fell silent. After a dramatic
pause, he took his seat. Father Tim then rose and signaled the
ushers to begin the collection.

The Liturgy of the Eucharist was a blur. Edie swam in
Easton's lay homily. She wanted to know him better.

She pitched her weekly twenty dollars into the basket and
then passed it along. Here was a man who also had left a
significant other. The little girl in her wanted to give him a
comforting hug, that innocent desire to let someone know you
were going through a similar experience, conveyed silently
through a moment of contact and shared breathing.

Her eyes followed a family of four as they brought forth the
bread, the wine, and the holy water. Easton Frost, he had the
same initials as her, Edie Firebaugh. She had a less innocent
desire to place herself before him and study his eyes. She had to
know the color of his eyes.

The Eucharistic ministers approached and gathered around
the altar, fussing over cups and bowls. What a gifted speaker.
What did he do for a living that made him so fearless at speaking
to such a large group? She could be lulled to sleep with his
voice, that rich timber, that confident cadence, that deep,
humming tone that sounded like it came from his feet and slowly
rose throughout his body.

The priest recited the transubstantiation ritual in his usual
loud voice, but she'd heard it plenty of times.

Edie hadn't yet decided if she would be attracted to Easton
Frost. He was too tall. But how could that make sense? He was
slender with a basketball player's frame without the muscles or
NBA tats she was a secret sucker for. If she ever did get to hug
him, it might be disappointing. She liked pressing herself up
against solid masculinity, to be wrapped up in an embrace, to
become lost in an unused, unnecessary strength, to feel arms
melt over her and to lose track of where they were placed
because they felt like they covered her.

What if she could feel his ribs when they hugged? What if his arms were as bony as they looked underneath his suit coat? What if she would know exactly where they were at all times?

But again, he was tall enough to rest his chin on the top of her head. She could fit into him that way. That might feel nice again. Edie couldn't remember the last time she'd hugged a man, outside of her family, who could do that. Corporal Anthony hadn't been able to, even in his issued shoes, standing on his toes. He'd been the ultimate small dog, willing to kill the enemy, to feel equal to taller guys.

Yes, it was worth the risk.

A hand patted her shoulder. She looked up and then realized it was an usher inviting her to rise and fall into the Communion line.

Would he be standing outside the sanctuary when Mass ended? Was he still sitting by the choir? No, he had disappeared into the masses, seated somewhere else. Probably next to his new girlfriend. No, that wouldn't work. What woman would sit in church and listen to her boyfriend lament the choices he'd made to leave a former love behind? Oh, yeah, a good cradle Catholic girl raised in the chauvinistic shadow of the church would.

"The Body of Christ."

"Amen."

She'd have to stay for the entire service then and not duck out after the priest concluded the Mass. Then she'd have plenty of time to pretend to look at bulletins, maybe sign up for the Habitat for Humanity build or schedule weekly debit card deductions to Feed All God's Children or Catholic Charities.

"The Blood of Christ."

"Amen."

But wait, the Cursillo ladies had set up shop for their women's retreat. Edie somehow knew that Frost would be stationed next to those flakes so they could vulture over all the other single women clamoring to talk him. Foiled by God again. Where was Mona when she needed her?

What was she going to do?

The kneeler slammed down. Edie blinked. Let's get on with it, she thought as she knelt and waited for the last few rows to clear through the Feast of Growing Impatience.

Without her noticing, the priest had concluded the Eucharist and had moved on to the announcements.

At length he said, "The Mass is never ended. It must be lived. Let us go forth to love and serve God. In the name of the Father, and of the Son, and of the Holy Spirit. Amen."

Just then the choir and band launched into a soulful, slow rendition of "Amazing Grace." It was an absolute killer. Half the church would feel compelled to sit through the entire song. The more aggressive single women would bolt for the door. They'd devour Frost. Edie had to save him.

But she fought through the temptation and stayed planted in her pew. In typical fashion, everyone sang along with the first verse and chorus then died off sharply with the second verse, most having no idea that the song told a full story rather than being an oft repeated spiritual refrain. Edie lost the fight not to roll her eyes.

How to time this? Timing was critical. Then a beam of epiphany hit her. Let the other women run to him. They'll get swallowed into the women's retreat, and while the three Cursillo night hawks encircled their prey, she would walk straight up to him.

She watched the priest and altar servers leave the sanctuary, led by the usher carrying the crucifix away from the cross.

The first section of pews was on the move.

Edie was in the third section, dead center in the sea of the cleansed.

The first section was full of old people though. *You're killing me, Smalls!* This was arguably their moment, their need for final fellowship and reconciliation in their apologetic eyes that said to Edie, "Oops, we did spawn the Baby Boomers, didn't we? Do you think Tom Brokaw still thinks we're the greatest generation?"

That mental rant had washed over the gradual emptying of the first section and the start of the mid-life crisis row's moderate-paced exodus, filled with parents and their barely conscious teens. Now, things were picking up.

Then Edie had another epiphany. Father Tim would be greeting people outside the building to spare Easton the older, more conservative followers grumbling at faulty hearing aid volumes about where the church was headed.

You're awesome, Father Tim! she thought.

Now came her section's turn to leave. Edie set her jaw and brow but then thought better of such a stern look. Lifting her eyes with her closed-mouth smile, she was assured that her face wouldn't seem too forward, too forthright, too desperate. She just prayed those wretched Cursillo cougars weren't humping his thigh.

She was past the holy water bowl.

Playing bumper pool with stranger shoulders, she shook her head at the usher handing out the bulletins and then cleared the sanctuary doors.

The outside air was clear. The church's front doors were open, providing much needed respite from the accumulated stench of Aquanet buns, Old Spice, and Stetson at nauseating war with the tween body sprays that made adolescent boys smell edible.

Edie loved Red when she was that age but had matured into a proclivity toward Eternity, reserving Obsession for true mammalian lust.

She shook her head. It didn't matter. Easton wouldn't be wearing any of those scents. He looked all in like a Drakkar Noir guy. Strong in the bar but leaving nothing to linger on the pillow.

She was judging. In church.

She banished her defense mechanisms to their dark recesses and scanned the lobby. There was the Habitat for Humanity table right next to the Feed All God's Children booth. The Cursillo three stood close by, chatting it up with their prey. The four women they'd ensnared were casting sidelong glances at Easton Frost.

Why did God have to make her right this time? Didn't he relish her being wrong?

Easton Frost was shaking a series of hands from a line of married men. What was that? Edie never imagined she'd be blocked by beer gutted, brat farting Minnesota men, confused with what flannel shirt best matched their Brett Favre Viking jerseys.

Just then the sea of goatees and armpits parted, and she had a clear line.

She approached, keeping her smile tight but her eyes bright.

His eyes were blue, really, unmistakably, angelically, sinfully blue.

"Hi, I'm Edie Firebaugh," she said and offered her hand.

"Hi, Edie Firebaugh. I'm Easton Frost. We have the same initials," he replied.

"Do you want to get coffee sometime?" she asked.

His eyes crinkled in manly confusion.

I'm an idiot, Edie thought.

Chapter Seven

Taylor's office was decorated with framed designations and degrees: CLU, ChFC, CPCU, CIC, LUTCF, a Bachelor's of Science in Marketing from the University of Northern Iowa, the Kellogg MBA. The pin-ups of his ego dwarfed the man when he sat behind his austere, company-issued desk. Stacks of folders and paperwork further imprisoned him within the tight picture of accomplishment and self-importance.

The office still brandished a full-length couch many regarded as an outdated faux pas throwback when rumors abounded of his female lackies winding down after an evening of number-crunching and sales report manipulation. At the far end, near the door he'd crammed in a small conference table with three chairs. It was the only functional, tidy area in the lair. It was here that Edie insisted on sitting for their one-on-one meetings.

Taylor was freckly bald, making Edie think of a football coach she couldn't name. Kennedy family rosacea tickled the man's nostrils and cheekbones. He was fond of his drink even though the drink's affection for him had long since faded.

He also had an eerie penchant for dressing down even when he met with the top producers from any channel. He was wedded to his navy blue blazer, wrinkled khakis, worn and blemished brown loafers, and the obligatory company-branded tie.

His grey eyes bore down on her just above the line of his steepled fingers. Edie had learned to relish the silent appraisal, refusing to speak first. She'd learned that lackies rushed in and vomited on their superiors in vain attempts to impress. She knew to measure her words and, more important, her reactions.

"Who are you targeting now?" he asked at length.

"For termination?" she asked to clarify.

"Yes, for termination. You've chopped off dozens in both sales divisions."

Edie squinted in thought. "I sense the real question is when do I anticipate making this pilot program, this ethical cleansing, replicable for other state offices with similar deterioration issues."

John Taylor cleared his throat. "If that's how you choose to answer the question, I'll listen."

"The systems have always been in place," she replied. "Not once have we requested additional resources. It's a thin expense model. Profitability can be better sustained going forward, considering the run off of bad business and improper risks. Within the next rating cycle, Siemens should be able to demonstrate the opportunity for rate relief in both auto and homeowners lines. This would also whittle away at the perception that rates here are kept high to subsidize the heavy mold losses in Texas."

Taylor winced at the reference. The company once commanded a twenty percent market share in his homeland. The Texas state office had retained a high level of full-time agents supplanting the moratorium on writing new homeowners insurance with life insurance, which, compensating at such a low commission rate, roughly equaled the commissions on home policies.

Edie knew though that there would be no positive rate changes. The Minnesotan was a loyal Nederlander who clung to Northwest Airlines despite downright abusive air fares prior to the Delta Airlines merger. The Minnesotan flocked to the Metrodome to see the Vikings not win Super Bowls and engage in horrible sex scandals and violent crimes. The Minnesotan held his State of Hockey dear even after the North Stars abandoned him and before the Wild came to play. The overall brand loyalty astounded Edie, but it came as no surprise to the company, which like many others had every intention of exploiting the insanity.

"Siemons would be a fool not to try," Taylor agreed at length. "But he would also be wise not to campaign too passionately."

Edie nodded. "I gather he knows the difference."

"Indeed."

"The model we've established is easy to repeat. It's a question of finding the right people who are willing to execute."

"The right people on the right spots on the bus," Taylor said.

It took a deep, inner strength to keep Edie's eyes from rolling. Everyone had been forced to read the book, *Good to Great*. The lackies read it in their cars waiting for the office doors to unlock and while cycling or treadmilling in the basement gym. The book held Gillette, the company that had decided to give away the razor and charge a premium for the blades, at the pinnacle of greatness. In Edie's mind, it was no coincidence that the quality and longevity of that company's product declined dramatically with the unsolicited endorsement. *Way to go, Harvard business school morons.*

"Precisely," she said.

"And do you think you could recognize this talent in our other regional offices as you did with your team from the Springs?"

Edie shrugged. "I was lucky to have worked with each of them before. Out of four hundred people, I knew who would work and who wouldn't. If you're asking me if I could select candidates for this career move, I'd have to ask you where you're looking. The Aurora Service Center has the worst work ethic. The Pocatello Service Center is plagued with a lack of population to support the upwardly mobile. The Tigard Service Center is flooded with former claims adjusters; they don't have the right temperament for the trade."

"That leaves Carlsbad, Baltimore, Austin, and Kansas City," Taylor said.

"Carlsbad is a cesspool of sexual harassment lawsuits. Women fresh from college jump into elevators just to rip open their shirts and claim unwanted sexual advances to pay for breast augmentation," she continued.

"That remains unsubstantiated."

Edie shook her head. "This is just the two of us talking. We would find good candidates in Austin, but given the circumstances that would decimate agent morale, particularly with the gubernatorial race so heated. Baltimore's too new. They just now have their first fully graduated career class with only a handful of agents running to daylight."

Edie hated that term. It was core to the diseased sales culture. When a career agent began his third year with the company, he could earn forgiveness from his subsidy and start-up loans through increased production. The system, however, aligned the amount of required new business with the plateau of renewal commissions that kicked in during the agent's fifth year, which enticed him to take an extended vacation on the long, straight road to mediocrity. Edie had proposed something more encouraging than escaping foreboding, enshrouding darkness. Something that comprised the themes of success from significance to prominence in the business and local community had much more uplifting appeal. Upper management not only didn't have the ears to hear, they barely had the nubs to sense the vibrations necessary to translate sound.

"Point taken," Taylor said as though he'd read her mind.

"Kansas City is the most likely place to implement a second stage. Siemens made a lasting impression there even though it was three relocations back for him," Edie said.

"Isn't there still work to be done in Minnesota?" Taylor cut it.

"Of course," she replied. "The St. Cloud and Brainerd districts have the highest amount of appointments selling away. There are forty additional termination cases that could be made there."

"Who's the next worst offender? Someone in the seven-county metro?" Taylor asked.

"Yes, Dennis Laurent's district in Mendota Heights. Of his fifty agents, twenty of them have direct competitor appointments."

Taylor winced. "Is there a way to sharp shoot your targets in St. Cloud and Brainerd so Laurent gets the message?"

Edie cocked an eyebrow. "Not without eventually consolidating those two outstate districts and removing one of the district managers."

"Who would you remove?"

"Need I say? Grudenberg in Brainerd is three times more competent than Otis in St. Cloud," Edie said.

"Would Siemens agree?"

"I can't see him siding with Otis. You know how he feels about obesity," she said.

"That's beside the point."

Edie again raised an eyebrow.

"What else is in the works?" he asked.

"We have the Sanders termination review board next week."

Taylor dropped his steepled fingers. "Thanks for prepping the news media sound bite on that."

Edie waved her hand. "I'm a sucker for big moustaches in sheriff deputy uniforms."

It was Taylor's turn to shed a surprised look. "Really? I didn't think you were old enough to appreciate a man with facial hair."

She immediately regretted her joke. "I'm not, John." Her tone was level and firm.

He waved it off with a gesture. "Do you think he'll make bail for the TRB?"

"His lawyer will recommend he post bond to show up," Edie said.

"But he was selling certificates of insurance for cash to launder drug money, right?" Taylor asked.

"It's still billable for the attorney, even if it never sees civil trial for wrongful termination," she replied.

"What else do you have going on?"

Edi sat straighter. "There is the matter with Terry Collins in Duluth."

"What matter?" Taylor asked.

"He assigned the entire Lundgaard agency to the agency's customer service rep and created a career agent out of her in thirty days," Edie explained.

Now, Taylor sat up. "When did this happen?"

"Apparently six months ago," she said. "Just when my team got here."

"Well, when did you find out?" His face reddened to camouflage his rosacea.

"A week ago, one of the agents on the policy assignment list called Mona and blew the whistle."

Taylor squinted into the near distance, letting his eyes relax. He was searching for motive, or the super motive as Edie called it. The motive that justified the actions of the true motive, much like Freud's sense of the ego. She'd seen this look enough to recognize it in Taylor's eyes.

"Who called it in?"

"Kerry Lutter," she said. "Both he and his office partner, Tom Hildebrand, were very upset. They both claim that Collins promised them the majority of the twelve-hundred-policy agency, but that he's been stringing them along and assigning the policies behind their back to Lundgaard's CSR."

"What does Siemens say?"

"That we should go up there and encourage Collins to resign," Edie replied. "Collins's recruiting is in the toilet and he's been riding on the high producing wave of his existing full-time agents for three years. Siemens has been pressing him for pending agent files, but his pipeline has been consistently weak from the start. If he turns in ten pending files, he'll see one reserve agent and no careers."

"So he hasn't grown the district at all?" Taylor asked.

"They have the best retention of any district, the best profitability, and the best new business in homeowners insurance. Plus, his existing agents write enough life business to keep him in the green. His auto new business is down," Edie explained.

"Does Siemens have a replacement lined up?" Taylor asked.

"He's been talking to two reserve district managers," she said. "One in Houston, and the other in Phoenix."

Taylor furrowed his eyebrows. "The one in Texas makes sense. But Phoenix? We're killing it in organic growth there."

"The Phoenix RDM is originally from Duluth, John," Edie said. "He wants to get back home."

Taylor nodded. "Sounds like a slam dunk. What's Siemens's time table for getting the new guy running?"

"Ninety days after termination," Edie said. "He wants to use the three months' district override to mend agent relationships and get some outsourced sales coaching."

Taylor nodded his approval. "That would pave a better landing for any new guy. Is there any way to recover the policy assignments from the CSR?"

Edie frowned and shook her head. "Not without litigation."

"But didn't Collins assign her the policies without our approval?"

Edie sighed. "Policy assignment was still under service center approval then. Siemens believes that Collins put the policy assignment in, knowing my team was arriving and would take over the assignment process at the state office level."

"So they've been approved?"

"Yes, they have been," Edie continued. "And they've been cherry-picked. So the few hundred that Lutter and Hildebrand received were the very worst, single line clients with profitability issues, wrong rate classes, and other foul things."

"So beyond being desperate for a new career agent, why else would Terry assign all the policies to an unproven CSR? Do we know how long she worked for Lundgaard?"

"Twelve years," Edie said. "She basically sustained the business, and by her claims she grew the business in the last ten years."

"Grew it by what percent?" Taylor asked.

"By about twenty percent," Edie said. "She claims she took it from a thousand policies to twelve hundred."

Taylor leaned forward, the thought of cracking open the mystery sprawling over his face. "So she grew the agency with poor quality, unprofitable business, and now sees a chance to slough off the bad business, especially to larger agencies like Lutter's and Hildebrand's, who can stomach the losses. It makes herself look cleaner, especially in light of you and your team changing the culture."

"Very perceptive," Edie said.

"You've already thought of that angle," Taylor retorted.

Edie nodded but remain silent.

"It begs the question..."

"All the business was written under the agent number," Edie said. "Lundgaard assigned her a writing CSR number or an agency producer number."

Taylor leaned back. That wasn't the question he had in mind.

Edie looked confused. "I'm sorry. I thought you were asking whether we had grounds to terminate her and then reassign the policies properly, keeping the renewal commission at the original assignment level of forty percent."

"That's an excellent point..."

"But it wasn't your question," Edie interrupted.

"No, I was going to ask if Collins and the CSR are intimate."

This time, Edie felt confident in rolling her eyes. "Even if they were, that's irrelevant to the case unless you could prove it in a court of law."

"Is she married?" Taylor asked.

"I'm not sure. The thought never occurred to me. I've only met her once, and she seemed priggish or lesbian."

Taylor slapped his knee. "Even better."

"I still don't see how that matters."

"Edie, quit assuming that everything will eventually go to court," Taylor snapped. "I'm looking for ways to get them both to resign."

"How would we ever come up with proof of an affair, however unlikely?" she asked.

Taylor pulled his BlackBerry from his jacket and punched in a note. "Leave that to me. I'll send Siemens an email. We'll use some old school tactics."

"Okay..." Edie cocked an eyebrow. "While you're sending out your supersleuth for soft-core black and whites, what should my team be doing?"

"Send Mona up there to bully Collins into a resignation. Also send Austin with her to placate Lutter and Hildebrand," he suggested. "If I can dig up something on the CSR and Collins, we'll put it in front of both of them and get her to resign."

"Won't we already have Collins's resignation in hand?" Edie asked.

"Yes, but they're not dead. They're just not a part of the company anymore, remember?" he said.

Edie felt a blush rise to her cheeks. "Sorry. Sometimes it's hard to tell the difference."

"I'm sure it is," Taylor said with a laugh. "So are we clear? Send Mona up there to get the resignation. Tell Siemens to bring up the kid from Phoenix, and then send Austin up there to booze up Lutter and Hildebrand and make them feel better about what's happening. Have her get them drunk and then have her tell them that we're going to have the CSR terminated or get her to resign. They'll have a vague notion of it but won't be able to hold us to anything."

Edie cleared her throat. "I understand, but I want to reiterate that Austin is very talented and you shouldn't see her as sugar-coating. In fact, there is another fraudulent district manager I wanted to assign to her to give her more experience."

Taylor took a tired, deep breath. "Who now? Don't say Laurent."

"No, not Laurent," Edie said. "Capote."

Alarm wrinkled across Taylor's forehead. "Capote's our top auto new business and premium district manager. He's a machine. Need I remind you that there are two renewal cycles a year in auto insurance and that's why it's so important to the channel?" he asked.

"No need to remind me," Edie said. "I sit on all the conference calls. But it's his agents, who care nothing for him, who drive the district's auto policy sales. He has no impact."

"Well, what's he been doing?"

"Getting his higher producing agents to write policies in his reserve agents' codes to get them to career," she explained. "The evidence goes even farther to suggest that he even appointed his agency manager and district life specialist as career agents to pocket the subsidy."

"He earns half a million dollars a year," Taylor said. "Why would he need to pocket the monthly fifteen hundred from agent subsidy?"

Edie shrugged. "He probably pays his agents who write the business out of the subsidy. You have to admit the subsidy is much higher than the monthly production requirements pay out. It's a good deal all around."

"Do you have enough evidence to terminate?" Taylor asked.

Edie shook her head. "Not yet. We can establish different IP addresses for the business being written online. We can tie those computer addresses to the agents' physical office addresses where the business was written. We can correlate the spike in business written by those agents to the rise in production that keeps the subsidization flowing but keeps the career agents under the success story radar. The only missing piece is whether the DM is forcing the agents to write the business or paying them to."

Taylor rubbed his face to hide his frustrations. "That's enough to pursue termination," he said with a sigh. "Tell Siemens we're going after Capote. Tell him I want the Houston RDM in Capote's district faster than the Homecoming King in Duluth. Don't pursue the agents Capote paid to write under the career agent codes."

Edie suspected Taylor gave her Capote to protect Laurent. He'd caved too quickly to the pursuit of Capote's termination. "Do you think it would be too difficult to get a subpoena or too costly to seek an injunction?" she asked.

John Taylor smiled and shook his head. "Not at all. The agents will get the message from putting a bullet in their district manager's head. But you know as well as I, they produce far too much auto new business to bring them under threat of termination. Besides, I guarantee Capote paid them off from his personal checking account, and all they have to do is move stuff out of their garage and into his and claim he bought it from them."

Edie leaned forward. "To be clear, John. They walk free, and we kill the DM?"

"Under heightened surveillance, of course," he said, his smile turning into perma-grin. "But they'll get the message."

Chapter Eight

Feed All God's Children was a Minnesota-based charity with six locations in the Twin Cities, the nearest to Edie's church being in Eagan. She'd attend two company-sponsored packing meetings when she'd first moved, and had been pleased to discover that her parish scheduled times throughout the month to serve and pack food for people in the most critical areas of the world. The outlet in Coon Rapids, north of the Cities, would please even the most skeptical donor with its nearly hidden entrance in the pit of a trucking complex. The Eagan location was equally barren. Edie had missed the turn twice, first following her GPS, and then again, reading from the printed directions in the church bulletin.

The temperature had plummeted since her meeting with Taylor. Its frosty foreboding was unwelcome when Edie parked and looked to the sky. In the Springs, the cloud cover mixed an eccentric palette of colors to foretell of certain snow. Electric green had been her favorite shade, ushering silent blizzards with thunderous accents. In Minnesota, the dozen hazy hues of gray hid the truth of their bounty, sometimes yielding eight inches of snowfall in a few hours, other times spraying an icy dusting. She sighed. Apparently here, the weather didn't need to concern people with amounts. Six months of unrelenting accumulation was enough to report. What did it matter if today brought powder and tomorrow weeping slush?

She peered into the charity's front office, scanning the windows for familiar faces. She didn't recognize anyone among the sixty or so participants. Several clustered together, forming workforce teams: Target employees in their red T-shirts and khaki pants, Best Buy employees in their blue T-shirts and khaki pants, Health Partners employees in their grey T-shirts and khaki pants. These teams would measure their competition in the number of total boxes packed, regardless of the number of players.

Once inside, Edie became more self-conscious of being alone. As the rosters coagulated, the smattering of individuals were sifted out to be assigned to stations like scabs brought in during strikes. She tucked errant strands of hair behind her ear and reminded herself not to slouch her shoulders. A middle-aged woman near the shopping counter, where packers could buy jewelry made in Haiti from recycled magazines, gave her a welcoming smile.

Then the woman raised her hand and called out, "First Presbyterians, let's meet up by the spare change drop!" Again, she smiled at Edie and nodded past her to indicate the array of fish bowls and antique vases where donors could away cast their coins.

"I'm not..." Edie mouthed.

The woman shrugged and gestured for Edie to join them anyway.

From behind, a warm, damp hand clasped Edie's shoulder. "She's with us," came a throaty, Northern accent.

Edie turned to see a large, short woman with orange bottle worn hair. "I am?"

"Sure, you're Risen Lord, right?" the woman asked. She then pointed to the emblem on her maroon T-shirt which carried the parish logo, celebrating the church's fortieth anniversary.

The Presbyterian smiled and turned to her flock, but Edie thought she saw a slip of disappointment shadow over her eyes.

"I'm Teresa," the parishioner was saying. "You aren't with the RCIA candidates, are you?"

Edie cleared her throat. "No, I converted before I moved to Minnesota. I'm new here."

"Oh, that's good to know," Teresa said, cocking back her head, crossing her arms, and cupping her chin in one startlingly fluid motion for her frame. "Because I'm a sponsor for our RCIA program. In fact, I finally convinced my husband of nineteen years to convert, and I don't remember ever seeing you at our weekly meetings with the candidates and their spouses."

Edie didn't miss the emphasis on her last word. Smirking, she shook her head. "I converted two Easters back in Colorado Springs. And I'm single."

"Single or divorced?"

"Single." The answer came before Edie could decide if the question were appropriate from a stranger. "I'm sorry. Did I come at the wrong time? Is this packing session reserved for RCIA?"

Teresa chuckled. "Oh, no. All are welcome, just like what the sign above the church says. Most of us are here for the public service requirement for RCIA, but there are a couple of others, too. In fact, Easton Frost's supposed to come."

Edie froze. It was a monumental internal struggle to keep her cheeks and the tips of her ears from reddening. She could feel every follicle in her head lurching to reject this ridiculous dye and free her red hair, which would at least justify the surge from dead pale to bloated tick red across her face in seeing him.

She had no doubt Teresa would chalk her up to Easton Frost's hangers-on, all those Cursillo women vying for a whiff of Frost pheromones. There would be no convincing this stranger of the accidental quality of the truth.

Instead, Edie decided to cast her gaze downward, straight downward, not to him and then away and downward, which would belie her interest to a schooled tell reader. This Teresa was a pry bar; she had the gift. Edie hadn't given herself one look in Frost's general direction. Nor would she as long as Teresa stole her oxygen and replaced it with bratwurst and mustard laced carbon dioxide.

"Were you at the nine o'clock on Sunday?" Teresa asked. "Did you hear his lay homily?"

"Yes, I was there," Edie said. "I spoke to him afterward."

"How long did you wait in line?" Teresa asked with a snort.

"I didn't see any line," Edie said.

"What did you talk about?" Teresa asked.

"Okay, everyone, grab a seat," a man yelled from the back of the meeting room, causing a musical chairs frenzy complete with a bulging Picasso of team jersey neogeometry.

It was a moment where Edie knew God liked her, like her personality, like her heart, gave her a thumbs-up for her sense of humor. Teresa had vanished from her side, scampering to join her husband and the full RCIA group. *The woman is dying to intimidate the Protestants,* Edie thought. A warm, chuckling approval caressed the inside of her neck.

Edie allowed the seats to fill and elected to stand in the back, along the walls of starry, magazine paper beadwork.

The man who had called the meeting to order walked to the front, carrying a grey discus high above his head. When he faced the audience, Edie outed him. His was an unapologetic sexuality that permitted his hips to sway proudly in decades old stone washed jeans. His Converse high tops were vintage and well worn. His belt buckle was hidden behind a belly that needed no introduction, and chest hair wolf manned out from the ridge of his volunteer grey T-shirt.

"Who here had dinner before they came over?" he asked the crowd.

Those who had packed before remained silent, aware of the presentation. Some from the corporate teams raised their hands.

The wolf man volunteer pointed to one lady. "What did you have for dinner?"

"A Hot Pocket," was the muted, dull response.

All laughed away their nerves.

"What about you?" the volunteer continued.

A tall man with black hair stepped in front of her. "Me? A chicken sandwich from Burger King."

"Is anyone here hungry?" the volunteer asked.

This was a new wrinkle to the presentation. Edie stepped forward, now abreast with the rude man who'd stepped before her.

The volunteer pointed his finger. "You? Yeah? A little bit, maybe." His voice trailed off. "How many of you ate this for dinner?" Now he brandished the grey disc again.

"How many of you know what this is?" he continued. "This is a mud cake. Women in Haiti and throughout the world make these and feed them to their children because it tricks their stomachs into thinking there is something worth digesting. People, it comes out looking the exact same as it goes in."

Edie lowered her eyes. The wolf man was a touch too theatrical, but the point was received.

"Here at Feed All God's Children, we started feeding people six years ago and were able to make, pack, and ship one million meals all over the world. This year, our goal is nineteen million meals." He turned his back and grabbed a packet of food. "Here is what we send. This packet has all the vitamins and nutrients needed to sustain life and let it flourish. In this we have dehydrated vegetables, rice, a vitamin supplement in powder form, and a small chicken flavor packet. This is what you will be packing once we go inside the packing area. Each person receives a cup of this mixture twice a day. In a minute, I will show you a video of the story of Baby Jonah so you can see the dramatic and direct effect your efforts have on people all over the world."

He paused to clear his throat and pat down the emotion welling in his voice. "We buy all of the material that goes into our packages from General Mills and local Minnesota farmers at a deep discount. Your cash contributions go directly to purchasing more food and to our shipping costs, which you can imagine, are the greatest expenses to running this not-for-profit business.

"Now, I can tell by your faces that you're going to pack several hundred meals for those in the most desperate need. And the more you pack, the more people will live. But the downside, and there is only one downside, is this. Your vigorous packing tonight will deplete our food supplies. So packing with us is only the first part of the equation. The second part is your donation either in cash or by shopping in our store where women all over the world hand make items to sell. Not having to worry about cooking mud cakes for their children, they too can learn trades and start businesses. Half of the profit from the sale of these goods is returned to these women so that they can build their growing businesses. The other half comes right back here to buy more food for the packing.

"Now let's take a look at the video that tells us more about Baby Jonah and how our organization saves and strengthens lives through the hard work of you and your fellow Minnesotans."

The volunteer bowed and stepped backward as a woman wheeled a TV and VCR on a cart to the center of the room. Ducking her head and squinting in the growing darkness from the setting sun, she pushed play.

Though Edie had seen the video twice before, she knew it would motivate her. Still it also didn't keep her from peering up at the man who'd stepped in front of her.

The tall figure with black hair was blanched by the TV's blue hues, but his eyes were unmistakable. They were blue on blue even before the screen's shimmer. Easton Frost had cut in front of her.

Dozens of questions flooded her mind. Should she jokingly ask him why he'd done it? What if he didn't remember her? She'd never really gotten an answer about getting coffee. She'd been one of two dozen women hovering around him last Sunday. But he had mentioned they shared the same initials. Surely, he'd remember that, right? But what if he wasn't alone? Who brings a date to Feed All God's Children? *A very considerate, selfless person who isn't afraid to open up and share himself with someone*, Edie told herself. *That's who.*

Against the horrific screams in her mind telling her not to, she cleared her throat dramatically and turned to face him. "You cut in front of me."

He shot her an apologetic smirk and shrugged. "I'm sorry. I didn't see anyone behind me. I got here a little late and didn't want to make noise." Then he crinkled his forehead and arched an eyebrow. "We met last Sunday at church, right?"

"Yes, I'm Edie..."

"Firebaugh," he said, snapping his fingers. "Yes, the lady with the same initials."

Edie hated being called a lady. While it was far better than being called a woman, it cloaked any interest he may have in her, which would have been obvious if he'd referred to her as a girl.

"Firebaugh," he said again. "That's a great last name. If I had that name, there's no way I'd change it or hyphenate it when I got married."

Edie recognized the attempt to determine her relationship status, and she had to admit it was clever. "That's right. I consider it a birthright and I'm not letting it go."

He cleared his throat and cast his gaze to the TV. "Sorry I wasn't able to talk to you about coffee. I sort of got pimped out at the Cursillo couples' and women's retreat table after Mass."

Edie kept her gaze at his temple, prepared for eye contact if he should turn back to her. "I know. I shouldn't have just blurted it out that way. I thought we had some similar experiences after hearing you talk. Don't worry about it."

"Well, you walked away before I really had a chance to think," he said.

"There were two people tugging on your arm," she replied.

"So you're not interested in getting coffee, like after this?" he asked.

He tilted his head toward her. That sharp nose threw a shadow over half his face, but she could still see his eyes. The picture was frozen in her mind.

"You aren't here with anybody else?" she asked.

He shook his head. "I'm sorry, are you? I should have asked."

"No, I signed up on the church's website," Edie explained. The tempo of her voice had a gallop to it. "I've done this before with work a couple of times."

Easton shoved his hands in his pockets and shrank down a bit so that they could continue to talk without drawing attention away from the presenters. "Yeah, they offer sessions at my job, too, but I felt better about coming with the church. I haven't been in Minnesota that long."

"That's what you said during the homily," Edie returned. With his well tanned face closer to hers now, she was gripped with the fear of bad breath. She'd been silent during the ride from work and then Teresa hadn't let her speak much during her interrogation. Edie sighed, knowing the longer you kept your mouth closed, the worse your breath became. It was her turn not to face him.

"Yes, that's right," Easton said. "I talk too much, so I have a problem remembering what I actually tell people."

"It happens to a lot of guys," Edie said and immediately regretted it for the unintended innuendo.

Easton coughed away his embarrassment. "Yes, I've been told on several occasions that as a gender we love to hear ourselves talk. There's just no sound with thinking."

Edie huffed. "There is in my head. You must not be thinking the right way."

Easton smirked. "I've been told that, too."

The video of Baby Jonah ended. Without warning, the wolf man volunteer was behind them, flicking on the fluorescent lights. The entire assembly squinted, their watery eyes magnifying the soft light.

"Okay, folks," the volunteer said. "Now, before we go into the packing area to divide up the work, we'll walk through the sanitation station. We are dealing with food preparation here, so it is important that you wash your hands thoroughly before entering your food prep station. Also, everyone is required to wear hairnets. If you don't feel comfortable, please remember, everyone is wearing one, and everyone looks just as ridiculous as you do. If you're still too vain, visit the shopping area, and make a large cash donation instead."

The three corporate and two church teams shuffled toward the sanitizing area. Bursts of excited conversation harmonized with nervous chuckles.

Edie felt a tug on her elbow.

"Hey, I was serious about getting coffee," Easton said.

Edie shrugged and prayed that her chin wasn't shivering. "Um, okay. I guess you're on unless you manage to have people prying you away at the end of this like you did at church."

He smiled. "Somehow, I don't think I'll be the center of attention here."

"Let's hope not," she replied, matching his smile. "There's a Caribou Coffee down the road."

"Okay, good," he said. "I'm not familiar with Eagan. I live in Minneapolis," Easton said.

"Minneapolis?" she asked. "Then why do you go to church in Apple Valley?"

"The basilica is just as conservative as the diocese in Saint Paul," he explained.

"So how did you find Risen Lord?" Edie asked.

Easton nudged her elbow again, marking the second time he touched her, and directed her to follow the group.

"Are we supposed to meet up with the RCIA people?" he asked when they'd finished washing their hands.

In answer, Teresa turned the corner and shoved a wadded up hair net into Edie's hand. "Hi, Easton!" she exclaimed and stood on her tip toes to throw a large, ricocheting arm around his shoulders. "I'm Teresa, one of the sponsors for RCIA. I'd love to hear more about your experience."

Easton's eyes darted from Edie to Teresa. Edie turn her shoulder away from Teresa and waited for his returning glance to roll her eyes. He rapidly blinked twice. Had they already started non-verbal communication?

"Maybe we can sit down before Mass on Sunday and talk further," Easton replied.

"Great, I'll reserve us a meeting room in the church offices," Teresa said. "Worst case, we can duck into one of the confessionals."

Her voice wasn't trailing off so much as the Doppler effect pulled Edie's hearing further away from Teresa as she glided into the food preparation and packaging center. She could only hope God would give Easton the strength to follow.

Waving her arms and sending a shrill whistle through her teeth, Teresa sidestepped Edie. "We're all meeting at station eleven. Easton Frost and Edie Firebaugh will be joining us."

"Frost and Firebaugh, that sounds like a law firm," Easton said.

"Funny, but if you reverse it to Firebaugh and Frost, it sounds more like a cop drama on TNT," Edie countered.

"I like it better that way," Easton said.

"So do I." But something remained unsettling with Edie. This Frost was being far too agreeable, too accommodating. Sure, after his discourse on his communion with others in heaven, she expected him to have a suave, soothing nature to his speech and mannerisms. But that didn't change the fact that he was a man, and men were goofy, clunky, unnecessarily sure of themselves, which gave them a slap-stick quality that some women grew to love. Easton Frost did not feel genuine. There was a gentle transparency in his gait and demeanor, but it was not enough to overcome her disquiet. Edie worried she might become fascinated with what all warnings foretold her was a flake.

She gave him a sideward glance and burst out laughing, not expecting the hilarity of seeing the tall man with a bulbous netting covering his affluent hair.

"Listen, sister," Easton said as his face crimsoned a blush. "You don't look so awesome yourself."

"It's for a good cause," she muttered.

The wolf man guided the group through the various stations of food prep, pointing out which measuring cups to use for each ingredient, how to use the funnel to fill the packaging, how to use the sealer to lock in the package, and how to weigh each packet. He then demonstrated how to pack a box, optimizing space for twenty packets.

Edie walked to station sixteen. Easton followed. Teresa had divided the RCIA candidates from their sponsors, and there was only one spot left to fill: weighing and sealing the packets. Edie stepped into position.

"Now, I need six strong men to volunteer to remove filled boxes and to replace supplies," the wolf man called out.

Realizing there wasn't a position left for the Risen Lord stations, Easton raised his hand.

The wolf man counted the volunteers and waved them to the storage area. "All right, men. This is actually the easiest job. Follow me."

Edie bit the inside of her cheek at hearing the emphasis the wolf man put on the word *men*. It reminded her of the raining men disco song, halleluiah. They were in his world now.

She was glad to see Easton go. She needed time to think. What would they talk about during their coffee? Would he continue to meander sinisterly down this Eddie Haskell path? Was this Easton Frost afraid to have a good time, to sin a little, because of what he saw? Edie found herself perplexed in her frustration. She couldn't figure him out, and she would be disappointed if she determined he wasn't worth her fascination.

Another thought pierced through all other bubbles. Had she been in agent termination mode too long? Did she need to go through some sort of mental detox? The world was still full of trustworthy people, wasn't it? Even here in the land of passive-aggressive, Minnesota nice wickedness?

The wolf man reappeared, the smile on his face aligned with her thoughts of northern mid-west deception. "Okay, people. Most sponsor volunteers leave it up to a vote for the music we listen to during our two-hour packing session, but I find late '80s arena rock to motivate the most production. Hope you don't mind Guns 'N' Roses, Poison, and Warrant. I have all their greatest hits CDs."

There was no time to argue. *Welcome to the Jungle* trickled through the speakers and grew louder. The wolf man added his own Axel Rose hip thrusts in time with the intro.

"Hi, I'm Stella," the woman next to Edie said.

"Edie Firebaugh," she replied.

They didn't shake plastic-gloved hands for fear of contamination, but their smiles equaled one another.

"Did they let you into the program late because of Joyce?" Stella asked.

"No, I'm not in RCIA," Edie explained. A man next to her handed Edie her first packet to measure and seal. "Thank you—I converted in Colorado Springs two years ago. I've only been here for six months."

Stella raised her eyes and nodded. "How was your RCIA class?"

"Strict, militant, by the book, painful. The Springs has military installations all around it." Edie replied. "How is it here?"

"Well, we started with Joyce, who was okay," Stella said. "I wasn't a big fan of hers. She's a musical genius who probably would have been a priest if she were a man. Her credentials are amazing. But if you asked too many questions, she'd drop the hammer and say something about that just being tradition and for us to accept it.

"Then we got Margaret. They asked Joyce for her resignation all of a sudden," Stella continued.

Edie smirked and placed her third packet under the sealer. She'd never worked this position, but it didn't take much concentration. "Sounds like there's a story there."

Stella nodded. "Well, Father Tim came to make the announcement one night and mentioned that due to state law, he wasn't able to say whether Joyce resigned, or quit, or was asked to leave, or got fired. We had no idea what she could have done. She'd been in the position for four years. She's a really devout Catholic, too. She has adopted five children from foster care agencies, and is raising them all on her own. She really walks the talk, you know."

Edie thought to be provocative. "But it sounded like you didn't like the way she taught the class or led the discussions."

"I didn't care for it," Stella agreed. "But I didn't dislike her enough to see her lose her job. Especially losing a church job." She leaned in closer to whisper. "I heard she left the church entirely and joined the Episcopals and is now becoming a priest for them."

Edie now understood. "Was she asked to leave because she had a partner?"

"A partner?" Stella asked.

"A life partner," Edie clarified.

"Did Teresa already tell you?" Stella hissed.

"No, but why else join the Episcopal church if you are such a devout Catholic?" Edie said with a shrug. "They don't have the hang-up about homosexuality, and they let women become priests."

"It is weird how chauvinistic the church is," Stella muttered.

"Why are you converting?" Edie asked.

"For my husband and children," she replied. "We've been married for twelve years, and now our oldest is going through first communion. So he's starting to ask really uncomfortable questions for my husband."

"Like why isn't mom allowed to get communion?" Edie asked.

"You got it," Stella said.

Paradise City rolled into *Sweet Child O'Mine* rolled into *Unskinny Bop* rolled into *Every Rose Has It's Thorn*. Edie didn't look up from weighing and sealing packets until Warrant's *Heaven Isn't Too Far Away*. The corporate teams competitively proclaimed each number of packed boxes. The Presbyterian table cast over the shoulder glares at the women at the Catholic tables with increased frequency when they found out these women were converting.

Edie spent her time people-watching, trying to guess who was married at the religious tables, and who was having affairs at the corporate tables. Then for a real challenge, which of the married couples at the church stations would be acting like the cheaters at the corporate stations if they were here under those circumstances.

If Easton had passed by her area to refill the rice or to take any one of their fourteen filled boxes, Edie hadn't seen him. She needed a clear mind for coffee. Driving directly from home office to this site, she'd decided, hadn't afforded her time to decompress and shed the tougher skin of working in agent graveyards, preparing more space in nameless catacombs. She knew that hers was a macabre way to earn a living. Even though she was successful at overcoming the first stages of guilt for supposedly destroying family lives, even though she'd blasted through the denial phase which prevented her from knowing the company had actually caused its own profitability issues, the frigid acceptance lingered. Edie imagined her soul also being able to see its own breath, and placed herself in Scrooge's future Christmas setting.

She couldn't be so hollowed out from the Drano of her profession or she wouldn't be able to attract a nice, normal guy. Edie hadn't felt she possessed a single attractive quality since...

since she had to dye her hair for this job. Before that, her loneliness had whittled her down to a sedentary, pajama lifestyle where reality TV governed the path of her week's worth of moods, only to be uplifted or validated with Ben and Jerry's.

Mona's and Austin's bar-hopping was no solution for Edie either. While she'd had her share of morning light shame-walking, Edie'd conquered the debauchery of the hook-up. Or at least, grew tired of its lessons, rote memorization of guilt that never needed repeating until one drank away the mnemonics.

Edie hadn't had sex since she'd broken up with Corporal Belligerent, sustaining herself with favorite childhood, cologne drenched stuffed animals for bedtime comfort and learning to ignore the pangs of needed intimacy.

She wasn't ready to start dating again. Edie couldn't believe she was deciding this very second. Inwardly rolling her eyes at the initial arrogance of assuming Easton wanted to date her, she told herself it was better to take herself off the proverbial market before any bidding started.

But she'd been the one to ask him out for coffee.

Certainly a mistake. She'd been overwhelmed with the collective Mass mentality during his speech. Edie was no stranger to Catholic men. Regardless if his bent was Irish Catholic, Italian Catholic, or even Latino Catholic, he'd assuredly cleaned up after his lay homily and wouldn't have felt guilty about it, feathering his lonesomeness and sorrow for driving his lover away within his physical need for assurance.

The priest, either Tim or Jim or any other for that matter, would have the words of absolution trickling out of their mouths before Easton had finished his confession.

Edie was no number.

She shook back her attention. Warrant's *I Saw Red* was humming along. The wolf man had taken their fifteenth box, and Edie now felt sure that the Presbyterians were spiritually transferring their anger and sense of rejection from the Catholic Church on to her.

No, Edie thought. God invented anger just like depression and joy. He knows its effects, and he intends for everyone to be subjected to it.

Easton was attractive though. His personality reminded her of a high school boyfriend, though Easton's looks far surpassed that. Why was it so hard to believe that some men were just genuinely that nice? America was now into its third full generation of women having arrogant jerks' children. Jerks begat jerks, thus swaying the balance against the diminishing number of nice men. Becca would say it was a downward spiral of geometric proportions.

Easton had those eyes. The rest was just too much to believe: tall, tanned, without blemish. She'd never gotten her hug though. That would be the final test, physically. That would be his Kryptonite. He wouldn't be huggable. Easton Frost was too skinny, would feel breakable, unable to protect or even make a woman feel safe.

Coffee was back on.

It was just coffee.

"Sixteen boxes with only thirty minutes left," Easton said somewhere just outside of her peripheral vision.

Edie took a deep breath but was far too focused to turn to face him. "It's a well-oiled machine."

"You sound a little tired," he said.

She wasn't about to let him renegotiate now. Edie agreed with Mona on one point. If a man offers to accept a rain check, the power of negotiation is still in his hands. He had the right to call you for the next month because he let you off the date. Edie recalled what Mona had told her once: that men and women experienced exhaustion differently. Men don't care if they're tired; they will still act a certain way, think a certain way, and are ready to have sex at any calling. *They have no true understanding of a woman being tired,* Edie thought. The ones who pretended to care were the worst perpetrators of underhanded dating negotiation. In short, if a man lets you off with playing the tired card, you will pay for it two-fold later, rang Mona's voice.

"Oh, no, Frost," Edie said, throwing gruff gusto into her tone. "You're going. It's just coffee and it's just down the street. Unless that's your way of saying you're tired, or you're really not interested in caffeinated conversation with me." Edie had enclosed herself in her thoughts for too long and it was prevalent in her speech. She'd gone too far.

"Oh, no, Firebaugh," Easton returned. "I'll drink you under the table. I'm talking black, no sugar, too, not that ridiculous stuff, ice cream swirl on top of a pureed cinnamon roll in a cup."

Finally, a hint of swagger.

"You're on then," Edie said.

Caribou Coffee, the Minnesota equivalent to Starbucks before the conglomerate's bid for global domination, was treasured for being unknown and taken for granted. Employees from both, however, were trained to grimace at a straight black coffee order.

The out state, lake cabin feel was reinforced with a gush of sawdust and pine aromatherapy, which some of the locals needed to settle their nerves at how big their suburbs had become. The made from branches tables and chairs were pretty to look at, but uncomfortable if one didn't have the proper northern padding.

Edie was eternally grateful that she was sans this rear cushion, but found herself wishing for the back fat necessary for comfort. Thus Caribou Coffee was a disease of the mind for inspiring such wishful thinking.

Easton looked at peace with the décor, poor lighting, and the local folksy never gonna be's piped in on overhead speakers.

"You don't look like you worked up a sweat, carrying all those boxes," Edie commented. She raised her mug to eye level with both hands, masking her smirk and steeling her eyes.

Easton shrugged and met her stare. "Not to brag..." He paused and cleared his throat.

"But you're going to anyway," she interrupted.

"Judge for yourself," he replied. "I was going to say that I was the most in-shape man who volunteered for the heavy lifting."

A smile won over Edie's face. "Okay, you're right. That's not bragging. Not here in Meenesotah, der den."

Easton coughed a bit, caught in the middle of a sip. "You do that well."

"Thanks, I've been working on my northern accent," Edie replied.

"I notice you don't have much of one."

"I'm from Colorado Springs," Edie said. "No accent there."

"I lost my Southern accent before I came here," Easton said.

"Where did you say you're from again?" Edie remembered he was from Oklahoma, but she didn't want him knowing that. Still, she cringed with how fake her question had sounded.

"Oklahoma," Easton said. "Not too many people care to admit that."

"Good news never escapes Oklahoma," Edie said. "You people keep some of the best secrets of the South to yourselves. The same holds true for Texas."

Easton brought his coffee mug hard onto the table, which startled Edie. She then rubbed down the rigid hairs along her neck. "You dare compare Oklahoma with Texas?" His look was sharp and seething with judgment, but just when Edie felt her confidence plummet, Easton's blue-on-blue eyes softened. "I'm kidding. But it is dangerous to make generalizations between the states."

Edie exhaled and chuckled, which did nothing to assuage her growing sense of unease. He'd just read her tells. *He's a player,* she told herself. Just this coffee meeting and that's it. "Are you talking about just Oklahoma and Texas or the entire South?"

Easton echoed her laugh. "Since the war, it's best not to make any direct state-to-state comparisons."

"The war?" she asked.

"Yes, the war between the states or the war for states' rights," Easton explained. "You may know it as the Civil War."

Edie rolled her eyes. "The predominant states' right was the right to own slaves, correct? That kills me. Like when that idiot Glenn Beck mentions the Civil War with those moronic euphemisms."

Perhaps she'd packed too much of a value testing wallop. Asking about racism and bigotry, lambasting the Great White Hope for the Tea-Bagging Party, and slamming down some solid vocabulary might be a triumvirate for turning a man off. But hadn't she decided to kill this off after coffee? Edie tallied the chess move as a further test of Easton's ability to read her facial and body language.

"Glenn Beck is an animal," Easton said. "I'm confident he will burn in hell for encouraging others to vote in ways that will lead them to burn in hell as well. He's definitely the second most false prophet in modern American times."

Edie leaned back and folded her arms across her chest. She then pursed her lips to hide as much of her enthusiasm as possible. "Round out the top three."

Easton smirked and shrugged again. "Rush Limbaugh is a deal with the devil demon incarnate. He doesn't even hide it anymore. And third is Sean Hannity. He's like the demon apprentice in *The Screwtape Letters*. Willing but unable to be as effective as his masters."

Edie cupped her chin in her hand and leaned forward. Not only had he read her non-verbals and responded on cue, he'd matched her vocab with the C.S. Lewis reference. "I don't believe it. I'm actually talking to a Southern gentleman, who claims to be visited by the Holy Spirit, who doesn't vote Republican but refuses to apologize for the Civil War."

It was Easton's turn to push his body away from the conversation. "Wait just a second, Edie Firebaugh. While I don't vote breed 'em, don't feed 'em, I don't feel it's my place to apologize for an entire war. You'll never convince me that the Civil War wasn't primarily a socioeconomic conflict with the North imposing its industrial dominance on the agriculturally based Southern economies. But who now would argue for slavery?"

He hadn't taken a breath yet. She'd struck something genuine within him, past his salesman bravado.

"The propaganda used for Operation Iraqi Freedom draws stark similarities," he continued. "No one would support a war with the slogan: Operation Cheaper and Safer Oil Interests. Just like back then, no one would rally around the slogan: Europe will use the Industrial Revolution to Overpower Us if We Don't Rebalance the Country's Economy."

"I agree," Edie said, holding her hand up to stop his rant. "All wars need propaganda."

Easton took a deep breath and a long sip from his mug. "Air-conditioning was the only thing that pushed the Southern economies into the twenty-first century."

"How so?"

"Before that, the North kept its industrial complexes above the Mason-Dixon line," he explained.

"Never thought of that," she said.

Easton turned to the side, crossed his legs, and refused to give her eye contact. "You also mentioned rather cynically my experience with God. If I didn't know any better, I would think you're trying to push me away before we even become friends."

Was she really being that transparent? Was she really this out of practice? There was no point hiding the blush, but being called out didn't signal a full surrender.

She waved her hands apologetically. "I'm sorry. I got a little carried away. I didn't mean to sound like I didn't believe what you said in church. It was meant more to be a comment on religious men from the South I've encountered."

Easton leaned forward once more, but kept his legs and posture crossed from her. "You have well honed corporate speech, especially for the passive-aggressive apology."

Edie cleared her throat. "I work downtown. Go figure."

"I'm not an evangelizer," he said.

Was he starting to pout? If so, was this a lure? Edie was analyzing the situation beyond any shred of enjoyment.

"I never said you were," Edie said.

"I'm sorry. I must have given you the wrong impression," he continued.

"What impression?" she asked. *Two could cast lures.*

"That I'm a sly snake charmer, looking to con his way into a church crowd for easy pickin's and make a fortune for good for what ails you snake oil," Easton said, dropping into a thick Southern accent.

"You did draw quite the crowd after your speech," she said.

"Does that intimidate you?" Easton quickly replied.

"Intimidate me?"

"I move to strike that from the record," Easton said. He squared his shoulders and placed his hands palm down on the table.

His lures didn't work, Edie thought. He literally had to reel himself back in. Even Vegas played odds on the percentage of time most women felt intimidated. For Becca, it was as constant and involuntary as breathing. Even Edie had her bouts with self-doubt. Was Easton reacting badly or was he being more honest than anyone she'd ever met? Did he have a history of intimidating people, women? Was he aware of this trait and compensated for it with the Eddie Haskell routine?

"Well, then for the record," Edie said. "No, I wasn't intimidated by your crowd at church. Doesn't everyone want to hear a story about a real, tangible experience with God?"

Easton smirked and nodded. "Then you believe me?"

"Of course, I do," she replied. "I believe in God enough that I don't question his ability to choose how he communicates with us. I especially believe the correlation to the description of heaven found in Matthew."

"You do?" His grin had exploded with perfectly straight, gleaming white teeth.

"Absolutely," she said. Now, she was reeling him in.

"While we're stating things for the record," Easton said, "the men were recruiting me to the Knights of Columbus."

"And the women?"

"Most needed someone to bake for..."

"Not *those* women," Edie said.

"The Cursillo ladies?" he asked and shook his head as a chill ran through him. "They're not my speed."

"What is your speed?" Edie asked.

He folded his hands together and leaned back. "I'm comfortable with a progressive, liberal trajectory. Not a race backward where people discuss supporting the annulment process and why women shouldn't become priests."

"So none of the Cursillos do it for you?" Edie couldn't believe she'd become so see-through. She didn't like the beat of this dance.

"I'm not seeing anyone, Edie," he said.

Edie squinted through the unreality before her. Had he just implied he was datable, date worthy, someone she'd be interested in seeing? "Excuse me?" she asked once the red rage dust cloud settled to the bottom of her sight.

Easton smiled big and cleared his throat. "I was just saying that I'm not seeing anybody right now. You seemed to be suggesting that one of the Cursillo retreat women had asked me out."

His speech was fast. His words were crashing into each other. "I'm really not over my fiancée yet, either. I'm not interested in jumping into a long-term relationship right now."

Edie looked down at her mug to keep from rolling her eyes. She then took a sip to stop her from clinching her teeth. It was a warning sign, telling her she was about to start growling.

Frost was an imbecile, at once as arrogant as France's Sun King, claiming to be divinely appointed, and as sickly sweet as any man who had convinced himself that he's devoid of ego. Further, he believed himself to be a genuinely nice person without motive.

Edie could see all of this in his blunder. Not that it was a difficult read. His dread was puffing his eye sockets. His realization of turning her off closed in his irises.

It was only coffee.

"That's certainly understandable," Edie said. "I'm still getting over a military schmuck, who insisted I convert to Catholicism for him." That should do it, she told herself.

Easton cast his head down and nodded. "There's unfortunately little distinction between faith and regulation," he said, "particularly when it comes to the sacraments."

"You mean particularly when it comes to you cradle Catholics," Edie said.

Easton looked up and chuckled. "That, too."

Edie polished off her coffee with dramatic flair and didn't bother to look across the table to see if Frost had finished his own mug. "I have a hectic schedule tomorrow," she said.

"Do you?" Easton asked.

Could he still be begging for conversation?

"Yes," Edie said with a sigh. She rooted through her hand bag to find some chap stick and gum.

"Where do you work again?" he asked. "Or did you already tell me?"

"I work downtown," Edie replied.

"So do I," Easton said.

"I know, you told me," she said. She placed her hands flat across the table and gave her eyes expectancy. Edie didn't believe in telepathy simply because people wasted most of their brain capacity, but she did think it possible to send basic messages from one mind to another.

"We could do lunch sometime," he offered.

No luck. She rose from the table. "Sure, I'll text you."

Chapter Nine

Plumes of fog rose from the lakes they passed. The morning light made the waters look like jagged shards of a broken mirror. The trees were emerging into radiant deaths: bleeding reds, bruising oranges, the yellows of decay, and the browns of acceptance.

Late fall was a fine time to travel to Duluth. It would save Mona a trip into Wisconsin, where her last warlock gamer had suggested they go for a date. She'd much rather travel with a purpose than stroll around, grinding out conversation with a guy who actually looked better when he kept silent.

The road rarely curved once she and Austin left the Twin Cities on I-35E. Mona had never been to the town on Lake Superior's edge but had always been fond of the song about the sinking of the Edmund Fitzgerald, a tune her mother would half-whistle, half-sing when confronted with stress. Also, Mona always thought Pearl Jam should remake the song. Eddie Vedder's vocal would make for a nice improvement, and she'd love to hear what Mike McCreedy would do for a guitar solo, not to mention Jeff Ament pounding out that ship swaying bass line with sea legs enough to withstand the forty-foot rogue wave that did the ship in.

Mona felt as though she were visiting a graveyard, and was excited for the history of it. She would be adding to that cemetery. They were off to kill themselves a district manager, a real dink of one too, to employ northern pseudo curse words. They'd get him and his little customer service rep, too.

As though on cue, Austin cleared her throat. "Did you ever meet Angelica?" she asked.

Austin had managed to add more fog to the company car's window, which thickened in a yellowing that was part cigarette smoke, part designer coffee, but mostly perfume emanating from her neck. Although Mona didn't care for Austin's choice of fragrances, they fit the woman. Mona butchered a movie line in her head. *This has to be the worst toilet water I've ever smelled. What do you get a free bowl of soup with this perfume? Oh, it smells good on you though!*

"No, I never met her," Mona replied.

"She's been to the last two town hall meetings," Austin said. "Once, when she was a reserve agent, and then the last time right after she went career. She seemed nice. Very outgoing. Very open."

Mona rolled her eyes. "Don't start with the poor old agent routine, Austin. She went in on a corrupt bargain. I've got no choice but to hang this guy and her along with him. I run policy assignment. If I don't shoot this one down, the rest will be running all over me, going straight to the Aurora Service Center with their politics and lobbying deals."

Austin pushed her sunglasses up the bridge of her nose and tore through her purse for another cigarette. "I just wonder what this Terry Collins sold her on."

"He sold her an agency for nothing but a career agent checkmark," Mona said.

"There must be something more to the story." Austin lighted her smoke and cracked the window. "You know, I only smoke when I'm around you. You know that, right?"

Mona could feel Austin's eyes on her. They felt like the eyes a girl beads down on a guy during a date to see if he'll look over at her while he's driving. Mona had learned early that guys have no peripheral vision outside of playing sports. If you want to get a man's attention, present your entire body to him and look away from him. Most women did the opposite. They focused their faces toward the man and their bodies away from him, feeling self-conscious of their forms. Mona had watched enough adult films to have a healthier sense of what men wanted.

Clearly, her mind wasn't on work.

Clearly, Austin had won.

"What's more to the story?" Mona asked. "Angelica didn't have the cajones to get her own license after working for her agent for twelve years. She fell into the codependent trap of retiring agent annuitization, working the business, keeping it afloat without any business-owner risk. Then when the time was right, when he announced his retirement, she perked up and volunteered to take over the agency. She'd worked her way into learning what everything costs, what her P and L would be, and what the increased take-home rounded out to if she just signed some paperwork with Collins. The business was generating enough for her to go from reserve to career in a month. Then not only was she getting the agency on forty percent renewals based on the policy assignment but she'd also validate the career subsidy program in half the time it takes a scratch agent."

Austin flicked her cigarette out the window. She'd managed to smoke the entire thing during Mona's eruption. "She worked under a beer gutted, barrel-chested, *don cha know* moron for the last twelve years. He hadn't coached a game or attended a Kiwanis meeting or even thrown in dues for the Chamber of Commerce in years. He'd come in at ten, leave at two, and not even show up on Fridays."

"Contractually, that was his right," Mona argued. "He'd built up his business. Rates are in the toilet, but with the hikes everyone gets a pay raise on the renewals. I had a conversation with him after he retired, Austin. That half-week stuff is all a fabrication..."

"No, it's not..."

"Even if it wasn't," Mona said, raising her voice to power down on Austin. "Even if it wasn't, it was his business. He started out from scratch just like every other agent does. Worked off prospects, mailers, and referrals. And all of a sudden after accepting a CSR salary for twelve years, Angelica Whatever catches the entrepreneurial spirit? Too bad we can't check her voting record because I bet she's a straight DFL party-liner."

Austin humphed. "What's that got to do with anything? Democrats own businesses, too."

"Other than in romantic comedies where the woman has a cutesy niche business where her and her gay friend just chat it up, never work, and watch the money come in, name one," Mona said.

"That's not fair," Austin said.

"Get in line," Mona retorted. "Oh, by the way, the line is Democrat-created."

"There are plenty of liberal business owners," Austin said.

"Looking for a name," Mona said. "Heck, I'd even settle for Jane, the other plumber."

"Stop!" Austin yelled. "I can't think when you're talking. You know, you really don't ever shut up."

Mona's knuckles went white on the steering wheel. "I thought you were the one who said women talk to think while men talk to hear themselves."

"That's right," Austin said. "You talk to hear yourself. I'm sick of you bullying me. Why can't you just accept that I have the ability to see things outside your hangman's view? You know, Edie relocated me out here, too."

"You don't mind the dyed hair, Austin."

"What's that supposed to mean?"

"Exactly what I said," Mona replied.

"I don't see why you refuse to see the agent's side," Austin said with a huff. "What if Terry Collins lied to Angelica? What if she was sold some pipe dream of owning an agency without the downside of default risk? What if Terry begged her to go along with it to save his neck because he hasn't recruited a soul in almost two years?"

Mona nodded. "I've thought of all that. I really have, Austin. That's why we're going after the DM and not the agent."

Mona tapped the eject button on the CD player. Out popped the second disc from Pearl Jam's greatest hits album, *Rearview Mirror*. Mona pushed it back into the player and skipped to the seventh song, *Nothingman*. "You need to listen to this song, Austin. I've been meaning to play it for you since we moved here. This is my motivation. Listen to the lyrics."

Austin sat straighter, no doubt intent on gleaning new emotional insight on her friend.

"What's the song called?"

"Nothingman," Mona replied.

Neo-crooner Vedder came in with a deep, reedy vocal just after the morose intro. Mona felt herself falling to another place, a little tender for having invited Austin to join her.

"Arms divided. Nothing left to subtract. Some words once spoken can't be taken back," Eddie sang.

Mona shot glances to Austin, but through the sunglasses, she couldn't get a read on her thoughts. She became lost in the song until the pre-chorus, which she felt necessary to join. "Caught a bolt of lightning. Cursed the day he let it go. Ah, Nothingman. Nothingman. Isn't it something, Nothingman?"

"So the agents are Nothingman?" Austin asked.

"They're nothing without us," Mona replied. "But be quiet. It's about to start back up."

"She once believed in every story he had to tell," Vedder continued. "One day, she stiffened, took the other side. Empty stares from every corner of a shattered prison cell. One just escapes. One's left inside the well."

Mona again joined the second pre-chorus. "He who forgets will be destined to remember. Ah, Nothingman. Nothingman. Isn't it something, Nothingman?"

Austin showed her mercy and remained silent until the end of the song. Then Mona turned off the player.

"So the company is the girl in the song, right?" Austin asked.

"You got it, sister."

"And we used to believe in the agents until we became unprofitable," Austin continued.

"Keep going."

"The agents are Nothingman because they are nothing without the company," Austin said.

"Yep."

"And catching the bolt of lightning was them getting the opportunity to become independent business owners and exclusive agents? Somehow I don't think that's the original intent of the song."

Mona wanted to thump Austin in the temple. "It's my motivation, sister. I never said that's why they wrote the song."

"It makes the company sound pretty arrogant for you to consider it a bolt of lightning," she continued. "So when the agent let it go is when what, he stopped caring about the company?"

"That's how I see it, Austin."

She shook her head. "You'll figure out a way to go after her, too."

"Who? Angelica?" Mona asked.

Austin nodded.

"That's not fair, Austin. It's our jobs."

Austin lit another smoke and cracked the window again. "You'll take those policies away from her."

"There is a system in place, a system Terry Collins circumvented," Mona explained. "I have to make it right so that the other agents have confidence in our production based, results driven method for assigning policies."

"But if Collins lied to the agent, doesn't she have a stake in keeping some of the policies he assigned to her?" Austin asked.

"Out of twelve hundred policies, who do you think cherry picked over them so that Terry Collins could assign out the worst two hundred? Do you really think his office manager had enough knowledge to spot the bad business from the good?"

"So you've just made up your mind that she was in on it," Austin said and took a deep drag from her cigarette.

"Yes, Austin," Mona said.

They shared a much needed but stifling silence.

"Edie brought me here to round out the team. I joined to balance you out. You'll kill everybody if I don't," Austin said.

Mona chuckled. "Not everybody, just the corrupt agents. This is the most corrupt state we've ever come across. We were brought in specifically to chase these idiots out. Let them run to the competition and take their bad practices with them. The Duluth district is one of the most profitable districts in Minnesota. These agents are some of the most loyal and dependable in the entire company. But their new DM, uprooted from Owatona, is just like the Twin City fat-and-happies. He could in very short time corrupt the entire district. At the very least, he's managed to uninspire and demotivate the good ones from producing at the high numbers they have for the past two decades."

Austin shook her head. "You can't burn the whole thing down, Mona. I'm just saying I'm not going to stop doing my job, just like you're not going to stop doing yours."

"I thought your job was to support the team's directives," Mona replied. "And our directives are to clean up the unprofitable corruption."

"You're just looking to force Taylor into promoting us so that you don't destroy the state's multiline channel," Austin said.

"Is that what Edie told you?"

"No, it's obvious," Austin yelled. "The way you rant about the other two northern districts. It looks like rage. It looks like a blitzkrieg, Mona."

Mona hated being angry, especially because there was the ever-present threat that she would start crying when the anger became uncontrollable. Nothing made her madder than being told she was in a rage. Austin believed she was brought into the team to be the agent's advocate to help avoid foreseeable law suits. But Mona knew that Edie had selected Austin for her ability to harness and manipulate emotions. She was wielding that awesome power on Mona. It was good that the road didn't curve, because the lanes were starting to blur.

"Your motivation is greed, Mona," Austin said. "You just want to make more and more money."

"We should be compensated a percentage of the profitability we restore," Mona replied. "And no, it doesn't have to be a large percentage. Are you seriously satisfied with a cost of living adjustment every three years?"

"The profit-sharing plan is pretty rich," Austin said.

"Which is also under question if the profitability issues aren't resolved."

"You can't even admit that you want more money," Austin said.

Mona pounded her fist on the steering wheel. "I just said we deserved a percentage."

"That's not the same as admitting you want more money."

Mona furrowed her brows in mock confusion. "What are you talking about? They're exactly the same thing."

She felt Austin's eyes burn into her temple.

"Yes, I want more money. Austin, aren't you just a little insulted that they made us all dye our hair blonde and forced us to office with the event planning bimbos so no one would get wise to our real purpose?"

"So that the company could maintain order and a healthy perception," Austin said, "I consider it an investment in the career."

Mona rolled her eyes, thankful they weren't watering. "A career where you aren't interested in advancement and want to coast for years on profit-sharing?"

"That's not fair," Austin said.

"This entire conversation isn't fair," Mona exclaimed. "We should be formulating a game plan. We just passed Cloquet, for god's sake. Instead, you're tricking me into your liberal, bleeding heart discussions. What's next, handing out flyers for the state communist party on 7th and Nicollet?"

Austin lit a new cigarette off her old one and flicked her bangs off her forehead. She didn't speak until half her cigarette had vanished. "Look, Mona. I'm not trying to be adversarial. I don't want you to think I'm working against you or the team."

Mona huffed. "Well, that's exactly what it feels like. Every time we discover some new wrinkle in all the fraud, some new scheme these bozos are pulling, you swoop in and try to rescue them."

Austin nodded, but kept her eyes to the road ahead. "Edie brought me in because I can empathize with agents. Does that mean I agree with their unethical decisions and practices? Absolutely not. But I understand how they run through the ethical decision-making process from analyzing their choice of actions, analyzing their ability to discern the consequences for the choice of their actions, and ultimately, the repetition of their unethical decisions."

"What more is there to know?" Mona interjected. "Either they think that everybody else is doing it, or they ask themselves: who will it hurt. What else is there?"

Austin took a final drag and pitched her cigarette out the window. "You've got me chain-smoking. I'm going to reek when we get to the office."

"It's too cold to roll the windows all the way down."

"What about a thirty-second burst?" Austin asked.

Mona rolled her eyes, but obliged her request.

"So you were asking about what's behind the justification of *everybody else is doing it and who will it hurt?*" Austin yelled, leaning close to Mona's ear as the crisp and bitter wind raged between them. Their blonde hair intermingled in gusts, Mona's ash blonde surmounting Austin's citrus strawberry locks.

"You give them too much credit," Mona said. "They're old high school jocks, used car salesmen, and burnt out mortgage brokers."

"Just because they can't understand how their emotions play into their decisions doesn't mean their incapable of being influenced by them," Austin yelled back.

Mona raised the windows. The relief from the barrage left an ache in her ears. It made her think of the last time she saw AC/DC. "I'm still listening, Austin."

"The *everybody else is doing it* rationale comes from two places, one, the fear of being left out or alienated and two, simple greed. Nobody's getting caught even though we all know it's wrong, so I'm going to get mine before time runs out," Austin explained. She rummaged through her grandma sized handbag for more body spray and perfume.

Mona prayed a quick, meaningless prayer. God had better things to do than save her from nausea. Soon, the misty cloud emanating from Austin's blouse and wrists was too much to ignore. Mona cracked her window for the freshness but then decided to cover up her disgust with lighting a cigarette of her own.

"I just reapplied here," Austin said.

"I don't care if I smell like smoke, remember?" Mona growled. "I don't care what fraudulent losers think of me."

Austin humphed and glared at her. "Anyway," she continued, "the question of who it will hurt comes more directly from greed but with a lingering respect for not damaging someone else."

"But what these agents and managers are doing is hurting the company," Mona said.

"Yes, you're right. Mother Company. I think there is a lot of weird, pent up mother-son issues in our sales culture," Austin said. "It's like fisherman giving their boats female names. Most of the agents do the same thing with the company."

Mona pointed to the horizon. "Like the Edmund Fitzgerald that sank in Superior."

Austin shrugged. "Sure, I guess...No, bad example."

Mona smirked. "I always thought men gave female names to anything they're attracted to but that's out of their control."

"And for fishermen, their lives depend on both," Austin added. "They're in love with their ship, but they have no control over its ability to provide for them or kill them."

"Hence, Mother Company," Mona said with a vigorous nod. Austin was making sense for the first time since they relocated. "So because the agents are exclusive, they depend entirely on the company to provide for them or to kill them."

"Office space allowances, marketing campaigns, subsidies for new agents, managers, and sub-producers, phone and internet, all the desktop computers and proprietary quoting and customer management systems," Austin said. "Not to mention the inability to sell a competitor's product as long as we offer it, no matter how different the rates and policies are."

Mona took a long drag, and visualized the dispersal of her smoke as clouds leaving her mind. "So you're saying that some of the justification to commit fraud is punishing Mother Company for jacking up the rates and trying to get profitable?"

Austin smiled but shook her head. "You're a step ahead of me. Most of the time when someone asks who will it hurt, the implied answer is no one. In some cases, when an agent asks who will it hurt, there's a different answer."

"Like all the agents in St. Cloud selling away from our products," Mona said.

"Yes, they could be deliberately selling away to hurt the company that used to stand by them and now is making them go out of business," Austin explained. "They feel used, rejected, abandoned, and the more you terminate, expendable."

"It still doesn't justify what they're doing. Most of them need to be terminated," Mona said.

"I agree with you, Mona. But you can't be so reckless with your vengeance," Austin replied. "These aren't the bad guys in one of your sci-fi movies. Nameless, faceless storm troopers that can be killed by the hundreds. The company made itself unprofitable, not the agents."

Mona furrowed her eyebrows. "What? You need to check the flavor of your Kool Aid." Was she being lulled down a path of acquiescence? Was Austin dating an agent on the side? This was more insight than she'd ever delivered before. It didn't feel right.

Austin clinched her fist in frustration and gave in to her own need to smoke another cigarette. "Why don't you trust me?" she said through a thick cloud of smoke.

Mona felt guilt shaded anger, partly at having displayed her distrust through a body language tell she wasn't aware of and partly because she was confused about trusting Austin at all. "Well, for starters, you just blamed the company for its own unprofitability issues."

"How am I wrong?" Austin asked.

"It was the agents who wrote bad business for years that created the strain on profits," Mona said.

"It was the company that accepted the business during that time," Austin said. "For twenty-five years, we had the cheapest rate in every city and every state. We were the discount insurance carrier. We gave discounts away like crazy. Then that earthquake hit Northern LA in the late eighties and we ignored the losses in California where we still have the highest market share of any multiline carrier."

"No, Austin," Mona said. "They raised the rates in every other state back then and cancelled the bottom twenty-five percent of every agent's book in California."

"But we never got back in the black," Austin said. "Ask Becca to show you the data she has on it."

"Where did she dig up that old stuff?" Mona asked.

"Where else? eBay," Austin said. "I was surprised to see retired employees selling off old reports, but it seems like every time they make cuts to the old pension program, here come the reams of perforated printouts."

"You've got to be kidding," Mona said.

Austin shook her head. "Nope. The management company that oversees all the separate insurance exchanges has been profitable, so the CEO was always able to report that to shareholders, but the mutual insurance companies the management company manages have never had a solid history of profit."

"So what's changed then, Austin? Why does the company care now about how unprofitable it is?"

"The losses on Texas mold claims have exceeded the billion dollar mark, so the exchanges can't afford to pay the management its fifteen percent to run distribution." Austin lit yet another cigarette.

"That's insane," Mona said.

"No, it's a fact," Austin replied. "The company had the exchanges raise their rates and cut off the toy vehicle, motorcycle, farm and ranch, and commercial lines simply to pay the management fee for the last three years while the exchanges could absorb enough additional premium to meet reserve requirements and be able to pay the management company."

"So what happens if the management company doesn't receive its fee? Doesn't it have its own operating capital in reserves?" Mona asked. "Who allowed it to get so thin?"

"Former CEOs, nepotism, and good old boys," Austin said. "But I don't know if the management company had reserves or when those dried up. I do know that if the fee doesn't get paid every year, all of distribution on the multiline side will be let go, both agents and employees."

"What about the life and annuity company?" Mona asked. "That's where we need to get to next. We need to leave this channel eventually."

"The company bought the life and annuity company in the sixties, and it's done very well from what Becca has told me," Austin said. "The life company has its own distribution system, brokerage and independent agent, so most of its profits pay for that. Only what the multiline channel sells in life and annuity comes to the management company for profit."

Mona was now impressed and puzzled at whom this new Austin was before her. "Have you talked to Edie about this?"

"Several times."

"Where was I?" Mona asked.

"Out serving termination letters."

"Do the agents know about this?"

Austin shook her head. "No, most of them don't. But it's not hard to figure out if you've been around long enough. When all of a sudden the company jacks the rates in home and auto by fifteen percent for four consecutive quarters, not only can you not sell anything, but your retention plummets and you start going out of business."

"So the main justification for all the fraud and corruption is to keep the business from going under?" Mona asked. "I don't buy it."

Austin took a deep drag. "I'm not selling it. You and I have never built a business, so neither of us can imagine the strain of seeing it vanish by twenty-five to forty percent in three years. We can't really know how we'd act if we were in their places."

"It's still wrong to fraud the company," Mona said. "And it's deserving of termination."

Terry Collins's office was an abandoned then restored service station behind the Duluth mall. The original couple who had owned it had lived on the second story. The former district manager had taken out the pumps and repaved the driveway for additional parking. Terry maintained the bullpen office for reserve and career agents on the first floor, but the space remained empty, a cemetery without headstones, for none had been recruited here.

Terry and his office manager, Karen, occupied a corner of the second floor, the rest of the square footage was wasted space, soaking up central heat and air and sending fluorescent bulbs to premature deaths in a vacuous training room.

To Mona, Karen was the gummy bear grandma type, who seemed more than willing to keep Terry from shivering with cold and fear in the lonely times of home office ill-favor. Judging by her desk, where Austin swarmed as soon as they were escorted in, the office manager was sans husband and had been for decades. Drawings and snapshots of a snaggletooth, Finnish gene pool, oozed from her filing cabinet and credenza.

Karen was an unfortunate, pear shaped woman, one who lacked the breasts to justify the hips, and this was the only source of pity evoked in Mona. She couldn't imagine life with such an upside down model, but then again, she wasn't a devotee of the "north country" where warmth mattered most and no one cared when the lights were low.

"Doesn't Terry know we're expecting him?" Mona asked Karen.

"I know he's expecting you," Karen reiterated, looking down bifocals teetering at the edge of her nose. "Is that what you mean?"

Mona leaned in to study a picture of the enumerated grandchildren and cracked her knuckles one by one. "No, I meant what I said."

Karen cleared her throat and threw Austin a look, glistening with impassioned plea. "Is this regarding Angelica?"

Mona chuckled. "Karen, you know we're not able to discuss the details of our conversations with office staff."

Karen clutched her throat as though she were tightening her Puritanical collar from a harsh and unexpected wind. "I realize that, but everyone knows what happens when you come sniffing around, Mona."

"What are you talking about?" Austin interjected.

Karen's look now bled heartbreak. "Oh, Austin, don't make me dislike you. You know what I'm talking about."

Mona cleared her throat. "I believe you were going to ask what will happen to you."

Collins then emerged from his hideaway office immediately behind Karen's desk, a sneer smeared across his face. To Mona, it was apparent he'd been listening to their not so small talk. Not that he'd installed high-tech surveillance gear. The walls were barely insulated behind '80s wood paneling. Mona imagined the original cellulose insulation held back by chicken wire, bristling and cracking from severe heat and cold over six or seven decades.

"If it isn't the ghost of Company Future come to pay me a surprise visit," Terry said. He flicked his salt and pepper hair helmet like the guy who played Kinnicki from *Grease* when he'd landed a role on *Taxi*. Terry's heavy drinking was bruised and splotchy across his nose and cheeks, leaving banshee white circles around his eye sockets. His slight build had always disturbed Mona in the few Town Hall meetings he'd graced. Sadly, she could see where petite women would find him attractive; but his waist, hips and buttocks were non-existent and he wore his golf shirts one size too tight, exposing his saggy, A cup man boobs for what they were, receptacles for loose skin and hair where muscles should have been for his physique.

He wasn't worth killing.

Until she factored in the next belt notch toward promotion.

"Terry Collins..." Austin began with an extended hand before he cut her off and turned toward Karen.

"That was the University of Minnesota Duluth on the line, Karen," he said. "That looks like a go. I'll definitely need help there."

Mona felt he was talking to his office manager for their benefit, but she refused to guess his angle without further prodding.

Karen's expression transformed, an invisible press lifted from her shoulders and back. She then looked down as though assessing her desk for how many boxes she'd need to vacate her space. "We'll do whatever we can."

"Get Larson on the phone as well," Collins continued. "I suspect I'll need to talk to him as soon as I've finished with these two."

"You got it, Terry," Karen said.

Now, Collins turned his attention back to Mona and Austin. "Okay, Barbie, Skeletor, I have time for you now." He stepped into his office but kept his back to them.

Karen snickered and shook her head, her eyes locked in a distant memory filled with flower petals and surprise love letters. It reminded Mona of the scene in *Superman* where the letter jacket morons picked on Clark Kent right before he punted the football to the moon.

Terry Collins was going to take the fun out of it.

Mona arched an eyebrow and mouthed *Barbie* to Austin as she motioned the blonde ahead of her.

Once inside the office, Mona stepped in front of Austin and headed for the chair on her right, which was Collins's left.

Austin moved to close the door.

"Leave it open," Terry barked. "Karen knows the score."

"Close it," Mona growled.

Terry grinned and shrugged.

"Fairly clean office for a district manager," Mona began. "In fact, I think this is the cleanest DM office I've ever seen."

Terry sat down on his burgundy faux-leather chair and steepled his fingers, reclining to an uncomfortably relaxed pose. His eyes were fixed on a single sheet of paper on the middle of his desk.

"Did you want to show us something?" Austin asked, taking her seat on Mona's left, right in Terry's view.

"I took the liberty of writing my own resignation letter," Terry said with a chuckle. "I'm sure you've encountered better written, but few so timely."

Mona leaned forward and dragged the paper across the desk. She glanced at it as though she were examining a dead rodent. "Cute."

"Cute?" he asked.

"Very well timed," Austin said after clearing her throat.

"I spent twenty years down in Owatonna, working for Federal Life and Protection before being conned into this gig," Terry said. His alcoholism became concentrated into a deep purple across his nose.

"I've read the file," Mona said.

He rolled his eyes and nodded. "Well, there's nothing here to recruit to," he continued. "I think I've proven that."

"By not recruiting for three years," Mona added. "That's like riding a pogo stick down a dirt road and then claiming moon travel is impossible."

"The University of Minnesota Duluth doesn't share your immature, irrational assessment, Mona," Terry said. He matched her condescending tone, but her stores of ammunition were far better stocked.

"They need a new recruiter for their school of business at the downtown location," he continued, unprovoked. "I've just accepted the position. Oh, and don't worry about Karen. I'll be taking her with me."

It was Mona's turn to chuckle. "We weren't worried about Karen. In fact, it would have taken our concern for her and several cups of coffee to lose sleep over it."

Terry whistled through gritted teeth as he watched Mona, with dreaded focus and determination, fold his resignation letter into an origami knot.

"The Company accepts your immediate resignation, Terry Collins," Mona said.

"That's a 90-day resignation," Terry growled.

"Not now that you've admitted to accepting another position that's in direct conflict with your assigned duties at district manager for district 15-64," she countered.

Terry picked up his head set and shoved it into his ear. "Karen, you got Larson on the phone yet?"

"His office called and said he was in meetings until..." came Karen's response on the speakerphone before he killed the line.

"Larson your attorney, Collins?" Mona asked.

"Yes," Terry said.

Mona then looked to Austin, but both knew the cue.

"Then this meeting is officially adjourned," Austin said.

"Don't worry, Mr. Collins, with your immediate resignation, it will make things much easier to terminate your one and only career agent for frauding the subsidy system," Mona said.

Dawning realization swept over Terry's face in waves of counter moves, regret, and anger. "What are you talking about?"

"It's none of your concern, Mr. Collins," Austin said. "The company has accepted your immediate resignation."

Mona bit the inside of her cheek to hide her shock. Was Austin finally succumbing to the dark arts?

"You can't do that to Angelica," Terry said.

Mona and Austin rose and moved to the door.

"We'll wait in the lobby until the Marketing Specialist can arrive in the company van," Mona said. Then she turned and smirked at Terry. "Skeletor. That's funny," she muttered. Gripped with an overwhelming passion, she inhaled fiercely and waved her hand in front of her face. "Toilet, Collins. Toilet."

Inside Grandma's Sports Garden, Mona and Austin watched Lake Superior's spume splash against the windows. Since dawn, the gales of November had been creating fourteen foot waves in the giant inland sea. Now nearing 5:00 pm, the winds were showing no sign of abating.

Mona and Austin had only spoken sporadically since their morning meeting with Terry Collins. The marketing rep boys had been thirty minutes late with the van, which made waiting for them in Collins' reception area all the more awkward. Even Mona had been close to an out-of-body experience, that removal of self where her mind and body knew what they needed to do but the disagreeable soul had floated a safe distance above to cast judgment on her acts.

Sipping her Jack and Diet Coke and inhaling the fresh lime slice's scent on her tumbler, Mona now sympathized with Austin's emotional state during terminations, resignations, and review boards.

"You've been quiet," Austin said. She scooted closer to Mona in their semi-circle booth.

"Are you reading my mind?" Mona murmured between sips.

Austin cast her gaze away and Mona followed it across the expanse of flat screens, each showing ESPN, Fox Sport Net, or the Big Ten Network. All the TV's were muted and scrolling close captioning. The bar's silence echoed their own. Even the kitchen was sullen save for the gentle hum of vents and fans.

Mona thought they were in the eye of a great storm. The splashing waves outside boosted the notion. The dinner rush wasn't on yet. Neither was the happy hour crowd. This was the time when the cooks were prepping for their rush, quietly cutting vegetables, making rouxes, and plotting specials. The bartender, a slender, pre-maturely balding man, who looked only four or five years older than Mona, broke the reverie's spell when he dumped a five-gallon bucket of ice into his sinks.

"Seriously," Austin asked again. "Why are you so quiet, Mona?"

Mona sighed and stretched. "Just thinking about today. About Collins' assistant, Karen. Thinking about being in one of the several restaurants named Grandma's in Duluth. Karen is a grandma."

"She's also a widow," Austin said. "And she just lost her job within two months of Christmas."

Mona downed her drink and slammed the tumbler on the table. "You think he really has a new gig with the University of Minnesota Duluth?"

"You'd better pray he does," Austin said. "Those were your grounds for accepting his immediate resignation over the ninety-day version."

Mona glanced at her watch. "How well do you know these agents we're meeting? I feel like getting smashed tonight and staying up here, but I don't want any funny business."

"Tom Hildebrand and Kerry Lutter are great guys," Austin said. "They're married. They coach little league football together. They're office partners, and two of the top four producers in the district."

"So salt of the earth guys who'll have a couple of Mich Golden Lights, listen to our story about kicking Collins out, and getting the policies reassigned to them, and bid us a fond farewell, huh?" Mona asked.

"That's the plan," Austin said. She gave Mona a reassuring pat. "Then I'll be your blocker." She retrieved her phone from her purse. "I'll even get us a room reservation in one of those hotels down the street."

"Either one looked decent," Mona muttered. "Thanks, Austin."

"No problem," Austin said while tapping on her phone. "I'm loving the revelation that you actually have a conscience."

Mona rolled her eyes and rose from their table. "In all the other cases, the marketing boys have the van hidden around the corner and ready to roll when we give the signal. It's a different thing having to wait for them and make sure the district manager isn't stealing or destroying company property."

"Then Karen started crying," Austin said, but she kept her eyes on her phone as though it were the most important thing in the universe.

"You saw that too?"

"And heard it. Very soft," Austin said. "Very tender, very personal. She's not a practiced crier."

"You saying it took a lot out of her?" Mona asked.

"I'm saying we get paid to terrify people," Austin said. Now she looked up from her phone. "I found the number for both hotels."

"We get paid to administer company justice," Mona said. "I'll get us another round while you call." She turned and used the bartender's glistening bald spot as her beacon.

"It terrifies the judged," Austin said under her breath.

"I heard that," Mona called over her shoulder.

The bartender poured her Jack and Diet Coke and Austin's whiskey sour without the slightest interest in their lives, for which Mona was grateful. She'd never understood the social mores that permitted bartenders and taxi drivers to be so inquisitive. Mona then imagined a world where plumbers, or even worse female OBGYNs, struck up conversations for the sake of commonality. So why were bartenders and cabbies exempt from such violations of privacy? *Pour the drink,* she thought. *Keep your eyes on the road. Fix my toilet. Check my plumbing. Stay quiet.*

Mona returned to their table to find Austin off her phone and standing to greet two large men. Smiling, Mona set their drinks down and offered her hand.

"This is Mona," Austin said. "Mona, this is Tom, and this is Kerry."

Kerry shook Mona's hand and Tom waved. Kerry was a head shorter than Tom, but what he lacked in height he more than made up for in looks and build. He had a compressed, bull dog stature, a buzz cut with a receding hairline, and muscles even his sweater couldn't hide. His slate grey eyes were captivatingly weird, and the space between his two front teeth created an endearing blemish on his stocky, stout façade. Kerry wasn't Mona's type, but she could appreciate objets d'art when she found them.

Tom wasn't exciting. Taller with a thinning hairline and a beer gut that boasted four kids, his eyes were too close together, and his angular facial features were at odds with his body's rotund motif. But he was clearly a sucker for the girl next door type and immediately sat next to Austin. Indeed, the two agents took the opportunity to sandwich Mona and Austin into the center of their semi-circle booth.

"Already drinking?" Kerry asked. "Must have been a heck of a day over at Collins's place."

Mona nodded and smiled. "I'm sorry. I didn't know you guys were here or I would have waited and gotten you drinks, too."

Tom dismissed her apology with a wave. He then stood and fished out his wallet. "We've got the next round or two anyway. We figure we owe you two that much because of what you're doing for the district." He pointed to Kerry. "The usual?"

Kerry nodded.

Tom disappeared behind a row of high-backed booths.

Kerry leaned closer to Mona. "So how did Karen take it?"

Mona sighed and took a bigger sip from her drink than she wanted. "She took it hard. But Terry said he already had a new job lined up for them with the university."

Kerry covered his mouth and chuckled. "Yeah, he's been hinting around about that when we've gotten him on the phone."

Austin cleared her throat. "So you both tried to get him to fix the policy assignment situation and play by the rules?"

Stretching his arms and popping his neck, Kerry chuckled again. "Yeah, that was a couple of months before we called Siemens and blew the whistle."

Mona stared straight ahead, but felt her second drink encouraging her to pay more attention to this Kerry Lutter. In most cases, she found the northern Minnesota accent unflattering and annoying, but the cheese grater timber of Kerry's voice melded well with his thicker than normal accent.

"So I guess that's when he called you guys in to see what the real situation was, huh?" Kerry asked.

Mona blinked herself back to the present and nodded. "Yep, I guess I don't know why you and Tom waited so long before telling us."

Kerry shrugged. "Loyalty for the district manager runs deep, I suppose. We didn't want him to get in trouble. We just wanted him to do what he promised to do. We've been waiting for four years for the next policy assignments. We made business plans around them. Tom and I hired two new gals to take on the new customers. We even built on to our office so we could have enough space for the filing cabinets and the two new ladies to work, you know."

Tom returned with their drinks. Two bottles of Mich Golden Light, one whiskey sour and one Jack and Diet Coke.

"I was just telling the girls here about all we did getting ready for those policies, Tom," Kerry said.

Tom nodded as he set the drinks on the table, placing the new cocktails next to Mona's and Austin's current drinks. "Yeah, we spent about ten thousand on the office build out and hiring Greta and Michele. We were counting on those policy assignment renewal commissions to pay for it. Heck, we had it in writing from Collins that we were next for the policies. I understand him needing to recruit new agents, but you don't have to go and give her twelve hundred policies to make her a career agent."

"Well, I accepted his immediate resignation," Mona said. "Even though he wanted to give me a ninety-day note. As soon as he brought up his new job as a recruiter for the university, I knew I had him. My next step is to reassign those policies back where they belong and do right by you guys."

Tom raised his beer. "Well, I think we should have a toast. To the company. For finally getting the right people up here in Minnesota to kick out all the corruption that's been bringing it down for so many years."

They raised their drinks and brought them together. Kerry slid his arm around the back of the booth near Mona's shoulders as they drank. As Mona set her glass down, she realized, she'd toasted her new drink rather than the one she'd gotten from the bar.

That was the last thing she remembered until the next morning when she found herself in a hotel bed, sleeping next to Austin. They were both fully clothed, but beyond the pounding headache and the feeling of still being inebriated, Mona didn't feel right. Something had happened.

Chapter Ten

Waiting for her next meeting with John Taylor, Edie reflected on her early morning conversation with Mona while she and Austin were on their way to Duluth to procure Terry Collin's resignation. Mona was becoming impatient. The team had chased out nearly ten percent of the full-time agent force in Minnesota, and now that they were looking at executing potentially five of the eighteen district managers, there wasn't much more to be done beyond mopping up the blood and waiting for subpoenas on the wrongful term suits.

"So you're still getting the stiff arm from Taylor on Laurent?" Mona had asked.

"Yes, but you need to focus on Collins this morning..."

"I know the drill, Edie," Mona growled.

"I just have a bad feeling. Something doesn't feel right. It's too calm."

"We've got this into a predictable rhythm," Mona had said.

"That's what's different. I don't want us to become blinded by our own confidence."

"You either mean me or Austin. Not the whole team."

"That's not what I said..."

"Look, Laurent has been my pet project for months, Edie."

"I know, but there are some apparent political angles we failed to see the first time I brought it up with Taylor."

"Maybe that's what's got you feeling queasy," Mona had said.

"Just be careful up there."

"Do we have the green light on Capote and his minions?"

"Just Capote, which is also why you need to be careful. Be the clinician, be surgical on Collins, Mona. We need it to be textbook. No surprises, no snide comments, no spiking the ball."

"Got it, boss!" Mona had yelled. "Seriously, I have it. You want to speak to Austin?"

"No, just tell her hello and let me know how she does."

Looking out the window in the reception area outside Taylor's office, Edie could see the evening shadows spreading over downtown. Her meetings with Taylor were always late in the day. Logic dictated this was to keep her team as undiscovered as possible, but something told Edie that Taylor wasn't a foreigner to evening meetings. He'd been in insurance his entire career, which started well before Anita Hill and Clarence Thomas.

She checked her texts from Mona and Austin. She hadn't seen or heard anything from them since the marketing reps had arrived to clean out Collins's office, though Mona had mentioned being encouraged by Austin's strength and solidarity during their discussion with the now former DM.

Taylor opened his door and waved her in with no audible greeting. His eyes looked heavy.

"Tough day?" she asked as she followed him in. Taking her seat in front of his desk, she looked up for his response. All she got was a deep sigh.

"Just trying to get the new no surrender charge life products to launch by the target date. They've been approved in most of the states now. Its compliance and finance that is giving me heartburn," he said and half-lunged, half-fell into his chair.

"Finance? Why would they be stalling? Won't those be a good short-term boost to sales?" she asked.

"It's the four-year commission chargeback for churned business that has her up in arms. Maggie wants to extend it to six years based on the cost of acquisition forecasts." He leaned forward. "You met Maggie Waller yet?"

Edie shook her head. "I know who she is, but we've never shaken hands."

"That doom is inevitable," Taylor said with a cracked smile. "Tell me some good news. How was the Collins resignation this morning?"

Edie sat up and opened her portfolio. "So far, so good. He notified Mona and Austin that he'd accepted a position with the University of Minnesota Duluth, which is grounds for immediate resignation."

"He try for the 90-day?"

"Yes, he'd handed the notice to them then mentioned the new job, so we have grounds to make the resignation immediately effective based on the district manager appointment agreement stating duties in direct conflict of the appointment's terms."

"Good," John replied. His smile was warming up. "And the crooked Career Agent?"

"That will be much easier to pursue now that Collins is out of the way."

"And Austin and Mona are meeting the other two agents to discuss correcting the bad policy assignment scheme?"

"If they're on schedule, they should have met with them a couple of hours ago," Edie said.

Edie felt she was getting enough buy signs to pursue the more difficult of topic of Denis Laurent. Taylor was yawning and nodding.

An idea jolted through Edie, an epiphany stranded for lack of hope. Mona's concerns were real. They would be finished with Minnesota in less than six months. Taylor had no more inkling of Edie's next career step than she did. She felt it throughout her. And if he didn't know where she would be next, he cared nothing for her team. They were after all relocated on the cheap, four single women narrowly escaping the mounting weight of regional office closures in Colorado Springs.

"There *is* the Denis Laurent file." There were two ways of advancing here: demonstrating your value as a profit center to the company, waiting for someone above your immediate superior to take notice, or becoming so strong, so convincing, so righteous that you might just take out every last imbecile if the company didn't promote you soon enough.

"He's untouchable," Taylor said as the smile dripped away from his face. "I'm sure as heck not going upstairs to champion his removal. He's done nothing wrong."

Edie leaned back and crossed her arms. "He's done nothing. That's what's wrong."

"For God's sake, he just had a stroke," Taylor said. His face was turning blotchy.

"Eighteen months ago."

"It warped the left side of his body," he continued. "The man can barely walk. You weren't at the last Town Hall meeting where he fell off the stage."

Edie tapped her pen against her portfolio. "But I was at the Halloween party where he was able to wear an end table with a lamp glued to it to become a 'one night stand.'"

"He's a third-generation district manager, Edie," Taylor said. "His is the largest district in the state. It represents ten percent of the state's full-time agent force."

"I'm aware of that, John," Edie said. "That's just a mirror fogging body count. In terms of overall production, according to the 1165 reports, his agents represent the least producing of the entire force minus the new career and reserve agents."

Taylor now crossed his arms over his chest. "They used to be top producing. Especially in homeowners and commercial lines."

"The dramatic decline in production is directly aligned with the occurrence of his stroke," Edie said. She imagined icicle shards flecking out of her mouth as she spoke. It was a technique she'd picked up in high school drama class, envisioning the physical manifestation of voice tone to produce the desired effect.

Taylor threw up his hands. "That's my point exactly, Edie. He's the grandson of the man who opened the company here. He's the grandson of the reason we moved the home office from Indiana in the sixties. And you're sitting there asking me if we can take him out. You're supposed to be guarding the company against fraud and unprofitable sales practices."

"Not recruiting new agents is an unprofitable sales practice," Edie said. "I think that's a direct quote from senior management."

"It is," Taylor conceded.

"Not running a sustainable business model in a district environment is an unprofitable business practice," Edie said.

Taylor nodded. His face had brightened a bit, but the weightless eyebrows looked forced. "I agree with you."

"Continuing to accept a district manager override that's well into six figures monthly while allowing your entire practice to fall is an unprofitable sales practice."

Taylor steepled his fingers. "You're failing to see this from all angles, Edie. Denis Laurent has a perception halo around him." He counted on his fingers. "Family values – pass your business on to your kids..."

"As long as they're acceptable to the company," Edie interjected. Laurent had repeatedly tried to appoint his daughter. She couldn't pass her securities license exams. Now, she'd been frozen out for life by FINRA. This, by contract, made her unacceptable to the company, never mind that she would become the fifth reserve district manager Laurent had tried to appoint in the last three years, representing over two hundred and fifty thousand dollars in lost RDM subsidy payments.

"Strong loyalty, a team builder with the district managers..." Taylor continued.

"Forget the backdoor conference calls Siemens hops onto once he's tipped off where Laurent is openly encouraging his fellow district managers to stop recruiting to force the company into a desperate state where we have to lower rates," Edie said.

"He's too juiced in," Taylor said. "Even if you threw all four of your four-inch case binders at him, he'd win in the court of public opinion. Sure, we'd get the Fox affiliate to listen to our side of the story..."

"Especially when we bring up that he declined our disability insurance coverage with its automatic business continuation and buy-sell options for nineteen years in a row." Edie said.

"But the NBC people would be weeping at his side like the bleeding heart, incestuous Swedes they are," Taylor said. Clearly, he was becoming tired of getting interrupted. "Laurent would run to the Pioneer Press after being ignored at the Star Tribune."

He held up his hand to silence Edie. "Hear me out. Yes, we could issue statements, but we don't need any more bad publicity. Yes, we've had to make some tough decisions. Getting out of the farm and ranch lines, and the motorcycle and toy markets being the top of even Siemens's list. Yes, we've had to take some aggressive rate actions, especially in the outstate areas and the new developments in the seven-county metro. Yes, Minnesota is one of three states in the country that has to deal with permafrost in evaluating new construction costs for total grounders…"

Now, the man was slipping into corporate speak, rattling off rallying cries from senior management. Edie had finally slit a nerve ending. At first, she thought Mona was chewing on a hang nail, building up a loathing for the way this particular district manager was worshipped. Edie knew the root cause of Mona's hatred. In the Springs, Ralph McSweeny was the only DM who could thwart Mona's attempts to block his politics laden policy assignments. Austin and Edie had to heal her ego with a healthy regimen of jokes about McSweeney possessing pictures of the Colorado State Executive Director and the Colorado Springs Regional Director in lewd positions.

The two were married three months after Edie's team relocated out. But even that couldn't quench Mona's extreme distaste for Laurent. She'd built the evidence library Taylor had mentioned by herself to bring down this moron.

"He acts as a shield for the others to gallivant around, acting like renegades," Edie said. Then she realized she had no idea what Taylor had been saying for the last few moments.

"He's coachable," Taylor said. "He's someone whom we can love up."

"Who's coaching him?" Edie asked. "Not the latest divisional marketing manager. Laurent's blown through three of those in as many years. The company is more fond of terminating full W-2 employees than it is statutory ones."

"Siemens should take it on," Taylor said.

"What's another trip into Minneapolis from Mendota Heights going to do for a guy like Laurent?" Edie asked. "I'll tell you what it would do. It would validate his misbehavior. He'd be paraded in front of his fellow miscreant DMs, who would all toast to his, the worst of all corruption, the corruption of sloth and complacence."

She'd oversold her enthusiasm, and she knew it. Edie had allowed herself to become emotional; however, scaling back would be admitting her error. Instead, she decided to pursue the blunder to its fullest.

"Senior management would like to throw him a retirement party," Taylor said, his voice almost a whisper.

"Is it tomorrow? Is it a surprise retirement party? Will his idiot of a daughter be persuaded to play host?" Edie asked.

Taylor humphed. "The new DMM is trying to schedule it."

"Trying to schedule it," Edie said. She leaned forward and started making karate chopping motions with her hands. "That makes no sense, John. Either you schedule it or you don't. There is no try." A strange echo of Mona impersonating that little green magician flitted across her mind.

"Just let that one breathe, Edie," Taylor said.

Edie rolled her eyes and let her boss see her do it. "All I have to do is send a zip file email to a certain Chief Financial Officer and it's on."

"I appreciate that," Taylor said. He rose from the table and gestured to the door. "But I think you have a full plate with terminating the other two district managers we've discussed."

"Will forty-five days be enough time for the other legitimate bottle blonds in event planning to throw a spectacular retirement gala for Laurent?" Edie said as she collected her things. "Or will I have to send that zip file on day forty-six?"

"I think forty-five days should be sufficient," Taylor said. His smile showed more of his veneers that he intended. "But by then you'll be well entrenched into your new assignment."

"We all dyed our hair these ridiculous shades for this one," Edie said. She opened the door and brought her voice to a whisper. "What will the next assignment call for, shaving our heads to make someone a wig vest, carving Xs in our foreheads and then turning them into swastikas?"

Chapter Eleven

E die's Monday morning had been filled with processing
Terry Collin's immediate resignation. When she arrived
in the basement level multiline office, she found herself
locked out of a closed-door conference call between Geoff
Siemens, John Taylor, and what sounded like a rather
impassioned Terry Collins. Fortunately, Geoff's administrator
kept Edie well-informed on such meetings for the cost of a
monthly lunch date or happy hour invitation.

Once the conference call concluded, she was called into
Siemens's office for half an hour of heated questioning about
what occurred the Friday before when she'd sent Austin and
Mona to Terry's office. Rather out of character, Edie was at a
loss for answers to half the questions; Mona and Austin had
decided to hit one of the famed Grandma's bars in Duluth and
had apparently split a hotel there, wise enough to their
inebriation not to attempt the two-and-a-half-hour car ride home.

She knew the basics. Mona had accepted Terry's resignation
as immediate once he revealed his acceptance of a new position,
which was in direct conflict with his district manager
appointment agreement.

As with every resignation of this magnitude, several issues
had arisen over the weekend. First, Terry's resignation letter
spelled out a 90-day resignation, not an immediate one. Mona
had failed to convince him to write a new letter. Second, the
University of Minnesota Duluth offer letter for Terry's new
position indicated a start date that coincided with the last day of

his 90-day resignation. Third and most likely the root cause for the other two issues, Mona had apparently threatened to terminate agent Angelica Myers for frauding the career agent subsidy systems with new business from her policy assignments.

Edie refused to cave to her stress level. She had assured both Siemens and Taylor to uncover all the facts and get Mona's and Austin's perspectives on the conversation with Collins. Both Siemens and Taylor reviled the thought of keeping Collins in the district for another three months, surely counting on the district override folios for that time, totaling over $36,000, to fund the next lead generation and event marketing programs for the entire state's benefit.

Mona and Austin had been hiding upstairs, camouflaged by the other dyed blonde coworkers. They had not responded to her voicemails or emails. Finally, at eleven thirty, she'd received a tentative, white flag text from Austin asking to meet them at the Chug 'N Choke, the nickname for the corporate cafeteria.

Corporate cafeterias are the Switzerland, the safe word, the panic room for all businesses, Edie thought as she stepped off the elevator on the fourth floor. A blast of Dawn dish soap and chili hit her nostrils. No one ever makes a scene in the cafeteria, she continued. They know they messed up. They probably blacked out from drinking in Duluth and have no consistent memory of their conversation with Collins. They think they'll be written up.

Passing the a la carte line, Edie tore through the side entrance and scanned the tables for her employees.

Austin found Edie before Edie saw her, but Austin's straightened posture and hushed whisper to Mona caught Edie's eye.

Mona kept her back to Edie as she approached. Austin served up an apologetic smile, her eyes widening to cartoonish proportions the closer Edie came.

"Hello, blondes," Edie said with a smirk. She sat between them and inhaled deeply. "How was your weekend?"

"Saturday hurt," Austin said.

"Until we came back to the Cities, that is," Mona added.

"How was Duluth?" Edie asked. She looked first at Austin and then toward Mona, allowing her eyes to glaze over with a clear, watery sheen of anger.

"The drive up was tense," Austin said. "Mona and I got into an argument about Angelica Myers."

"Really?" Edie replied. "What about her?"

"Whether she knew she was frauding the subsidy system," Mona said.

"Easy to find out, right?" Edie said. "We can have Becca examine the number of rate class changes from sevens and nines to qualify as new business, as well as the number of cars she's reinstated from older client accounts, which makes the entire household's policies appear as new business."

"Doesn't that only serve to roll the assigned policies into full renewal commission status?" Mona asked.

Edie shrugged and kept up her wicked smile. "In the system, new business is new business. So if there is a high level of those transactions, especially after her career date, then we would have enough evidence to terminate without having to speculate on her motive. Isn't that right, ladies and gentleman of the jury?" She settled her stare on to Austin for this final comment.

"Never thought of that," Austin murmured.

"Too preoccupied about saving her somehow?" Edie asked.

Austin shook her head, but Mona nodded. Austin gave Mona a betrayed look.

"I think we all know the scheme was Collins's idea," Austin said.

"She agreed to it," Mona replied.

"She might not have known everything she was getting into," Austin returned.

Edie cleared her throat. "Need I remind you both that we stick to what we can prove in court? In the future, stop arguing over guilt. It is not for us to determine. We only recommend termination where appropriate."

"Does Becca already have data on Angelica's sales record?" Mona asked.

"She does now," Edie said. Her smile was starting to hurt her cheeks. "After Terry had a conference call with Siemens and

Taylor to let them know you threatened to terminate her next, Mona, I asked Becca to pull the records."

Mona shook her head and rolled her eyes. "It wasn't a threat. I simply said it would be easier for us to terminate her after his immediate resignation."

"Which has now come into question because of his new position's offer letter," Edie said.

Mona gripped the side of the table. "Which could have been altered after our meeting with him."

"Can you prove that?" Edie asked and looked Mona down until she cast her gaze to the floor. "No, you can't. But you could have certainly provoked defensive action with your snide comments."

"What does it matter if they push back his hire date?" Mona growled. "He admitted to accepting the new position."

"If his start date isn't for three months, then the conflict of interest might not occur until that time," Edie explained.

Now she was able to drop her smile.

"I'm sorry, Edie," Austin muttered.

Edie nodded and threw her a genuine smile. Then she turned back to Mona, whose silence was growing more daring.

Mona was not going to apologize. Edie settled into the stifling silence, waiting for Mona to speak next.

"The record will show that District Manager Terry Collins had not consistently recruited new reserve and career agents during his three-year tenure in the Duluth district," Mona said in her opening argument voice.

Edie leaned forward and steeled her eyes on Mona, taking advantage of Mona's willingness to acknowledge her with eye contact. "The testimony for the defense will show that Mona Stott, an employee of the company, charged with the duties and responsibilities to terminate underproductive and unprofitable career agents, threatened my client, Terry Collins, with the pending termination of one of his agents upon receipt of his 90-day resignation letter."

A bellowing silence followed.

Transforming from dry, red-veined anger to watery remorse, Mona's eyes lost their direct challenge.

Austin blinked profusely and pretended to people-watch.

Edie nodded her head, pursed her lips, and basked in the quiet.

"We'll always be made to be the bad guys, won't we?" Austin asked.

Edie nodded. "Trial lawyers love insurance companies for our willingness to settle out of court."

Mona squared her shoulders and straightened her posture. "Even when we have a case? Even when we can prove our righteousness?"

"There is no being right," Edie said. "I've told you this before. Our only option is being dead right. The only good publicity any insurance company can hope for is showing how fast it paid claims after a disaster. Like the California wildfires, the Oklahoma tornadoes, or even the mold issue in Texas."

Austin cleared her throat. "Any other time we're in the press, we're painted as the deep-pocketed evil corporation mismanaged from the top for pure profit."

Edie snapped her fingers and pointed to Austin. "You got it, sister."

"So what's going to happen now?" Mona asked.

Edie folded her hands together and rested her wrists on the table. It made her look as though she were praying or pleading. "We won't be able to terminate Angelica Myers."

"What the..." Mona growled.

Slapping the table lightly, Edie stalled the protest. "Calm down and listen, Mona. Siemens and Taylor will never agree to the termination after a threat."

"Well, then..."

"Let me finish, Mona," Edie continued. "I have a way out for you." She paused to allow Mona to take two deep breaths.

"A way out for me?" Mona asked at length.

"We propose transferring Myers out of the Duluth district and into the St. Cloud district," Edie explained.

The lines in Mona's brow dispersed with her bright realization. "Policy assignments must remain within the district where they were originally written."

Edie nodded. Austin smirked and shook her head.

"So we propose transferring her so that the new district manager doesn't have to deal with pre-existing bad blood," Edie said. "By procedure and contract, the policies will then need to be reassigned to the rightful agents in the Duluth district."

"What happens to Angelica after she gets transferred?" Austin asked. "The St. Cloud DM is no better. He plays dumb to his agents selling away."

"One of two things will happen," Edie replied. "She'll either resign within short order, or over time she will be contaminated with their practices and eligible for termination."

Mona drummed her fingers on the table. "Then we'll have two strikes against her."

"Exactly," Edie said. "And it will provide a natural lead into investigating other agents in St. Cloud."

"That can't be Taylor's or Siemen's plan," Austin said.

Edie smirked. "It's not. You two want to advance to the life and annuity side, right?"

Mona shrugged. "As long as either the action or the pay is better."

Austin rolled her eyes then squinted. Edie picked up the tell. Austin wanted a cigarette.

"We've gotten rid of Collins," Edie continued. "We've gotten verbal approval to go after Capote. I'll keep hitting a wall if I continue to target Denis Laurent, but no one in Home Office will argue if we can prove that the company's business in St. Cloud remains unprofitable and the agents there are selling with competitors. The assumption will be that the better business, with better risk and cheaper rates, will gravitate to the competition."

"That's our ticket to promotion," Mona hissed.

Edie rubbed her hands together. "If need be."

"So will they uphold the immediate resignation for Collins?" Mona asked.

Edie shook her head and paused. She needed Mona's pugilist style to remain honed, but Edie couldn't allow her to realize that it was exactly this type of aggressive disregard that would force Taylor to send them higher up the proverbial ladder, preferably to a rung where the unreimbursed expense of blonde hair dye was no longer necessary. "No, Mona. They will honor his 90-day resignation."

"So he'll pocket the district override for the next three months," Mona said with a huff.

"Unfortunately, yes," Edie said. "And unfortunately, that counts against our score of improved profitability."

"It does?" Austin asked.

"To the tune of $36,000," Edie said. "Which is not huge given the terminations we've processed so far."

"What are the estimated savings to profitability?" Austin asked.

Edie shook her head although she had the number, tickling eight-digit range, stenciled into her mind. "Hard to say with only the first auto renewals coming up. We'll need to check with Becca. It's well into the millions."

Mona's entire body looked relieved.

Austin extended her chin so the pudgy patch underneath wasn't so pervasive. "Where is Becca? Why isn't she here?"

"I have her working on Capote's termination recommendation letter," Edie replied. "We're just waiting on a few last details. Once the career agents business is cross-referenced with established agents' books of business and then layered with the effective dates, we'll be able to draw stronger conclusions."

Austin took a deep breath and scratched her head. "So, I'm confused. Are we looking for policies where say two cars were written at the same agent office location with similar effective dates but with different agent numbers for production credit and commissions?"

"Yes, that's exactly what we're looking for," Mona said.

"Even better would be if a homeowners policy was written within the week with the original agent number and all the autos were written under the career agents' numbers," Edie explained. "If this has been going on as long as we think it has, we'll have enough renewal cycles to determine if the policies were ever reassigned back to the original agent."

Mona licked her lips and bounced her shoulders, anticipating the kill. "But wouldn't the stream of commission repayments back to the established agents need to continue? Wouldn't Capote have a long payroll history for that?"

"That will be the threat that will get him to resign," Edie agreed.

"Resign?" Mona asked. "I thought you were drafting the termination recommendation letter."

"I'll need approval to terminate before Capote will recognize the gravity," Edie explained. "We all know how much of a bluffer the man is."

"When do you anticipate sending me out to him?" Mona asked.

"Within two weeks," Edie said, "and I will accompany you."

Mona's dark eyes narrowed. "Is that a Taylor or Siemens request?"

Edie smirked and then reset her jaw. "No, it's an angle toward redemption. Capote's monthly override is around $45,000, compared to Collins at $12,000. You and I saving that override for the next three or four months will show a positive effect on distribution expenses and not just direct policy profit."

"So if you and I nail Capote," Mona said, "you'll run back to Taylor and Siemens, tell them how professionally I executed the agreed upon resignation..."

"Which will mitigate your unfortunate flub in Duluth," Edie said.

Mona's eyes grew into slits. "So now it's a flub."

"It became a flub when you allowed Terry Collins to get the better of you," Edie corrected.

Mona rolled her eyes.

"You're falling in love with the kill, Mona," Edie continued. "Don't let it take you down with it."

Mona's stare was incredulous. "What are you talking about, Edie? I'm not in love with the kill."

Edie froze. Something had tickled her peripheral vision. The flash brought Frost to mind. Was that him in the a la carte line?

"Edie, what's wrong?" Austin asked and grabbed Edie's forearm. "You look terrified."

Edie cleared her throat and shook her head. "No, I just thought I saw someone. Someone who goes to my church."

Mona craned her neck to follow Edie's eyes. "Sounds like a man."

"You've been holding out on us," Austin said. "You have a lot of explaining to do, Ms. Firebaugh. You've been coming in grouchy and horny on Monday mornings for months. How long have you been seeing him?"

Edie raised her hand to stop the geyser of words erupting from Austin.

"Which one is he?" Mona asked. "Oh, no. I can tell. The one with the mauve and blue striped shirt, right?"

Edie rolled her eyes. "You mean the short, bald one? Isn't he from Accounts Receivable?"

Austin picked up on Mona's joke. "Wait, Mona. You're wrong. It's that tall gent in the gray slacks and tan shirt."

"With the scraggly beard?" Edie gasped. "He's an actuary."

"Then who is it?" Austin asked, turning back to Edie.

Edie couldn't calm her pulse. She also didn't know why she was nervous. It was just coffee and it was the first and last time they would have just coffee. But She felt most comfortable in her work environment, and Frost was violating that.

The man she'd been eyeing turned to face them. It *was* Easton Frost. He wore a navy pin-stripe suit and chocolate brown shoes. He's black hair adopted the blue tint in its shiny gel. His tan had faded a bit, but he'd kept that olive complexion.

Mona volleyed her eyes back and forth from Edie to Easton. "No way, Edie. No way, sister."

Austin took a deep breath. "I'm going to need to cigarette if you tell me you've been seeing that man in the blue suit with the Superman hairstyle."

Edie pressed her hands flat on the table. "It was just coffee. We met accidentally at a Feed All God's Children event and got coffee afterward."

"Just coffee?" Mona asked in disbelief. "I would have closed that deal."

Austin nodded emphatically. "Yeah, I would have nailed him too, Edie. He's good looking enough to forget about other guys you might be seeing."

"Maybe for you blonde heathens," Edie said, "but not for me."

A smile of recognition sprinkled across Easton's face and he waved to Edie.

She exhaled with sinking shoulders and waved back.

"Do you need alone time?" Mona asked. "Because you're not going to get it."

Austin rifled through her handbag. "Where's my phone? I have to get a picture. No one in the Springs is going to believe this."

"Believe what?" Edie asked. "I'm not seeing him. I never started seeing him, and I have no interest in dating him."

"Is he a jerk?" Mona asked.

"You still could have slept with him," Austin replied.

"He's not really a jerk," Edie said. "It's just weird. I don't get a good vibe from him. He's hard to read. Like he's a reader, too, so he knows how to mask himself."

"Sounds like your perfect challenge," Austin said.

"You know he's coming over here," Mona said, bringing her voice to a whisper.

"Yep, as soon as he finishes paying for his food," Austin said.

Edie waited until Frost looked down for his wallet then grabbed both Austin's and Mona's arms. "Don't even think about leaving me."

"Did you know he worked for the company?" Austin asked.

"I never told him where I worked, but he said he worked downtown," Edie hissed.

"And you met him at your church?" Mona asked. "I gotta start going to church. God's chosen people got hot without me knowing."

"No, Mona," Edie said, biting her lip not to laugh. A laugh would become a school girl giggle when he made it to their table. Edie knew that's what Mona wanted. "The rest of us are still plain God fearers."

"Has he always gone there?" Austin asked.

"No, he relocated with the company from Oklahoma," Edie said.

"Is he from there?" Mona asked. "He looks a little Native American."

"I can't remember right now, so just shut up. Here he comes," Edie growled.

Without another thought, she rose to greet Easton, her hand outstretched to put him off guard. "Easton Frost, this is a strange coincidence."

Smiling broadly, he looked for a place to set his food and take her hand.

Edie didn't flinch, keeping her eyes locked and her hand ridged.

"You can join us," Austin offered. She scooted closer to Mona, giving Easton the empty chair next to Edie.

"Thanks," he muttered. He set down his food and took Edie's hand.

"Good to see you again," he said. "I didn't realize you worked here, too."

Edie shook her head. "Me, neither. Where do you work exactly?" She motioned for him to sit.

"I work in specialty markets," he said. "I sell annuities directly to businesses."

"Introduce us," Mona barked.

Startled, Edie felt blood rush to her face. "Oh, I'm sorry. This is Mona and Austin. They work with me in the multiline channel."

Austin shot Edie a warning look. "We're event planners."

Easton chuckled. "That explains the hair then."

Edie wanted to die.

"Yes," she said after a moment of regaining composure. "We're the event planners for the multiline channel."

"You're really a red-head though, right?" he asked Edie.

Edie enjoyed the frown she displayed. "You got it."

Confused, Easton furrowed his brow. "Is there a lot of event planning for the multiline channel?"

Austin coughed and kicked at Edie under the table. "Actually, there are the three agent and district manager incentive trips: Summit Club, Champions, and President's Table. We also have the town hall meetings. They're every six weeks or so with eight across the state."

Easton opened his black Styrofoam container, revealing a large salad, heaped with cottage cheese, ham, eggs, and bacon bits over ranch dressing. "Were you still eating?"

"We ..." Edie began.

"We just finished with a meeting before lunch," Mona said. "We need to get back to the office." She tugged on Austin's shoulder until Austin gathered her things.

Edie rose. "Yes, we need to get back. It's fascinating. Not only we go to the same church, but we work for the same company, Easton."

He shoveled in a huge mouthful of salad and shrugged. "Sorry, I'm starving," he said, covering his mouth. "We all have to work and worship somewhere, right?"

Edie smiled, though repulsed by his lack of manners. "That's true. Good to see you again. Probably see you Sunday morning," she rattled off as she watched Austin and Mona exit the cafeteria.

"Wait a sec," Easton said. He'd at least stopped chewing and rubbed his mouth with a napkin. Cottage cheese and ranch where dribbling down his chin.

Edie turned her full attention back to him. "Yes?"

"We should get coffee again sometime," he said. "I think I gave you the wrong impression."

"Um, sure, okay." Edie was desperate to leave… and write up her direct reports for abandoning her.

"Do you office with the multiline state office or are you up with the rest of event planning on the sixth floor?" he asked.

"Upstairs," she muttered. Anger reined her every thought. She was enraged for being left.

"Good deal. Maybe I'll stop by after work sometime and we can get more coffee or dinner," he said, looking up at her for the first time.

"Don't you travel a lot for your job?" she asked.

"Constantly," he said. "But I'm always here on Mondays and Fridays."

Edie crossed her arms and shook her head. "Well, great. I'll see you around then." She wanted to scream at him that she wasn't gaming hard to get. Edie truly didn't care for him.

"Later, Edie Firebaugh," he mumbled over another mouth of food.

Austin and Mona were dead. Mona first, which would torture Austin with painful anticipation.

Chapter Twelve

A ustin and Mona had the sense not to pester Edie for the rest of the week. As far as Edie knew, they hadn't even mentioned the unfortunate Frost encounter to Becca, although it wouldn't have surprised Edie if Becca had been informed and simply didn't care to ask.

To Edie's relief, her team spent four days gathering the last evidence on Rich Capote's termination, and submitting the final recommendation letter. Edie focused on cleaning up the Collins mess. Taylor and Siemens had decided to honor the 90-day resignation, as Edie anticipated, but they also agreed to reassign Angelica Myers to the St. Cloud district. Edie then charged Mona with collecting the policy assignments given to Myers for the pending reassignment the day following Collins's last day.

It was a sound strategy to give Mona the onerous task. It would remind her that her primary responsibility continued to be policy assignment management. It would also prevent the terminator from fixating on her next kill.

Edie further suspected that when Mona wasn't casing a particular nerdy man online or in the bars, she became even more zealous about destroying agents and district managers. So Edie agreed to barhop with her team on Friday. There was no going home to change. They were to head straight for the warehouse district and then crawl toward the Target Center, stopping at the Hard Rock Café and dropping Austin and Mona off at Prince's club, 1st Avenue.

Edie craned her neck from her cubicle to see if the weather was still cooperating. The fall had been more snow than rain, but a darkening, overcast gloom had squatted on the cities. Edie couldn't remember the last time she saw the sun.

That afternoon, she put the finishing edits to the Capote termination recommendation letter and emailed it to Siemens and Taylor, knowing neither would officially look at it until Monday morning. Taylor would approve it before lunch. Siemens would acquiesce after a weekend of whiskey, fretting about his reputation in the face of the squirrelly son-in-law of district manager legend.

Edie and Mona would be heading to the Lakeville district office on Tuesday morning, termination letter in hand. She'd spend Monday afternoon arranging for a security escort, a group of marketing gents, and a company van to pry Capote loose from the premises.

But now it was time for Edie to shut off that part of her mind and attempt having fun. Locking her computer to its docking station and bicycle lock, she rose from her desk and gathered her folders and cutesy little event planner work backpack. It was the second worst part of the disguise. What was so wrong with carrying a laptop case?

Edie popped her neck and slung the backpack onto her shoulder. She was ready to quit working, dump her stuff in her Rav-4 and meet Austin, Mona, and Becca in the lobby. But she thought to check with Austin first rather than waiting downstairs and chancing a run in with Frost.

Austin was poring over her computer monitor when Edie knocked on the cubicle wall. "Can I come in?" Edie asked.

She always felt awkward asking to enter a cubicle space. Her team had been strategically blended throughout the maze of event planner cubbies. None of them sat near one another. It presented quite the privacy challenge, which continuously kept Edie locked inside conference rooms.

Austin looked surprised and then guilty. "Sure." She scuttled around her desk for her mouse. It sounded to Edie like she'd been watching a streaming video.

"What's that?" Edie asked. "You downloading porn at work again?"

Austin laughed a little too quickly and too much. Then she tucked her hair behind her ears and looked away. "You promise not to get mad?"

Edie crossed her arms, now alarmed by Austin's body language. "Depends. Were you really looking at something naughty?"

Austin shook her head with renewed vigor. "No, I'm not an idiot, remember? Besides, if anyone were tempted to do that, it'd be Mona." She dropped her voice to a whisper. "Although I think Becca has some wild cat secrets." Austin snorted and jokingly bounced her eyebrows up and down.

Edie knew she was being worked up. It was one of the proverbial arrows in Austin's emotional intelligence quiver. She'd busted Austin in the middle of something, and although Edie couldn't deny the friendship vibe Austin was evoking, she needed to find out what Austin had been watching.

"Tell me what you were downloading," Edie said again.

"You have to promise not to get mad," Austin demanded.

Edie grabbed the guest chair and sat down. "Or I can write you up for insubordination."

Austin squinted and huffed, trying to make Edie feel pathetic.

"Let's have it, Austin."

Austin sighed and maximized two windows on her monitor. "Okay, we've been trying not to bring it up since Monday, but that guy is way too cute for you to pass up."

Edie pinched the bridge of her nose. "How much time have you spent looking him up?"

"A couple of hours." Austin smiled an apology.

"A couple of hours for a Google search?" Edie growled. "Is he like that beer commercial guy, the most interesting man in the world? I can't believe this."

"Sorry, Edie," Austin said. "Mona and I have been finding different YouTube links and emailing them to each other. Your Frost is amazing."

"Yeah, right," Edie said. "Amazingly annoying and bizarre in an Eddie Haskell kind of way."

"He stopped a guy from kidnapping a little boy in an Office Max," Austin said.

Edie leaned forward. "What?"

Austin turned to her desk and clicked on her media player. "It was during one of those Code Adams when the store locks down because a kid goes missing."

"Play it," Edie demanded. "What are we watching?"

"There are two links. This one is the actual security camera of the parking lot showing Easton tackling the man with the four-year old in his arms," Austin explained.

Edie peered at the screen. Amid the grainy black-and-white, slow-motion footage, a dark figure charged out of the store. Edie could make out the child's head and shoulders dangling away from the man's body, trying to wrestle free. Then another man in a white shirt and black slacks sprang into the shot to leg tackle the dark figure. The three fell to the ground. The man in white ripped the boy free, but the hooded figure took off running. The man stayed with the child as others from the store ran to them.

"How do you know it's Frost?" Edie asked. Her heart was racing. The sheer terror of seeing an abduction threatened to bring her nightmares.

Austin clicked on another link. "Here's one of the evening news interviews with Easton."

"Where did this happen?" Edie asked.

"Oklahoma City," Austin said.

They fell silent to watch the reporter interview the man. Sure, it was Easton Frost. Who else could it have been? Batman? Superman? Ironman? *Was this why God sent Frost visions? Was he really some superhero?*

On the screen, Easton described what happened. His voice was shaky, and he wrung his hands. "I was just walking into the store for paper when this guy ran out with the little boy," he said. "My first thought was that the boy, that it was an emergency, like he might have fallen or something. But in a split second, I saw the look on the boy's face and it was..." He paused to clear his throat. "He was terrified. He knew he was in real danger." Easton covered his mouth and shook his head. "I don't ever want to see a look like that again. So I just took off after them."

The video cut to the security camera footage, but Frost's voice continued. "I knew I could take out his legs, and I thought I could strip the boy from his arm like when I used to strip running backs at UCO."

The reporter thanked Easton and turned the broadcast back to the anchorman who made a comment that Easton should have played ball at OU instead of the University of Central Oklahoma if he could make those kinds of plays. The anchorwomen ignored the moron and looked genuinely relieved the boy was safe and unharmed.

"See," Austin said.

Edie shrugged. "I'm not saying he's a bad guy. But he gets on my nerves. I think he knows he's *that* good-looking."

A new idea washed over Austin's face. "You afraid he's a pre-mature shooter? A lot of really cute guys are, that or they have really small..."

"No, Austin," Edie said. "I really hadn't thought that far into it. He's so annoying I never bothered to wonder about his junk."

Austin took the comment in stride and pointed to her screen. "There's more."

"What's more?"

"He rescued a woman from an assailant, too," Austin answered.

Edie rolled her eyes. "Yeah, right."

Austin ignored her and brought another link into her media player.

Edie slapped her knee in disbelief. "Of course, there's footage of this, too. Why wouldn't there be? Do you expect me to believe this guy was in the right place at the right time twice?"

Edie fell silent when the video started. In this shot, another security camera angle, outside a K-Mart, a white, windowless van pulled behind a woman walking to her car. The van's side door flew open and a man clad head to toe in black grabbed the woman.

Edie let out a small shriek. Two samples of nightmare fodder in five minutes. She was going to get plastered tonight. When she closed her eyes, Edie felt her mind already processing the horror. The man in black looked more like a tarantula wrapping his arms and legs around the woman.

"Edie, you're going to miss it," Austin said. She rewound the footage with her mouse.

Edie opened her eyes. Just as the van door was sliding shut, another man in a jogging suit dove into the van. The jogger kicked the door open and rolled out with the woman in his arms. Then he jumped up and blocked her with his body, but the van had sped off.

"And there's a news story on this too, right?" Edie asked. "How else could anyone verify that it was our hero hottie, Easton Frost?"

Austin stared at her in utter confusion. "What's your problem with this guy, Edie? I'm starting to think you're the one with the issue, not him."

Edie had nothing to say, so silently she nodded for Austin to play the footage.

The same news anchors and reporter covered this story. Edie could tell time had passed by their hair styles. Frost looked the same in the face, only his clothes were different.

"Incredibly, Easton Frost, the same brave individual who saved a small boy from being abducted outside an office supply store, has done it again," the reporter announced. The camera shot widened to show Frost standing next to her. "This time, the victim of the assault and attempted abduction was a woman. Now, the footage we're about to show you is not only miraculous but also very disturbing."

The video cut to the security camera footage just like before.

"It's the same story," Edie said. "It's the exact same."

Austin rolled her eyes. "Why are you being like this? It's the evening news. Of course, it's going to be the exact same format. That's kind of the point, isn't it? The same guy in the same situation is being reported a few months later but on the same news affiliate."

Edie set her jaw and allowed the waves of dejection to flow over her mind. Their commitment to her private life held the same fervor as terminating bad agents. Edie had clung to a conscious denial that she could keep her personal life hidden. But they had become too close in the last few months for her to keep her loneliness a secret.

Austin continued to blather about superhero Frost as Edie's hearing returned to the present.

Edie held up her hand to stop the flood of words and exhausted breath. "Okay, Austin. Okay. I get it. You know I had trouble with Captain Shorty Fantastic..."

Austin shook her head. "Nothing more than short man syndrome there. This is different."

"Listen, Austin. Calm down," Edie returned. "I'm not ready to be with anybody right now. And I don't want you to get any ideas."

She could see the romantic comedy unfurling in Austin's mind. But there would be no change of heart. If Frost started showing up unexpectedly and unannounced, Edie would define him as a stalker, not a mysterious hunk with awesome, do gooder eyes who donated shoes to orphans because he had so much time on his hands. There would be no melting of emotions or thawing of the senses when he saved her favorite cat or niece from a burning building while he happened to be in the area. There would be no climatic moment where his frustration and passion would get the better of him, and he would give her the tough love straight talk she needed when she was doing the dishes from a meal he guilted her into making for him at her place because he'd stood outside her door in the rain fondling himself.

"What are you talking about?" Austin asked, but the notion was crawling all over her lips, chin, and eyebrows.

Edie snapped her fingers. "I'm serious, Austin. Not pretend, secretly hoping for a rescue, serious. Dead serious," she said. "Do not try to set me up with this guy."

"You have to get over Cappy Dwarf America," Austin argued.

"I realize that, Austin," Edie said. "But I don't like going out on pointless dates, some leading to humiliating make out sessions, just to get over a guy. It's a waste of time and money."

"Okay, Edie," Austin said and threw up her hands. "I get it. I get it."

Edie wasn't convinced. "Just so we're clear. I don't want to talk about him tonight. I don't want Mona tampering with things or Becca feeling awkward because you two have your minds between the sheets."

Austin looked away, her eyes watering from the lecture.

Edie could tell she was making Austin mad. She reached out and grabbed Austin's hand over the mouse. "I really appreciate it. I do. But I don't want to get close to anybody. One of the most attractive reasons for coming here was so I could be left alone and not drive by the air force base on my way to work."

Austin refused to look at her. Instead, she closed the media player and the Google link. "I just want you to be happy. It's like you're either depressed or angry all the time, Edie. You're getting so used to it you don't even notice."

Edie shook her head. "I'm starting to realize that just because you're really good at work doesn't mean it's any less stressful."

"It's more than that," Austin said. "Sure, you come out with us on Friday nights and every other mid-week happy hour, but then you disappear. No one hears from you until Monday. You don't answer your phone or send back texts."

"I don't like being hung over in church," Edie said with a joke in her tone. "It makes the wine taste bad. I once retched on the blood of Jesus from partying too hard..."

"You could still check in with us and let us know you're alive."

"Oh, I'm sure Mona is typing away at her phone while she's banging one of her nerds from Saturday night bar trivia. And Becca becomes a ghost on weekends, too," Edie says.

"I can find them both through Facebook updates," Austin said.

Edie furrowed her eyebrows. "What? Mona posts her conquests on Facebook? No way."

Austin chuckled. "She's developed a code language referring to a time of day and color for successes, failures, and prospects. She was actually dating one of them for a couple of months."

Hearing that surprised Edie. "Really? Is she still dating him?"

"No, she dumped him. He was getting too clingy. Wanted to meet parents and spend the entire weekend together. Walks around Lake Calhoun and wine tasting in Hastings," Austin explained.

Edie nodded, no longer perplexed. Then something else occurred to her. "Becca's on Facebook?"

"Begrudgingly," Austin admitted. "But she'll respond to emails as long as you don't ask too many questions."

Edie patted Austin's hand again. "I know that must be difficult."

Austin laughed and shut off her laptop. Then she rose to gather her things. "You have to admit though, it's pretty amazing that the same guy saved two people's lives within three months because he's either so courageous or so dumb to throw himself into danger."

Edie cocked an eyebrow and shot Austin a threatening look.

Austin shrugged. "I'm just saying."

"He was a football player," Edie replied. "You've seen how those guys dive after each other just to make a tackle. It's in his head."

"Do you really think he played football?" Austin asked. "He's too skinny."

Edie nodded. "Probably got 'roided up or used a bunch of protein shakes in high school. Those guys always deflate like cheap birthday balloons once they quit the game."

Austin sighed. An amused pout formed on her lips. "They deflate everywhere, don't they?"

Edie rolled her eyes. "I think the 'roids take care of that before they stop using."

Austin had finished packing up her laptop and filing away her loose paperwork. "Just admit that he's brave."

"No question," Edie replied a bit too quickly. "You should have heard his speech in church. He even had *me* groveling to meet him."

A thought flashed across Austin's eyes. She did everything she could to hide it: check her purse's contents, reapply chap stick, pluck at errant hair. But Edie had caught the tell.

"Groveling?" Austin asked. "And he's in specialty market sales. So he's good-looking, heroic, successful. So seriously, all things being equal…"

Edie thumped Austin's elbow to encourage her to leave her cubicle and grab the other two bottle blondes. "Yes, he's hot. I think he's too skin and bone for me. But on paper, yes, he's a catch."

Austin slung her purse and laptop bag across her shoulder. "That's all I wanted to hear. It's good to know you're still alive."

Edie gave Austin the last word, knowing that as soon as they rounded Mona's cubicle, Edie would have to navigate through another onslaught.

Mona was ready and waiting, wearing her laptop and small handbag, when they greeted her. "You two ready to get Becca?"

"Sure," Austin said.

"Where are we heading again?" Edie asked.

"That Green Bay Packer bar," Mona said. "I think it's on 8th. I know how to get there regardless."

"The Packer bar?" Edie asked. "Isn't that sacrilegious, being in downtown Minneapolis?"

Mona huffed and waved her hand. "I've been a Bronco fan since Terrell Davis played for them, and I liked Ed McCaffrey and Bill Romanowski, too. Almost everyone on that team was hot. So I could care less about the Minnesota Vikings and their four Super Bowl losses. Besides, I'm in the mood for some local counterculture, even if it is still football."

"Okay, Mona. Calm down," Edie said. She could hear the translation in Mona's voice. Mona had been scurrying around all week, working out her redemption for the Terry Collins debacle. She'd pulled the Rich Capote file together in record time for such a tenured district manager, and now, she needed a night out, especially if she were on the prowl again.

They meandered the cube maze to Becca in silence.

Then Mona cleared her throat. "So Austin, did you send Edie those links?

"I saw them at her desk," Edie said, keeping her eyes focused on the narrow hall before her.

"She's not impressed," Austin said.

Mona humphed. "Maybe you need to contact the employee assistance program for your six free shrink visits because that makes you certifiably insane, Firebaugh."

Edie turned to Mona. "I never said I wasn't impressed. I'm just not interested. On any level. We had coffee once already, and it didn't go well."

Through a discussion Edie hadn't heard, trailing half a block behind Austin and Mona with a preoccupied Becca, they'd somehow suddenly decided against the Packer bar. The one they now entered was nameless and quiet. This isn't our typical bar scene, she told herself. Austin and Mona wanted to talk, to conspire against Edie, to convince her to pursue that idiot just because of what they'd dredged up online. Perhaps they wanted to gain back her favor from the botched resignation in Duluth and their bar hopping afterward. Whichever the case, Mona had been avoiding Edie's eyes since they stepped out of home office and trekked these four short but bone-chilling blocks.

Once they'd settled into their seats, Mona rushed to the bar to get their drinks without asking anyone what they wanted. Something was amiss. Sure, Mona was aggressive, but now her demeanor was cagey, trapped, cornered into staring at darkness.

Facing Austin and Mona's empty seat, Edie brushed her hair behind her ears and leaned forward. 'What's with Mona? What's going on? Is she still upset about the Duluth thing?"

Austin's eyes bulged. "Has she already told you?"

Edie felt like nodding her understanding, but figured she'd get Austin to reveal more by remaining stoic.

Austin feathered her fingers through her short hair and rubbed her neck. "It's really for her to tell you. Let's wait until she gets back."

Edie cemented her gaze on Austin and remained silent.

Austin fidgeted beyond her usual checkpoints. It reminded Edie of third base coach signals in softball: pinch both earlobes, check earrings, brush imaginary lint off tip of nose, rub both arms in self-hugging embrace, cough and clear throat, rock legs under the table.

Mona reappeared with their drinks.

"Austin tells me there's more to the Duluth story that what I got from Siemens and Taylor," Edie said before Mona had a chance to pass out the cocktails and take her seat.

Mona chose not to glare at Austin. Instead, she fixed her watering eyes on Edie and struggled to swallow. Then she cleared her throat. "Yes, we wanted to tell you before the agents' story came through the state office, but it's been hectic prepping the Capote termination recommendation and you fixing the Collins' resignation with legal…"

Edie took her glass of red wine from Mona and sipped it, allowing ample time for the other blondes to get the wrong impression. Then she carefully set her glass down on the blood red table top. "This place looks like that Hell's Kitchen breakfast joint down the street," she said at length. "It's all black walls and red tables."

Austin leaned forward but looked down.

Edie shrugged. "I was wondering why you two chose this spot."

"It's quiet..." Austin said.

"It's dark..." Mona said at the same time.

"So you went drinking with the two agents who tattled on Collins for the policy assignment fiasco last Friday afternoon," Edie said. "You also stayed the better part of Saturday."

"Do Siemens or Taylor know that?" Mona asked.

"No," Edie said. "That's what you two told me, remember?"

Austin nodded. "Oh, yeah. That's right."

Edie took another patient sip of her wine.

A long silence followed where three pairs of eyes volleyed for who would speak next. Becca remained quiet and aloof, oblivious to the unintended body language and blatant tells.

Unable to withstand the passive communication, Mona broke the silence. "Something happened that night."

Edie leaned back and crossed her arms. "What happened?" Given Mona's tone and reluctance and the time lapse between that night and now, Edie feared the worst. A cascading decision tree of informing human resources of impropriety if not grounds for termination flowed over her mind's eye. Her executioner and comforter, usually diametrically opposed, had come together to create the perfect storm of unforgiveable blunders; they'd slept with two agents.

"My drink was spiked," Mona said. "The way I felt the next day and how I can't really remember anything makes me think it was a rufie." She crossed her arms over her chest and looked down.

Edie turned to Austin. "Was your drink spiked, too?"

Austin shook her head. "No, it wasn't. Thank God. But I'd had three drinks before I noticed something was wrong with Mona. We were planning to get hammered that night anyway," she added quickly. "We wanted a night on the town without those agents, so we planned on having a quick drink to let them know our next steps on reassigning the policies and then we were going bar-hopping. I'd even reserved a hotel room so we could crash."

"That's where we woke up the next day," Mona said. "But it was spur of the moment for us to stay up there. We just wanted to unwind. The meeting with Collins was difficult. The marketing guys were late, so we had to stay in the office alone with Collins and his assistant for thirty minutes. It was over-the-top stressful."

Edie patted her hand on the table top to regain control of the conversation. "So let me get this straight. Mona's drink was spiked with rufies, but Austin's wasn't. Who do you think spiked your drink, Mona? One of the agents?"

Mona coughed and leaned forward. "We talked about it the whole way back on Saturday. We had a toast with the drinks Tom Hildebrand brought us, and that's the last thing I remember. Either he spiked it or the bartender did for him or the bartender was acting alone."

"Was Tom hitting on you? Making any moves?" Edie asked.

Mona shook her head. "No, he had intentions on Austin. The other agent, Kerry Lutter, was sitting next to me."

Now, Austin jumped in. "So we think Tom spiked the wrong drink and wanted to drug me up."

Edie fought to keep her breathing normal and not roll her eyes. "Let's cut to the chase..."

"We didn't sleep with them," Mona said.

"Are you sure?" Edie replied. "Because you just said you didn't remember."

"Austin took care of the situation," Mona said with less conviction.

Edie turned again to Austin. "How did you take care of the situation, Austin?"

Austin rubbed the back of her neck again. "I got Mona back to the hotel. When the agents saw how out of it she was, they split..."

"They left you two there at the bar?" Edie stammered.

Austin nodded. Her face was puffy.

"How did that happen?" Edie asked.

"Mona chased them off," Austin said in a near whisper.

Edie rubbed her forehead and sighed. "Why do I feel like I'm prying this out of you two? Just come clean, ladies. I thought you said Mona was drugged."

Austin looked apologetically at Mona who shook her head and stared out the window. Then Austin faced Edie. "Mona pulled her knife on them."

The revelation was too much to process, so Edie guzzled the rest of her wine, stalling for time to think. When she set her glass back down, she wasn't any closer to clarity. "You pulled your jack-knife on them?"

"It was my switchblade," Mona muttered.

"Your illegal, smuggled-in from Mexico switchblade?" Edie asked.

Mona nodded. "Look, I don't remember it. But they had it coming, drugging me like that."

"Had they started hitting on you then?" Edie asked them both.

Austin nodded. "They were getting pretty handsy. Lutter went for Mona's boobs and that's when she whipped out the knife. I have no idea how she got it out of her leg holster that fast, but it was against his throat in like two seconds."

Edie chewed the inside of her lip to avoid anxious laughter. "While you were drugged, you were able to pull out your knife and threaten the jugular of a man who had his hands on you? Yeah, right."

Still staring out the window, Mona fought off her own smile. "I practice a lot."

"Self-defense classes?" Edie asked.

"With my heavier stuffed animals," Mona admitted. "You remember that five-foot tall Teddy Bear and the white tiger in my room? They're both pretty stitched up."

Edie took another deep breath. "So then they left you guys there? Did you make a scene?"

Austin patted Mona's shoulder, but Mona shrugged it off. "Mona had some choice threats about calling their wives and castrating their sons. So they excused themselves and we never saw them again."

"And you escorted Mona to the hotel room?" Edie asked.

"Went nowhere else," Austin said. "I was afraid the cops were after us."

Edie popped her knuckles. "And you're both afraid that these agents will call Siemens or Taylor and tell them that you threatened them?"

Both Austin and Mona nodded.

Edie placed her hands flat on the table and leaned forward. "Here's the count, ladies. No more drinking with agents. Ever. Not even at holiday parties. You could both be fired for getting yourselves into that situation to begin with. Next, Mona, go to the doctor and get a urine and a blood test done to see what they put in your drink. You'll need to have documentation that something was in your system."

Mona shook her head. "It could have cleared out by now."

"When's the last time you dyed your hair?" Edie asked.

"About a month ago," Mona said and unconsciously combed through her roots.

"Then get a hair sample test, too," Edie demanded. "Now let me finish. Chances are the agents won't say anything to Siemens or Taylor. Our first strategy will be their word against yours until they produce evidence, say a picture from a camera phone."

Mona leaned forward, now ready for the fight. "But it was in self-defense."

"Sure, it was," Edie agreed. "But you just admitted practicing on stuffed animals, which gives way to pre-meditation. You can't prove who spiked your drink; you just know it was spiked."

"What about the policy reassignment?" Austin asked.

"It goes as planned. I'll have Becca work on it so it won't be conflicting for you, Mona," Edie explained and nodded to Becca whose hands were trembling and whose eyes were fixed on the floor.

"So they get the policies anyway?" Mona bellowed.

Three people at the bar froze in silence, and the bar tender shook his head in warning.

"Check your anger, Mona," Edie advised. "We are going to reassign the policies. Had this not happened, which we're pretending it didn't, we would be assigning them anyway. You want them to come up with a story on you? Best way for that is not to assign the policies."

"This is ridiculous," Mona growled.

"It's covering your butts," Edie said. "This is the last time, you two. Any more renegade stuff, and I'll fire you both."

Mona clenched her jaw and caught furious tears on her fingertips before they could fall from her eyes. "It's been a long time."

"Since what?" Edie asked.

"Since I had a rage cry," Mona said. "I hate this feeling. I hate crying. I hate this assignment. I'll get those agents back. I will make them pay."

Edie cleared her throat and deadened her gaze into Mona's eyes. "I'm never going to say this again, because this conversation never took place." She waited for Austin and Mona to nod their agreement. Even Becca looked up and shook her head. "Do it on your own time with your own resources, and make sure it has nothing to do with the company."

Chapter Thirteen

Edie glanced up at Mona in the brisk morning light. Edie was only a social smoker but she humored addicts, especially Mona and Austin. Although stinky, Mona was much more pleasant after replenishing her nicotine levels.

Edie felt she'd become pampered in Colorado Springs, where the need to preserve crisp mountain air prevailed over smokers' convenience. While living there, she'd witnessed the banning of smoking anywhere inside, within 100 feet of facilities for children, and even in one's own vehicle in Boulder.

Edie was nervous for their visit to Rich Capote's office and recognized her mind's need to wander. She watched Mona bend down and extinguish her third cigarette in a row. The once black-haired woman then dug through her purse for chewing gum, body spray, and perfume. Edie wondered if the body spray would evaporate or freeze before it touched Mona's skin. Perhaps early December wasn't quite that cold, but today's sudden drop to a high of twenty degrees wasn't anything to laugh about.

Mona yanked open Edie's rear passenger side door and threw in her backpack and purse. The two bags slammed against Edie's milk crate full of files for Capote's termination, which she'd brought along in case Capote's was a more intellectual debate over his innocence.

Then Mona hopped into the front with Edie. "Morning, boss," she breathed. The three pieces of gum almost hid her breath. By the time they reached Capote's office in Lakeville, no one would be able to tell.

"Morning, Mona. How was the rest of your weekend?" Edie asked.

Edie had left her three teammates early Friday evening after getting a call from Taylor that he'd approved the termination recommendation before waiting for Siemens's nod. The detour from protocol had guaranteed Edie a working weekend, fine-tuning the meeting in her mind. She'd buried herself with work until Sunday morning Mass, which Edie spent looking for Easton Frost, and then avoiding contact with him.

"It was okay," Mona said. "Hung out with Austin most of Saturday."

"You did?" Edie's tone was as accusatory as it was curious.

"Well, I basically wound up crashing with her Friday night," Mona admitted. "You didn't miss much after you left. We went to the Packer bar. Overweight, jersey wearing Germans from Wisconsin ordering cheese curds and sauerkraut."

"So neither of you hooked up with anyone?" Edie asked.

Mona laughed. "I got into a debate with a guy about the Super Bowl when the Broncos beat the Packers, where the final play of the game was a give up check down pass from Favre to Mark Chmura, the tight end, that had no hope of reaching the end-zone. He wound up buying us two rounds because he was so impressed with my knowledge of the game."

"Really?"

Mona shrugged and glanced to her neighbor's now vacant townhome. "Yeah, I'm pretty sure he fantasized about me, being the most intelligent, football-watching woman he'd ever met, but it wasn't in the cards."

"So he didn't get angry with your trash talking?" Edie asked.

"Every Packer knows it was a check down give up pass because the routes were blown and there was nothing left to do," Mona explained.

Entirely disinterested in football and knowing that Mona only enjoyed the sport for the builds and the butts, Edie cleared her throat to change the subject. "I meant to ask you on Friday how it's going with your neighbor's family? Do you talk to them?"

Mona stared straight ahead as Edie made the turn out of the neighborhood and headed toward southbound I-35. "Make a left on 42 instead of taking 35," Mona said. "I haven't really seen much of them. One of her sons came by about a month ago. He met with a realtor and they checked the place over. Then the realtor lady stuck that sign in the lawn and left. I was outside smoking so I spoke to him a little."

"How was he doing?" Edie asked.

"He seemed sad, but also preoccupied," Mona said. "I think he was worried about the market downturn for houses, especially the townhome market. Made me glad I'm a renter."

Edie grimaced and nodded. She, too, was appreciative of not owning a house. She had intended to buy when they first relocated, but the team had become so enamored with cleaning up the state office that Edie had put off house hunting. "How much has that market declined?"

She turned left as Mona had instructed.

"Anywhere from seventeen to twenty percent depending on the age of the townhome," Mona answered. "Mine was built in the '80s, so it's on the greater side of the decline."

Edie whistled. "That's tough."

"There are a lot of empties sitting around the neighborhood," Mona agreed. "And I thought of something else a couple of days ago. When January hits, you're going to see a lot of busted pipes."

Edie shook her head. "Good thing it's too cold for mold here."

Mona humphed. "I wouldn't count on it."

"Where am I going now?" Edie asked.

"In a couple of miles, you'll run into Cedar Avenue," Mona said. "There you'll take a right. It will eventually turn into County Road 23 which will takes us to the side of Lakeville where his office is."

"How do you know about this short cut?" Edie asked.

"I cased the joint on Sunday," Mona said. "You know, like visualization of free throws in basketball. I like envisioning myself making the termination so I have better control over the outcome."

Edie rolled her eyes and bit the inside of her lip. "Is that what happened in Duluth?"

"Hardly," Mona said. Edie couldn't find any embarrassment in her response. Perhaps Mona had recovered from the mistake and learned its lesson. Perhaps she was ready to emerge stronger with fresh battle scars from her most recent near-death experience.

"Austin had my mind tumbling through all sorts of empathies," Mona said. "Angelica Myers being hoodwinked into becoming an agent. All that stuff."

Edie nodded. "Did you expect her to act any differently?"

Mona looked out her window and brushed lint off her black pants. "Not really, but she did toughen up with Collins."

Edie recognized her opportunity to coach a listening Mona. "I think the biggest hurdle for you to get over is that Austin is a great asset."

"She's too soft on them," Mona muttered.

"No, she thinks like they do," Edie said. "She's their June Cleaver. Her need to make excuses for them anticipates the same excuses that defense attorneys bring to trial." Edie cleared her throat again to mimic a deep Minnesotan accent. "I wasn't trained all proper, doncha know. I supposed I could see how dat was wrong. 'Bout as wrong as jacking da rates der den on de homeowners and car policies. Dat guy der, my district manager, told me it would be okay as an exception basis type ting."

Mona snickered. "That might be valuable to our lead counsel or to your boss, but it just gets in my way."

"It's designed to get in your way, Mona," Edie said.

Traffic was thickening as they neared Cedar Avenue and their turn into Lakeville from Apple Valley.

"Why is it designed to be that way?" Mona asked.

"What Austin does ensures that we continue to make the company sustainable and more stable," Edie said. "If you were able to simply terminate Angelica Myers and Terry Collins, or even shove an immediate resignation down his throat, you would provoke a lawsuit. Even if we were able to settle out of court, it would damage the company's reputation. Senior management would become gun shy on future termination opportunities, and the rogue, renegade agents would run more amuck than they have been."

Mona rubbed her temples. "See, I just don't get that, Edie. I see it more as a war, and in war, you expect to have casualties. Out of court settlements should be factored into the equation, the rare lawsuit should be, too. Our reputation is for price-gouging the rural areas and for penny pinching claims. And internally, its reputation is for driving people to burn out and replenish human resources with college kids moronic enough to graduate with liberal arts degrees like the four of us did."

"At least Becca has a Bachelor of Science," Edie said. She did enjoy Mona's rants. Edie couldn't resist stoking the rage a bit more.

"In criminal justice," Mona growled.

"Which is why she's such a great investigator," Edie replied. "But the problem with your war analogy is this: the company is a business. It's a corporation managing mutually-owned companies. It doesn't have limitless resources to devote to a war like a country does. We have to be rational to become profitable again."

"You and Austin review all the potential agent and district manager terminations with Siemens and Taylor before you assign Becca to investigate," Mona said.

Edie scanned the horizon. "Mona, are you sure we're going the right way?"

Mona looked up and nodded. "Yep. It's all farm land east of Lakeville until Farmington. You'll see a big auto dealership on the right. Turn at that intersection."

Edie sighed off her disquiet. Not knowing her exact way frazzled her. But Mona's need to direct them to Capote's office outweighed her own need to know where they were going.

"We review the ramifications of a heavy amount of terminations," Edie explained. "We have people from the legal department review our methodology and business justifications. But Austin's input is still necessary on a case-by-case basis."

"But Taylor and Siemens have always backed us, even when they felt strongly that the agent would sue the company," Mona said. "Remember one of those first terminations where the agent was inputting phony social security numbers to avoid surcharges for bad credit ratings? In fact, the one I'm thinking of came from Capote's district."

Edie nodded, seeing the car dealer ahead.

"Weren't Taylor and Siemens reasonably sure he was going to sue for his contract value, trying to prove it was a form of deferred compensation in a retirement program and that he was a statutory employee rather than an independent contractor?" Mona asked. She took a deep breath having run out of air with the question.

"Yes," Edie agreed. "But no one was positive about what he'd come up with. He couldn't go down the route of wrongful termination without the division of insurance catching on to his fraud. Who do you think coached him on bringing the agent appointment agreements into question?" Edie took her right and headed due west toward Lakeville proper.

Mona coughed and chuckled at the same time. "Capote?"

"It proves how dangerous he is," Edie continued. "Minnesota has a nineteen-part test to determine if someone is a statutory employee or a contractor. If even one of the nineteen parts of the test fails, the state considers the person an employee. Then all the benefits offered to the agents would fall under employment law. Contract value, the value of the agent's books of business, would then be treated as deferred compensation. The company would have a crippling tax bill on its hands. It would also hurt the agents because they would have to pay income tax on the plan for their final years in business."

They passed a dilapidated bowling alley.

"Are we getting close?"

"Too close," Mona replied. She leaned forward. "See that red corvette in front of that weird looking building?"

Edie nodded.

"That's Capote's car and that building is Capote's office," Mona said.

"Should we pull in?" Edie asked.

Mona gave Edie their first eye contact of the morning. Edie's eyes held several questions. Did Mona need another cigarette? Did she need to make sure she didn't smell like cigarettes? Was she ready to face Capote and hand him his termination letter?

Had she bounced back from the reprimand about Collins's resignation?

Mona's dark brown eyes held all the answers. She'd visualized handing him the termination letter hundreds of times over the weekend. She'd roll played their dialogue over the same visualizations. She was a true student of short-comings and failures. She was adept at changing her style and approach to fit the situation. And yes, she needed one more smoke for a variety of reasons. With a cocked eyebrow, she told Edie that she didn't care if she were stinky in Capote's office.

"I'll turn into that gas station down the road," Edie said.

"Good deal," Mona replied.

"So Capote drives a corvette?" Edie asked as they veered south again and pulled into the convenience store parking. "How do you know it's his car?"

Mona had her cigarette and lighter in hand before Edie could park. "He's offered me rides back to home office from the last three town hall meetings."

Edie bunched up her chin in surprise. "He has? That would have been important to know before we set out this morning."

Mona hopped out of the car and slammed the door behind her.

Edie left the engine running and stepped out herself. The brisk wind's knuckles caught her face and seized her throat.

"Yeah, it's cold," Mona growled. "So he's hit on me a couple of times. It's not that big a deal."

Edie swallowed to warm her throat and then coughed. "I have to ask..."

"Are you kidding?" Mona blew an enormous cloud of smoke into the air. "Even if he wasn't married to the daughter of the district's former manager, even if it was just a convenience marriage and they didn't have kids, the freak looks like Howdy Doody. Ginger red hair..." She caught herself. "Sorry, you know what I mean."

Edie rolled her eyes and crossed her arms. "I'm not a ginger. I just have red hair. I don't have that many freckles, especially below the neckline."

Mona took a drag to avoid laughing. "Okay, okay. I'm sorry. Anyway, he dyes his hair dead brown, but the freckles are there along with the buck teeth and rubbery cheeks. He likes to hear himself talk about as much as that puppet, too."

"Wonder whose hand is up his butt working his mouth parts?" Edie asked.

They shared a nervous laugh.

"Laurent," they then said at the same time.

"So Capote is Denis Laurent's pawn," Mona said.

"And Capote's aware of it because he treats his agents the same way," Edie said. "But tell me about him hitting on you."

Mona took another drag and shrugged. "The first time, he was driving a Volvo. It was pretty harmless. It came across as being friendly or wanting to get to know the new home office employee in charge of policy assignment."

"Sure," Edie said. She studied the length of Mona's cigarette and prayed that within three drags, they'd be back in the car.

"Then the second town hall meeting, he drove the Corvette and wore a fitted golf shirt and sun glasses," Mona said. "It was like a high school reunion from an '80s afterschool special. He was playing big man, hugging and hi-fiving agents, putting his arms around some of the other women from the state office, like Catherine Monte and Elaine Lovelace."

Edie understood. "So when he approached you, he'd already established his territory and loved up other women in similar positions."

Mona snapped her fingers. "You got it. But this time, when he sat down at my table, it was time to play twenty personal questions, designed to get me to realize how lonely this icy state can be."

"How did you fight off his overpowering advances?" Edie asked.

Mona took her final drag and smirked. "I told him I hadn't shaved my legs or underneath my arms since we arrived."

"And he hit on you a third time?" Edie asked after wiping tears of laughter from her eyes.

Mona nodded wearily, flashing the age of her soul. It was the first time Edie had seen it. "I became a challenge then."

"Is that why you still wanted Austin to come with you today?" Edie asked. "Instead of me?"

Mona stamped on her cigarette butt and ripped open the car door.

Edie exhaled with relief and followed Mona back inside.

"They all underestimate the gravity of their terminations when they're staring down her cleavage," Mona said.

"You could work the cleavage angle if you wanted," Edie said.

"Don't insult me," Mona said. "Even without her, I figure Capote's ego won't be able to register what we're about to spring on him."

Edie reversed her Rav 4 and eyed her route back to Capote's ramshackle office. "So that's why you suddenly didn't care about smelling like smoke."

Mona clapped her hands. "Bravo, boss. The thought hit me while we were just talking. Also, from an *Art of War* perspective, he'll unknowingly admit defeat when he brings up his disappointment that I smoke."

"How so?"

"If all he can come back with is a personal attack, his strategy is lost, and he's desperate," Mona explained.

"I can't see him acting like he's lost even the battle, much less the war," Edie said.

Mona shrugged. "Capote is a guaranteed law suit. He'll never admit defeat. But there's an advantage in providing your opponent a trap to walk into. Even a small one that shows weakness but keeps the enemy alive."

Although the lot was empty save for an older truck, dripping with rust, they parked next to Capote's red sports car.

"I can't believe how dumpy this office is," Edie said.

The parking lot had huge potholes and divots from crumbling asphalt. The lines for parking spaces were barely visible.

Nothing came close to how toothless Capote's storefront appeared. Modeled after a Swedish farmhouse, its arched roof bowed outward from a center tip, designed to push snow accumulation to the ground on its own weight. Edie could almost make out the original red trim. The exterior walls had been replaced in a late '70s patchwork of windows. Edie could see into all three floors. That's where the toothlessness became more apparent. The lack of uniformity of desks and office furniture facing the windows was unsettling. Even worse were the overflowing filing cabinets and the boxes of computer paper lining one office's floor. Company signs were scattered everywhere. The window decals were pealing. Capote had not invested in his business in decades, and it showed.

Edie was first out of her SUV, but Mona wasn't far behind. Sensing that Mona was psyching herself up for their inevitable confrontation allowed Edie to straighten her back and double the strength she felt in her shoulders. She turned to Mona. "You ready?"

Mona cleared her throat. "Yes, I am." The fierce stench of Mona's cigarettes hadn't abated. Instead, it surrounded her, the foul odors encircling her torturous aura.

In her mind, Edie cued the force majeure house music as she faced the office. She then took her first step forward in time with the thunderous downbeat that blasted sound and light from the explosive jam. Her stance widened as she impersonated the female detectives in cable cop dramas. Edie couldn't tell if they walked bigger because they liked carrying guns on their hips or if they were pretending to be men with large units, but Edie always found it hilarious.

Without warning, she stopped. Mona was probably playing a similar song her own head. Except Mona wouldn't see any humor in her preparations. Just then, the once jet-black brunette collided into her.

"Ugh! Why did you stop?" Mona asked. "What's wrong?"

"Nothing," Edie said. "I thought I saw something."

"Let's get inside," Mona said. "He's already spotted us. He knows why we're here."

Mona scurried along, scraping her heels against the pavement as she opened the front door for Edie.

"Thanks, Mona."

"Seriously, don't mention it," Mona muttered.

Once inside, mildewed heat blasted their faces from a furnace that smelled as though it hadn't been serviced in Edie's lifetime.

Mona had slowed her paced and closed her eyes, basking in the humid heat to open her pores, oblivious to the rotgut smell permeating the entry way.

Edie crinkled her nose and scanned the scene. From the doorway, the entrance split to a stairway leading to a lower level and another heading to the second floor. A narrow corridor between the split level led to the rest of the main office.

"You've been here before, right?" Edie asked Mona.

"No," Mona hissed. "I've only driven by. And that was last night."

Edie stamped her foot, more in frustration from the wicked combination of Mona's breath and the misery of Frankenstein's foyer than anything else. "Well, then, where do we go?"

Mona looked past Edie and eyed a woman working on the second floor.

Edie followed her gaze. Mona hadn't spotted a person. She'd spotted the ankles, knees, and (to her disappointment), beyond of a woman sitting in a reception area.

Rolling her eyes, Mona knocked on the glass between them and the woman's calves.

"Yes? Can I help you?" came the irritated response. The knees, toes, and woman faced them. The calves didn't move.

"We're here to see Rich Capote," Mona said.

Edie found herself studying the legs. They bristled with the black dots of two days without shaving. The woman wasn't wearing hose. She must know that men have a direct path to her legs, thighs, and upward. Otherwise, she would feel more self-conscious about her calves being exposed. *She's caught men looking up her skirt*, Edie thought. That's why she keeps her legs stubbly, wears neither hose nor longer skirts.

Edie motioned for Mona to validate her logic.

Mona peered up the glass, then, looking impressed, pounded on the window. "You going to tell us which office is his, landing strip?"

The woman rose from her desk with a loud sigh and a string of muttered phrases ending with, "I'll gladly show you Mr. Capote's office."

Within seconds, she was bounding down the stairs in her high heels. The woman was something to behold, for a cougar. Her hair was curling iron flattened. It had been colored blonde for several decades, but her roots had won the final battle evicting the bleach near her crown to reveal salt-and-pepper patterns. She had a larger, top-heavy frame and her breasts, though ample and sure to encourage attraction from all ages of men, were low on her chest. Her white sweater made the flowing leap from her chest to cover her gut which disappeared into a long black skirt, under constant pressure to split along the zipper. Her legs, muscular and taunt to perfection, were a metaphysical feat, being so slender and well formed yet finding the will to support her bulbous frame.

She was upon them in moments.

Mona gave her a similar evaluation and then looked back to Edie as if to say the woman reminded her of Austin in twenty years. Edie rolled her eyes, but she knew Mona wasn't done.

"I'm sorry," Mona said. "Maybe that was a Hitler 'stache I saw, or maybe racing stripes."

The woman ignored her and focused on Edie.

Edie offered her hand. "Hello," she breathed with an embarrassed smile. "I'm Edie Firebaugh. We're here to see District Manager Capote. But we do not have an appointment."

The woman squinted her glare at Edie. "We all know who you are, and why you're here."

"Great!" Mona interjected. "Then you can show us to Capote's office."

"That's why I came down."

Edie withdrew her hand. "Do you work for one of his agents?"

The woman thumbed over her shoulder to a sign reading: How many referrals have you sent to Gonyea? You owe it to yourself, to your friends, and to your agent for taking such great care of you. "I work for Peter Gonyea, top auto and homeowners salesman in the district and the division."

Mona frowned. "Ah, the Great Rebater!"

The woman mirrored the frown until she placed the reference. Then she cleared her throat. "I'll show you to Rich's office. Follow me."

"How long have you worked for Peter?" Mona asked while placing her footfalls centimeters from the woman's. "Didn't he get into trouble with the state division of insurance for rebating with gas and gift cards for referrals?"

"Peter's been exonerated from all that," the woman said.

"Yet he's still the top producer in the land," Mona said.

The narrow, panel coated hallway left little opportunity to breathe, but as soon as they had entered it, they were coming out the other end.

Edie, paying more attention to her feet, nearly walked into Mona, who had stopped and was whispering something in the woman's ear. Edie was close enough to make out the following:

"Don't get me wrong. I'm not playing for the other team. But you got my curiosity up. Is it a 'stache or a stripe? I know you've caught guys looking up there. I know you like it. The flashy-flashy of it. Let me know and I promise I won't go after Gonyea for all his shady dealings. Especially with what we're killing Capote on."

Edie cleared her throat but caught a glance of the woman's horrified expression. It was a look not of being busted with a secret but of losing her job through her agent's termination.

"None of that will be necessary," Edie said. "I'm sure a stern warning will suffice."

The woman, petrified with shame, looked down and muttered. "It's the German one."

Mona's wicked smile brightened further. "Excellent. Mums the word, here. Don't worry. You'll have a good Christmas."

Edie had lost her train of thought and her composure in the face of such bargaining. *Was this how Mona operated in the field? Surely, this wasn't just an act for Edie's benefit.* Mona was still plotting her Duluth revenge.

The woman cleared her throat and pointed to the closed-door office on the other end of the hall. "That's his office. He's been here since before I clocked in."

"Thanks!" Mona beamed victoriously.

The woman didn't need an invitation to vanish.

In a moment, Edie and Mona were alone.

"Did you seriously just ask how that woman kept her pubes?" Edie growled.

Mona shrugged. "I didn't get the angle on the part I saw. I wanted to know if it was vertical or horizontal."

"What does it matter?" Edie hissed.

"Hey, if she's going to wear a skirt with a long split without hose or underwear, then I have a right to ask."

"Ever heard of sexual harassment?" Edie demanded.

Mona ignored Edie's question, and Edie regretted asking it. It was something better saved for private counseling. They needed to focus on the behemoth before them.

The office door was now ajar.

Edie led the way and gave her strong five-count knock on the threshold before they entered.

"Yes, come in," came Capote's invitation.

Edie and Mona entered as almost the same person existing in the same space. Capote smiled when he saw them, but refrained from getting out of his chair. Instead, he waved them in and scrolled through the ESPN website, finishing an article about the Minnesota Vikings.

"Edie Firebaugh and her lovely policy assignment guru, Mona," he said, keeping his eyes fixed on the computer.

Mona took the left chair facing his desk.

Edie remained standing. Then, with deliberate and calculated motion, she extended her hand. "It's good to see you again, Mr. Capote."

Seeing Edie's refusal to be seated, Mona rose to her feet.

Capote smirked and shook his head at her hand. "Oh, no. We don't need to be that formal. You've no doubt seen how my in-house agents choose to present themselves." He swiveled from his desktop to face them and threw up his hands. "That's the beauty of being independent contractors. I can't really tell them what to do. I can only advise them and lead with example."

Edie peered into his face for tells as she acquiesced to taking her seat. His round face was a stony façade. His bottom lip held the imprint of his teeth while his upper lip dropped to cover his large bucks. It was an altogether odd arrangement of mouth parts. One she'd seldom encountered in sales, perhaps because people with such asymmetrical faces weren't usually successful in sales careers.

Edie reminded herself that Capote had inherited his district agency from his father-in-law. It made him compensate with arrogance and belligerence that which he could not defend with a history of personal production or prior experience in sales management.

Edie and Mona wouldn't get a word in.

"So how is Mona?" Capote asked. He leaned back in his chair and folded his hands behind his head. "We haven't really talked since the last town hall meeting, correct?"

Mona dropped her eyes. Edie could feel her friend hiding her blush.

Capote's eyes showed concern, but it was masking his sense of a dominant edge. He grinned and then took a deep, sniffing breath. "I don't remember you being a smoker."

Mona looked up from her wrung hands and matched his gaze. "Probably because you and I aren't really that well acquainted."

"You're right about that." Capote looked at his wrist watch and then leaned forward. "So what can I do for you two today? Is there some new event you're planning? A new marketing tool that will be so awesome that we'll forget how horrible our rates are? Or did Siemens send you for more nefarious reasons?"

Edie cleared her throat. "We're here to deliver your notice of termination." She removed from her suit coat the envelope which carried his notification letter and the first of three equal payments totaling his district agency's contract value. Edie had looked at the check and was amazed that the company was willing and able to pay him nearly $167,000 in three installments even after the evidence of embezzlement they'd submitted.

Capote rocked back in his chair. "Really? You're here to terminate me." He snatched the envelope from Edie's hand and tore it open. His shoulder relaxed when he reviewed the check's total first, but the rest of his body was tense, preparing for the conflict.

"It's effective immediately," Mona said.

Edie had been waiting for Mona to add that bit. It established solidarity before Capote could launch into his attack.

Capote tossed the letter and check across his desk and returned to his position with his hands behind his head. "I suppose I'll need to reserve my reaction and comments until I talk to my attorney, but at the same time, I believe I'm in my right to know what grounds this alleged termination is based upon."

Expectantly, Mona nodded. "The letter indicates the grounds as embezzlement of company funds and resources."

"Are you at liberty to be more specific?" he asked. His eyes narrowed to slits.

Capote's demeanor reminded Edie of the Judd Nelson movie, *From the Hip*, where John Hurt lunged at his attorney, Nelson, with a gruesome looking hammer and then settled back into the witness stand and play acted insanity.

"Your misuse of the company's career agent subsidy system," Edie explained. "You created career agents almost entirely supported by the other agents' production to ensure that the subsidy payments would continue to flow."

Capote shook his head. "What would be the advantage of frauding the company with phony career agents? I can't see making any money on two or three agents receiving the fifteen-hundred-dollar monthly stipend."

"It has allowed you to keep your district recruiting goals in the black," Edie said. "That's the number one goal for which you are measured. It keeps the district folio, near $50,000 a month, coming into your bank account."

"It keeps me employed," Capote said.

Neither woman took the bait. "It's kept you in business as an independent contractor acting as a district manager for the company," Mona corrected.

"If you can prove that in court," Capote said, "I suppose it would have to have kept me in business."

"We have records indicating that your career agents were submitting business in other agents' offices, outside the district office but within the district's agency force," Edie continued.

Again, Capote shrugged. "The computer network allows any agent to access the system from any terminal so that all agents can service any customer who walks in the door. I've always arranged for my reserve and career agents to use my full-time agents' offices to submit business after meeting with customers and prospects." He counted on his fingers. "It enables faster service, timely placement of policies, customer peace of mind, and convenience for my agents, which is value-added from me."

"It's very altruistic of you," Mona said.

"Thanks, Mona, for seeing it that way," he returned.

The sarcasm was nauseating.

Edie continued. "There are checks leaving your folio account and going into your personal bank account that have the same totals as the commissions that were paid to the career agents for the business they wrote in your full-time agents' offices. We have several counts of this."

Capote's jaw dropped until he could no longer keep his sneering smile hidden. "That is an incredible coincidence."

"We're prepared to subpoena your personal bank account statements to determine if checks totaling the same amounts were paid out to your full-time agents," Mona said.

Capote turned his gaze to her, wicked condescension threatening to erupt. "You can't prove something that simply doesn't exist. I've never paid full-time agents any funds from my personal checking accounts for business placed with the company. Now, sure, several of my agents are personal friends of mine and we've done things together on our personal time that would require money changing hands like football games, fishing trips, trips to the cabin. But nothing like what you're describing."

"Even if they were cash transactions," Edie said. "You won't be able to account for the coincidence of your last six failed career agents."

"Another coincidence?" Capote interjected. "Sounds like quite a bit of circumstantial evidence to me."

"All six were cut off the subsidy program within a month of ceasing to place business in the offices of your full-time agents. Each then started writing business in the full-time agents' offices the next month to regain their active status on the subsidy program," Edie explained. "Each then yo-yoed between no production, removing them from subsidy, and high levels of production that earned their current subsidy as well as their subsidy in arrears."

"And the volume of folios to personal bank account transactions that total the same in new business commissions to these career agents is consistent for nearly two and a half years," Mona said.

Capote raised his hand. "Let's be clear. I'm being immediately terminated after nearly fifteen years of service based solely on the supposition that I have been paying my full-time agents to write business in my career agents' agent codes to fraud the small, ineffective subsidy system? This in turn allowed me to avoid, indeed, prevented my termination at an earlier date due to the lack of successful recruitment and appointment of new agents within my district, which I would not have been able to do without having devised and executed this scheme. Do I understand you correctly, Edie Firebaugh?"

"You do, indeed," Edie said. "You just mentioned ten minutes ago that the rates for our products are too high for new agents to be successful."

Capote brought a finger to his nose. "No, we need to be clear there. I made a quip about a new marketing tool being such a magic bullet that the agents would forget how uncompetitive our pricing is right now."

Mona shrugged. "Either way, you admitted your belief that our rates are uncompetitive, which makes recruiting and appointing new agents more difficult for you than it has been in the past."

Capote chuckled. "I guess that will become my motivation for having committed this fraud?"

"It certainly could serve for justification," Edie answered. "We can't speculate on your motivation beyond keeping your business running."

"Which of you will be taking over my office?" Capote asked. "Because frankly, this is nothing more than a witch hunt. Just like the several dozen other agents and district managers you've managed to con into resigning or wrongfully terminating."

"You're certainly entitled to emote and to seek validation for your emotions," Edie said. "But neither of us is interested in becoming district managers or taking over your business. We're confident in our career paths."

Mona smirked and nodded her agreement.

"What if I threw you out of my office right now?" Capote asked.

"I think our time here is finished regardless," Edie said. She rose and motioned for Mona to follow.

Edie turned back to Capote before she crossed the threshold of his office door. "But we do have our van and a few people from home office here to reclaim your district office files, systems, technologies, and accounts as indicated in the termination notification letter."

"I don't necessarily have to allow them in either," Capote said. Now his face was glowing with suppressed lashings and anger drenched abuse. His hold on his outbursts was diminishing.

"We will seek a court injunction to support the actions detailed in your termination notification letter, former district manager, Rich Capote," Edie replied. "Any prudent lawyer would advise you to allow all parties involved to adhere to the provisions of your appointment agreement to facilitate termination."

Edie turned away from Rich Capote and glided down the corridor, down the stairs, and out the district office's front door. Waving in the marketing men, waiting with hand carts and furniture pads, she felt Mona's excited breath on her neck.

She hoped she'd won Mona back.

Chapter Fourteen

The state office was now as buried with calls from irate and frightened agents as it was buried underneath six floors of home office personnel who pretended it didn't exist. News of Rich Capote's termination spiraled through the remaining district managers, many of whom had phoned Geoff Siemens to inform him that they would be suspending their recruiting efforts until they came to a full understanding of what Capote had done wrong. The undercurrent of mutiny wasn't lost on Siemens who spent the next week and a half touring the metro and out-state territories explaining how sophisticated the company's ability to conduct thorough investigations had become since Edie's team arrived.

As a result of Edie's team being "thrown under the bus," an oft-used, favorite cliché throughout the company, Mona had submitted a daily request to return to her natural hair color. Edie suspected that Becca was passive-aggressively allowing hers to grow without dyeing it again. Edie wasn't ready to revolt with her team. What choice did she have? Add red highlights to transition from blonde to strawberry-blonde to her nearly ginger, Irish heritage? She couldn't allow her roots to break free because she'd start to look like a patient with a head wound who'd somehow lost her bandages. Going straight for the red hair dye was bullish and optimistic at best. No one ever matched the bottle to a natural red.

Only Austin seemed content to remain a blonde.

For the short term, Edie kept Mona and Becca calm, reminding them that promotion out of the scourge meant they needed to remain incognito a while longer, especially if the next assignment came from the independent general agent sales channel.

Mona's email requests gradually dwindled in inverse proportion to her workload of reassigning the fraudulently written policies back to Capote's full-time agents and encouraging the career agents involved to resign. The career agents' choices were clear: resign without question, and the company would write off the fraudulent subsidy payments, or continue appointment until a full investigation, including division of insurance support, was completed. All six career agents had resigned, leaving Mona tasked with the policy reassignments, and a new wave of out-of-district reassignments for the legitimate business the career agents had written. Both Siemens and Taylor felt it prudent not to reward the full-time agents with these policies after their involvement in Capote's scheme.

Austin had spent the same time winning the hearts and minds of the dirty full-time agents. Journey's *Open Arms* always fluttered into Edie's mind when Austin gave her daily updates. Most pled ignorant, blaming a member of their office staff. Few admitted their guilt. All were assured of their continued appointments, which solidified their loyalty to the company rather than to Capote and his attorney.

The commotion Capote's removal caused was heading toward perpetual inertia. District Manager Denis Laurent had made three unannounced visits to the state office to unveil his new recruiting, marketing, and succession plans for his agency. Terry Collins, at first belligerent, had swum through the stages of grief like an Olympian. He was now catching his breath with quiet acceptance. Much to everyone's surprise the St. Cloud district's home and auto sales had spiked, hitting a watermark not seen in five years and setting a new high each business day.

To keep Becca busy, Edie had her track the sales groundswell to the timing of Geoff Siemens's district visits.

Edie knew that a key measure of her team's success was the swift and violent changes their actions caused, but it saddened her to equate careers ended, jobs lost, and company-created turmoil to the positive, reinforcing, encouraging warm fuzzies of a job well done.

She was in the middle of just such a rationalization when a new email popped up in her in box. She was adept at prioritizing emails and phone calls, enabling her to remain focused on her daily agenda, but this one caught her eye. It was from Easton Frost.

Edie experienced a surge of adrenaline without an emotional justification. She thought to her freshman psyche class when they studied William James' classic assertion of running making one scared versus being scared making one run. Edie had always thought the 19th century shrink an imbecile until now. Her skin goose fleshed. Her hair rose on her neck and arms. Her vision became brighter and she could smell everything more clearly. She was in the thralls of fight or flight, but she couldn't tell if she were excited, angry, or frightened.

She despised Easton for making her feel this way. She decided to punch out a quick, cold response to kill whatever he wanted.

But then she also had to read the email.

Edie,

How are you doing? How's the multiline world treating you? Any cool events in the works? Actually, I know what your real assignments are, and I think it's great that you're taking such a strong stance.

Any way we can get lunch today?

Easton Frost
Sales Vice President
Specialty Markets

Now, Edie had emotions to assign to her biofeedback: repulsion, disgust, paranoia. How had he found out what they were actually doing? His specialty markets sales channel was three degrees removed from the multiline channel, with the affiliated life and annuity and the brokerage life and annuity channels between them. It was very unlikely he had contacts or cohorts in her area, regardless of the hideous, nearly satanic coincidence that they worked for the same company in downtown Minneapolis.

Edie reached for her cell phone and found Mona's cell number.

"This is Mona," she answered.

"Did you tell Easton Frost what we actually do?" Edie asked.

"What?" Mona barked. "Is this Edie? Why are you calling me on my cell phone? Aren't you here today?"

"Yes, I'm here," Edie snapped. "I didn't want to call you on the office line. Just answer the question. Did you ever tell Easton Frost what we do?"

Mona sighed. "Well, I gather he knows something by the way you're acting. But no, I didn't. I haven't seen the guy since that time in the cafeteria."

"Except on YouTube downloads," Edie replied.

"So... he knows," Mona said. "What, did he call you or something?"

"He emailed me on the company server," Edie said.

"So answer him back," Mona said. "Ignore his speculation and ask him what he wants."

Edie rolled her eyes. "He wants to go to lunch. Today."

"Sweet," Mona growled. "Then go to lunch with him. Find out how he knows and what he knows."

"I'm calling Austin first." With that, she hung up on Mona.

Austin wasn't much better.

"I swear I didn't say anything to him," she said thirty seconds later.

"Have you talked with him at all?" Edie asked.

"Not about work stuff," Austin said guardedly.

"Austin!" Edie coughed into her hands, having swallowed wrong from a shocked gasp. "When have you been talking to him?"

"During smoke breaks," Austin said. "I've only ran into him a couple of times."

"I thought he traveled a lot," Edie said. "What's he doing hanging around home office?"

"Edie, you know I have no idea," Austin replied.

"What have you talked with him about?"

"Just normal small talk, chit-chat," Austin said, her voice drifting in and out. "Weather, Vikings, Minnesota Wild tickets he was giving away."

"You were talking about me, weren't you?" Edie demanded.

"He brought you up a couple of times, yes," Austin admitted. "*I* didn't mention you. *He* did."

"So in a couple of conversations, he's asked about me at least twice," Edie said. She rubbed her temples and closed her eyes. "What did he ask?"

"If you were seeing anyone," Austin said.

"And what did you tell him?"

"The truth. That you haven't been."

"I've got to go," Edie hissed.

"Wait, Edie. Are you mad at me?" Austin asked.

"Yes, Austin, I am. He sent me an email asking me to lunch," she spat.

"That's awesome!" Austin replied.

"No, it's not. I specifically asked you not to talk to him, especially about me. The man seriously creeps me out."

"Then tell him that at lunch," Austin said.

"We're not finished with this, Austin Jenkins." Edie then hung up on her, too.

Then she turned back to her email.

Easton,

Nice to hear from you. I can't have lunch today. In fact, my whole week looks packed. Sorry. Maybe some other time.

Thanks,
Edie Firebaugh
Marketing Specialist
Event Planning

Within seconds, he'd sent a reply.

But I'd like to talk to you about your real job. I think I can be of help. Aren't you looking for a promotion out of multiline?

Edie froze. Deafening blood flooded her ear drums. Her heartbeat pounded in her temples. What did this man know? Why was he so interested in helping her?

Thousands of scenarios and spindles of next steps fractaled through her mind. Maybe he thought she was nothing more than her job and was willing to do anything to get ahead. Perhaps he assumed she was a pure corporate junkie who would have been impressed with him finding out as much as he had. Maybe he was calling her bluff. Then again, she could be reading too much into the note. What if Frost was trying to draw her out, get her to reveal something she shouldn't? Everyone had a job title and an actual job. He was probably just joking about her job title and the real work she and her team did, the grunt work of event planning, never getting to go to Italy or the Virgin Islands for spot inspections. He could have as easily been thinking about a new assignment within the event planning department, something for his channel.

Why was she so panicked? *Because this was invasive*, she told herself. It's as scary and weird as a random home invasion. She felt that her privacy had been violated.

Then, for some reason, her mind sprang to the internet videos of Easton rescuing that little boy and woman from abductions. Had she invaded his privacy by looking into his searchable, online past? What if he'd done the same to her?

She shook her head, disagreeing with her inner dialogue. He wouldn't have found anything.

Edie struggled to catch her breath and relax her heart rate. The best course of action was to meet him as soon as possible and find out exactly what he knew and what he was propositioning.

Besides, he probably just ran into one of the multiline channel's ex-agents she'd terminated. He couldn't be *that* juiced. Frost was no home office rat. He was in the field. He was in sales. Sales people are categorically opposed to home office operational types like her and her bosses.

She turned back to her laptop and email.

Frost,

I can meet you for lunch today. Cafeteria. 11:30 am. I only have half an hour before I need to get to my next appointment.

Thanks,
Edie

She glanced at her clock. It was already 11:15. By the time she visited the restroom, crossed the street through the underground tunnel to the company cafeteria, it would be 11:30. She didn't have time to wait for his response.

It was time to scare this imbecile away.

The cafeteria looked darker and drabber than it had before. With winter creeping into the land, its institutional grey walls and suspended ceiling were depressing. Beyond the random clattering of dishware and stainless steel in the kitchen, all sound was devoured. Edie thought it was a perfect model for a Stanley Kubrick version of hell; one devoid of activity yet boiling over with torturous anticipation. The mounting pressure of something's got to give and this too will pass was enough to split atoms and synapses, and cause the soul to implode upon itself.

Edie felt fully prepared for this particular kill.

She surveyed the terrain, and soon decided on a two-seater table in the farthest corner, overlooking the six-floor building where she worked. Her building's arches and architecture would draw her attention away from Frost, something he hopefully wouldn't appreciate but would read well enough.

Edie took the inside seat, giving her full view of the cafeteria. Her back was to one wall, sure, but she had two windows to peer out with marked disinterest. Once seated, she yanked her Blackberry from her purse and pretended to be deep in email and corporate chatter. He needed to get the impression that she had no time for his help, had no time to be friends, had no time for Mr. Easton Frost.

Even if she hadn't caught a glimpse of the lanky, boyish man as he turned the corner from the a la carte entrance, she would have sensed his presence. His was a rippling effect as he traversed from one point in distance and time to another, with a trajectory and tempo marked with the silencing of conversation, the raising of eyebrows, the opening of irises, the coolness of open pores, the quickness of breath, and the turning of "oh, my" faces from other women. Those who TiVOed their "stories" while they worked, that is.

Edie further belittled him in her mind. Yes, that's exactly the fit for Easton Frost (what kind of name is that anyway?). He is much better suited to be one of those perennially shirtless doctors on *Days of All Our Hospital Patients*.

His walk sped up as he passed the check-out station with two cups of coffee. He'd seen her. Edie focused on her fictitious email, mimicking her hunt and peck with the cadence of his footsteps.

She refused to look up until he was upon her and then only briefly. She would not look into his eyes. She would not let him see into hers.

"Edie?" he asked and cleared his throat.

She threw up an index finger, asking for a moment more of silence. Then, with animation, she hit send on her bogus message and glanced at him. "Easton. Thanks for being so flexible and yet so persistent in deciding to meet with me. On such short notice, too."

He set the coffee on the table.

Edie realized she didn't stand to greet him, or beat him to the handshake like she preferred. Inwardly, she was impressed with herself as she hadn't consciously thought to avoid this action. It only proved that all of her intentions, both upfront and deep within were in accord.

"I know you're busy," he was saying. "Thanks again for meeting with me. I'm about to leave on a sales trip so I wanted to catch you before then."

"Sales trip?" she asked and looked out the window nearest her.

"Yeah, can I sit down?" he asked.

Edie nodded and leaned forward, dragging her eyes away from the Minneapolis skyline. Then she took a breath and looked up at him, staring at the ridged contours of his forehead rather than his eyes. "So when you leave for a sales trip, how long are you gone?"

Easton smiled and straightened his posture so their eyes could connect.

She cursed herself for their small talk. Men almost always took small talk as a measure of interest.

Easton cleared his throat to get her attention. "…so most of the time I'm in the field, living out of a suitcase. It's really unusual for me to spend so much time in home office. It's driving me crazy. We've just had so many new product launches I needed to get things ironed out."

"Your emails this morning were decidedly poignant," Edie continued.

Easton dropped his smirk. "Did I startle you?"

Edie rolled her eyes. "I found your cloaked messaging distracting. I have a very hectic week."

"I'm sure most of your weeks are hectic, Edie," he said. "I understand there are a lot of shake-ups in the multiline channel, particularly in the Minnesota State Office. I know you and your crew aren't event planners. I report directly to John Taylor, too."

Edie stared through him.

"Believe me, it's a good thing to work directly for Taylor," Easton said. "He's a good rabbi, a good person to have on your side, especially from a senior management perspective."

Edie clasped her hands in front of her face and rested her chin on her knuckles. "Well, I don't want to sound self-involved or conceited, but it seems as though I came up in conversation with Taylor."

Easton nodded. "You got it."

"And the gist of this conversation was?"

He took a large, dramatic sip of coffee before answering. Easton looked as though he were mentally surmising his discussion with their boss, but he'd known the score from the beginning. Otherwise, he wouldn't have demanded this meeting.

They shared a parish. They shared a place of employment. Now, they shared a boss.

"Taylor is very impressed with you, Edie," Easton said. "He said you'd made a name in Colorado Springs for improving your region's profitability with some strong and consistent distribution decisions."

"I'm a terminator," Edie said. "I realize you're aware of that now, so we can skip the euphemisms."

Easton wagged a finger at her. "That brings up another point he made. He mentioned that you kept him on his toes. That you've been pushing the envelope."

Edie shrugged. "I owe it to my team to advance them as much as I can and to provide them the best opportunities available."

"All four of you dyed your hair to blend in with the event planner clique," Easton continued after another gulp of coffee.

Edie grimaced and watched for Easton's reaction. He gave her none. "I'm not too pleased with that aspect. None of us really are. It borders on workplace sexism and harassment. But we believe in what we're doing, we're committed to the opportunity and we do our jobs very well."

Easton leaned forward. "But I understand there is limited opportunity working within other state offices for your channel and going to another regional office would feel like a lateral move."

"Taylor would like to replicate the model I've built with other problem states," Edie admitted. "But I'm not a bouncer. I don't like to skip all over the country like you sales people."

Easton smiled. "So what does that leave you?"

Edie squinted and thought of how much she should reveal to Easton. She decided to be as direct as possible. "Why are you so interested?"

He dropped his façade. Now, he was cold and unreadable. Edie thought of an errant quote from the musician Sting about the notes not played being as important or more than the notes played. The same held true in business and the language of the street. There was value in not reacting to certain things. It could give you an edge on your adversary, especially if he were inclined to make assumptions.

"I like helping people," Easton replied at length. "I feel like I know someone now in home office that isn't directly affected by my sales. I just thought I could help you get to where you're already going."

"Oh, I know you like helping people," Edie said. Two could become blunt and icy. *She* wasn't making any assumptions. She actually had no idea what his motivation was, and Edie wasn't about to believe he wanted to date her. There was something more to his angling.

"What's that supposed to mean?" Easton asked. But he couldn't hide his *Singles* Matt Dillon smile.

"Austin and Mona googled you," Edie said. "And then spent an afternoon watching your rescues in Oklahoma on YouTube."

Easton became the lamb. The blush in his cheeks was insulting. She knew he was playing her. He knew what was out there. Could he be more Narcissistic? "Oh, you saw those, huh?"

Edie nodded. It was time to kill. "Yes, so if you want to help me, figure out a way to get that afternoon of lost productivity back for my team."

The pretense vanished in his eyes. "Hey, I just wanted to see if I could help you get promoted out of the multiline basement work with your ridiculous dyed hair dos. If you don't want my help, I understand. I'll just walk away and get on my plane."

Edie created a power triangle with her elbows and rested her chin on her knuckles. She'd struck the first blow, a warning shot. Her next would result in a defensive wound, but she now had his attention.

"I don't trust people I barely know acting like they know too much about my little known assignment," she said. "Rumors fly. Most come from the field, especially in the career and affiliated channels because those sales forces feel the closest to us. It's not my identity I'm guarding, Easton. It's the perception that the company is using a hatchet instead of a scalpel, to use recent political campaign lingo, to make itself more profitable."

He slapped the table softly, but it was still a sign of frustration and a certain display of power, even if it was a tad bit metrosexual. "So you don't trust me."

"I don't know you, Easton," Edie said.

He raised his hand to count his points. "We go to the same church. You know about the vision I had. We attended the same charity function. We then got coffee and talked. A few weeks later, I come back from the field to discover we work at the same place. You at least know I saved two people's lives in Oklahoma right after college. You agreed to meet with me to discuss ways I can help your career. How don't we know each other? What have I done to make you not trust me?"

Edie loved to employ mimicry after a counterattack. It mocked the articulated offensive, matched mêlées and parries with precision. Slowly, she, too, raised her hand to count on her fingers.

"There are six thousands members of our parish. You were swarmed with people after your lay homily. You show up to the same event. You came on too strong during coffee, hinting that you weren't seeing anyone. Then, it turns out, you work where I do. You send me suspicious, alarming emails at random. I don't know you, and you're behaving like a stalker."

Easton grimaced. "A stalker?"

Edie nodded without blinking.

"Are you that cynical to think that no one, including people you share so much in common with, can be your friend, can be trusted?" he asked.

"Hello! I'm in terminations," she replied. "Everyone has an angle to play. So I have to ask. What's your angle? You barely know me. I've made every indication that I'm not interested in you, and yet you still appear. Please don't tell me you're playing this out in your head like it's a romantic comedy."

Easton rolled his eyes and shook his head. "I don't want to date you, Edie Firebaugh."

"Good because you're not..."

He cleared his throat with flare and slammed his hand on the table. "You strike me as someone who needs a long-term relationship. That you take dating more seriously. Like you've got the right man in your head and no amount of shoe-horning is going to make anyone else fit."

Edie felt two inches tall, and the reasons were abundant. He'd got her making assumptions she'd sworn not to make. He was more perceptive about her than she'd anticipated, and he did so without much effort. It made her feel open and vulnerable and frightened.

Being naked emotionally was far worse than physically. She shook that last notion from her mind. No, nothing was worse than really being naked when you didn't want to be. Nobody killed herself in the nude.

"When you said you weren't dating anyone, I thought that meant you were interested," Edie said. "And you're right. I'm not either."

Easton shrugged. "We had coffee. It was your testing ground. Either I didn't pass, or you decided something on your own without my help." He rolled his eyes again. "Either way, I've spent too much time thinking about it already. Look, I just wanted to still be friends, and to let you know that there was someone outside of your work sphere you could talk to. It's a lonely world working in the field, only eating what you kill. And don't start thinking anything else. I meant professionally lonely. Not snuggle and watch a rental lonely."

"Got it," Edie said. "I'm sorry for being such a heel, Easton. I really did think you were pursuing me, and I don't want that right now. From anybody."

"I'm not pursuing you, Edie," Easton said. "I like single-serving girlfriends..."

"That's from *Fight Club*, right?" Edie asked.

Easton smiled and cast his head down in a silent chuckle. "You got it. I chased away my perfect woman. Right now, I can't decide if I don't deserve to find anyone, or if I'm being a pig and enjoying the company of too many barely memorable women."

Edie cocked an eyebrow. "You and Mona need to get together and go bowling... And that's not an invitation to hook up with a member of my team."

Easton shook his head. "If the other women in your department are anything like you, I'll stay away."

They shared a laugh coated with new understanding.

"So let me ask this," Edie said. "Do you have women in all the cities you do business? You know, like a little black book?"

Easton nodded. "It's a Blackberry rather than a black book, but yes. I love the note pages you can add to the contact listings."

"Good memory joggers?" she asked.

"Just like with business prospects who think they need a real relationship to do business," he replied.

"Good to know." Having an amoral man who knew not to mess with you as a friend was almost the same as having a gay friend. Edie felt as though the threat had disappeared.

The tension had risen from her shoulders. Now, she allowed the elbow power triangle to crumble. "So would it sound conceited if I ask you to tell me more about what Taylor said?"

Easton guffawed and clapped his hands. "Yes, it would. But I'll humor you."

The relief in both of their voices was pleasant. *Maybe they could actually be friends,* Edie thought.

Easton looked above her head to recall the conversation thread, sipping his now lukewarm coffee as he did. "Taylor agreed that he didn't want you hopping around from state to state."

"That's a relief," Edie replied wryly. "We've discussed moving to special investigations for the brokerage channel."

Easton nodded. "That's what he said."

"He must really trust you."

"He knows I'm harmless," Easton said. "But yes, he trusts me. I think he also sees me as a confidant. I'm always in the field, removed from the politics internally. I hear a lot of his brainstorms."

Edie drew the immediate connection. John Taylor saw Easton Frost as a younger version of himself, the proverbial son he never had, or didn't have time for earlier in life. Both were womanizers and moving targets. Taylor lived through Frost's conquests, and in return, John let Easton in on the intimate details of home office lore and strategy.

"So what can you help me with, Easton?" she asked at length.

He shrugged. "I understand you're getting too close for Siemons. He won't be able to hit his recruiting and agency development goals if you kill off any more district managers. Taylor is worried about morale and revolt. There is always safety in numbers. If all of the district managers sit on their hands in recruiting, the company will go after Siemons."

"So it's getting political," Edie said with a huff.

"I don't think they expected you to have the stamina or the passion to keep up your current pace," he continued. "Your work is taxing. But you and your team use it as fuel. It's also rare to find women in your positions, taking risks, demanding to be heard." He gave her a sheepish grimace as though he wasn't trying to sound so chauvinistic and merely making sad social commentary.

Edie cleared her throat and focused her mind on getting all the information from him that she could. "How can you help me?"

"Taylor really does have your career path in mind," he said. "You're one of two success stories for him in recent years."

She decided to ignore his plea for an ego-stroke with the assumed follow up question. "So is it the direct producer channel or the brokerage channel for us?"

"I don't know." He leaned back and sipped on his coffee. "But whatever he offers you, take it. Don't negotiate. It's your ticket out."

Edie furrowed her brow in disgust. "So you accept the original terms of any offer the company makes you?"

"Well, no," Easton said. "But I'm in sales. Most of my pay comes from commissions and renewals."

"So you have more to leverage in risk and therefore more to lose?" Edie said. She'd had enough. She rose from the table and checked her watch. "I have to get back."

"Wait," he said and grabbed her arm. His grip startled her, the strength in its boniness.

She wrestled free and kicked his shin. "Don't you ever grab me!" she hissed.

Easton threw up his hands. "Sorry. Sorry. I didn't mean to scare you."

"You didn't scare me, but you're way out of line, Frost."

"I just mean you need to take the position to get out from under the multiline channel. There are some last ditch effort type things about to come out. Don't go down with a ship you're not the captain of."

"I have a meeting coming up in a few days to discuss a certain district manager termination," she said. "You know something about that, don't you?"

"Just don't act surprised, whatever you learn," Easton said in a fervent whisper.

She shook her head. "Thanks... for... whatever," she muttered. "This might be the single worst help I've ever received professionally, Frost."

Chapter Fifteen

Even in mid December, the company's austere approach to property management left Geoff Siemens' office frigid. Edie watched as her team's noses reddened in the Spartan, L-shaped office. They sat along the conference table at the bend in the L, designed for semi-private discussions where Siemens conducted his infamous "between these four walls" browbeatings with under-performing district managers. The coffee Becca grabbed for them was their only defense against the ceaseless freeze.

Siemens had scheduled the meeting to debate Denis Laurent's fate at 6:30 am, in part to discourage Edie's team's participation, in part to keep the meeting hidden from state office staff and home office speculation, and finally, in part to make John Taylor more than usually cranky and close-minded to the idea of sacking the heralded, third-generation district manager.

While the office had been open for the team to set up their presentation and research, Siemens wasn't to be found. Judging by the lack of his distinct odor, too much Old Spice antiperspirant after a grueling ten-mile morning run, Edie knew he hadn't arrived.

If she had a man on her team, Edie would have sent him into the restrooms in search of both Siemens and Taylor. The men's restroom trumped all water cooler conversations. Although it was generally accepted that men didn't speak while relieving themselves, some men, senior leadership in particular, took advantage of a longer break for non-existent yet potent side dialogues.

Edie wondered which of the two were taking longer then decided it must be Taylor given that Siemens ran almost every morning and had conditioned his bowels accordingly. Taylor, on the other hand, was nearing Metamucil age. Disruptions to his regularity such as pre-dawn termination meetings would not be taken lightly. Clearly, it was another part of Siemens' subversive strategy.

Scanning the conference table, Edie checked their presentation portfolios and eyed the four boxes of supporting evidence, dating back five years and cataloging the annuitization of Laurent's district to supplement his semi-retirement income. Becca leafed through the proposal, no doubt searching for a final chunk of concrete that would overcome Taylor's and Siemens's emotionally charged defense.

Mona, the head researcher on Laurent's sweeping inattention to his business, popped her knuckles and sipped loudly at her coffee. Edie sensed she was growing impatient.

Austin, stationed the farthest from Edie and the closest to where Taylor or Siemens would sit, bridged the debate's body language gap. She, too, was flipping through her proposal copy, which consisted of a forty-eight page termination recommendation letter and several dozen exhibits ranging from career agent recruiting pipelines, career agent success rates, and subsidy charge-backs to the district's production count reports across all lines of business, and marketing resource utilization rates.

This would be the largest and most meaningful termination in multiline channel history. Or, Edie hoped, it would be the bottle blondes' ticket into the special investigation department.

"Where are those two?" Mona growled.

Edie blew warm air in her hands and chuckled. "Don't dwell on it, Mona. They're most likely talking last-minute strategy in the restroom."

"It's disrespectful to call this meeting so early and keep us waiting," Becca said softly.

"It's intended," Austin said before Edie had the chance to reply. "It's part of their strategy: to make us feel beneath them, under-confident in our approach. Don't be surprised if they become fatherly right before they tell us no and thank us for wasting our time on such a worthless quest."

"Well, now we know Austin's weakness," Edie said with a joking tone. "Lack of sleep kills all optimism and positive reinforcement."

The door opened and closed with enough pause for two people to enter. The four bottle blondes stopped talking, but Edie scoured her mind for something to say that didn't convey that the women had been talking about the case. *Then again*, Edie told herself, *they had been doing the same thing.*

"Good morning," Siemens said at high volume before he rounded the corner to the conference table.

Edie rose and motioned for her team to follow.

Austin rolled her eyes, undoubtedly thinking how unladylike it was to rise to be greeted by men. But Edie knew Austin understood the drill. Everyone was equal at the termination table.

"Good morning, Geoff," Edie said once the Bic bald head birthed the bend in the office. "How are you this morning?"

"Fine, Edie. Thanks," he replied. Siemens barely looked her in the eye when he shook her hand, distracted by both Mona and Becca fidgeting with their watches to make sure it was 6:45 am.

"John, good to see you as well," Edie said and offered her hand to her boss.

Taylor's hair looked more coifed than she'd ever seen it. Edie realized she'd never see her boss before 2:00 pm.

Taylor placed his cold, fat hand in hers and shook it softly. "Hello, Edie. Thanks for agreeing to meet with us so early. I think we can all appreciate the sensitivity."

He then turned to face Edie's team. "Since this is our first meeting, let me see if I can name your team correctly." He stood with his back as erect as he could make it, which unfortunately jutted his growing gut further past his beltline. Edie was embarrassed for him. His stance suggested that he'd been to an executive body language seminar that stressed the imminent connection between posture and posturing. While a slumped back made a gut look massive and burdensome, standing too stiffly gave the impression of pride and obtuseness.

Taylor coughed in his hand and cleared his throat. Then he stepped forward and greeted the blonde closest to him. "You must be Austin."

"So nice to meet you finally," Austin replied. Even in the dim office light, her whitened teeth sparkled, and the cold office provided a rouge to her cheeks.

Taylor then turned to Mona. "And I'm positive you're Mona."

"Nice to meet you, Mr. Taylor," Mona said. Her tone was deep and heavy and its effect wasn't lost on him.

"You're the legendary sword wielder from the costumer party. I remember someone making a comment about that," Taylor said.

"Rich Capote said something once," Siemens muttered.

Taylor snapped his fingers. "That's it. During that conference call when he informed us of his intention to seek legal counsel." He rolled his eyes then smiled. "And by process of elimination, you're Rebecca."

Becca blushed and took his hand. "I go by Becca."

Taylor maintained his smile. "I like that." He took his seat next to Austin with a sigh of relief that held a palpable amount of wind.

Forgetting to shake the rest of the team's hands, Siemens joined Taylor immediately. Austin and Taylor shared a corner of the table, Edie and Siemens faced off with Mona sitting to Edie's left and Becca sitting on Mona's left.

"Well, as John said before, thanks everyone for agreeing to meet with us so unusually early," Siemens said.

"Agreed," Edie said with a nod.

Siemens wasn't quite ready to give her the floor and so continued his introduction. "Edie, your team has had tremendous impact on the company's profitability, specifically in terms of the multiline distribution model, which has been filleted in business journals as an extinct business model. I don't believe anyone here would have trouble admitting that the channel's mismanagement over the past several years has contributed to the analysts' position. We've had to make some necessary changes to the product offerings to ensure profitability and future stability to the exchanges. These changes, many abrupt and seemingly out of corporate identity, have encouraged some of our sales force to make poor decisions about how they continue to run their businesses."

Taylor placed a hand on Siemens arm. "Admittedly, these agents needed to be dealt with swiftly and justly, which is why we relocated your team to home office," he said. "You're helping us change the culture."

For Edie, this discussion was taking a turn for the surreal. It sounded as though they were about to relieve her of command and her team of their duties.

"With your leadership, Edie, we've eliminated that fringe element where corruption and one-sided business decisions prevailed," Taylor continued.

Nearly ten percent of the full-time agency force has been removed from the field," Siemens added, "removing the worst contributors to the misrepresented and under-profitable elements to our home, auto, and commercial lines of business."

Taylor leaned forward. "You've done an outstanding job, Edie. And your team is one of the best small business units I've ever seen constructed."

This coming from someone who simply guessed their names by reference in private meetings, Edie thought. She kept her head poised with a slight tilt and nodded imperceptibly to each of their bullet points.

"Thank you, John," she said after a pregnant pause in the hopes that they would sense her frustration.

"Yes, job well done, team," Siemens echoed, probably after a kick under the table.

"Thank you, too, Geoff."

Taylor rubbed his hands together. "Now, to the matter at hand. I believe we're here to discuss the potential termination of District Manager Denis Laurent."

Edie leaned forward and lifted her copy of the proposal, indicating for Taylor and Siemens to do the same. Neither glanced at the document. She cleared her throat and began, resolved not to be deterred. "As you both know, Laurent has been running a defunct, under-performing district, having only one career agent in the last five years, despite significant improvements to our recruiting platform.

"Ten out of his fifty agents have been nominated by either the state office or the service center for the deteriorating agency rehabilitation program." She felt her eyes slip away from Siemens's and Taylor's and to the proposal for support. "The same agencies, which led the entire company in commercial lines production in the 1990s, now rank among the bottom quartile of all five hundred districts within the thirty-eight states where we do business. Laurent's life insurance production, although historically low, is now best described as non-existent with the average agent in the district writing only 2.4 life policies annually."

Taylor remained stoic during these opening statements, composed and in tune with his rebuttal. Siemens clenched his jaw and checked the chew along his bottom teeth with his tongue, hungry for a chance to interrupt and derail her. Neither were listening to her arguments.

Edie was determined to overcome the blatant disrespect and patronizing attitude that sizzled along their foreheads. "Further, removing last year's home insurance rewrites, when the state of Minnesota made us create a new exchange to house our policies, Laurent's auto and fire production has dwindled to the performance of districts in this state a quarter his size. For these reasons as well as innumerable other examples of Laurent's inability and unwillingness to support the company's direction from his position of leadership we recommend the 90-day termination of his district manager's appointment agreement."

She set down her proposal and pressed her fingertips flat on the table, splitting her stare equally between Siemens and Taylor.

Taylor spoke first. "How many agents made the Summit Club last year?"

Becca cleared her throat. "Fourteen, sir."

"Fourteen?" Taylor asked. He contemplated this with a scrunched chin and a smug expression, reminding Edie of a younger Robert DeNiro. The look wasn't working for Taylor though. "That's nearly thirty percent of this district, right?"

"John, the majority of last year's Summit agents canceled their old homeowners business and wrote new policies rather than rewriting the existing business in the new exchange," Edie explained.

"The majority?" Siemens asked. His tone was ripe with disbelief and condescension.

"Twelve out of fourteen," Edie replied but kept her eyes on Taylor's. "The only two who qualified through normal, non-subversive means where Zoe Zimmerman and Marv Williams."

"They're perennial President's Table members." All self-assuming expression had evaporated from Taylor's face. "Are you telling me that twelve of Laurent's agents knowingly went against our rewriting process for the new insurance exchange and instead canceled the existing business and wrote new policies for existing customers?"

"Thereby generating new business commissions rather than renewals, creating new policy fees and premium loads for their customers, and using the ill gotten production to qualify for the all expense paid company incentive trip," Mona added. "Yes, that's what we're saying."

Taylor turned to Siemens. "Were you aware of this?"

To minimize the severity of the revelation, Siemens coughed in his hand and shook his head. "Division Manager Michaels mentioned something to me about this a few weeks ago."

"Mentioned it?" Taylor repeated. "How did he discover it? What steps is he taking to resolve the matter?"

In mimicry, Edie coughed in her hand and nodded to highlight the corruption for what it was. "Becca brought it to Michaels's attention three months before the Summit trip."

It took mere moments for Becca to hand out copies of the original email, the subsequent email chain between her and Michaels, and the actual memo where Becca had cautioned Michaels of the total cost of the trips for these agents as well as the expense associated with their new business commissions versus the renewals they'd been receiving. The total cost had been highlighted in orange at the bottom of the memo: $237,658.

Taylor fished out his bifocals and angled them between the memo and his face. "Geoff, is this correct?"

Siemens fixed his eyes on Edie. "I'd have to have someone from my office verify the numbers."

"Meaning it hasn't been done," Taylor asked, "even though we concluded the Summit meetings six weeks ago?"

Siemens leaned back and rubbed his stubble along his head. "Division Manager Michaels informed me that he had established a repayment and chargeback cycle for these agents with the service center accounting department immediately after the trips."

John Taylor now faced Siemens rather than shoot him his trustworthy, sideward glances. "He made the decision to allow these agents to attend the Summit meetings?"

Siemens squared his shoulders to match Taylor's stiff posture. "According to the travel company, it was beyond the cancellation date, so the company would have incurred additional expenses for the short notice cancellations..."

"Which could have also been recovered in the same chargeback plan he supposedly instituted after saying bon voyage," Taylor snapped. "It sounds as though you need to inform your newest Division Manager to grow a pair of... earlobes to support company initiatives. How can we expect our district managers to support the company direction, however contractually obligated they are to do so, if your own second-in-command doesn't have the stones to do the same?"

"I'll look into it with him today, John," Siemens said with deadened calm dripping from his voice.

"See that you do," Taylor muttered before turning his attention back to Edie. "It would seem to me that twelve agents who had been caught with sales churning, which isn't only against company policy but also illegal, might be appreciative that we allowed them to keep their jobs and be compelled to pay back every last cent they owe the company."

"I'll conduct a full investigation personally," Siemens said.

Taylor cleared his throat and pointed to Edie. "No, Edie will head up the investigation, while I know Mona would love the score to be twelve terminations to zero saves, I suspect your

Michaels would tip the scale the other way to zero terminations and twelve saves."

"Understood." Siemens pretended to make a note.

"Continue with your proposal, Edie," Taylor said. His smile was as genuine as the smiles of the bad guys in those '80s dance off movies who experience a change of heart, and realize just how much better the Karate Kid is than they are and that there really wasn't anything to fear. Edie's suspicion that adult work behavior was actually based on child's play was confirmed.

"For the record, it was not our intention to discuss this district's Summit Club investigation today," Edie said.

"Noted," John said. "I brought it up."

Siemens uncrossed his legs, adjusted his suit coat and leaned forward. "And we know why you did, John. It's important to recognize how highly decorated Denis Laurent is for the achievements of his district and his leadership. In thirty years of being a district manager, after taking over for his father, who also took over the district from his father, Denis has qualified for Summit Club twenty times. In those twenty times, he served at the President's Table for ten consecutive years. He's netted thirty-five full-time agents from the career agents he's recruited, even after having five agents reassigned to other district managers twice. So instead of starting out with twenty-five full-time agents when his father retired, he started with twenty, added ten, lost another five and then over time added twenty-five."

Taylor's face was clinching back up. Edie imagined she could see the words from *God Bless the USA* float between his ears.

Siemens, sensing the same change, continued his rant. "Rather than looking at his lagging commercial lines production, I see the original potential he saw when he increased his production by training his agents how to write that business. Denis Laurent single-handedly elevated his district to the top in that production line, all while consistently delivering auto and fire new business, impressive recruiting results, and even sound life sales numbers."

Siemens was finally out of breath, so Edie seized the opportunity to interject. "It appears as though Denis has reached the pinnacle of his family's business cycle within the district.

Five years prior to Denis inheriting the district from his dad, the district had forty full-time agents who produced astounding life insurance numbers. Denis inherited an underperforming district that had lost fifteen full-time agents without any replacements."

Siemens sucked in air. "He's retained fifty agents. He hasn't lost anywhere near the agents his father lost."

"Perhaps in part due to company oversight,' Taylor murmured.

Siemens was undeterred. "I believe Laurent has brought the district manager model to its fullest efficiency. I personally don't believe that the company's founders ever dreamed of a district growing to that size, especially with a population base like here."

Edie painted a puzzled expression on her face. "Geoff, you have always been a supporter of expansive business practices. You're always encouraging the district managers to remain students of the business: to learn when to recognize expansions and contractions within business cycles, especially when it comes to making the decision to hire more district staff."

"Exactly, Edie. That's precisely my point," Siemens said. "I feel that Laurent, with the full history of the company behind him and his family, could spearhead a campaign to create a super district office: one that could support twice the number of agents he has now and employ double the number of office personnel he has now."

"And you feel Denis Laurent is in a position to do this?" Taylor asked.

Edie was relieved Taylor had asked the question. Coming from her or one of the other bottle blondes, Siemens would have mired them in the muck of prejudice against disabled Americans. Nothing could distort reality more. District managers were independent contractors, not employees of the company, so the American with Disabilities Act did not apply to them. But in the battle of hearts and minds, perception was everything, and if John Taylor sensed that Laurent's stroke was the catalyst for the termination proposal, then there wasn't much hope.

In an apparent reversal of convenience, Taylor had prompted the question.

"I'm not sure I understand," Siemens said, clearly goading Taylor to fall into the same trap he'd prepared for Edie and her team.

"He's had five failed reserve district managers, two of whom he's given large, unapproved policy assignments when they'd failed the district manager training program," Taylor explained. "And as I understand it, his daughter, Alyssa, has failed the Series 26 securities exam for the final time."

Siemens became very still. He didn't rock, adjust his suit or cross his legs. "I'm not aware of any other prospects he has in the current environment," he began after a few moments in deep, dark meditation. "But were we to surround him with specialists for each facet of his business, I believe he could manage them for a time prior to selecting the frontrunner of that group to take over the district."

Taylor leaned forward and caught Austin's eyes. "What Geoff is referring to is something we've been debating on the sixth floor for the multiline channel," he explained. Oddly, he kept his attention fixed on her rather than spread it around the table.

Edie felt Mona's and Becca's questioning looks but could only shake her head in silence. This was the first time she was hearing of this new model.

"We're looking at internalizing district operations," Taylor continued. "While we agree to start this conversion process in the most under-productive states and the most under-performing districts, the debate still continues whether to implement this strategy here or in Ohio or Michigan."

Edie nodded her growing understanding. Minnesota vied for third to last in nearly every category of measurement with those other states. The question then became if either of those states had a district that represented ten percent of its sales force, which would yield enough in district overrides to put a beta program in place.

Taylor was explaining this as Edie thought it. "Unfortunately, neither Ohio nor Michigan has a fifty-agent district, much less one that is so substantially under par, like Laurent's."

Despite her conscience telling her otherwise, it was time for Edie to interject. "Give us a second to digest this, John. This is the first any of my team, including me, has heard of this."

Taylor nodded with an apologetic grimace.

Edie pressed on. "There's an overriding proposal to take over a district operation and staff it with home office employees, who are specialists in the different lines of business we run?"

Siemens cleared his throat. "That's correct. You'd have a personal lines specialist, a life specialist, a commercial specialist, a marketing and lead generation specialist, and a recruiter, all reporting to the district manager in place..."

"That remains to be decided," Taylor said with a wagging finger. "We don't know if the district manager would still be an independent contractor or a home office employee under a different title."

Siemens turned to Taylor and squared his broad shoulders again. "But for what I'm proposing, John, we would keep Laurent as the district manager, have him announce all the decisions we were guiding him through in the back office. He could make his daughter his recruiter, he could bring back two of his failed reserve district managers as specialists in life and commercial lines, and we could help him hire the other specialists."

"Bring back the failed prospects?" Edie asked.

Siemens threw her a threatening look, the first stretched tawny with muscle since the meeting began. She felt that this was the moment the discussion had been leading up to. It was her turn to be shot. Her turn to be executed. With her team to stand witness. They had been too good at their jobs. They'd been appointed as hatchet women because no one suspected them and no one had placed any faith in their success.

"There is a soft skill set you haven't grasped yet in your short career, Edie," Siemens began. He folded his fingers together and rocked back in his seat. He'd been planning this, fantasizing about the words streaming flawlessly from his mouth, down to the look on her face and shining wells in her eyes.

Taylor coughed and cleared his throat, warning Siemens to be more delicate.

"Yes, Geoff?" Edie asked. Her voice was unwavering, not from a spring of anger, but from an inner strength to present herself as impenetrable before her team.

"At the core of what remains to be developed in your skill set is perception and how to manage it," Siemens said. "Denis Laurent's case is a perfect example. You and your team have been laser focused on the black-and-white, the chunks of concrete, the gathering of evidence to prove your case. You've behaved well as prosecutors."

Siemens, in full relish, placed his hands on his chest and eyed each member of her team in turn. "Forgive me because I'm a passionate guy, so I get a little rambunctious and abrasive."

Becca and Mona nodded. Austin held her expression motionless, no doubt terrified. Edie kept her posture rigid, her hands neatly folded, and her face expectant.

Siemens checked Taylor then continued. "We have eighteen districts. Two about to become empty, a sales force depleted by over ten percent. Our attempts to keep your work under deep home office cover has been thwarted not only by the agency rumor mill, but also how visible you've been in the processes of termination."

Taylor leaned in. "We didn't expect you and your team to volunteer to hand out termination letters or accept resignations."

"Anything to get out of the pep rally glee club you guys call the event planning department," Mona said.

Becca snorted a laugh and then shook her bowed head.

Edie silenced them both with a twitch of her shoulder. "We'd grown accustomed to handling those aspects of the job in Colorado Springs, which I believe I made clear to both of you before we accepted this new assignment."

"Indeed, you did," Taylor replied quickly. "Perhaps we thought that the division managers under Geoff were better situated to make those unhappy field visits."

Edie reached across the table and tapped the stack of documentation Becca had presented concerning Laurent's Summit Club agents. "We soon learned that our resources were needed in that area, too."

Siemens stirred once more, and Edie leaned back, giving him the floor. She'd anticipated his need for it.

"Edie, as the head of your team, you possess more of the skill of perception enhancement than your teammates, certainly a reflection of more visibility and time in front of senior management," he explained. "However, getting back to the point about Laurent, as you clearly want us to, discarding a third-generation district manager with the pedigree, company history, and record of success such as his would prove detrimental to the company's sustainability in its domiciled state. We wouldn't be able to recruit new district managers to the positions you helped vacate once word of Laurent's termination, resignation, or forced retirement hit the spin cycles and distorted realities of agent chatter."

Edie sensed her chance to speak in Siemens's need for oxygen. "Instead, are we to continue to burn through rookie division managers, the latest costing the company nearly a quarter of a million dollars with this so called perception enhancement skill?"

Taylor shifted his weight and his concern of the case toward Siemens.

"John is completely aware that over the last eighteen months you've had three division managers in the division to which Laurent is assigned in addition to the three in the other Minnesota division in the same timeframe. The four former division managers are no longer employed by the company after serving an average of six years in various high-flying capacities," Edie said. "I'm sure Becca would be willing to work with HR and one of your marketing specialists to create a balance sheet of investment in reserve district manager training expenses versus the costs in developing internal talent to partner with district managers at the divisional level."

Siemens leveled his now demonic eyes at Edie. All the remnants of Greek compassion had vanished from his pupils. "Again, you're thinking in black-and-white, Edie. Step into the light. Step into the world of color." He chuckled. "Each of those unfortunate position changes has been documented with HR, including a list of circumstances not directly associated with the demands of the job."

"So we will not, in fact, terminate Denis Laurent," Edie said. "Instead, we will promote his newfound support of this brave new company initiative: a new, stronger partnership with the state and home office, the arranged marriage of state office employees reporting to Laurent to capture his business-building wisdom and wherewithal to build a super-district operation, a joint venture destined to succeed with sales force business savvy and the limitless coffers of the insurance company at its back."

"Do you think Laurent needs to keep working to provide for his retirement or his estate?" Siemens asked.

Edie had made the blunder of dropping the pretense of professionalism. Siemens's jabbing had worn her down and he was stepping into his upper-cut punch.

Siemens looked to Taylor and shook his head in disbelief. How dare this woman and her three female teammates directly defy the stamina, endurance and virility of Geoff Siemens? "Laurent has enough money to retire ten times over. He works for the pride of his family history and to protect his unseasoned and unskilled daughter, the only hope he has to make sure his family's legacy doesn't die with him, given how much a pansy, electric lawnmower owning liberal his son is.

"There's value in knowing that," Siemens continued. "There's leverage to provide lift. We go in with your stack of business reasons to terminate. I appear as Laurent's savior. I'll give him my infamous, 'Today, I'm your best friend' speech. Within one hour, *one hour*, he'll have agreed to sign over his district overrides, unrestricted, back to the company in exchange for his daughter being on the payroll, and being assured of her lead position in the new operation. Hiring back his failed reserve district managers makes it look like he's still in control, like he's calling all the shots. It will be seen as his idea to merge his district with the might of home office. He'll politicize his district as the city on the hill."

Taylor grabbed Siemens elbow to calm him down. "And when the time comes, when the venture is off and running, Laurent will announce his retirement," Taylor said. "We'll throw him a huge party, fly in his district manager chums from all over the country. Our beta test will be well on course. Our most dismal district will have been rehabilitated from home office's direct involvement. Other district managers will agree to the more robust engine and sign over their districts to become fully vested employees. We'll be able to run our sales force directly and ensure that the levels of unprofitability that remained unchecked for decades never happens again."

In the ringing silence, Edie took a ten count before deciding which tact she should take. Then she dropped her stoicism and beamed the brightest, most genuine if not affectionate smile she could muster. In the back of her mind, she wished there was a security camera in the office just so she could finagle the footage of her award-winning performance from the guard on duty. "Boy, when you talk about changing the culture, you really change the culture, John."

Taylor stiffened.

Siemens looked edgy.

"Edie," Taylor began slowly. "When we first brought your team to home office, we really had no idea the massive changes your presence would bring about. Sales counts are up in every line of business in nearly every district. By all measures, the quality of new business has seen an uptick. There has been a fifteen percent reduction in the underwriting queues while the increase in production is at five percent all in."

Edie shot Becca a quick glance to verify what she was hearing. Becca nodded slightly. She was aware of these results. Edie took this to mean that while Becca had been surveying these metrics, she lacked the confidence in claiming credit for her team's contributions. Edie noted the coaching opportunity for another time.

"The only area where we haven't seen any impact whatsoever has been in recruiting and agency development." Taylor's tone became harsh and he cast sideward sniveling glances toward Siemens. Catching himself, he raised a cautionary hand to Edie. "Don't misunderstand me, Edie. Your team has no involvement with that process."

"You're the weed whackers, we're supposed to be the fertilizer," Siemens said with his hand on his chest again and that feces eating grin.

Edie nodded but let the smile run away from her face. "I'm not sure where this discussion is going. Let's review what we know now. One, we're not terminating District Manager Denis Laurent. Two, contrary to the termination process my team has initiated and spent immeasurable time, energy, and resources on, we will approach Laurent with this revolutionary operational model combining home office resources with field experience to create a super district office. Three, while my team has contributed not only to a huge restoration in profitability by all projections through our termination, rehabilitation, and policy reassignment processes, underdeveloped until we arrived in Minnesota, my team and I lack the soft skill of perception enhancement and management to see the bigger picture of running this state office or even the company. As an aside to that statement, my team and I have no designs or current aspirations of running any state office or becoming a part of senior management without first being accepted and groomed into those positions. To that end, we are not privy to senior management discussions, including those that grant a higher access view of the company's planned direction, regardless if we're lacking in a certain skill set, Geoff. Finally, despite our lack of refined skills, we've actually impacted new business in terms of quality and increased production, which far exceeds any expectation established for us with our primary focus being to ensure profitability on the existing book of business not the acquisition of new business."

Edie leaned forward and steepled her hands in a prayerful position. "Have I provided an accurate summary of our discussion to this point?"

Taylor's face had whitened, pale and sucking in light despite the budding sunrise glaring over the piles of plowed snow that caked the basement's windows. "As though you were dictating a memo," he said.

Edie threw a smirk to Becca and then nodded. "Then in conclusion, from our side," she said, "I hereby advise my team to stop dying their hair."

Siemens must have swallowed incorrectly as red and choked as he suddenly became.

Edie continued without even raising a concerned eyebrow. Geoff Siemens could aspirate on his own saliva. "Either the company can make an announcement that the event planning staff is celebrating the diversity Barbie embraced over twenty years ago, or it can make the announcement that my team is moving into its own division of special investigations."

She looked at Mona, Becca, and Austin in turn. "If any of you would like to remain blondes for the enhanced perception of the event planning department, you are certainly free to do so. Come morning, I will have restored my natural tint."

Edie turned her attention back to Taylor and Siemens. "Is there anything else that needs to be discussed with my team today?"

Siemens rose and readjusted his suit coat so that it clung to his form yet fell straight to his sides. With an unbearable grin, he leaned over the table to shake each of the women's hands in turn. He kept his gaze fixed on Austin, most likely having direct view of her cleavage. "Edie, it's a pleasure as always. I look forward to working with you on setting up this opportunity with Laurent. Have Becca or Austin set up the meeting for the two of us along with Michaels to meet with Denis."

"Will do," Edie lied and rose to shake his hand at an equal level rather than give him the pleasure of stooping down to her.

Siemens nodded to Taylor who waived him off. He then vacated his own office.

Edie turned to her team and gave them a signal to start gathering their proposals and supporting documentation. She sensed in their eyes the need for an extended coffee break somewhere in the bowels of the skyway system slithering through Minneapolis. Edie could also feel a not-so-happy hour in their near future. Judging the looks on their faces, not even Mona was impressed with Edie's act of defiance in counseling them to return to their normal hair colors.

The disappointment Edie felt had no bottom, no end. It was for her the crown jewel of leading this team, standing up to the rampant sexism so readily in bloom at every insurance company she'd heard of. She'd taken a position, crossed her arms, and hadn't budged. Taylor and Siemens hadn't even acknowledged the act. The least her team could do was give her some encouraging smirks.

"Just a second, Edie," Taylor said behind her as she turned her back on him to gather her laptop backpack.

"Yes, John," she replied, keeping her back to him.

"I dismissed Siemens so that we could discuss another topic that pertains to your team," he explained. "Please sit. I know you'll want to hear what I'm going to propose."

Midway into slinging her backpack onto her shoulders, Mona set down her things and returned to her seat. Austin, the piddler, wasn't close to leaving, electing to check her lip gloss and hair in a compact before leaving the office so to be as presentable as possible to the state office staff. She quickly closed her makeup shop and tucked her purse under her seat. Becca, the nearest to escape, swiftly turned around, dropped her belongings, and tried to disappear between her own shoulders as she shrank into her seat. At last, Edie turned back to Taylor.

"What proposal?" she asked.

"Your next assignment," Taylor said with a smile and a chuckle. "You're perfectly correct. We need to increase and expand your visibility throughout the enterprise. You're the greatest success story of the last two years, a small start-up, covert subdivision with such dramatic impact, led by an admitted first-time manager, who created new roles from virtual thin air. The company needs to hear this story's first chapter and witness its second."

Edie leaned backward, her mind still oscillating between her deep disappointment at not being able to terminate Laurent, which she would always feel was a grave mistake, and her team's lack of confidence in her to the unbelievable extent of not following her version of the end of *Spartacus*. "Second chapter, John?"

"We'd like to move your team, as you suggested, and quite frankly, as you've propositioned, into special investigations," he replied. "No more subversive tactics, no more hiding in event planning and pretending to work on town hall meetings for the multiline channel. I'm talking about moving the four of you into the independent brokerage channel."

"Doing what exactly?" Edie asked.

Taylor's smile broadened. "Investigating potential churning of business, replacing life and annuity policies after their surrender periods have expired, looking for potential money laundering situations."

Not only could Edie feel her team bristle with excitement, she could see them twist and fidget. She thumped the side of the table to send a vibration along their line. The team stopped moving.

"I thought the brokerage channel *had* a special investigations unit," Edie asked. "Are we to be adjunct or additive to that?"

"In a certain way, both," Taylor said.

Edie glanced at her watch. "Before we start talking about how wonderful this opportunity is and what it could mean to our careers, what is the targeted increase in compensation?"

"I believe we locked it in at a twenty percent increase with a variable component of fifty percent base salary for meeting established goals," Taylor said. His smile was infectious as though he'd expected her to ask such a brash question so early.

"Go back to HR and get a thirty percent base salary increase, keep the bonus the same, and then let's schedule a follow-up meeting to examine the new role in its entirety," Edie said.

With that, she swept up her things and headed straight for the crease in the room and to the office door. In her excitement she forgot to see if her team was following her. "Any of you non-blondes care to get some coffee with me? I think we have a time dividend for being in so early this morning," she called over her shoulder.

Chapter Sixteen

The first opportunity Edie and her team had to meet her new boss, Delores "Tiny" Campbell was the celebration of her fortieth anniversary with the company. The event was held in the large training room centered between both first floor lobbies. Most in attendance squinted in the midday light bleeding through slits between the elongated windows' vertical blinds. These people were also not used to seeing the sun.

Edie leaned on the fake wall toward the back of the room which cloaked a coat closet and small kitchenette adequate enough to hide the surprise cake and disposable utensils. Seeing her restored red hair in her periphery still startled her much like the frames on a new pair of glasses. She grinded out the surge of anger between her incisors. Edie was humiliated by how accustomed she'd become of the bottle blonde do.

Over the two weeks between her cataclysmic meet with John Taylor, Edie noted the trepidation of her team to return to their natural hair colors. Carrying boxes and totes from her office on the sixth floor to the basement, Edie brandished her reclaimed identity the very next Monday. That Thursday, she'd seen Mona's black hair for the first time in months as her weapons master unpacked her belongings in her new fluorescent lighted dungeon cubicle. What startled Edie was Becca's change the following Thursday. The auburn was still tinged with too many highlights, but the bottles' damage had been nearly eradicated by a professional salon experience. Edie would have lost untold sums had she wagered, placing Austin ahead of Becca for the re-dye.

Two full weeks, and Edie had not even shaken her new boss's hand. This Tiny Campbell, the care bear grandmother of the retail compliance department, had been on a Grecian vacation. Only through brief hallway dialogues with the presumed members of their larger unit had Edie learned of the anniversary party. The rest of their last ten business days had been spent unpacking, learning new names, and erasing their memories from the multiline state office. The latter's success was a feat impossible to fathom given that the Minnesota state office shared floor space with Home Office compliance.

On four distinct occasions, Geoff Siemens had refused to look Edie in the eye. On two of them, he'd been walking with his division marketing manager, the very man who'd allowed corruption to continue in Denis Laurent's district. She hadn't taken the ritualized snubbing personally.

The surviving multiline agents hadn't wanted to know any of them. Alyssa Laurent had sent a bouquet of congratulations flowers, but the arrangement looked more suitable for a funeral, no doubt her true intent.

Mona now entered the training room, catching everyone's eye, including Edie's. Her hair now fully accentuated her olive skin tone; the white business dress under a black, knitted sweater vest underscored the power of her natural beauty. She was as fiercely intimidating as she was iconic and coveted.

Edie gestured to catch her attention, and Mona quickly joined her by the wall partition. "What's the word, boss?" she asked Edie.

Edie shook her head and covered her mouth to whisper back. "You know everything I do. Delores Campbell has been with the company for forty years. She has no idea that they are throwing this party for her. We're all supposed to yell surprise when they bring her down."

"Then what?" Mona asked.

"We eat cake. Perhaps introduce ourselves when she makes the rounds."

"When do we actually get back to work?" Mona growled.

Edie smirked, looked down to hide her grin, and crossed her arms. "I have a suspicion that this Tiny has something in mind for us already."

Mona popped her knuckles. "She better. This is a ridiculous reassignment. We were getting too close to cashing in big in the multiline channel."

"We still have it in writing that they owe us the residual retention and profitability bonuses," Edie explained.

"I don't trust Taylor and Siemons to honor that," Mona said.

"What better area to be in than compliance to monitor and track the reports and payments," Edie said. "Besides, the raises have already hit our paychecks."

Mona pretended to ignore her and waved Becca to join them when she walked through the room. "Having to look for our real hair is bizarre."

"Just be glad we're back to normal," Edie said.

"Processing system-generated termination letters for churners is a huge price to pay to return to normal," Mona said.

Edie couldn't argue. Eight of the twelve in compliance prior to her team's assimilation spent most of their time monitoring submissions of 1035 exchange forms. These IRS forms enabled an in force life insurance policy to be exchanged for the same cash value into a new life insurance policy. While these created red flags for company policies being exchanged for a competitor's policy, no one seemed to notice or mind the unreported millions of new premium dollars coming in from exchanges from other companies. The intense scrutiny was justified by comparing the age of the insured to the amount of time left for surrender charges on the original policy. If an agent or broker tried to exchange a policy that had passed the surrender charge period for a policy with a new surrender period (usually ten years), compliance would have to approve or reject the submitted policy exchange. Exchanging an eighty-year-old's original policy with no surrender charges for a new one with ten years of surrender charges was considered unethical and examined thoroughly. Never mind the suitability for newer policies that were cheaper for the customer. Never mind the profitability of the original policy being seven times that of a new policy. It was the ethical behavior of the broker that had compliance concerned.

"It's pretty straight forward," Becca was saying.

Edie blinked out of her reverie and nodded to Becca as though she'd been listening the entire time. Becca's highlights were lost in her tied back hair, but Edie detected a hint of rouge and lip gloss tickling across her face. Further, she'd upgraded her wardrobe with the first of their new paychecks, now sporting a silver skirt and black heels.

"Yes, I'm sure you're in heaven," Mona replied. "Data mining for bad guys and checking their frequency of fraud."

"It's ice cold," Becca said. "It's process driven and systematic. After we reject three exchanges, the agent receives his warning letter. After the fourth rejection, we process his termination and assign home office personnel to service his existing policy base."

"And then home office coordinates internal policy exchanges," Edie explained. "No new commissions, no new surrender charges, all the profitability of keeping old business on the books."

"And they pay us a lot more to do this," Austin said. "I'm fine with it."

Edie hadn't seen Austin join them. Mona chose not to hide her look of disgust at seeing Austin's blonde hair. Becca couldn't be bothered to notice.

"It also means we're stuck in Minneapolis," Mona growled.

Austin glanced around them to see if any of the other employees had heard Mona. "What's wrong with that?" Austin said with an apologetic smile.

Mona stepped in front of her and squared her shoulders. "If it's all systems and letters, then why can't we move back to where the sun shines?"

Edie chuckled. "Perhaps you can someday. Tiny Campbell has been here for forty years. She'll have to be retiring soon. Set your sights on her job and move the unit to Colorado Springs when you ascend to the throne."

"Yeah right," Mona replied. "In the meantime, there's no sunlight, no juice, no action, and a little bit more money."

"Don't forget your black hair," Becca added.

The gathering erupted with "Surprise" then thundered out applause. Edie and Mona turned and stood on their toes to get their first glimpse of Tiny Campbell. Although she was short, she was nowhere near petit. Even through smiles and laughs, her face remained bulbous and pugilistic. Thick lenses in heavy dark brown frames hid her eyes from this distance, and her arm fat danced separate jigs with each bear hug given to her coworkers. Tiny's outfit was equally unremarkable, something she'd picked up at Dress Barn, a purple and brown flowing blouse. Designed to cover her Minnesota beer gut, the garment stopped just shy of her knees where brown corduroys billowed out over sandals.

Mona leaned in to whisper in Edie's ear. "That's our new boss?"

"It looks like it," Edie said.

"We're doomed," Mona said. "We're banished to compliance and stuck in Minne-hoser for eternity. You played your hand too aggressively with Taylor. He's punishing us for it."

Edie nodded and laughed to maintain appearances. "I can't believe you just accused me of being too aggressive."

"You need to find a way to get us out of Home Office and back into the field," Mona hissed.

Austin and Becca were having a separate conversation, but Edie couldn't make it out over the din of congratulations and people asking Tiny if she really had been surprised.

The rest of the celebration became a blur of roast like speeches and squares of cake being passed from person to person. At some point, an agent presented a twenty-year-old video of Tiny and him singing karaoke to "Twist and Shout" at a sales convention. Edie thought that version of Tiny looked much warmer and less reptilian.

Their new coworkers either ignored Edie and her team, or sneaked sideward glances and smirks at them over bites of cake and ice cream until Tiny singled Edie out of the crowd having made her rounds of thank yous to everyone else in the room.

"So you're my new assignment?" Tiny said in a gruff voice. Edie felt as though Tiny were looking straight up her nose. Edie had at least a head over the woman. Mona might as well have been a WNBA star.

Edie offered Tiny her hand. "Edie Firebaugh, Mrs. Campbell. It's a pleasure to finally meet you."

Tiny grabbed her hand and pumped it roughly. "Don't ever call me that again. It's Tiny or nothing for me." She then took a step back to size Edie up. "I can see why they sent you to me. Well, I can see why they think they sent you to me and why they really sent you to me."

"What's the difference?" Edie asked.

"You were too good. No one expected you to outlast Home Office's appetite for bloodletting," Tiny explained. "And they thought four women couldn't possibly handle the stress of wrecking agents' lives."

"We are the job," Edie said.

"You *were* the job," Tiny corrected. "Now you have a new job. Working with me. I'm an arrow, Edie Firebaugh. You'll always know where you stand with me." Tiny rubbed her face and picked at her nose before shrugging. "Okay then. Time to kill this shindig and get back to work. Come up to my office after lunch. There are some items we need to discuss."

"The whole team?" Edie asked the back of Tiny's head as she bowled down an aisle between seats.

Barely turning, Tiny threw Edie an impatient and condescending look.

It would only be the two of them.

Tiny's office rivaled the outbreak of reality shows on hoarders and the people who dealt with them, the complete opposite of what Edie expected from the head of the company's compliance department. An arced valley between spires of notebooks and stalagmites of three-ring binders allowed safe passage from the doorway to the lone seat before the desk. A spring showering of pastel elementary school folders lined the shelves behind the desk. Somewhere buried under reams of dot matrix printouts was the standard three-person conference table. Edie could see its outline under a thick blanket of hanging file folders and manila files. That corner of the office would have reminded Edie of a snow-covered and fir-lined mesa, if she still had the right set of eyes.

Was this garden gnome of a woman hiding in plain sight among all the things she kept? Now Edie understood why their meeting was one on one. Necessity demanded it.

"Feel free to take the seat when you're finished drinking in the soaring views," a voice said behind her.

Edie turned to see Tiny's bulldog waddle traverse the valley pass. Her body seemed to fold itself inward to scale across the mesa's high cliff wall and spin to her orange felt seat.

Staring at her new boss's chair, Edie reached for the other seat and slid into place. Layers of tape lined its arm rests. All types where represented: duct, masking, scotch, packing, electrical. Tiny's chair had been lopsided before she's settled into it as though over the years the metal support and frame had bent to the increased and sedentary weight. Without thought, Tiny righted herself into a position of perfect balance, the village's old medicine woman in deep meditation.

Tiny leaned forward with a smirk and half a Snickers bar hanging out of her mouth. "I know what you're thinking. That answer is yes. This is a portal where time and space do not abide the fundamental laws of physics. Here everything defies gravity." The woman bit off a chunk of the candy bar, sending a nougat covered peanut down her front. "Well, almost everything," she muttered as she retrieved the errant snack.

"It's impressive," Edie said. "Like surveying a tornado's path of destruction on The Weather Channel."

Tiny leaned back again and crossed her arms under her chest. "I like that. Think I'll make a sign with a quote. You don't mind if I steal your words, do you?"

"Quite the ethical question coming from compliance," Edie said with a chuckle.

Tiny shook the remains of her candy bar at Edie. "I was right about you. I *am* right about you, and I'm *going* to be right about you."

Edie glanced down at her notepad, the weight of embarrassment bowing her forehead. "How so?"

"Describe your fondest memory of John Taylor's couch?" Tiny asked.

Edie bristled. "Not sure I have a fond memory of that couch."

"Was it awkward then?" Tiny continued. "Not pleasant. Felt like taking one for the team."

"I don't belief I ever even sat on that couch," Edie replied.

"Don't tell me Taylor's becoming spryer at his age. They haven't invented a pill that makes the rest of the body more flexible while making one area more rigid."

Edie found the strength to look Tiny in the eye. "I've never slept with anyone at work."

"What about the rest of your crew, kid?" Tiny grunted.

"We're all clean," Edie said. "I'll stand by that."

"What about that remaining blonde? She looks like fun."

"Austin has never compromised her professional integrity by mixing up work and her personal life," Edie said.

Satisfaction danced across Tiny's face. "You know why I'm asking though, right?"

"I have no idea," Edie said after clearing her throat. "Other than some ridiculous rumors circulating around the multiline state office to trash our names."

"Good guess, but those haven't surfaced yet." Tiny spread her arms wide and smiled again. "Welcome to where careers come to die, Ms. Firebaugh. I've been down here for twenty of my forty years. Every young starlet who has a chance encounter with John Taylor finds her way into my Hades."

"You're kidding," Edie muttered. Shame seared her eyes and cheekbones.

"No, not today, thank you kindly," Tiny replied. "There have been exactly seventeen before you spending their final days here. I tend to think of it as the company's hospice for incurable dreams of industry success."

"You're saying that seventeen women over the last twenty years have been reassigned to your department after having worked too closely with John Taylor," Edie said.

"Not just worked too closely with him," Tiny said with a chuckle. "Most fell in love with him. Believed him when he said he was going to leave his wife or succumbed to other lies."

Edie took a long slow breath. "So naturally, you're assuming that one of my team, namely me, worked too closely with Taylor, became a threat to him and is now banished to your department."

"You got it, sister," Tiny said.

Edie let her notepad fall to the floor as she tucked her new hair behind her ear. "Well, we must have become a threat in some other way, because none of us ever slept with him."

"What about Siemons?" Tiny asked. The grin on her face had become sinister.

"None of us," Edie said.

"Then how do you explain being shipped down here?"

"Before we relocated from Colorado Springs, Taylor mentioned to me that one career path would be to move into either the direct producer channel or the brokerage channel and continue our work in improving the company's culture," Edie explained.

"Terminating fraudulent agents," Tiny added.

"Precisely."

"You terminated nearly ten percent of the Minnesota agency force in just over six months, Edie Firebaugh, including two well established district managers."

"Yes, we did," Edie replied. "You said it yourself not two hours ago. We were more successful than anyone anticipated."

"It's a career shop over there in the multiline channel," Tiny said. "Those agents are almost company employees. We provide them medical, dental, and retirement benefits."

"Yes, I know..."

"In exchange for exclusive first rights to any new business in lines we carry," Tiny continued.

"I understand..."

"So how many were selling away with these new online and over the phone auto insurance carriers?"

A silence followed while Edie catalogued the lesson of never interrupting or talking over her new boss.

Tiny, for her part, adjusted her thick glasses and popped her knuckles.

"We could have wiped out the other two northern districts, both St. Cloud and Brainerd, with the outside appointments and heavy loss of auto policies we've experienced there in the past three years," Edie explained.

"So in addition to the ten percent dead loss," Tiny said. "In addition to the beheadings of two district managers, you could have exposed what, another thirty-five agents with grounds for termination?"

"With that one contract violation, yes," Edie said.

"What else?"

"Another fifteen percent of the agents have their own auto policies rated in the personal use only rating while they continue to use the vehicle for business purposes, inspecting homes to insure, attending marketing events, buying office supplies," Edie said.

"And of course, those agents are still claiming their vehicles as a tax deduction with the IRS while paying substantially less premium to the company they work exclusively with," Tiny added.

"That's correct."

"Sounds like the death count could have been a full third of the agents." Tiny cupped her chins in her hand and snorted. "But that's not why you were promoted to the brokerage channel watch club."

Edie shook her head. "We took a serious swing at Denis Laurent."

Tiny clapped her hands above her head. "Finally, the truth! Denis Laurent? *The* Denis Laurent, Mr. third-generation district manager himself? You realize his grandfather first convinced the company to relocate the entire multiline sales channel home office here."

"Poor performance is poor performance," Edie said. "Unprofitability is unsustainable."

"Tell that to Taylor," Tiny muttered. She then shook a thought out of her head. "So you made your case on Laurent with Siemons and Taylor. They, of course, knew you had files on the misrated auto policies and the agents selling away as your next areas of corruption to tackle."

Edie folded her hands in her lap and nodded.

"So they sent you to me so I could bore you to death with running reports on system-generated terminations in the other sales channels."

Edie remained still.

"Well, you're a first for me, kiddo," Tiny said at length. "Taylor's never sent me a success before. We're a kill it in committee type outfit. I mean I wasn't surprised to see the raises he gave all of you, but you and your team thought of this as an actual promotion."

"If you don't mind me asking, what's Taylor got on you for you to do his dirty work, chasing off the women he had affairs with?" Edie asked.

"The first ten didn't last ninety days," Tiny said. "It's a little known company policy that your new supervisor can start your first ninety days with the company over again with each promotion or raise. I tracked their attendance and timeliness, and called for their resignations over firing them with HR. It was a blur back in the nineties. There must have been one a year. At first, they were barely above entry level positions, so I chalked it up to them being pretty and talentless. Like I was doing him a favor. It wasn't until later I realized that he was sending them here because they'd become emotionally attached to the idiot."

"So there were seven that you knew had had affairs with him and yet you still chased them off," Edie said. "Why?"

"Because I want to take down John Taylor my own way," Tiny said in a low deep voice. "I don't want to go whistle-blower, you know, press conferences and awards banquets for doing the right thing and two weeks later being led out to pasture with a farmers' rifle at my back. I want to go toe-to-toe with him."

Edie's mind was spinning. It was impossible for her to have earned this woman's trust so quickly. Unless, of course, Tiny had conducted her own thorough due diligence on Edie's team during the last two weeks she was supposedly on vacation.

"Other than being unfaithful to his wife, what's John Taylor done?" she asked.

"I couldn't care less about his wife," Tiny said. "It's the potential lawsuits I've saved the company. Plus, there are other things I don't have access to that I should in order to properly conduct our annual audits and satisfy our regulatory requirements with the states."

"What don't you have access to?"

"The specialty lines sales channel, for one," Tiny explained.

"I know one of their sales reps, Easton Frost," Edie offered.

Tiny leaned forward and pulled her frames away from her face. "He's not one of their sales reps. He is the only sales rep for the entire, multi-million dollar annual revenue sales channel."

Edie pinched the bridge of her nose to steady her racing thoughts. No amount of rationalization could help her route the deluge. She decided instead to pursue honesty. "Why are you telling me all of this? I'm new to your team. I have no background in compliance or regulation. You don't know much about me or my team, and you're willing to reveal your bull's eye on my former boss's back?"

Through wrinkles on wrinkles, Tiny furrowed her brow. "I'm blunt, but you already know that. The first lesson for anyone new to compliance is that you do every last bit of your research on someone before you even speak to them."

"But you've been on vacation..."

Tiny held up her blackberry. "You're new to having subordinates. One day you'll learn that you can delegate ninety percent of your job to your employees. I have tendrils in human resources because we have to supervise the securities registered employees. I got your full backgrounds from a friend. My team has also been observing yours for the last two weeks."

"Granted," Edie replied. "So the last gut check was to make sure I hadn't had an extracurricular relationship with John Taylor?"

Tiny coughed then shrugged. "Pretty much."

"All that still doesn't explain the immediate trust in me. Revealing that you're out to bust John Taylor with something major? Bring him down?"

"How did you get along with Taylor before he promoted you?" Tiny asked back.

Edie grinned and felt her face redden. "Honestly, I think I intimidated him. Although I respected his position, I ignored his ego and always leveled with him."

"Did he ever hit on you?" Tiny asked.

Edie crinkled her brow in thought. "Not really. Nothing serious. A couple of late evening meetings in his office where he poured himself a drink and sat on his apparently infamous couch. But I never joined him. I always sat by his desk."

"Did you know anything about his reputation before you walked into my office?"

"With women?"

"On anything, any topic," Tiny said.

Edie raised her hands, palms open. "We were intentionally sheltered from the rest of Home Office. Most people in the building barely know we exist. We had to dye our hair blonde to fit in with the event planning department. In fact, Taylor set that up as a cover for us so that other departments wouldn't get alerted to our real objectives."

"So you never really spoke to anyone say in licensing and commissions, or underwriting and new business, or any wholesalers from the other sales channels?" Tiny asked.

Edie shook her head. "We were pretty myopic."

Tiny rose from her seat, which tilted precariously back to its warped position. Crossing her arms over her chest, she paced between the edge of her desk and the file covered conference table.

Edie cleared her mind as best she could, sensing a lecture coming on.

"The CEO and Board are getting wise to Taylor, Firebaugh," Tiny began. "It all starts with succession planning retreats where senior management gets to know the heads of all the sales channels and the operational teams. That's the tipoff that something is out of place.

"The profitability of the entire company has reached unsustainable levels," Tiny continued. "The multiline channel is increasingly expensive to support, and since the nineties, we've gotten less and less business from those agents, even though they aren't supposed to sell outside of the contract. The direct producer sales channel focuses on premium finance cases using no surrender charge policies that only stay on the books an average of eighteen months, when we need them to stay on the books for seven years minimum to earn any profit. The brokerage channel continues to commoditize our products while asking for more and more commissions for their aggregated production. They are soaking up all our premium reserve requirements, which disables our ability to invest in new, competitive or innovative products."

Tiny continued to pace. "Given the decade long bear market and the recent recession, we're not earning any investment income to provide relief to the massive amounts of guaranteed products we're selling in the brokerage channel. And even though we have a competitive advantage over the Canadian and European-owned companies, no American bank is lending money right now to borrow against our reserve requirements."

She spun around to face Edie as though Edie had said something. "You're crazy if you think any of the European banks would lend us money over lending to their fellow European insurance companies."

Edie coughed in her hand to cut Tiny off. "So the company is being poorly managed and the board is looking to make a change for the president of distribution.

"Taylor is an old dog with some fight left in him, but his ride it out approach only worked in the high interest rate environment in the eighties and the great bull market of the nineties," Tiny continued. "After ten stagnant years, his only answer is making the products more competitive, hence less profitable without unrealistic sales volumes, for the brokerage and direct producer channels.

"That's why he brought you and your team in on this beta," she continued. "There are basically only two levers to pull in managing a company. Increase revenues or cut costs. Taylor's methods for increasing revenue have become short-term solutions in this economic environment. The revenue looks good to the shareholders, but there is no sustainable profitability."

Edie's mind honed in on the exact same thought she had earlier in the day. "I completely understand."

Tiny nodded her approval. "I figured you would. The multiline channel has always been a good punching bag for distribution. Its costs are high but fairly fixed and predictable. Now that we're only getting two-thirds the production we used to from that channel, it's easy for Taylor to take shots and celebrate his cost-cutting strategies."

"That channel can't really be the most expensive though," Edie said.

"You've got it. It's actually becoming one of the cheapest. The brokerage channel is driving up the cost of doing business with its greed for exorbitant commissions and payouts. It was originally based on a model where the company paid out everything in straight commissions and gave absolutely no field support. Now, we hold sales incentive and award trips in Europe for producers and their wives. We have a full-scale service model for processing new business. Our underwriters spend hours reviewing informal policy applications when we only get a four percent policy placement, and we have a fully staffed sales desk with sixteen external wholesalers."

"Sounds like the exact same as the multiline support model," Edie muttered.

"That's because it is the exact same," Tiny said. "While we get sixty percent of what we used to get from the multiline channel, in our best year, according to industry-wide statistics, we only got about eight percent of the business from the brokerage channel. All this while paying an additional forty-five percent commission to that channel over the multiline." She waved her hand and rolled her eyes. "Don't get me started on the differences of policies staying on the books in multiline versus brokerage."

"So Taylor makes cuts to multiline through incentive trip, medical and dental benefits, and retirement plan contributions in order to afford paying the brokerage channel the higher commissions? Even though the support models are nearly identical?" Edie asked.

Tiny clapped her hands then rubbed them together, deep in thought.

"Is the multiline model the second most expensive then?" Edie asked.

"Depends on the year," Tiny explained. "The direct producer model can go from two hundred sixty percent sales goal in one year to forty percent in the next, depending on what product line the external wholesalers are exploiting."

"Then what's the cheapest model to run?"

"Specialty markets," Tiny said. "Like I said. They have only one sales rep, your friend, Easton Frost."

"He's not my friend," Edie clarified.

"Good, because as near as I can tell, he's a ghost. He belongs in the spirit world. He's a moving target, a rolling stone. He's untouchable."

"Why is that?"

"He brings in millions of dollars of premium single-handedly each year," Tiny said. "He's squeaky clean from a regulator's perspective. Specialty markets is the only thing keeping John Taylor alive."

"How profitable is the business for that channel?" Edie asked.

"I wish I knew," Tiny said. "I was hoping you and your team could help me find out."

Edie frowned, then a smiled snaked across her face. "How can you not know? I thought you had tendrils everywhere."

"Ivy can scale walls, Edie, but it's been impossible for me to get those numbers. I'm guessing their outstanding, because whatever Frost is doing, he's an absolute cash cow. I've been told we pay him nearly two million dollars a year in cash. I won't tell you what his options and deferred comp arrangements look like. You'd pass out."

Edie huffed. "He doesn't act like he makes that much money."

Tiny returned to her seat and steepled her fingers under her nose. "How well do you know him?"

"He goes to my church in Apple Valley," Edie explained. "I actually asked him out after church once. We ended up having coffee after a church volunteer function. But that was before I discovered we work for the same company. Since then, when he's in town, he pesters me to meet him for lunch in the cafeteria."

Tiny's eyes had widened enough for Edie to see them through her glasses. She had muted brown eyes.

"Other than that," Edie continued. "Apparently, he's a hometown hero in Oklahoma. My team did a YouTube search on him..."

"Yeah, yeah, I saw the videos," Tiny said. "The ones where he saved a kid and a woman from getting kidnapped."

"So that's all I know," Edie said. "I think he wanted to date me, but I put a stop to that once I..."

"Sure, sure," Tiny said. "You know he's very close to Taylor. I'd say as close as two hetrosexual men can get at work."

Edie felt her face blush. "He's very attractive. I can see how he'd be successful in sales."

"Oh, yeah," Tiny agreed. "He does it for pretty much everybody in Home Office."

"Please don't ask me to get any closer to him," Edie said.

Tiny shook a look of disappointment off her face. "First, I'd never ask you to do that. Second, he's close to Taylor, so he already knows you've been reassigned to me. It's no secret that I've been looking for the sales and retention reports for that channel since its inception four years ago. No, we'll have to employ a difference strategy. I think I have the perfect approach in mind."

Chapter Seventeen

It amazed Edie how quickly two weeks could vanish. Although the team was humming at maximum potential while transitioning into their new assignments, ten work days, bookended with dismal, forgettable weekends, slid past her with a torturous grace. The menace of time's persistency was formidable in its lure and lull.

But they had moved things forward, projects had been delivered on time, each member managed to put in two different evening shifts to impress their commitment upon her. Austin had been on time and free of eyelid bags last Monday, but she suspected Mona of starting a sleep aid regimen. She'd lost her crisp, ear-splitting focus. Her drive had slackened. Only Becca remained consistent with her work, having cleared her schedule to lunge into the company's life insurance and annuity products, with special devotion to this mysterious world of no surrender charges.

Some brokers and agents made a very fine living replacing or exchanging policies for the same clients. This was known as churning and was grounds for immediate appointment termination, fully backed by the law in most states. Edie still couldn't understand where the long-term profitability manifested itself with policies specifically designed to be one hundred percent liquid and available for immediate exchange to another carrier.

Her discussions with Tiny had validated her concern. Surrender charges were any life company's way to keep a policy on the books long enough for the premium to outlast the costs in product development, underwriting, customer acquisition, and agent commissions. Even with a decreased agent payout, Edie couldn't yet rationalize why the company was entering such a shifting marketplace.

The simple truth was those policies bulked up quarterly sales numbers in premium dollars and made CEOs and boards of directors look great to shareholders, most of whom wouldn't own pieces of the company when the short-term successes didn't equate to sustainable growth.

But that's what they were to discern this morning. Becca had created a presentation to explain these products, starting on the life side. Edie glanced around the conference room, scanning for approaching footsteps. Her eyes fell on the clock. 8:05. All of them were five minutes late.

Why did most employees consider getting coffee and asking about someone's weekend actual work? It was compensation for absolutely no productivity. At best, it was a parade for women to present new wardrobe additions. The men were oblivious unless a blouse or vest was more revealing than normal.

8:07 am and finally Austin and Mona breezed in, feigning breathlessness as though the bus had been late or the parking garage was already full.

"Good morning," Edie said with a fake smile.

"How was your weekend?" Austin asked.

"I'm here on time, so it was boring," Edie replied.

Mona and Austin exchanged a questioning look.

"8:00 is 8:00, ladies," Edie said.

"Well, this meeting promises to be cheerful," Mona murmured. "Where's the princess of punctuality then?"

Edie cast her eyes to the LCD projector she'd come in early to set up. Plugged in, ready to go, its laptop connector looked lonely. "Not sure."

"You know how nervous she gets when she's about to give a presentation," Austin said.

Mona snorted. "Yeah, she's probably in the bathroom puking."

Edie leaned forward, cocked an eyebrow, and steepled her fingertips together. "Then go check on her."

Mona set down her coffee and coughed as she left the conference room.

"So your weekend sucked?" Austin asked.

"How was yours?" Edie replied.

Austin took a deep breath. "Fine. Met a guy. It was one of those multiple clubs under one roof, so we hopped from club to club in time with the slow songs: country, rock, hip hop. All his request. Then we wound up at that rooftop bar on Hennepin. It's a cigar bar, so there were a bunch of gold diggers prowling about."

"Sounds like he was trying to seduce you," Edie said.

Austin harumphed. "His loss, free drinks and a peck on the cheek. He was a decent dancer though."

Edie cleared her throat, searching for something positive to say and more than a little surprised by a not so subtle tinge of jealousy.

Becca and Mona burst into the conference room. Her throat visibly clenched, Becca was a post-shriek banshee. She hugged her zippered portfolio to her chest, which wrinkled her grey, pin striped power suit and dark blue dress shirt.

Edie realized she had more immediate concerns than dwelling on why she was so acutely jealous of Austin's fortune with men. She knew she wasn't envious of Austin's looks or charms. It was more the ease in which they became enamored of her. Edie's teenaged inner voice demanded to know why Austin and why not her, but Edie brushed away this tempting stream of consciousness and fought not to roll her eyes. She would buy a puppy, violate her townhome lease, and move into a rental house before she allowed herself to devalue Austin's contributions over something so petty as loneliness. Being alone was fleeting. She hoped.

"Becca, how was your weekend?" Austin asked.

"I don't remember," Becca mumbled, looking down at her shoes.

Edie rose from her seat. "I've already set up the projector for you. It's only the four of us; you can relax."

Becca sat down and unzipped her portfolio. She took a heavy breath and exhaled through her nose. Her eyes drifted a bit as though she were counting down numbers before she decided to speak. "I think it's because... it's just us that I'm so nervous."

Mona sat to Becca's left at the table, directly across from Edie. "What would you do if Edie had asked you to present in front of Taylor or his bosses?"

"I would have resigned," Becca snapped. Not a trace of sarcasm lingered.

Edie leaned forward and placed her hand on Becca's arm. "I would never have asked you to do that." She shot a bristling look toward Mona, who only cocked a defiant eyebrow.

"But you feel comfortable enough to admit you're nervous," Austin said to Becca. "We must be growing on you."

Becca nodded and lost the battle with her smile. It broke free with a light but billowing gust. "That must be it."

Edie winked at Austin so that Becca wouldn't see. Austin acknowledged her without diminishing the look of concern given to Becca. Once again, Austin had said the perfect thing at the perfect time. That was more worth Edie's envy than any slow-dancing, crooner wannabe.

"Where's your laptop?" Edie asked Becca.

Mona lifted a computer bag Edie hadn't seen her bring in. "I carried it in for her."

"It's on inside the bag," Becca said.

Mona removed the laptop and handed it to Becca, who lost no time connecting it to the projector. In a few seconds, she'd brought up her presentation and was passing out her note pages.

"I'll try not to be convoluted, but it's pretty murky," Becca said.

"What is?" Edie asked, guiding Becca to be clearer.

"This notion of no surrender charge products," Becca said.

"Why don't you start from the beginning?" Edie suggested. "We were property and casualty hatchetwomen. We need a crash course."

"That's the challenge," Becca said. "It's a much more sophisticated product. The agent has to be better trained for what it takes to run illustrations on our sales software. It's not like playing with an antiquated quoting system to exploit programming flaws."

"Okay," Austin said. "You lost me at 'sophisticated.'" While her face remained deadpan, the team sensed the joke, and everyone paused for a brief chuckle.

"What I'm trying to say is that the product behaves very differently than traditional life insurance products," Becca continued.

Edie cleared her throat. "Start from the beginning, Becca. Give us a review of life products first. You know, term versus permanent, renting versus owning. Show us the way the multiline agents are taught to sell it. Then we can get into the differences with this new market."

Becca nodded and blushed a little. "Okay, so there's term insurance, which means that it insures a person for a term of time like ten, fifteen, twenty, or thirty years. Pretty straight forward. It's what most middle-income people buy for final expenses, college funding, income replacement for their spouse, mortgage and debt payment, right?"

"Got it," Mona said.

"But usually, if someone buys a cheap thirty-year term policy when they're thirty and keeps it until the term is up, they aren't nearly as healthy when they're older and still might need life insurance coverage. It becomes much more expensive to buy another thirty-year term when you're sixty than when you're thirty," Becca explained.

"With you so far," Austin said with a wink.

"So that's where district managers train their agents to talk about the difference in term and permanent insurance from the perspective of renting or owning a house. With permanent insurance like universal life or even variable universal life, the insured has the potential to build equity within the policy called cash value. This creates flexibility so that in later policy years the cash value can be used to pay the premium rather than the owner continuing to pay or being forced to pay to keep the policy in force."

"Yep," Mona said. "So far so good."

Becca took a deep breath. "The buildup of cash value inside the permanent policy is a result of premium payments above and beyond what is necessary to cover the actual cost of insurance, and the policy fees, and charges. This additional premium is credited with an interest rate, which gives the product its name, current assumption universal life. The additional premium sits in a general account and earns this interest tax-deferred. The policy owner can even take out cash value loans at very favorable interest rates and keep the policy in force by either continuing to pay the premiums or paying back the cash value loans."

Edie nodded. "Good so far, Becca."

Becca smiled her appreciation to Edie. "Thanks, boss."

Mona raised her hand. "I've always wanted to know what happens to all that cash if the insured dies."

"It depends on the selected death benefit option," Becca said. "If the death benefit is what's called level, then the policy's face amount death benefit is paid to the beneficiary and the company retains the cash value." She rose and opened the cabinet that hid the dry erase board. Popping the top off a red marker, she wrote an example case.

With Becca's back turned to them, Edie grinned to Mona and Austin. Becca had forgotten her nerves, now enraptured with her need to report and train.

"It's a method of self-insurance," Becca said. "Let's take a five hundred-thousand dollar face amount case with a level death benefit and fifty thousand dollars in cash value. If the insured dies, the beneficiary receives the total five hundred thousand dollars. The insurance company retains the fifty thousand of cash value, effectively paying out only four hundred fifty thousand in actual loss. The insured is in essence ten percent self-insured."

"Why would anyone pay more premium than necessary to keep a policy in force if they knew the company would take the money?" Mona asked. "That's insane."

"The death benefit is still ten times the amount of the cash value," Edie said.

"I understand that, but why would anyone select a level death benefit if there were another option that gave them the death benefit and the cash value back?" Mona asked.

"There is another option," Becca said, drawing an arrow in green marker from her first example to her second, which anticipated Mona's question.

Becca acts like Radar in that old TV show, *Mash*, Edie thought.

"Let's take that same example, same original death benefit, same cash value, only this time, the insured had selected the increasing death benefit option," Becca was saying. "Only now when the insured dies, the death benefit has increased to say five hundred thirty-five thousand..."

"Why not five hundred fifty to reflect the death benefit and the cash value?" Austin asked.

"There are a number of factors that don't allow the cash value and the increasing death benefit to align exactly," Becca said.

"Like what?" Mona asked.

"In current assumption universal life, the cost of insurance, also called COIs, can increase during the life of the policy based on the company's experience in death claims," Becca said. "Those increases can be mitigated with increased premium payments, which would preserve the amount of cash value or the insured could continue to pay the same premium he's always paid, and the difference caused by the increase in COIs would then be deducted from the policy's cash value."

"What's another factor?" Edie asked.

"Outstanding loans and loan interest," Becca said.

"Is that all?" Austin asked.

"Well, ultimately, life insurance enjoys a tax-free death benefit status. The beneficiary isn't taxed when he or she receives the death benefit, unlike being a beneficiary of an annuity or someone's 401k," Becca continued.

Mona clapped her hands and rocked back in her seat. "Check out the big brain on Becca."

Becca blushed and coughed into her hand. "It gets worse. I pinched a couple CLU books from one of the life specialist's desk."

"CLU?" Austin asked. Her eyes were growing wider and more despondent.

"Chartered Life Underwriter," Becca said. "It's a designation. You have to take eight courses in life insurance to get it."

"Nice," Edie said. "Go on."

"Well, as I was saying, life insurance death benefits are tax-free. It also enjoys a tax-preferred treatment for cash value," Becca continued. "Insurance premiums are generally not deductible for individuals, so the cash value has already been taxed. But the buildup in cash value above basis is not taxed at withdrawal because it's viewed as a policy loan rather than a full withdrawal like in an annuity."

"So why would anyone invest in an annuity or mutual funds or stocks?" Mona asked. "Those things are all taxed, right?"

"It makes sense to diversify your investment products based on your goals and how they are taxed," Becca explained. "The primary, if not sole purpose of life insurance, if you're talking to a regulator, is to insure against the economic value of a life, a person's ability to transfer part of his or her life into income. But some have viewed life insurance as a natural tax shelter, and in the past, people invested huge sums of money, beyond the cost of insurance into policies for that reason."

"How the rich stay rich," Mona said, shaking her head.

"One way they used to," Becca said. "Then the government instituted regulations where premiums paid in the first seven years had to pass one of two tests to meet the definition of life insurance. If you pay too much premium in the first years, the IRS stops regarding the policy as life insurance and it will be taxed as an annuity to the beneficiary."

"Anyone need coffee?" Austin asked.

"And a smoke," Mona said.

"No," Edie said. "We've just started."

Mona groaned. "This is too much, Edie."

Edie was shocked. "Are you serious?"

"As serious as information overload on a Monday morning," Mona said. "I'm getting a headache."

Edie glanced at Becca, who confirmed her worry with downcast eyes and fidgeting.

"Becca, explain the difference between increasing and level death benefit," Edie said.

"But there's another option that a lot of people choose in these no surrender charge products," Becca all but whispered.

"You're killing me, Smalls!" Mona said.

Edie knocked on the table. "Calm down, Mona."

Mona sat up from rubbing her temples and squeezing her eyes closed.

"This is important," Edie said, "and we've been working too hard lately. I'll buy the first round at an early happy hour."

This made Austin sit up. "I call Mona as my wing woman then."

"You two sound like those idiot fighter pilots at the end of *Top Gun*," Edie said.

"Is that the underwear and volley ball movie?" Becca asked.

All heads turned to her.

Becca blushed again. "What?"

"The underwear and volley ball movie?" Mona repeated.

"Is it?" Becca asked again.

"It is," Edie said, a giggle edging through her voice.

"You know how I am with movie titles," Becca said.

"That's not what's surprising," Edie said.

Becca crossed her arms. "What? I *am* a hot-blooded woman."

Austin laughed loudest. Becca pinched the bridge of her nose, and Mona started digging in her bag for cigarettes.

Edie slammed down her hands, more to get their attention than to startle them. "Let's get through this."

Becca shrugged. "It's dry material. I like researching this stuff, but I know it's not for everybody."

Aiming the pointed toe of her shoe in Mona's general direction, Edie kicked at her executioner and fought to keep her shoulders motionless with the effort.

Mona winced when they connected. "Sorry, Becca. It's just so new. It's hard to take it all in."

Edie buried her chuckle. Her kick would cause a bruise, even on Mona's dark skin. It would be slacks at the bar tonight.

"Yes, sorry, Becca," came Austin's predictable, self-deprecating addition. "I'm just the one who flirts with the inmates before their trials."

Becca smirked, and Edie thought she saw her roll her eyes. Was everyone becoming jealous of Austin? In Colorado Springs, they'd all stayed well within their lifestyles. With relocation, the four were stumbling onto one another. Work/life balance was non-existent. Morale was unraveling.

"So," Edie said. "Becca was telling us the difference between level and increasing death benefits."

"Level death benefits stay level, keeping the COIs lower even in later policy years," Becca said, rushing the natural cadence of her speech. "If you want to buy a policy for its cash value growth, you may want a small death benefit which doesn't cost you as much so that more of your premium dollars go to your cash value. If you believe your death benefit need will increase through your lifetime in line with your expenses, responsibilities to your family, and your asset base, you may choose the increasing death benefit so that as your cash value increases your death benefit also increases in an actuarially pre-determined pace."

"Actuarially pre-determined pace?" Mona asked. "Do you have a crush on the life specialist you nabbed that book from?"

Becca coughed in her hand. "He's not bad. I'd go out with him. But there is a third death benefit option, sometimes called Option C, where you can get back your entire death benefit and all the premium you've paid into the policy. It's call the return-of-premium death benefit option, and it is used to provide business insurance solutions to partnerships and small to medium sized corporations."

Edie leaned forward. "Excellent, Becca. Let's talk about why business owners and shareholders of corporations might need life insurance."

"It all stems from the tax treatment of life insurance death benefits and cash value buildup," Becca said. "You can use life insurance as additional benefits for executives, as in a simple bonus policy paid by the company and owned by the employee. You can even fund what's call non-qualified deferred compensation with life insurance."

"What's non-qualified deferred compensation?" Austin asked.

"When someone is paid at such a high level that they can't contribute to their 401ks or pension plans at an even pace for their salary and their retirement goals, they can use non-qualified deferred compensation to fight against the reverse discrimination that IRS regulations cause on company-sponsored retirement plans," Becca said.

"We're entering a whole new world here," Edie said. "These are pretty advanced sales concepts."

"Which means the crooks are more sophisticated," Austin said.

"It's like moving from street vice to white-collar drug trafficking," Mona said. She clasped her hands together and made a gun. Holding it close to her face, she peered through slits. Then she started humming the theme to *Miami Vice*, complete with the drum breaks and the squealing guitar.

"Mona, be serious," Edie said.

"You're right," Mona replied. "It's better to see it as working random drive-by gangbanger killings to Vincent D'Onofrio and *Law and Order: Criminal Intent*."

"Yes, that's more appropriate," Edie said. "Now, can we get back to Becca's report?"

"I don't see where no surrender charge products come in yet," Austin said.

"If I'm the CFO of a company that's looking to fund non-qualified deferred compensation on ten executives using ten life insurance policies, my company is planning on spending a great deal of money on premiums. While the executive will have access to the policy's cash value at retirement, the company will be paid the death benefit on anyone who dies prior to or after retirement, which helps the company's cost recovery for the expenses," Becca said. "With a traditional surrender charge product, the cash value is held in check by the percentage of the surrender charge in the first ten years of the policy. Because the company would have limited access to the cash values, it has to hold the life policies on the liability side of its balance sheet."

Mona glanced at Austin with widened eyes.

"I know this is heady," Becca apologized.

Edie waved her hand. "No, Mona and Austin accepted their new roles and their raises to bust the top players in their wicked schemes. It's the price of admission."

"Okay, so anyway," Becca continued. "With a no surrender charge policy, the business can claim the life policies as assets to offset the liability side of the balance sheet which reflects the premiums paid for the plan."

"But how do insurance companies make a profit if there's no surrender charge to entice the policyholder to stay put until the premium payments exceed the costs?" Mona asked.

"It's tentative at best," Becca said. "There is a schedule of commission chargebacks to the writing agent if the policy is replaced or cashed out. Usually in the first four years."

"Four years doesn't sound like enough time to become profitable on a policy," Edie said, encouraging Becca to expand her explanation.

"It's not," Becca agreed. "But these sales make quarterly numbers look good for CEOs of publically traded carriers. Don't get me started on whether or not shareholders care about long-term profits or the sustainability of businesses anymore."

"And we're publically traded, right?" Mona asked.

"The life company demutualized like most everybody else in the eighties," Edie said.

"So a mutual insurance company, like those supposedly owned and controlled by the policy holders, don't make these types of products?" Austin asked.

If Austin were going to start dropping sound logic on top of her uncanny intuition, the team's budding jealousy would reach tuning fork vibrations sooner than Edie anticipated.

"They certainly could make these products," Becca said. "But a mutual company's focus is on long-term profitability, and they don't have the added pressure of creating consistent quarterly dividends. So this type of product doesn't hold much attraction."

"So why did we develop it?" Edie asked, though she knew the answer.

"Short-term sales growth," Becca said. "It would appear that every company in this market has convinced itself of these products' security in one of two ways. First, the higher degree of self-insurance given the larger premium payments offsetting the actual death benefit..."

"Which is totally negated by the return-of-premium death benefit option," Edie interjected.

"What is the second piece?" Mona asked.

"The ability to monitor policy exchanges and replacements and to thwart the agents who make a career of churning the business after the four-year chargeback cycle when they can get a fresh stream of first year commissions," Becca replied.

Their extended silence was not spent in confusion. Each was making the pertinent connections in her mind.

Mona spoke first. "But as long as the agent can make the argument that a policy replacement is in the client's best interest, then compliance can't justify preventing the replacement or terminating the agent for churning."

Edie nodded. "And without a new surrender charge created in the new policy that replaces the original policy, the agent can make the case that the current interest credited to the new policy is better."

"Or that the costs of insurance are less in the new policy because people are living longer and the mortality tables are becoming less expensive to the insured," Becca said.

"So who benefits from these kinds of policies?" Austin asked.

"The insured, the businesses that own the policies, especially those that can afford Option C, the agents, and the life company's senior management because it makes the company stock more attractive to investors," Becca explained.

"But the company doesn't profit," Mona said.

"Not in the long-term, but with a balanced product portfolio, the intent is that other products provide long-term sustainability while these products achieve short-term growth expectations," Becca continued.

In unison, the three sitting at the table leaned back in their seats.

"How confident are you that the brokerage channel has the company's best interests in mind by selling a balance of the product portfolio, Edie?" Mona asked.

"Not at all," Edie said.

Mona rubbed her hands together. "This is going to be brutal. We'll be bathing in broker blood now."

"You're forgetting the no surrender charge annuity product though," Becca said.

Mona had risen and started gathering her portfolio and notes. "No, I'm not. I get the drift here. We can dive deeper on that later. We have a month before the products launch. Great presentation, Becca."

Edie shot black ice into Austin's and Mona's eyes. "I'm disappointed in your cavalier attitudes." Then she turned to Becca and smiled. "Great job, Becca, for your research and training. Thank you for taking this seriously. We haven't arrived anywhere, ladies. We have no laurels to rest on. We're either going to be caught failing upward or we'll continue to defy expectation. I hope you two will come to understand that."

Austin and Mona shared a somber look but remained silent.

Austin and Mona aren't feeling guilty for dumping on Becca, Edie thought as she arrived at the GameWorks bar with Becca in tow. *They're still trying to skate by on our recent successes. They're still in celebration mode.*

Becca remained hard to read, but Edie could sense her agitation for their lack of interest in her research and for being dragged to another team building happy hour. The small introvert literally refused to let her now light brown hair down, keeping it tightly tucked into its bun from this morning. While Edie had encouraged Becca to go home when she turned Mona and Austin loose to freshen up, Becca elected to stay in the office with Edie until six. Edie then offered to pay for a cab to the loud, obnoxious, testosterone filled bar. Becca remained silent for the trip, cleaning her teal blue designer glasses until they arrived.

"Everything okay, Bec?" Edie asked after paying the cabbie ten bucks for the seven-fifty fare.

"Everything is fine," Becca said.

"You sure?" Edie asked. "You've been quiet since the training."

Becca looked down at the pockmarked sidewalk, splattered in the rainbow of GameWorks' neon lights. "Aren't I always quiet?"

Edie nodded and sensed that Becca wasn't ready to go inside. "Do you want to talk about it?

Becca shrugged and pressed her glasses up the bridge of her nose. "What's there to talk about? You have to bribe or coerce the other two into listening to the very information that will enable them to do their jobs. I'm the butt of their jokes." Becca waved her hands in front of her in mock apology then rolled her eyes. "I know, I know. I'm supposed to be oblivious."

"Have you ever thought that Mona and Austin are intimidated by you as much as you are of them?" Edie asked.

Becca crinkled her nose as though she anticipated the after school special speech from her mother but not Edie. "What am I supposed to do with that?" she asked. Her gentle eyes had turned into a full glare.

"Just something to consider..."

"Oh, consider how the other two are secretly horrified by my brutal intelligence and my mad skills of computing and analysis?" Becca interrupted. It was the first time she'd done that, although she'd countlessly watched Mona interrupt Edie.

"Want a cigarette?" Edie asked. "We've been standing out here long enough to draw looks."

Becca considered it, then a smiled crept across her face. "Promise not to tell the other two?"

Edie felt like she was in middle school again, agreeing to keep unimportant secrets. Becca felt it was important for the other two not to know she enjoyed a rare smoke. *I need to respect that,* Edie told herself. Maybe that was when Becca's social development had been arrested. Some deeply embarrassing slumber party where she came to realize she didn't fit in or wasn't allowed to.

257

Girls were cruel after all. For Edie, there had been times when she'd played both perpetrator and victim. But perhaps, Becca hadn't been given the encouragement to go to the next slumber party and the next.

Edie fished out a crumpled pack of light cigarettes. "Don't tell Austin or Mona about these," she warned. "They'll never let me off the hook."

"No problem." Becca pried out a gnarled cigarette and placed it between her lips. "Just don't tell them I bummed it from you."

"Deal," Edie agreed. "Besides, they're so stale now, they'll probably taste more like Trident and chap stick." She found her book of matches, also deformed, and managed to light one.

Becca took the matches, grimaced, and inhaled. "Thanks," she muttered with a stifled cough.

They shared silence.

Then Becca cleared her throat and exhaled above their heads. "So you really think I intimidate Mona and Austin?"

Edie nodded. "Absolutely."

Becca took another drag and swayed. "I may get loopy."

"You already are," Edie said and patted her friend on the back. "Don't worry. They're both on their third drinks. They'll make comments about you and I actually showing up, but then they'll forget it. Mona will ask you to do a fly by over a table of comic book geeks. Austin will ask me to take her to the ladies' room. It'll be routine."

Becca took a deeper drag and nodded.

Edie moved her hand from Becca's back to her shoulder. "Make no mistake, Becca. I need you here. The team needs you. It's more important that you know how life and annuities work than those two. Mona needs to know who to stab and Austin needs to know who to make out the Hallmark card to. You're the engine. Don't let them belittle you. I know what you're worth."

Becca blew out smoke. "I don't like everyone else in the company knowing what I'm worth. It feels forced when you sing my praises, as you call it, to Taylor and now to Tiny."

Edie eyed her with a pensive glare. "Does it make you feel awkward?"

"It makes me feel fraudulent and arrogant," Becca said. "I don't consider what I do to be that special. It's what my degree is in and what I know how to do it. That's all."

"You are more talented and more intelligent than people who have been in your position for a decade," Edie replied.

"I've been trained on more updated software systems," Becca argued.

"You're using the same antiquated reporting they are. In the Springs, the whole office was using thirty-year old computers." Edie took a long drag to temper her argumentative tone.

"I was lucky that the DOS systems still made sense to me," Becca said. "I don't feel comfortable grandstanding, and it feels twice as ridiculous when you do it for me. It sounds contrived."

Edie threw up her hands. "Okay, Becca. I'm sorry. I won't make such a huge deal of your talent to the boss anymore. A little bit of that really juices up Austin and Mona. It's been a good motivator for them."

Becca stomped out her cigarette. "Then why does it surprise you that I don't care for it, given the conversation we just had?"

That gave Edie greater pause. "You're absolutely right, Becca," she said at length. "Which is why what I have to tell you next will seem like a monumental kick in the teeth."

"Give me another cigarette then," Becca demanded. She took the smoke with twitchy fingers.

"It's okay for us to talk like this," Edie said as she handed her the match book again. "You don't have to get so worked up."

"You know I don't like confrontation," Becca snapped.

Edie put on her best disarming grin. "I don't consider it confrontation. You're just giving me candid feedback about how I manage your performance."

"You're stalling, Edie," Becca said with the cigarette between her teeth.

"Tiny wants to farm you out on a special assignment in the financial department."

Becca took a long drag and rolled her eyes. "Under Maggie Waller? You're sending me to work on another team?"

Edie grabbed Becca's elbow then patted her shoulder. "No, you'll still report directly to me and still under the compliance department."

"Then why does Tiny want me to help Maggie's team?" Becca asked. "Are they friends? Because I've heard mixed things about their relationship."

Edie cocked an eyebrow. "So have I. Enough to make me think I shouldn't make any assumptions on whether they're adversaries or allies."

"So what will I be doing?" Becca asked.

"I don't know yet. We're meeting with both of them first thing next Monday."

Becca covered her mouth. "I can't believe you did this to me, Edie."

"I thought I was giving you more exposure, more opportunity," Edie said quietly.

"I don't want it," Becca growled. Her eyes started to water. "I want things to calm down and be normal. I can't stand this pace."

"Okay," Edie said, "but we're committed to this one."

Becca looked up and away. "Please make it the last one for a while, Edie. And by a while, I mean, six months or better."

Edie nodded, her head floating from the adrenaline rush of being so horribly wrong. "Fair enough," she said gruffly.

"You're buying all of my drinks, boss," Becca stammered.

"You got it," Edie said.

Becca pitched her cigarette into the street and stormed into the bar.

Chapter Eighteen

Austin felt like she was drooling though she knew she wasn't. She'd checked the cool area where the end of her pen met the corner of her mouth. Still, in her mind, she could feel the water torture drip of her saliva hitting her desk.

The four unblondes had been at their new assignment for thirty days. Austin felt they were literally in the cubicle underworld. While the gnashing of teeth was indeed great, the silence was more fiendish and incendiary than any horrific, pain-drenched scream. Yesterday, the entire compliance department murmured their way through the Happy Birthday song for one Charles Eichten, a lifer with twenty-six years of sales preventing service. It had reminded Austin of a Meryl Streep movie where she played a homeless woman having to sing for her supper every other evening. The mumbling wasn't out of disrespect or apathy so much as it was from a lean economy of energy and caloric expense. Sudden bursts of positive emotion would startle the herd.

Thirty days of fake ferns baking under flickering fluorescent lighting. Even with Christmas behind them, if the sun had shone itself with its vindictive promise to return in May, the department wasn't privileged with garden level windows. Austin missed the Minnesota state office. Their side of the basement had the windows. Compliance, on the other hand, had been buried alive decades ago. The maintenance men made sure there was just enough oxygen pumped in to keep the unit alive and active. The zombies thrived only on the brains of corrupt brokers and independent agents, so the risk of outbreak throughout the Home Office complex was distinctly minimal.

Austin's eyes were drying out, so she told herself to blink. Five seconds passed before she was able to refocus on the spreadsheet report. She tried to minimize her blinking so she could keep her place on the rolling list of new business cases versus historical data for the red flag brokers she'd been assigned. Her tasks weren't that different from her prior duties, though now, she felt like Jodi Foster's character in *Contact*, looking for patterns within the utter randomness of a dryer tossing around clothes. In compliance, she was looking for reasonable doubt or even beyond. Something in the patterns of business replacement notifications that would somehow justify the business leaving the company for the betterment of the customer and not the broker.

On Tuesdays, Becca would scoop up the updated data from the competitive analysis team and merge this with the competition's product names on the replacement business submission forms. Austin would then start her day just like every other. Dock her laptop. Log into the network. Open the spreadsheet. Sip her Caribou Coffee. Compare costs of insurance between the existing policy and the competitor's new policy. Compare differences in premium payments, annual fees, death benefit amounts, additional riders added, original riders removed.

Sure, the company could have written a program to review all of the data, and Becca did an outstanding job matching all the data fields, but the level of pattern recognition within the variable subtleties of comparing the apples still took human application.

After three weeks of reviewing policies, sipping coffee, and waiting for her bladder to fill enough to give her something else to do, even if for five minutes, Austin understood how this work would drive John Taylor's troublesome, scorned ex-lovers into resigning. That is if they were all to believe what Tiny had revealed to Edie. While Austin knew Edie, and the rest of the unblondes, to be instantly trustworthy, not only in their appearances and demeanor, but in their very beings, she couldn't believe that Delores "Tiny" Campbell had revealed so much of her intentions to a new subordinate. Especially after a history of killing off every other John Taylor reject. She would have to warn Edie again to protect herself. They were all expendable. They were all worthless.

Sighing, she blinked again and flexed her bladder muscles to see if it were time to go urinate. *Not yet, apparently*, Austin thought. Watching for the clock to strike 11:55 am flooded her with middle school in-house suspension memories. Austin had found herself in the days' long detention several times, chiefly for skipping classes to go to lunch with the sophomore and junior boys who would pick her up outside the gym. Just like back then, the melting of time scorched her nerves and tempted her stream of consciousness to drift into sexual fantasy. Unlike those glory days where all it took was a heavy make out session, now those same thoughts left Austin feeling worn down, resentful, lackadaisical for having to take care of her needs after work.

Someone wrapped on the metal framing of her cubicle wall. Austin looked up and smiled at Mona. "Hey, girl," she said.

Mona lunged into the seat next to Austin's small desk. "What's up, lady?"

Austin noted the exhaustion spiraling throughout Mona's aura. She left her work screen and folded her hands together on the edge of her desk. "How are you doing?"

"I'm dying, Austin," Mona muttered. "I'm actually dying of boredom."

Austin shrugged and scratched at a hangnail. "I don't know what to say without it sounding like an *I told you so*."

Mona nodded. "I know. I know. I never thought I'd miss it. You and Edie were right."

"It can't be just the kill, Mona," Austin said. "I miss the action, too. The interaction, you know. Feeling like a part of the larger team."

"Everyone despises compliance," Mona said. "It's a prison sentence."

"It's a death warrant for the career," Austin agreed. "That's why they set us up with such good raises. They figured we'd quit soon, so they wouldn't have to pay us very long. At least, we can leverage the higher salary in looking for a new job."

Mona leaned forward and laid her head on her forearms. "You can't seriously be considering a resignation. Where would you go? Do you really want to stay in Minnesota?"

"Not at all," Austin said.

"I don't want to look for work in this economy," Mona said.

"Neither do I," Austin said. "No one's hiring to a relocation, so we'd have to pay for our own tickets home."

Mona looked up again. "I don't want to go back either."

They shared a moment of silence, only communicating with their eyes.

"I get what you mean," Austin said at length. "It would feel like retreat or a step backward."

"So in the meantime, how's your savior job working out?" Mona asked.

Austin shot a disgusted glare at her computer. "I haven't found anyone I felt justified in saving since those first four three weeks ago."

"The anomalies?" Mona asked with a huff and she shook her head. "It actually startled Tiny that you found someone to justify suppressing the auto-term letter."

Austin crinkled her nose. "Been a little gun shy since then."

"Guilty until proven innocent, Austin," Mona said. "It's much more black and white, too. There is no benefit of the doubt."

"There is no doubt at all," Austin said. "A broker shows up on a report for the third time replacing a policy for a client older than eighty, he's out. How is the letter generating side of the business going?"

Mona rolled her eyes. "About as riveting as the orphan policy assignment side."

"Still getting grief from that supervisor in policy services?" Austin asked.

Just as Austin had hit serious flak bringing four possible kick outs from the systematic appointment terminations, Mona had encountered some egotistical resistance from a supervisor at the life policy service center in Minot, North Dakota. Mona had intentionally circumvented the traditional assignment procedures for the policies left behind by the terminated brokers and independent agents. In this sales channel, they weren't assigned to the most deserving agent or the one who coughed up the most payola. Instead they were transferred into house accounts governed by Home Office directly. The insureds and policy-owners were notified of the change and given contact numbers, links, and PINs to access their policies directly. The customers were also now known as orphans given their lack of agent representation.

Mona had recognized the danger of the policy holder leaving the company after the reassignment. She'd spent her time over the last month evaluating which people on the orphan policy service team would be proactive enough to sell the internal exchange policy to the existing customer. After discovering a handful of go getters, she'd started assigning policies with the most likelihood of being replaced or canceled outright to those who could most successfully pivot a service call to the internal exchange program and tell the client the features and benefits of getting into a new policy, one in which no one received any sales commissions.

The supervisor, typical of service center mentality, had been close to cardiac arrest for the breech of protocol and had placed a call to Tiny as soon as she became aware of the change.

"I told you she called Tiny right away, didn't I?" Mona asked after rolling her eyes.

Austin nodded. "Did Tiny talk to you about it or did she go through Edie?"

"She went through Edie."

The growl in Mona's tone was not lost on Austin. "What's Edie doing about it?"

"She's making me write a proposal as to why the change to my way would be better for the company and its most profitable blocks of business."

Austin rubbed her fingers together and winked at Mona. "That's where the real money is, these ancient policies with their jacked up cost of insurance charges where old people are still paying through the nose to keep their policies in force for their loved ones."

Mona looked over her shoulder and peered out Austin's cube. "Don't say that too loudly."

"Why not?" Austin asked. "They're trying to get us to quit. At least Taylor and Siemons are. We're squeaky clean. Firing us would create a media tornado."

"Even with what happened in Duluth?" Mona asked.

"Totally unsubstantiated at this point," Austin said. "It's their word against ours."

"I pulled a knife on him," Mona said.

"After he spiked your drink," Austin replied.

Mona narrowed her eyes as her mind drifted into hazy memory. "Edie made it sound as though they could prove pre-meditation because I wear my knife for defense."

"You think you're the only woman that idiot's drugged for attempted date rape?" Austin returned.

"Is that why they're trying to get rid of us?" Mona asked.

"It has to be part of it. That and the Laurent file, the fraudulent auto rate classes for the agent's own policies, and the selling out of contract in St. Cloud and Brainerd," Austin explained.

"So you buy into what Edie told Tiny?" Mona asked.

Again, Austin shrugged. "We did have the files. I'm sure Becca still does somewhere."

"Implanted onto her brain." Mona snickered.

"Do you think Edie trusts Tiny too much too soon?" Austin asked.

Mona bristled and sat up straight. Soon, her arms had slithered across her chest. "I know she never trusted Taylor or Siemons."

"Which is what makes it suspicious that she trusted Tiny so quickly, and that Tiny trusted her just as fast," Austin replied.

Mona spent a moment in silent thought. "Is Tiny Edie's first female supervisor? I can't remember."

Austin followed Mona's thought progression. "We all reported to Jeff Silver in the Springs. I know Edie was fresh out of college when she took the job just like you and I."

"Becca had been there longer than us though," Mona muttered.

"About a year in portfolio underwriting when we joined," Austin added. "Then another year or so before moving over to marketing with us."

"Maybe Edie is giving Tiny too much credibility because she looks up to her," Mona offered. "Edie could be looking for a kindred spirit in a woman high up in the company who has to manage others and endure rumors and accusations along the way."

Austin chortled. "You really think Tiny Campbell ever had a rumor about sleeping with someone?"

Mona cocked back a shoulder and huffed. "We have a rumor threatening right now and neither of us want to advance any farther."

Austin looked away and stared at her monitor. "You're right. You're seriously thinking about quitting, too?"

"Where would I go?" Mona asked.

"You could find a head hunter and fill in your resume as the hatchet," Austin suggested. "There are plenty of other companies that need cleaning up."

"I don't want to start over."

"You don't want a fresh set of enemies at the bridge looking over your trail of dead," Austin said.

Mona chuckled. "You been listening to heavy metal?"

"They're just the words I use when I'm around you."

"Thanks, Austin." Mona gave her a genuine smile. "I appreciate that acceptance of my persona. And you're right. If I'm going to become a career hatchetwoman, I'd rather be a contract employee. In and out, tactical insertions and strikes. No real identity at work. Nothing anyone can use against me."

"Could you work alone like that?" Austin asked. "Without a team?"

Mona started to answer then caught her words. She glanced sideward to Austin then shook her head. "I don't know."

"Don't spare my feelings, Mona." Austin felt a jolt of excitement. Mona had come to confide in her. Did Mona feel beholden enough to Austin that she actually had considered Austin's feelings? Austin felt a pinch of cheesiness flitter through her thoughts, which caused her to stop just shy of thinking the discussion was a breakthrough in their relationship.

"I'm not," Mona barked. "I think I'd have to be in charge, call the shots."

"That much is clear," Austin agreed.

"If that's met, then I think I could use another person or two on the team, but like I said, it would be contract basis only."

"Of course," Austin replied. She felt an emotional opening in the lull. *Time for her to validate Mona and gain more of her confidence.* "I think you're right about Edie and Tiny. Edie is probably looking to relate to a woman more successful than she is. All women in high corporate positions are getting desperate to find protégés, I think because they feel the dual pressure of finding talented people to develop and of avoiding finding and developing their replacement, especially a younger, more attractive version of themselves."

"Yes, but that doesn't explain Tiny revealing so much to Edie," Mona said. "Even Edie's more attractive than Tiny..."

"I don't think Tiny's looking at Edie as an heir apparent. I think there are others in line for that," Austin explained. "But Tiny could still get credit for playing the good corporate citizen and gaining another protégé, helping another woman advance her career."

Mona checked over her shoulders again. "Or maybe Tiny thinks we really are expendable. She uses Edie to take her shot at Taylor. If it works, Taylor's gone tomorrow, and Tiny retires in front of a bronze bust of herself in the lobby. If it doesn't, we were all sent here to quit anyway. Everybody who lives by the hatchet gets led to the gallows eventually."

Austin tapped her pen on her desk. "That's what I think, too. The next chance we get, we need to tell Edie to be more careful in whatever she's doing with Tiny."

Mona nodded and grinned. Then a pause melted her smile away. "When did you and I start thinking the same way?"

"When we became cellmates in the compliance department," Austin said.

Mona snapped her fingers. "That has to be it." Her tone held no sarcasm.

A new knock arrived at Austin's cubicle. Both Austin and Mona locked their expressions and thoughts.

Becca's face appeared just over Mona's head. Austin smiled and exhaled and waved her into the cubicle. Mona followed Austin's eyes before turning to see who was joining them.

"Oh, it's just you, Becca," Mona said as Becca took the seat on Mona's right.

"Yes, it's just me," Becca said.

Austin heard distress in her small voice. "What's wrong, Bec?"

Mona, now apparently convinced that Becca wasn't suspicious of their nerves and body language when she knocked, leaned back and put her arm on Becca's shoulder. "Yeah, Bec. What could possibly be wrong? Your data feeds are flawless. Austin hasn't found any more questionable or circumstantial issues warranting suppression from the termination lists, and my letters are flying out of here at the normal, pre-determined pace."

Becca cast her eyes down. "Though I understand you still have issues with the orphan policy assignment procedures."

Mona remained unfazed. "Yes, I was going to stop by your desk later today and ask if you could help me with the numbers in my proposal. I need to prove that putting people in new policies after internal exchanges ensures they stay with the company even longer versus simply allowing their policies to expire or be exchanged or sold to a life settlement company."

Becca caved in her shoulders and folded her hands. "In a normal market from say five years ago, that would have been nearly impossible to accomplish, even without paying a new commission, the costs on the new mortality tables are so much cheaper than the 1980 tables, there's virtually no profitability in internal exchanges."

Austin leaned forward and furrowed her brow. "What's changed?"

"The rash of life settlement companies and stranger-owned or investor-owned life insurance," Becca said. "It's also called STOLI or IOLI for short."

"That's what those things stand for then," Austin said. "I've heard some of the others use those terms."

"Yes, now that there are companies out there that buy life policies for cash and keep the policies until the death of the insured, there's a new level of competition for the premium dollar," Becca explained. "You probably have a good chance to change the policy assignment procedures, Mona."

Austin sensed tension building around Becca. "But that's not why you came to see us, is it, Becca?"

Becca shook her head but kept her eyes to the ground. "I know you guys sometimes call me Radar behind my back, but I had no idea Mona was going to come see me this afternoon."

"Then what's wrong?" Austin asked again.

"Yeah, Becca, you're starting to scare us," Mona said.

"Edie and Tiny want to assign me a mentor," Becca hissed. Her eyes scanned an invisible line six inches from her face as she recalled the pertinent facts from a recent conversation.

"What's wrong with having a mentor?" Austin asked. "So you have to read a couple of new business books or take a couple of online courses in the company's virtual university."

"It's with Maggie Waller," Becca said in a nearly inaudible whisper.

"Maggie Waller?" Mona asked just as softly.

Becca nodded.

"Do you think she's gay?" Mona asked.

"Definitely," Becca said.

This insistence startled Mona and Austin, especially coming from Becca.

"What's going to be the nature of her mentorship?" Mona prodded and poked at Becca, jabbing her shoulder, neck, and back with sharp fingernails.

"That's the problem," Becca said. "Tiny and Edie feel that I've made so many improvements to the efficiency of the compliance reporting schedules that I can lend a hand to the finance and sales reporting wings under Waller."

Austin snapped her fingers at Mona to stop pestering Becca and then placed her hands flat on her desk. "Well, hey. That's not bad at all, Becca."

"Yes, it sounds like you're the only one who has prospects for getting out of this prison," Mona agreed. "Funny though, the one person who doesn't feel imprisoned is the one they shine some daylight on."

"I think there's more to the responsibility than that," Becca said.

"Is she going to deliver conjugal visits to you in the dungeon?" Mona asked.

Becca rolled her eyes. "Get real, Mona. Play out your bi-sexual fantasy on your own time. I'm meeting with Tiny and Edie Monday to go over the details."

"So now it's an assignment?" Austin asked. "It's not a voluntary program? That does sound troubling."

"What should I do, Austin?" Becca asked. "I don't want to turn down the opportunity, but I don't want to be coerced into doing something unethical, either."

"Who said anything about unethical?" Mona asked.

Becca swallowed and looked to the ceiling to blink frustrated tears out of her eyes. "I have a bad feeling based on how Edie's been acting."

Austin shot up from her desk and threw her arm around Becca. "Hey, it's okay. What's wrong? What's worrying you?"

Becca, for her part, didn't shrink from the hug, but rolled her eyes. "I feel like I'm being traded."

Mona crossed her arms and huffed. "It's called leverage, Becca."

Austin swatted at Mona's arm with her free hand. Mona recoiled from her, but caught Austin's warning look. "What's making it feel that way, Becca?" Austin asked.

Her tone had taken on a deeper, throaty edge. She felt the effervescent sympathy cry warming her chest and moving into her face.

"It feels like when we were in the Springs and all of a sudden I was Edie's best friend because she needed a data head," Becca explained. Her voice warbled with a hurt deeper than this latest round with her boss. "I'm just so used to being ignored. Then, without warning, I'm necessary, I'm needed, I'm important."

Austin gently pushed on Becca's shoulder to guide her into a chair. "Becca, we all owe you a lot. I know Edie probably doesn't let on how much you have done for us."

Mona shifted her weight, scooted away from the table, and then stared at the far wall.

"No, she tells me," Becca said. "In the Springs though, I just ran profitability reports on agents and then sent them to the state offices for the marketing specialists to deal with. The specialists would take the portfolio underwriters in the field and train the agents on what they needed to fix. I was overlooked. I was just a cog in the wheel, but it felt safe. I didn't want any attention. I just wanted to do my job and go home every night."

Austin pushed her own chair to the table and joined Becca. Once she was seated next to her, she reached out for Becca's hand and patted it with a slow double tap someone might use to comfort an infant.

"Then comes Edie, shouting down the halls and making presentations with the regional director about how great I was," Becca continued.

"You did save our rears on that one termination where we accepted the resignation when we shouldn't have," Mona said.

Austin gave Mona an encouraging smile, knowing emotionally enriched episodes were difficult for her.

Becca also glanced up at Mona and nodded. "I know, and that was awesome to be such a huge help for you guys. But I don't like being turned into a big deal. I don't like being the center of attention. It makes me feel used or cheap. Like my buttons are exposed."

"Manipulated," Mona murmured. "Leveraged."

"Yes, I guess that's corporate-speak for it," Becca agreed. "So then we moved up here and I got to tuck myself in and away again. But it didn't take long for Edie to start her showboating again, once the reports justified the terminations. Then I had to sit in on the review boards and document the discussions for Siemons to read, and hack through, and criticize."

She looked up again as though fighting the anger down and shook her head. "Then we get promoted out from under all that, but it feels weird now. It feels like we're all being used for something more than what we're being told. And Edie's singing my praises to the new boss. I'm in the spotlight again, and I hate the attention." She crossed her arms. "It's always been better for me to be ignored than to feel used. I hate feeling like this. It makes my skin feel dry and dirty."

Austin cleared her throat. "So you feel like Edie's using you to advance the team?"

"More to advance herself," Mona said.

Austin locked eyes with Becca. "Do you feel that way?"

"I think it's both," Becca said. "They are one in the same with her. She convinces herself she's advancing the team so she doesn't feel selfish for promoting herself."

"She's a mid-level manager, Becca," Mona said. "They all do that."

"But in operations, it's a long, slow drip. Just a couple of droplets a year during performance appraisals and anniversaries with the company."

Austin nodded. "It's not as aggressive in operations. You're right, Becca."

"We're making almost double the money now than we did in the Springs," Mona said. "And the cost of living isn't really that much higher. So she's basically done right by us."

"Yes, the money is good," Becca agreed. "But it feels so rushed. I don't trust the pace. I wasn't really comfortable before, and now that we're in compliance, it's all frenzied. I mean, Mona, you haven't even finished unpacking."

Mona chuckled. "Probably won't ever. You know how I am. Always having to keep an escape bag packed."

"What did Edie tell you she and Tiny agreed to?" Austin asked.

"Not much," Becca said. "Only that I would be working part-time with Waller's team. But have you two heard about Maggie Waller? No one lasts on her team for long. She down-sizes herself twice a year. She acts like she's doing it to cut costs, but I've heard that once someone on her team shows more proficiency in something than she has, they're gone."

"Did Edie say you were being fully transferred?" Mona asked.

"No, she said I was still her direct report," Becca said.

"Well, there you go," Austin said. "Maggie can't cut you. She can only tell Tiny and Edie that she doesn't need your help anymore. I'm sure Tiny is aware of how Maggie works."

"Yeah, that does sound like a safe play," Mona said. "So just roll with it. It's probably nothing more than these two old bags wanting to get a leg up on each other."

Austin continued to pat Becca's hand. "You just have to give it time. Watch it play out."

Mona stepped forward and rubbed Becca's shoulders. "Hey, listen. I know I've been a jerk to you. Especially during your training on the new life products, but Austin's right. We all owe you for half of the opportunities we have. Edie set all this up, but you're the one empowering us. I'm sorry for treating you rough about it. Sorry for making jokes and pretending like I didn't care. I never wanted you to feel like you didn't matter."

Becca looked up to Mona and grabbed her hands. "Thanks, Mona. That means a lot, coming from you."

"I'm sorry too, Becca," Austin said. "I try to keep things light and airy, but I'd be totally lost in all the technical insurance stuff without you. None of us should ever have ignored you, or taken you for granted, or pointed at you when you were in the spotlight, like you said."

"Thanks, Austin," Becca said.

"Are you feeling any better?" Austin asked.

Becca nodded. "It's spreading over the ache."

"Sounds like a line from an eighties hair band ballad," Mona said. "Meaning I like it."

They shared a laugh. Mona kicked at Becca's chair and grinned. "Now, what's the story on the life insurance rep nerd who loaned you his books for that training?"

Becca gritted her teeth and growled. "That's exactly where I want you to ignore me, Mona."

Mona slapped her knee and chuckled again. "I know. I'm only kidding."

Chapter Nineteen

Meandering the sixth floor maze annoyed Edie. Before the promotion, she remembered being intoxicated by its grandeur. Now she kept her eyes fixed on the back of Tiny's head until she realized it might give off the appearance that she was looking down and frowning. Instead, Edie surveyed the area to smile at random coworkers, knowing Tiny would ignore anyone who crossed her vision and Becca would bore holes into Edie's shoes.

The southeast corner housed their former headquarters, the event planning department, neighboring the tax attorneys and advanced sales concept wholesalers on the east side and the rows of internal wholesaler cubicles to the south. In the center of the floor plan were offices for directors and officers for the various sales channels. Here was the head of the internal sales support department, there the presidents of the broker, direct, and multiline channels, the latter being Geoff Siemens's boss.

She'd never met the man, had never even seen him until this moment, but his appearance answered certain lingering questions as to why Siemons commanded direct audience with Taylor. Siemons towered over this man, Henrik Fasen, a penciled, Doonesbury caricature, who looked nothing like Taylor's usual minions. Fasen had been in place before Taylor's ascension and had obeyed enough to remain in power. Siemons, conversely, was the strongest executive director in one of the worst performing states. A little more clean up and culture-shifting, especially with the new district office model Geoff had championed, and he'd have Fasen's position.

"You should have seen it before the remodel," Tiny muttered ahead of her, misreading Edie's silence. "The ceiling was twice as high and everything was painted white. For thirty plus years it was literally the ivory tower."

Edie cleared her throat. "I've heard that before."

"About a year ago, Rieser came in from corporate in Atlanta and gutted the place," Tiny continued, "making the entire floor sales support. You should have seen the officers' offices before that."

"I'd heard that back then Taylor's office had a bedroom and full bath," Edie said and immediately regretted making the statement.

Tiny looked over her shoulder, rolled her eyes, then turned back and shook her head. "Is your mind where it needs to be?"

"I believe so," Edie said.

"That's not forthright enough," Tiny muttered.

"Yes, it is."

Edie watched the back of Tiny's head nod. "Good. Maggie Waller is a tough sell on everything, especially ideas that are not her own, especially when they are coming from compliance, especially when they are coming from me."

The three turned the northeast corner where the directors' offices came to an end. The hall provided an entryway to two conference rooms. One was the original board room, preserved in its solid wood luster complete with the original soaring ceiling and paneling from the 1970s. Edie peered into the open doors. As they crossed before the boardroom, she sensed Becca doing the same. Edie had never been invited to a meeting in there.

Tiny remained stoic and motioned to the next, smaller, modernized conference room called the Fish Bowl, where they would meet with Maggie.

"Should we head in and wait for her?" Edie asked.

"No, we'll pick her up and bring her over," Tiny said. Her voice had lost weight, but sounded like she were sucking in her gut to sound lighter.

Edie hid her admiring smirk. She liked her new boss's power play. Picking up the chief financial officer at her office and escorting her to a conference room. Only compliance could wield such a brash, vulgar display. There was strength in displacing ego and acting ignorant of the chosen weaponry. Taking sudden measure of her experience, Edie realized she'd never liked any prior superior, feeling as though she had merely tolerated the person's position, but Tiny Campbell was finding a new place inside Edie's esteem.

They rounded the next corner and were forced to line up against the glass store front of Maggie Waller's office as Tiny knocked on the sliding door. The door rattled at her insistence. Maggie Waller swiveled her chair to face them, dental floss woven from one index finger to the other and buried somewhere in her top row of teeth. The image of faceless onlooker herds with their noses against zoo animal exhibits shot across Edie's mind.

Maggie rose, leaving the floss to dangle in her mouth and motioned for them to enter. "Delores, come on in. I thought we were meeting in the conference room."

She stepped from her desk. She was the same height as Tiny, but held less grandmotherly girth and underarm jiggle. Still, Maggie Waller had a thousand years, a thousand tears behind her eyes. Silver and grey streaked her pure black Ancient Egyptian straight banged hair. The shoulder pads and dark brown elbow patches dated her hounds tooth jacket. She wore her pants 1990's high, and her white blouse looked stolen from Puritans.

There was something in the way she looked at Tiny, something in her tone of voice that belied a deep history between them. That errant, nearly imperceptible sigh, plummeting down a canyon without the returning echo coupled with a what-now expression and the shackled shoulders of stockyard humiliation.

"You know I don't like to be kept waiting, Margaret," Tiny said. "And knowing how punctual you are, being kept waiting would be an insult, and would start us off from a bad place."

Neither offered their hand for shaking.

They used to be friends, Edie thought. *This feels familiar. Like I'm looking at Becca greeting Mona in thirty years. Theirs is a salaried tolerance.*

Maggie pulled the floss from her mouth and stuffed it into her pants pocket. Side stepping both Tiny and Edie, she fixed her attention on Becca. "Are you Becca then? I've heard impressive things."

Becca bent her head and extended her hand. "Yes, it's a pleasure to meet you, Maggie." She hesitated on calling the superior familiar but hadn't wanted to offend the woman with Mrs. versus Ms. The subtly wasn't lost on Edie, but she hoped the others hadn't picked up on it. Equally offensive might be the assumption that no one of healthy mind and body would propose marriage to Maggie Waller.

Maggie took her hand. "Good to meet you, too. Let's head to the Fish Bowl. We can talk about the project there."

Tiny exited first. Edie held Becca's elbow to allow Maggie to follow next, fearing Becca, in her nervousness, would be oblivious to the chess match before them. Maggie took large steps to catch up to Tiny.

Edie counted to two and then nudged Becca forward. "You okay?" she whispered.

"Fine," Becca mouthed. "I still don't think this is a good idea."

"I don't either," Edie agreed. "But it's not our idea."

"As long as we can document that," Becca said.

They entered the stale, cold Fish Bowl without a word. Tiny took the chair at the head of the tan and black granite table. Maggie took the seat to Tiny's left. Edie and Becca stepped behind Tiny and took the places to Tiny's right in order, Becca unloading her portfolio and binder of reports before sitting down.

Tiny leaned back and folded her hands in front of her belly, her square-rimmed glasses edged the tip of her nose. "Thanks for meeting with us, Maggie. I know around here no one likes to be assigned a protégé, but Becca is running circles around my department in terms of improving reporting efficiencies, and I think her talents can be leveraged in your world, too."

Maggie cast a slight glance toward Becca then froze her eyes on Tiny. "Well, like I said over the phone, I implement cuts in my own department before asking others to do the same, particularly in a sluggish sales cycle, like what we're seeing now. I let two of my analysts go last week before making the announcement that each department in sales needed to shed two positions from their full-time staff."

Tiny grunted and threw her head toward Edie. "And yet, I got to absorb an entire team from the event planners."

Maggie nodded. "Another oversight error from Taylor. But the numbers made sense. Event planning lost four from its staff, two extra over what was needed. Your department then netted two additional staff because two positions were eliminated from special investigations."

"Makes sense," Tiny said. "So with this new team, which you and I both know never should have been hidden with the event planners, and the loss of your two positions, I thought the best efficiency would be to create this mentor program, and offer you a chance to guide Becca's development in exchange for addition person power."

Maggie smirked at Becca. "I got volun-told to take you on."

"Thank you," Becca replied.

Maggie then motioned to Tiny but kept her eyes on Becca. "I know your experience has been in the multiline channel, focusing mainly on portfolio underwriting and profitability reporting, but I've been waiting for an opportunity to get someone with experience at the regional office level to work with us from a financial perspective, so don't take my bad joke the wrong way."

"I didn't," Becca said.

"We've been sorely missing the perspective of how our sometimes difficult business decisions impact the field, change the behavior pattern, et cetera," Maggie continued. "This last year, we've been chiefly focused on changing how the external wholesalers in the direct producer channel are compensated. Two years ago, we experienced a fire sale on our guaranteed universal life products, a huge increase in 1035 exchanges from other carriers' current assumption products into our product line.

This was paired with favorable interest rates compared to internal crediting on our no surrender charge products for premium finance cases..."

"There were two wholesalers who actually made more money than Taylor based on the bonus model at the time," Tiny explained with a chuckle. "We can't have people three or four rungs down the ladder making more than the distribution's CEO, can we?"

Maggie coughed in her hand to regain the flow of the discussion. "The financials and forecasts were way off mark and did not anticipate the large volume and massive premiums from these cases. The past model was based on anticipated weighted annual premium. We switched to an actual or earned weighted annual premium model."

"Which resulted in an average reduction from seven hundred and fifty thousand in total gross compensation to the wholesaler to two hundred fifty thousand," Tiny said.

"There are forty external wholesalers," Becca said softly. "That's a twenty-million dollar adjustment."

"On average," Maggie agreed. "I'm glad to hear you use the term adjustment."

Becca nodded but cast her gaze downward. Edie scooted a foot from her chair's casters and tapped on Becca's shoe. Becca shook her head minutely, then leveled her eyes at Maggie, who had been staring at her and waiting for her selected response.

Maggie took a deep breath and threw Tiny an I-knew-it glance. "It's helpful to look at overall distribution as a fund portfolio with certain allocations based on risk tolerance, much like what we support inside our variable universal life products. We have a three channel model in place on the life insurance side, so I like to look at the allocation as the broker channel being cash and cash equivalents, the direct producer channel as the equity portion given the annual volatility in actual sales, and the multiline channel as the bond portfolio with a mix of government and corporate debt." Maggie ran out of air and took mental note of Becca's fierce scribbling. Edie mirrored Tiny's posture, keeping her hands folded in front of her.

"This will sound cynical," Maggie continued. "But the broker channel is like a water faucet. If we want more production, we simply relax underwriting guidelines, or if we really want a boost in sales, we increase commissions. When we want to curb the volume, we turn the faucet off. Hence the liquidity of this business."

"Brokers are hookers," Tiny grunted. "They'll wear anything to attract the John as long as the cash is flashed up front."

"It's more appropriate to view their business model as transactional," Maggie said with a raised voice.

Tiny chortled and flicked Edie's shoulder, but Edie only smiled and kept her eyes on her hands.

"The direct producer model is volatile because it reacts to outside market influences like competition, interest rates for premium finance, politics on death benefit proceed taxation, and laws concerning estate taxes and liquidation," Maggie said, now fixing her speech on Becca. "Throw in the move from the 1980 mortality rates to the 2000, which most companies fought until a couple of years ago, and you have the two hundred and sixty plus percentage sales goal results versus forty percent from last year on the same goal."

Becca nodded and continued to take notes. Edie beamed internally, knowing that Becca would thrive under this new tutelage.

"Then that leaves the multiline channel," Maggie continued. "The bond portfolio, the steady-eddies. Of course, the management company loves the monthly premiums coming in from home and auto, but that only serves to fund the exchanges the management company manages. The channel's profitability comes from their life insurance sales. The moratorium on new homeowner's insurance in Texas stopped the bleeding for the exchanges, and opened up a huge opportunity for the Texas agents to write record-breaking levels of life insurance just to keep up their revenue and income."

Becca looked to Edie to confirm what she'd been thinking for months. "So the exchanges suffer from the massive losses in Texas, but the management company profits because it directly owns the life insurance company."

"Precisely," Maggie said. "The financials and forecasts support selling off the property and casualty exchanges to competitors or European companies looking to enter that domiciled market, but the board doesn't want to do away with the grandfathered structure of policyholder-owned exchanges managed by a publically traded company. The model was established in the late 1920's and was made illegal less than a decade later. We've enjoyed said grandfathered status since, and we're the only remaining company still in business with that particular model."

Maggie looked to Tiny, established elongated eye contact, and then lowered her voice. "I agreed to take you on for one reason, Becca. It's in the company's best interest to sell off the exchanges, retain the multiline agents on the life side as captive, and allow them to broker out their auto and home business. It's an easy sale to them because they'll get to replace the business after a pre-negotiated do-not-compete clause with the buying entity. The agents would receive new business commissions at a higher brokered rate from the new companies they represent, we could increase their commissions on life and annuity to just under broker levels costing only a small portion of the retained operational expenses of supporting their actual brick-and-mortar, and ultimately, we would divest the risk of the exchanges not being viable enough to pay the annual management fee to us."

Edie looked up slowly as Maggie listed off her rationale. The CFO wanted to reengineer the multiline channel and rid the company of the property and casualty business. This was quite a different perspective on the future of the channel than what Geoff Siemons envisioned and sold to John Taylor. The ramifications fractaled in Edie's mind before settling on her perspective's only truth. Her team's work to improve profitability and Geoff's vision of the in-house district model were the last chance strategies for the dying business model. All the while, if Siemons's proposal failed, the company would then be prepared to sell off the exchanges in a negotiations process that had begun simultaneously with his project.

Edie's arms bristled and goosefleshed. She and her team were through the looking glass. Literally, sitting in the Fish Bowl, the inner circle, beyond even Taylor's direct reach.

Maggie had lowered her voice even further, now just above a whisper. "I need you, Becca, to run the financials on the projected profitability improvements from the potential replication of what your team has done in Minnesota, in part to determine the channel's sustainability, and in part to determine if the increase in revenue could fund the venture of finding an appropriate buyer and enter into negotiations."

Becca put her pen down and looked up. "We'd have to account for catastrophic losses forecast on a geometric equation."

"Yes," Maggie said.

"The likelihood of the hundred year flood in several locations, the impact of hurricanes hitting the Gulf of Mexico versus the Atlantic coast line, the projection of major earthquakes in California, Pacific Rim volcanoes," Becca continued, "and add in past trajectories of wild fires and tornadoes."

"Yes," Maggie said again.

"How do we get access to that data?" Becca asked.

"The question is how do we wrestle that away from the actuaries?" Tiny said.

Maggie straightened and crossed her legs. "There's a good chance I already have."

Tiny huffed. "A good chance?"

Maggie gave her a weighted look. "Very good chance."

Tiny nodded and pushed her glass back up her nose. It was her turn to sit straight and rub her chin. "This will all take considerable resources, a significant investment."

"Agreed," Maggie said. "Ever since my department's budget moved under sales, I've been captive to the ups and downs of production. I haven't been able to keep a consistent team. And until now, I haven't had direct access to the multiline actuaries on non-life business."

"But with Becca's help, with my help," Tiny said with a pregnant pause, "you'd be able to build your proposal and sell it above Taylor to the board and corporate in Atlanta."

Maggie nodded.

"And in turn save your deferred compensation from draining away when the management company has to dip into the general fund to continue to manage the exchanges," Tiny said.

Maggie stiffened, her earlobes reddened, and she clenched her teeth. "Yes, Delores. There are dozens of us nearing retirement, you included, all too far down the trough to watch our savings and investments dwindle away with so much pugnacious, traditionalist bravado. Atlanta is too focused on the BRIC strategy and emerging markets."

"Brazil, Russia, India, China," Tiny rattled off, explaining the acronym.

"We are the cash cow," Maggie continued. "But we've caught mad cow disease, and the gentlemen at the top have been well taken care of with their golden handcuffs and parachutes. I am not this company. I don't view it as the men like Taylor and those on the board do. They all believe that the company is one with their spirit, and when they retire or move on, watching it smolder in ashes from their yachts will bloat their egos."

Tiny grinned and peered at Edie and Becca.

"I want the company to move into the future without us," Maggie continued. "I don't mind being forgotten as long as the company prospers."

"I don't want to work for the company forever either," Tiny said after a deafening silence that witnessed the white return to Maggie's ears, neck, and face. "But this type of thing is hard to keep secret for long."

Maggie, now clearly aware of overplaying her position, rolled her eyes and sighed. "Here it comes."

Tiny leaned forward. "Yes, here it comes. I want access to the sales reports for the specialty markets."

"I can send you the encryption on the life reports as soon as I get back to my office," Maggie said.

"No, Margaret," Tiny said. "I want the annuity sales reports. I want to see exactly what Easton Frost has been up to. I want to see what sales he makes, to what companies, what he makes in commissions, everything."

Maggie shook her head. "Tiny, look. You don't know what you're asking for."

Tiny slapped her hand on the table and coughed. "I know exactly what I'm looking for. And you know exactly what I'm looking for." She motioned to Edie and Becca. "And these next gen ladies would already know what we're looking for if they'd dug further into their YouTube searches. It's now a matter of time before they know what I'm looking for."

Maggie drummed her fingers on the table. "With all due respect to you, Becca and Edie," she said. "Delores, you cannot trust them. They've only been in your world for a few weeks..."

"They're squeaky clean, Maggie," Tiny said. "They are as do-gooder girl scout as you and I used to be when the Kool Aid still had sugar in it."

"There's no possible way to know that..."

Tiny slammed her hand down on the table again. Then she took a measured breath and in a low, barely audible voice said, "None of them have known John Taylor in a biblical sense."

Something shot through Maggie Waller's spine. From the distant look on her face, a tell so deep and personal no amount of training could mask, she was reliving both a mental and muscle memory. *Here resided the thousand years, the thousand tears,* Edie thought. *Maggie Waller was the original* La Jetee.

"You'd better be one hundred percent on this, Tiny," Maggie muttered.

"You know I am," Tiny said, matching the soft ache in Maggie's voice.

"I'll send what I have later this afternoon," the other woman said.

Edie's thoughts were challenging to corral from the sudden conclusion of her meeting with Tiny, Becca, and Waller. Crossing the street above ground, rather than taking the tunnel between her building, and the one that housed the company cafeteria was failing to clear her mind. Her skin felt energized, activated in the rare sunlight; her pores were open and breathing for the first time in what felt like weeks. She knew what she needed to tell herself, what she needed to hear, but the impulse to ignore it and plunge into this new depth was loud and exhilarating. The adrenaline was drowning out the logic. The initial dose of surprise was now sustained with a sudden dramatic surge.

Squinting at the sparkling, icy shards of the sidewalk's plowed snow, she cleared her throat as though to speak aloud to herself. Her logic demanded a slow gate, wading in albeit with heavy stones in her pockets. They'd been in their new roles for six weeks. Certainly, her team's reputation balanced against taming new boss ego, and respecting compliance department tenure. Edie knew that women like her and her teammates were often promoted more on past performance and measured results than on potential and risk tolerance for the next assignment. *That's what feels foreign,* her electrified perspective suggested in counterpoint. *You don't know what it feels like to be given so much autonomy so rapidly. Everything up until now has been earned, fought for, taken.*

Edie glanced at her watch. She had ten minutes before meeting Easton Frost at the pre-arranged, and Tiny suggested, lunch. Mona and Austin hadn't dug deeply enough in researching him. But that hadn't been their motivation. What would have driven them to ask questions beyond the questions? Inwardly, Edie cursed the missed opportunity. She should have asked more. How had hero lightning struck twice for the same man?

No, Edie thought. *Those cynical, suspicious inquiries would have sprung from a personal source, not a professional one. What else was there on the open internet connected to Frost?* She was now meant to find out.

It was also time for him to describe in detail his position. How long had he been there? What was his promotional history? How long had he been so close to Taylor? Of course, *the answers could be as simple as dollars*, Edie thought. *Taylor and Frost could have nothing in common other than one being able to make large sums of money and the other being able to channel the energy into something profitable and name making in a corporate environment.* Edie's inner voice disagreed.

So it would be a friendly chat, an ego stroke, an opportunity to ask for mentorship or sponsorship in an indirect way. She'd ask for help understanding Taylor's decision-making process for promoting her team so quickly after so many stymied attempts at getting him to divulge his thoughts on her career path.

Selling off the exchanges scared her. Getting caught in the middle of an extremely unpopular project was a terrifying risk. Her years with the company, her track record, her ability to continue to climb could be shattered in nanoseconds. Were Maggie and Tiny playing her inexperience and eagerness like penguins pushing one another toward the edge of the ice flow, waiting for her inevitable fall into the cold, dark depths so they could peer over the side, scanning the black waters for bubbling crimson?

She would need to get Becca's mentor program in writing with language stating "other various projects as directly assigned."

Still, the notion of curing the disfigured model, of swooping in and preserving the future of the company for a couple of decades was intoxicating. If it were successful, she would peer over the snow banks, dare to look at opportunities in other companies, other industries even. If one could fix a cancerous, conservative, glacially crawling insurance company...

The actuarial data would uphold Maggie's position. The mutual exchanges could be viable under self-management, especially if allowed to be directed by actual policyholders like in normal mutually owned insurance companies. The good insureds would support the actions of running off high risk business with the resulting lower premiums on their own policies. The high risk insureds would continue to gravitate to the online auto insurers and non-standard companies. The captive sales force would make much higher commissions on brokering that business to other companies invested in buying up market share. The plan would work on paper and in actual practice.

Of course, the Unibomber's parents probably were happier before someone told them they were the Unibomber's parents. Taylor and the board would obviously react negatively and aggressively when their perpetual, death-defying child was exposed as the anti-Christ.

Edie realized she had mindlessly traversed the street, parking lot, building entrance, and elevator. She had no memory of pushing the button for the fourth floor. She was now seconds from the cafeteria and her lunch appointment.

What was Tiny really looking for? Why was Edie so readily accepted as the golden child, the chosen one, the new messiah? What is really because she and her team hadn't slept with anyone in the company? Had there really been that many women before her who were willing to do that? Edie deeply hoped that her justifications for taking this new risk weren't based on such a platform. The world was well into a new century. The sixties, seventies, eighties, and nineties were over, right?

The cafeteria was bustling with clatter and conversation. Matching the den was the aromatic pollution of daily specials and cleansing agents. Easton was waiting for her outside the corridor of elevators, fidgeting with his smart phone. Edie nearly had to invade his personal space for him to notice she'd arrived.

"Oh, hey," he muttered as he glanced up. "Sorry. Didn't see you there."

Edie smiled and motioned to his phone. "Did something come up? Last minute fire drill?"

Easton let out a held breath and grinned. "No, nothing I can't handle after lunch." He looked frazzled, distracted. The affect was alien. Beyond the pin stripe suit, shiny shoes, white on white shirt, and solid red tie, was asymmetry. The gelled back hair was as lopsided as his grin. His eyes weren't equally open, the left drooping a bit from lack of sleep or staring at a computer for too long.

"Thanks for agreeing to meet me again," Edie said before turning and heading for the salad buffet.

"Um, yeah," came his response immediately behind her. "I was a little caught off when I saw your email. I didn't think our last discussion went so well."

"It didn't," Edie admitted. "I became defensive when you offered the unsolicited career advice." She grabbed a tan tray and cold, damp plate for her greens.

"But now that's changed because you've been promoted," he said. "Your whole team is now outed from the event planning decoy."

She fixed her eyes on the choices of lettuce. "We don't feel exposed from it. In fact, quite the opposite. It's very liberating. Like being paroled. Although I don't have any experience in the penal system."

He chuckled.

Her face felt hot and red. She muttered an instant prayer that he wasn't giggling at her word choice.

"Was it so bad working undercover?" he asked.

She'd moved on to the diced veggie selections, nudging the person in front of her with an elbow. "Ever had to dye your hair for a promotion?"

"I've had to update my wardrobe, cut my hair, lose some weight, start running, learn how to play golf..."

"Not the same," she said. "Not even close."

"You're right," he said. "You sound as though you're getting defensive again."

She dropped the tongs onto the roma tomato slices and stood straighter. "You're right. I guess I'll be angry about that for a long time, but it wasn't your decision. You had nothing to do with it."

"For the record, I advised Taylor not to force the issue," Frost said. "I thought it wasn't necessary to bury your team at all. But let's just say John doesn't have the stomach for being the bad guy, the enforcer. He's more a politician, a crowd-pleaser."

"How did you become so close to him?" she asked.

"He found me," he replied. "I was working in the bank-owned life insurance department. There were two of us, two producers. They only needed one. And the regular corporate-owned life sales position was taken. Emerson does a fantastic job there. He brings in serious premium. So there was no need to displace him."

"So Taylor saved you from a down-sizing?"

"There was a new opportunity I wanted to create in specialty markets. On the annuity side. It meant working one on one with him for nearly two years just to R&D the marketplace and bring the products from inception to launch," he explained.

"A lot of pre-selling, getting the right prospects to nibble?"

The rapid questioning had brought them to the end of the salad line. Frost veered toward the deli. Edie grabbed a bottle of Diet Coke and headed for the cashier.

"I'll meet you at the table," Frost called out.

Edie nodded. "I'll just pick the first two-seater available."

She paid for her lunch and found a table while running through her current strategy. *He's frazzled about something,* she told herself. *Something's shaking up. It's good to stay on the offensive and keep control with questions.*

Sitting down facing away from the cashier was also a suitable move for her objectives. Keep him back, keep him interrogated. She opened her drink and guzzled before unwrapping her silverware and raking over her salad.

Easton set down his tray on his side of the table and was seated fast enough to stir up a cologne coated breeze. Edie identified the scent as Obsession.

"So what were you asking before we split up?" he asked.

"Did you have a lot of pre-sales with prospects?" Edie took a huge bite to force herself time to chew. The more she ate and he talked, the more control she maintained.

"Yes, well, that's been the single most successful piece," he said. "We were able to build a great deal of the product under key prospects' specs. It is a buyers' market. But the operation is so small, we can be very nimble. Also, you wouldn't believe the referrals I get now. When some executive leaves one company and goes to another, he usually implements most of the same strategy and tactics. It's been so consistent that we are starting to model sales projections on the timing of expired do-not-compete clauses."

Edie had swallowed the enormous mouthful of salad. "So are these retirement annuities?" Then she shoveled in another large bite.

Frost gave her a confused look as though he expected her to know the type of products he sold. "Not at all. They fund corporate promotions in their various retail spaces."

Edie furrowed her brow. "How does that work?"

Easton humphed. Leaning forward, he folded his hands together. "You've seen those fast food places that have the million dollar grand prizes?"

Edie nodded over another mouthful of food.

"Well, those are generally paid out fifty thousand dollars a year for twenty years," he continued. "So they are either self-funded from the fast food company, or they could be backed by a single premium immediate annuity, a SPIA."

"How does that work?"

"Well, with the system we have set up, the company running the promotion doesn't actually buy the annuity until the winner has been selected..."

"Once they win the right game pieces or pull the right tab off their drink?" Edie asked.

"Exactly," he said. "So because they don't know the age and sex of the person until the winner emerges, the company holds off on buying the SPIA. Then we price the product to the age and sex of the annuitant. We sell it as a fixed annuity, meaning that it doesn't follow an index or have any portion invested in a portfolio. We lock in the current assumption as the guaranteed interest rate for the life of the annuitized payment streams. So the company saves money because the cost of the SPIA is considerably less than the actual million dollars in prize money. The winner still has the ability to receive a total of a million dollars in payments."

"What happens if the winner dies before one receives the total payout?" Edie asked.

Easton squinted, then scrunched up his brow, masking his tell with a questioning look. "Well, there is no death benefit."

"So the person's husband or kids don't get the rest of the payout?" she asked. "Like if someone had received two hundred thousand of the payout and then dies, then what happens to the other eight hundred thousand?"

Easton chuckled. "There isn't really eight hundred thousand earned yet."

"On the annuity contract there is," Edie said.

"Yes, on the contract that offers no death benefit," he replied.

Edie shook her head.

"Okay, so I can tell you haven't had much experience with annuities," Frost said. "When someone buys an annuity, they aren't just putting their cash into a savings account with a better interest rate. They are buying accumulation units inside the annuity. Once annuitization occurs, the accumulation units convert to annuity units."

"I understand that part," Edie said.

Frost grinned out his disbelief. "That part of an annuity sale is the greatest issue from a compliance standpoint. Most people don't understand that an annuity acts as a guaranteed income stream. It doesn't act like a savings account. It isn't a liquid investment. You are actually buying a product and your funds are locked into that product."

"That's why there are surrender charges for annuities like with life insurance that offers cash value," Edie said.

"Exactly, but with our SPIA, there is a large one-time surrender charge because the annuity starts payment on the income stream immediately," he continued. "So the surrender charge is basically the loading of the cost of acquisition and processing for putting the annuity in place. If someone were to surrender a SPIA after receiving the first income installment, they would receive the total of their funding into the annuity less the surrender charge and the total of the payments received."

"So why isn't there a balance of the future payments to be paid out when someone dies?" Edie asked.

"The value of the accumulation units hasn't accumulated to the total of all the payments. The remaining units that haven't been used to make the annual payments to that point are still earning the guaranteed interest rate."

Edie pointed her fork at him. "And the units are priced based on the age and sex of the annuitant?"

"You got it," he said. "So if the winner is someone who's a seventy-year old man, the units are much cheaper because the life expectancy is much less."

"Only so many seventy-year old men make it to ninety," Edie added.

"Right again, but on the other side a forty-five-year-old woman has a much greater likelihood of seeing sixty-five and receiving all the payments of the guaranteed income stream." Now, Easton paused and took the first bite of his own salad.

"And you developed the market for these products?" Edie asked.

He motioned for her to give him a moment to swallow his food.

She put down her fork and gave him his time.

"Yes, that's the key. The big companies like Subway or McDonalds don't need to fool with insurance companies," he said. "They have the profit margins to cover their promotions."

"So where's the market then?"

"Mid-sized regionally based companies who want to compete with the big boys in their target demographics," Easton said. "Those are who I go after. You have to give them a value-add from the savings they'll see using our product. Like enhancing their other giveaways."

"Like what?" Edie asked.

"Like take a grocery store," he said. "In fact, the most recent one I landed was a chain in the Mountain West region, you know, Idaho, Montana, eastern Washington, Utah."

"Okay."

"Grocery stores have razor thin profit margins, but they are also big on celebrating local stores anniversaries," he said. "So they might offer a half-million dollar grand prize giveaway to the millionth customer to shop in that store. With the potential money they save in buying our SPIA, they can offer small giveaways to get more people to shop toward the big reveal. It's all about getting more returning customers."

"What are some of the other businesses you target?" Edie asked. Her mind was flooded with realizations and rationales. Her view of Frost was much clearer now. Either he was proverbially born on third, thinking he hit a triple, or his ego was actually earned from developing this business initiative and carving out such a niche position for himself.

"New car dealerships, payment streams on houses large real estate partnerships give away, professional sports teams, minor leagues, mainly," he said. "Someone has to fund the half-time, half-court shot prize money. The same for the shots on goal at mid-ice in the hockey rink or the punt, pass, and kick competition at college bowl games."

"That's crazy," Edie said.

Easton shrugged. "Like I said, someone has to fund it. Lots of times, smaller businesses get their local banks to extended a line of credit for those kinds of promotions because that's the traditional 'safe' method of funding." He added air quotes as he rolled his eyes. "But the opportunity is getting bigger and bigger. I've also leveraged my Oklahoma roots with the Native American casinos. That's taken the greatest amount of time and investment. And there are a lot of tribal courts and state regulations you have to get through."

"Was that how you first came up with the idea?" she asked.

Easton nodded. "It takes a few casinos to buy in before you can take it to the competing tribes. The tribes have been warring for longer than the United States has been a country, then we pushed them all together into two territories and systematically took back most of their land, which caused them to fight and sign treaties with each other. The casinos are a real game changer. Now, they compete for the white man's money. And their clientele aren't the high rollers in Vegas. Most are taking people's social security, disability, and welfare."

"That's sick," Edie said.

"It's a brilliant way for Native Americans to get their piece of the redistribution of wealth," Frost said a bit too quickly. "Not to get into a political discussion on economics over lunch."

Edie gave him the laugh he'd earned. "Sure. We don't have time for that."

"Let's just say that now a portion of the social security or welfare check goes to the tribe instead of all of it going to Wal-Mart, or the grocery store," Frost said. "And Oklahoma gets a higher rate of taxes from the casino than the local cities or counties get from sales taxes at retail shops."

"So as long as the state gets a cut of the profits from the casinos, they're happy," Edie said.

"Pretty much," he said. "So all I have to do is convince the state that we're not going to cut into their action, and it gets approved, as long as the state income tax level is on par with the casino's tax bill."

"So you brought this idea to Taylor, and he got you the funding for it?" Edie asked.

"About five years ago or so," Easton said. "It's been a lot of hard work. I started in the Denver office on the life side, like I said, working in the COLI/ BOLI market. Then we decided I'd be able to penetrate the casino market more successfully if I relocated back to Oklahoma. I came here once we set up enough relationships to keep it going. Now, we're trying to leverage that with some of the big Minnesota casinos. But as you can imagine the state of Minnesota is a little more liberal and asks a lot more questions than Oklahoma does."

"I came from the Colorado Springs regional office," Edie said.

"How long were you there?"

"A couple of years, so there wouldn't have been any overlap from when you worked in Denver," she continued.

Easton shook his head. "I never had a reason to go to Colorado Springs."

"Spoken like a true Denver citizen," Edie said.

Easton smirked. "Yes, most people in Denver avoid the Springs. But beyond that, the multiline channel was about the farthest thing from what I was doing as it gets."

"Trust corporate randomness for us to run into each other in Minneapolis," Edie said.

"So how's the promotion going so far?" Easton asked.

"Who's asking?" Edie returned.

"Both of us," Easton said. "I'm just asking for conversation. Unofficially, Taylor would like to know, too."

"I get the feeling that we weren't promoted as much as reassigned because we were becoming troublesome." There was power in acting as though one was putting everything on display, but Edie also didn't want to stretch the notion of needing to be rescued. The play would get her the ego reaction from him, but she didn't need him overextended into her personal world.

Easton nodded. "There's not a long life span for the hatchet."

"I knew that going in," Edie said. "I think we were more successful and bullish on cutting out the corruption than anyone planned."

"That's an understatement."

Edie sighed and made her eyes look tired. "It seems that Taylor has shuffled off a lot of protégés to compliance over the years."

"That's Tiny talking, isn't it?" Easton asked.

"You know Tiny?"

Easton grimaced and looked away. "Yes, I know Delores Campbell. Not a big fan of my line of business."

"Why is that?" Edie asked.

"Because she can't control it," he said, again a bit too quickly. "I'm basically an in-house sales agent. And I'm the only one, and I happen to write more business in premium and in number of policies that any other agent or broker in the company."

"We just had a meeting with Maggie Waller," Edie said. "She mentioned restructuring the life external wholesaler compensation."

Easton's face started to flush. "Yeah, well, the external wholesalers don't work as hard as I do, and they don't bring in nearly the direct business. Also, my commission is only two percent on the SPIA which is half what a producer in the field could make on it. Not to mention there is no override to pay to a general sales manager in the field."

"I don't know anything about what the wholesalers make," Edie said. "But apparently, a couple of them made more than Taylor that year..."

"They make half or three-quarters a percent on all premium coming in on their agents' and brokers' sales," Easton explained. "All for going to a couple of meetings and pushing the hottest product. Beating the company drum that doesn't need much beating in the first place."

"I'm sorry," Edie said. "I think I hit a nerve."

Easton faced his salad, then pushed it away. "Just watch your back. With both of them, Tiny and Maggie."

"Okay," Edie muttered. "I will."

"And you're right," he said. "They have a history of killing off people Taylor tries to promote."

"How so?"

He rolled his eyes and snickered. "They probably told you that I'm the star, the golden boy, right? It's not like Taylor hasn't tried to help other people develop their careers. He once told me he thought that compliance and finance were good 'tested in the trenches' assignments for six months or so. So if you can play their games for that long, there's probably a position on the other side waiting for you."

Edie's sense of guilt was alerting her. Easton hadn't been this easy to play before. Had she really stumbled upon such a highly sensitive, tender subject or was he playacting her like she was him? Clearly, he had no idea of the plan to sell off the channel. "Like what kind of position?"

"Haven't you discussed replicating your new model in other states?" he asked.

"Yes, but it appears there's only limited opportunity," she said. "Especially with the new project of internalizing the district manager offices inside the company."

"Yes, but even if Siemons' plan gets the green light, the company won't want dead weight being carried into the model."

Edie shot him a confused look. "If that were the case, why did we get reassigned to bird-dogging replacement business? Why not send us to another state to work the same program?"

Easton cleared his throat and pushed away his tray. "A couple of reasons. One, to give time for the improved profitability numbers to come in. Two, to move you and your team out of Siemons's way. He could blame you as a distraction for his project if you were still dragging him into termination review meetings. This way, if his project fails, he can't blame it on outside influences or bad agent morale."

Edie raised her eyebrows. "That actually makes sense. So your advice is to keep my head down until the dust settles on Siemons's project?"

"That's what I'd do," Easton said. "Trust me, if you can survive all the picking gnat turds out of pepper with Tiny and Maggie, then you'll have your choice of states to work."

"Won't they know where to roll out the internal district model by then?" she asked.

"Sure, but you'll be out of home office and Minnesota. And you'll be insulated from Tiny and Maggie from earning their trust."

"I feel as though they've already let my team in," Edie said. "They have us working on some pretty deep R and D."

"Don't trust it," he said. "It's like an elementary teacher handing out a thick stack of busy work. They're giving you stuff to observe how you work. Let me guess. They just handed you some top secret assignment that they've told you is something Taylor isn't aware of, or even better, something he doesn't actually approve of that they want to take over his head if the numbers make sense."

Edie channeled most of her adrenaline into remaining still to prevent showing any conscious tell.

Easton brought his blue eyes to bear. She allowed him her thought processed face, but remained otherwise stoic. Then she laid down the grateful damsel in distress, hoping it would derail his passive-aggressive tactics. She was counting on him reveling in his own heroism, clouding his objectives with his own inflated sense of awesomeness. "Thanks for having lunch with me, Easton. I know I wasn't very open to your help earlier."

"Don't mention it, Edie," he said. "I just caught you on a bad day."

Her laugh came out higher pitched than she wanted it to, but she followed through with it, willing her eyes bigger and her smile brighter. "Most likely, you did."

He returned her smile and then looked at his watch. "I should be getting back. I'm heading out to a couple new closings in Oklahoma tomorrow. I need to finish up a few things before I go."

Edie looked at her own watch. "I should be getting back, too."

Easton rose and pushed his chair back to the table. "Do you still go to the nine o'clock at church?"

Edie smiled again. "I've been going to the Saturday evening mass lately."

"You're kidding," he said with a chuckle. "You're far too young and attractive to be going to that service."

"I see a lot of people our age at that mass," she said, ignoring the compliment.

"Yes, but they're the ones who get it out of the way because they're too hung over to make it to church on Sunday," he said. "The rest are with their teens."

"That's probably true," she admitted.

"You should start coming back to the nine o'clock," he said. "I could use your help."

She rose from her seat and gathered up her things. "How so? You sign up for being an usher or Eucharistic minister or something?"

He rubbed the bridge of his nose. "Nothing like that. I'm not judgmental enough to dish out the crackers and wine, and there is a definite old man pecking order to ushering I'd upset if I volunteered."

"Then how exactly am I supposed to help you?"

"You could sit with me during mass," he said.

"I don't think we need to go to church together," Edie said. "I don't know you well enough for that. In fact, that's about as forward as I've ever had anyone come across."

Easton laughed as he put on his overcoat. "I didn't mean to suggest you going to church with me. Just meet me there and sit with me. What's so forward about that?"

Edie flexed her fingers into her gloves. "How would I be helping you?"

"I need some blocking and tackling," he said. "You know, like the opposite of a wingman at the bar. You could block me from getting pounced on. All those Cursillo ladies, and the grandmas looking to set me up with their granddaughters, and the other cougars looking for well... things best kept out of the church."

Edie couldn't shut her mouth. "You're suggesting that I block you from getting hit on at church by meeting you there and sitting with you?"

He threw up his hands. "Yeah, what's wrong with that? I know you have absolutely no interest. But you know... you're good looking enough for people to think something more is going on. That would make sense to most people."

She turned from him and started a brisk pace out of the cafeteria.

"What? It makes even more sense. You of all people are pretty immune to death ray looks and jealous murmurs, seeing how you don't lose sleep terminating agents in high volume."

Edie swiveled back on a heel. "So is that the price of getting your advice on how to handle my team's new promotion?"

"No, I was just asking for a favor," he said. "Has nothing to do with work stuff. At all. I swear."

"You're an idiot, Frost." The elevator bank couldn't have appeared further away.

"I bet that felt good to say," he said, clapping his hands and buckling over with laughter. "I bet you've held that in for a long time."

"You have no earthly idea," she growled.

"So I park on left side as you're entering the church," he said to the back of her head.

"Never going to happen, Frost."

"See you at nine o'clock then. Sunday. I sit on the far left toward the middle of the pews but on the far end of the row," he continued. "Or we could meet in the fellowship hall in the basement. There's a set of doors down there that lead out to the parking lot. Kind of a backstage entrance. We don't need to hold hands or anything. It *is* church, after all."

Chapter Twenty

"**E**die, got a minute?"

She could see half of Tiny's head jutting out of her doorway. An electric charge shot through her. She hadn't expected to see her boss this early. "Um, yeah. Yes," she said with a huff.

"Did I startle you?" Tiny asked as she opened her door further.

"Yeah, kinda," Edie said. "I'm on my way to a training session on annuities." She followed Tiny into the hoarder's labyrinth. This time, Edie noticed that all of the stacks of paper and file folders were roughly the same height. All stood about a foot taller than her new boss. *That's as high as she can reach,* Edie thought.

"There is a method to all this," Tiny said, anticipating a comment on her elaborate mess. "I can't fit another filing cabinet in here, and the company won't allow me a bigger office. The stacks are cases and supporting files from two years back to present. My filing cabinets are two to four years back. Years five to seven are in the department's storage room."

"No need to explain." Edie took the seat in front of Tiny's desk once Tiny had motioned for her to sit.

"You're heading to a training session on annuities?" Tiny asked. "Who's doing the training?"

"Becca. It's just for my team."

Tiny rubbed her jaw and scratched her chin. "Gearing up for the new product launch?"

Edie nodded. "Yes, I've had her do some research on the no surrender charge life products. Now, she's presenting on the no surrender change annuities."

Tiny harumphed. "Has she uncovered how insane that kind of annuity is?"

"Yes," Edie said. "I still have no idea why we'd offer one. Not sure what the exact market is for that type of product."

"It's designed only for specialty markets," Tiny replied. "Speaking of which, how was your lunch last week with Superboy? I never heard anything more."

"Yes, it's been a hectic week," Edie said.

Judging Tiny's non-plussed reaction, Edie realized that she wasn't making any time for excuses.

"The lunch went fine," Edie continued. "I got him to talk about what he does for the company. He explained how he developed the specialty market annuities with Taylor to fund promotional liabilities with fast food chains and grocery stores."

Tiny raised her eyebrows and nodded. "Did he saying anything about the Native American casinos?"

"Yes, he mentioned them, saying that was why he had been spending more time in Home Office," Edie said. "Something about going to the casinos here now that they've gotten some sales from the ones in Oklahoma."

"He must really want to impress you."

"Like I said, the last time I spoke with him he was offering career advice on how to handle Taylor," Edie explained.

"And that was totally unsolicited?" Tiny asked. Her tone dripped with distrust. She waved a dismissive hand. "Sorry. It's just, when's the last time you ever heard of a man offering a women mentorship without wanting something else in return?"

Edie leaned forward. "Well, it's not as uncommon as you might think, but I understand where you're coming from."

"You're still able to resist his snake charming?" Tiny asked.

Edie fought the notion to roll her eyes. "Yes, Tiny. I'm not interested in him..."

"Still don't find him attractive?" Tiny barked. "Not getting shool-girl giggly with him?"

Edie cleared her throat. "Yes, as we've discussed before. He's a very nice looking man, but he's too syrupy. And he knows he's physically attractive, which makes him pretty repulsive..." She abruptly stopped her explanation. A shock of discomfort coursed through her. This conversation was nearing inappropriate... again.

"Okay," Tiny said. "I'll take your word for it. What else did you two talk about?"

"He asked how things were going," Edie said. "I knew he was asking for Taylor, so I tempered my responses. But he completely assumed we're all miserable. He encouraged me to tough it out for another few months until Taylor could get Siemons's project on the internalized district office model off the ground. Then he mentioned that Taylor would want us to replicate our janitorial services to the other states."

Tiny sighed heavily.

"He's no fan of yours or Maggie's," Edie said to gauge Tiny's continued reaction.

Tiny's scalp pinkened under the rows of her spiked, highlighted hair, and she scrunched up her face. Otherwise, she remained silent.

"He was well aware of Maggie's work to retool the life wholesaler compensation, and he became very defensive about his own compensation."

"Really?" Tiny asked.

"He had a lot of planned responses for me," Edie continued. "Asking about you and Maggie, talking about his department and how he felt about you rolled off his tongue without much pause."

"You have any idea what kind of money he makes?" Tiny asked. Despite her attempts to remain stoic, Edie found Tiny's tells becoming defensive: heavy breathing, the redness about her face, the veins crawling around the edges of her drying eyes.

"You said around two million," Edie said. "But we haven't been able to find anything else on YouTube."

"Taylor had to elevate Frost's title to president over specialty markets to avoid causing unwanted attention from shareholders on the quarterly reports."

"That's a lot of money," Edie said, now acutely aware of her own tells.

"Also, he has full access to the deferred compensation plan like the other officers and wholesalers," Tiny said. "And he's maxed out on his 401k."

"He mentioned something about his commissions being half of what brokers and agents make on regular fixed annuities without any overrides going to a general manager like what usually pays out to the field."

Tiny now leaned forward and grinned. "That's also something he doesn't know." She rose and approached one spire of paperwork. Tonguing a thumb, her fingers crawled up one precipice. "Maggie sent me over the compensation model after we'd negotiated the terms of loaning out Becca." As though making a move in Jenga, Tiny pulled out a green file, two full inches under the top without agitating the rest of the supporting documents. "Taylor takes a full percentage point above Frost on his production. It was almost a million in cash for him if Frost only makes two million." She opened the file folder, leafed through it, and handed Edie a print out.

"That's crazy," Edie said.

"Of course, there's no reason for anyone else to know that right now," Tiny warned.

"Understood."

"Good." Tiny returned to her desk. "I know I'm keeping you from Becca's training, but there are a few more things we have to talk about."

Edie shrugged. "As long as she brings Austin and Mona up to speed, then we're good."

Tiny nodded and turned to her laptop. "I'm sending you a file on the raw experience data for the specialty annuities. They've been on the books for about four years. It's a dense file, showing the annuity payments and the function of the accumulating units converting over to annuity units to make the payouts happen."

"Okay."

Tiny coughed and swallowed something thick. "I don't have the right kind of eyes to make sense of all this, but my gut tells me Becca does."

"Most likely," Edie agreed. "Did Maggie send you that file then?"

"Yep."

"We need to get Becca's temporary assignment with Maggie's team in writing. Something that spells out the agreement..."

"I'm working on that," Tiny said. She kept her face bathed in her laptop's soft light.

"Need any help drafting the language..."

"No, Edie. I have it written."

"Then what's the next step? Is Maggie reviewing it?"

Tiny swiveled back around. "Yes, Edie. It's in review."

Edie looked down and nodded. "I don't feel comfortable having Becca continue to work on anything with Maggie until we have that agreement fully written and signed off."

"We're doing a lot of this on the fly, as you know."

"That's why we need the road map in 3D before we get too far," Edie said, cringing at the extended, tired corporate metaphor.

Tiny reassumed her lounging position in her strained chair. "Don't worry. On this, I trust Maggie completely."

"On this? Not on everything? Why the difference?"

Tiny chuckled. "Because on this Maggie is working on saving her own money and not just the company's."

Edie shook her head. "I can't rest on that alone."

"Well, you're gonna have to find a way," Tiny said.

"Frost was a full disciple of you and Maggie having it out for Taylor," Edie said. "He was fishing about projects you had us working on. Seemed to be speaking from experience, a history of you trying to turn Taylor's pets against him."

"Except you came to me before Taylor made you a pet," Tiny said.

"I don't like feeling like a pawn," Edie said. Her mind was reeling from her recent discussions with Becca on putting her in the spotlight.

"You and your team are the first crystal clean group he's sent us," Tiny said.

"Why have you been so dependent on the talent Taylor finds?"

"He squashes all our attempts to add positions and find people outside the company," Tiny said, increasing her volume and inflating her shoulders. "He claims that it's a developmental process for marketing and sales people to get experience in compliance so they can carry themselves better in the field. The shareholders and CEO buy it like snake juice."

"I'm the new kid here, Delores," Edie said. "I'm just trying to figure out what's going on. We're having to navigate through decades of brooding and plotting. Every little thing we say causes some ridiculous ripple effect."

As soon as she freed herself from her heated discussion with Tiny, Edie checked her mobile for the email containing the raw actuarial data on the specialty annuities. The file was too large to open or download, but being in the epicenter of the company's VPN enabled her to forward it directly to Becca.

Edie then checked her watch. She was nearly forty minutes late to the training session she'd scheduled. Recalling the last training session and the fall out from Becca caused Edie to grind her teeth until they popped. A calming sense washed over her as she had more time to explore the reflection of what had troubled Becca.

Being the center of attention had up until now served as an incendiary motivator. Edie's assumptions about the motivation's effect on Austin and Mona had been on target. But she had failed to determine fully what inspired her data head. Becca was more prototypical for corporate operations. Only marketing, sales support, and sales were narcissistic enough to crave accolades and hardware. Everyone else: new business, underwriting, product development, claims, HR, compliance, licensing, commissions, and training were prairie dogs, able to bark and squeal to alert others to danger but unwilling to do anything about it as individuals.

She stepped into the restroom to give herself time to think. Finishing with the necessities, Edie washed her hands and stared at herself in the mirror. The normal dark circles under her eyes were being replaced with puffy bags. She hated how hot her face became when she was angry or surprised.

She'd been given a full blast of seeking attention's downside. In Tiny's mind, in light of the history of running his death camp for the dishonorably and shamefully discharged, Edie and her hatchet women would have no lingering loyalty to John Taylor or the multiline channel that brought them into the corporate world. Tiny's logic had several flaws, Edie admitted, but the end result was terrifyingly close to reality. Edie did not feel much loyalty to Taylor.

He hadn't provided her any indication of further advancement.

He'd sent his minion to keep watch over her.

He'd failed to act ethically, choosing right now over right regarding the Laurent termination proposal.

He'd refused to be her mentor and had shattered the trust of being her sponsor by taking Siemons's position.

He hadn't expected her to live up to her potential. His experiment had been too successful. He had discarded her and her team as he had done dozens of times before. Only Edie hadn't made such an unforgettable mistake. She hadn't become emotionally compromised or physically entangled with the man.

Having no experience to rely on fully, she couldn't determine if she had more reason to support Tiny's unapproved inquisitions or less motivation to enact revenge on John Taylor. Edie refused to feel hurt. Betrayed? Yes. Disappointed? Certainly. Willing to kill... Mona would give an emphatic affirmative laced with cuss words. Austin would tell her no and ask her to find a deep inner will to rise above, to overcome. Becca would provide information, hold up a mirror, and force Edie to arrive at her own decision.

Edie blinked moisture back into her eyes and shook her head until it returned to this more pertinent state of consciousness.

Becca's training session. She revved her hope, thinking that Mona and Austin would treat Becca more fairly, more appreciatively. Edie was in no mood to placate them. She braced herself instead in the resolve of handing them both written warnings for general insubordination if they had so much as snickered or rolled their eyes during Becca's presentation. Guilt was a sharp weapon. Guilt for missing the bulk of the meeting and not being there to defend Becca coupled with anticipated resentment for more of Becca's grief for forcing her into greater responsibility was enough to run Austin and Mona through, to impale them both with stinging documentation.

She fidgeted with her hair and straightened her shirt and pants, then pushed through the restroom door, heading toward the small, boxed in conference room.

Austin huddled over her smartphone. Mona, legs propped up on the table, cradled hers. They both did little to hide their texting dialogue.

Spreadsheets whirred across the projection from Becca's laptop. Becca, herself, was lost in the insurance matrix. Her lips and eyeballs were drying and cracking.

"What's going on?" Edie asked gruffly.

"Just finished," Mona muttered. "Where were you?"

Edie took the seat opposite Becca and her pivot tables. "Tiny pulled me into her office."

Austin looked up from her phone and set it down. "Judging from how you look, that didn't go very well."

"It was fine," Edie said quickly. "She was just looking for an update on Becca's special project with Maggie's team."

"I've queried the forecasts and ran all possible Monte Carlos," Becca said. She refused to tear herself away from what she was working on. "Should have the probabilities back early next week. Then we can solve for a high and low on retention and sales forecasts using the standard geometric rates to determine future viability."

Mona and Austin gave Edie their widest eyes.

Never mind, Edie mouthed. I'll tell you later.

"We're all finished with the crash course in annuities," Austin said in a louder than necessary volume.

"How did it go?" Edie asked.

Mona pulled her feet from the table and sat up. "Better than the life insurance session."

"Yes," Austin agreed. "Annuities are much more straight forward. Much less confusing."

"Easier to sell," Edie said. "It's much more exciting to sell the growth and guaranteed money than the heartache of dying young."

"That, too," Austin said.

"I think I could sell life insurance," Mona said.

"That's because you don't mind talking about death," Austin said.

Mona shrugged.

"How did it go, Becca?" Edie asked. "Did they listen to you?"

With starry eyes, Becca nodded. "These relationships are opposite their usual correlations."

"What?" Edie asked. "Are you waxing eloquent on our refined, ever evolving group dynamic?"

Austin looked lost. Mona had mentally dismissed herself.

"What are you working on, Becca?" Edie asked.

"That file you sent me," Becca said. "On the specialty market annuity experience over the last four years."

Edie leaned forward. "What are you seeing?"

"The hockey stick production increase cliché is demonstrated somewhere between the eighteenth month and twenty-first month of the product's life," Becca said. Her voice was eerily devoid of connotation or emphasis.

"Is that normal?" Edie prodded.

"For annuities and other commoditized life insurance products like term, yes," Becca said.

"How long has she been working on this?" Edie asked Austin.

"Ten minutes or so," Austin said. "As soon as she received it from you."

Edie cleared her throat. "What else do you seen, Becca? Where are the correlations different?"

"There is only intrinsic profitability on SPIAs," Becca said. "Because they pay out immediately once issued, the remainder of the lump sum purchase is invested by the company in various portfolios while only crediting the policy with the current interest rate. On this product, it's locked in for the life of the payment stream."

"That's what Frost told me the other day," Edie said.

"The company's profit on the product is in the positive arbitrage between the investment experience on the funds minus the current assumption on the interest rate credited to the policy."

Edie nodded. "The company bears the investment risk for its own profit while providing the insured with a guaranteed payment stream backed by the larger risk pool of thousands of other annuitants."

"That's not true here," Becca said. "The profit margin is massive."

"Okay, so what's different?" Edie asked again.

"The larger the purchase of accumulation units, the greater the profitability," Becca said.

Edie looked to Mona and Austin, but they weren't able to keep up with the conversation. Edie reminded herself that it was like speaking directly to a computer. Or a know-it-all on those ridiculous forensic whodunits like *CSI: Cleveland* or whatever the baby boomers watched these days.

"So the larger the lump sum going into the SPIA, the more profitable the risk?" Edie asked.

"Yes," Becca said. "That's an inverted correlation from normal experience. It's not that smaller SPIAs aren't more profitable. It's that the investment risk bourn by the company is much less on a hundred thousand dollars than on a million dollars given the regulations insurance companies are under for their investment portfolios."

"So what's making these specialty SPIAs more profitable on the heavy end?" Edie asked.

Becca finally looked up from her work. She blinked away the blur and visibly swallowed. "The mortality experience on the larger SPIAs."

"Meaning what?" Edie asked. But her body already knew the answer. Whether she was subconsciously reading Becca's body language: the dilation of her pupils, the quivering of her lips and voice, the trembling of her overworked fingertips, the jilted pattern of her breathing, the erratic pulse from her jugular. Or the hollowness of her own being: in the marrow of her bones, the emptying of her face, the plummeting of her stomach, Edie knew the reason.

"The annuitants in the larger SPIAs are dying," Becca said.

"At what percentage?" Edie managed to say.

"Nearly one hundred percent," Becca whispered.

"Does it track with their ages?"

Becca shook her head. "There is no actuarial reference point..."

"English, for crying out loud!" Mona bellowed.

"It doesn't matter how old they are," Becca said.

Edie looked down and willed herself to remain still. She took a deep breath and returned her gaze back to her team. "Is there a tie between how long they hold onto the policy before they die?"

Becca's fingers flew over her keyboard and the pivot table shifted to portray different data. "They all die sometime after receiving the second annual payment but before receiving the third."

"And who receives the death benefit?" Austin asks. "Are the beneficiaries listed in that report?"

Edie covered her mouth. "There is no death benefit on these SPIAs."

Becca looked back up. "The remaining income stream is reabsorbed by the company."

Mona bolted from her chair. "Who else knows about this?"

"That's not the most important question," Edie said.

"Who knows we know?" Austin asked for her.

Chapter Twenty One

"I don't want to know where you are," Edie hissed on her cell phone to Austin. "And you can't know where I am or anyone else is either. Not until we know what we're dealing with." She hung up without saying goodbye.

She and Becca had found a small, windowless conference room deep in the second floor hallways that housed the new business processing and underwriting departments. Once inside, she'd propped a chair underneath the door handle and slid the room's only table against it. Then she turned to Becca. "Will your internet cord reach if we sit at the table like this?"

Becca, catching tears from her eyelashes with the flesh of her thumbs, nodded.

Edie grabbed her shoulders and squeezed them. "We're okay. No one saw us leave the sixth floor."

Shaking her head, Becca pointed to the ceiling. "They have us and everyone else on the security cameras."

The hum of the fluorescent tube lighting overhead was deafening. Edie's heartbeat wailed against her chest and neck. She could feel every hair on her arms. "Okay, but let's think about this. So we know they could track us on the cameras, but they don't have a reason to yet. Even Tiny doesn't know what we've found, and she sent me the file to send to you. She doesn't even suspect that we were going to find what we found. We're still safe. As long as we don't overreact..."

Edie straightened her back and dropped her hands from Becca's shoulders. Then she smeared on a smile and dragged an empty chair to the table.

"They still have record of you barring the door," Becca said, remaining motionless.

Edie crossed her legs and extended her smile. "Yes, but they don't know what they need to be looking for. Please sit down and plug your laptop back in."

"I have the file downloaded onto my computer," Becca explained. "I don't need to be connected to the VPN. I don't need to access the shared drives."

"Okay, then. Sit down and explain to me how you know what you know."

Becca set down her laptop and brought the last chair to the table. "The first thing I noticed is the final annuity payment dates for each annuity." She opened her computer and pulled up the spreadsheet.

"Then what?"

"Then I correlated the number of payments since the inception of the policy."

"And that's when you noticed that most don't last past two or three payments," Edie said.

"Yes, and because there is no death benefit payable to a beneficiary, the company retains the balance of the annuity units," Becca explained. "We're netting the balance between the single premium paid to purchase the annuity and the total amount paid out to the promotion winner."

Edie peered into Becca's computer screen. "Can you run a total number of annuities sold, the total in premium, and the net retention the company is keeping?"

"Give me a second." Becca's fingers rattled over the keyboard.

Edie watched her work and made a mental list of her new, tentative strategy. There was no written procedure for how to handle this. No one to call, no anonymous tip line to human resources or legal she could turn to. She'd confiscated the company-issued smartphones and tablets from her entire team and had locked them into a drawer in her office. She'd told Austin and Mona to scatter, warned them only to use their personal phones, and not to access any company website from them. She'd insisted they turn off all GPS and navigation systems, told them not to let each other know where they were heading, told them to hide out in libraries, or coffee shops, or better yet in eyeshot of a police station, told them to stay in public, stay in the seven-county metro area, but stay away from downtown and uptown Minneapolis.

"There are over eight hundred total policies," Becca said, snapping Edie back into the present.

"He's written over two hundred a year?" Edie asked.

Becca shrugged. "It's an annuity. You don't actually have to be in person to close them. You can email the contracts, have the owner sign, scan, and email them back. Most don't even have issued checks for the payments. Just account numbers and authorization signatures on the application."

"What's the total amount of paid premium?"

"Just a second," Becca muttered. "It's just under six hundred million."

Edie held her head in her hands. "You've got to be kidding me."

"Average premium is around seven hundred and fifty thousand."

"On promotional payment streams?" Edie asked. "That's crazy."

Becca nodded. "It's hard to imagine. Also, we've paid out just over one hundred twenty million."

Edie's throat clinched. "What's two percent of the six hundred million? Just use round numbers." She could hear the clattering of keys, but she couldn't comprehend any sense of timing with this new gravity enshrouding her body.

"It's twelve million," Becca said.

"We've paid him out twelve million." Edie shook her head as she recalled what Tiny had told her earlier that morning. "And Taylor's supposedly taken an additional six. Tiny has it wrong. They must be hiding the rest of the commissions."

"Edie, the acquisition costs on these are higher than a three percent commission. It's more like five percent all in," Becca said.

"It's that in line with industry?"

"It's hard to tell," Becca answered. "I don't have any other actuarial data to run it against. But..." Her pause took light-years. "The column for premium taxation at the corporate or entity level is blank."

"We're not paying taxes on this business?" Edie asked. "Good lord, this gets thicker and thicker."

"Do you think they are killing these annuitants?" Becca whispered.

"How many still have active payment streams?"

More key rattling, then, "Six hundred and ninety-two."

Edie's eyes lost focus and her head felt like it had taken flight. "How many are deceased?"

"One hundred twenty-one," Becca said.

Edie's fingers vibrated against her mouth. "They've killed one hundred and twenty-one people?"

"There are one hundred and twenty-one people who are showing as no longer receiving payment streams," Becca said. "That's all the data shows."

"Give me a scenario where they aren't dead, contractually speaking," Edie said.

"There really isn't one, Edie."

Edie leaned back, and, closing her eyes, rubbed her temples. "So if I just won a million dollars in twenty installments of fifty thousand, and I'd received one hundred thousand for the first two years and then in the third year, I didn't receive anything, my first step would be to call the fast-food chain's corporate office."

"And they'd tell you to call the issuing company," Becca said.

"And if they didn't pay me, I'd be screaming to high heaven about it," Edie said. "I'd be getting an attorney like in those claim settlement commercials. The ones where the old guy yells 'It's your money. Use it when you need it!'"

"And there'd be some sort of public record of the lawsuit being brought against the company in whatever state and county the contract was executed in."

"Which would be Hennepin County because our home office is located in Minneapolis, right?" Edie asked.

"Most likely," Becca said. "We should be able to do a basic Google search on active cases against the company and cross-reference the annuitant names with the plaintiffs."

"Couldn't we also do a search on death certificates or related stories on accidental deaths?" Edie asked.

Becca nodded and chewed a hangnail on her thumb.

"How long would that take you?"

Becca spit out a piece of dried skin. "A couple of days max."

"Do we have that kind of time before anyone gets wise to what we know?"

"Depends on how long you want us to stay away from the office," Becca reasoned. "You have to decide if we're really in physical danger coming to work."

Edie stood up and then grabbed the back of her chair as the blood drained from her head. "Good God, this is crazy. Okay. Let me think. Okay. So…Maggie sends the file over to Tiny. Tiny sends it to me. I send it to you. I dismiss my team within forty-five minutes of sending you the file."

"Someone has to be on the inside, Edie. Someone in Claims would have to process the receipt of death certificates in order to stop the payments," Becca explained. "Someone other than Taylor and Frost."

"Well, there's plenty of additional commission in a slush fund somewhere," Edie said. "If Frost is making sure these people are dead, or orchestrating their deaths..."

"We don't know any of that," Becca said. "You're jumping all over the place. Stick to what we can prove, Edie. Come on."

"There's enough money in this to get all of us killed, Becca."

"I know that," Becca snapped. "But we can't go around making assumptions. Taylor could be paying to kill these people out of his cut."

Edie shook her head. "They're too close, Taylor and Frost. If one of them is in on it, both of them are."

"It still could have nothing to do with either of them," Becca argued. "We have no way of telling at this point. You need to focus on giving us time to find out more about these deaths."

Edie shook her head to clear her mind. "You'll have a pretty good idea in a few hours, right? It won't take you two full days."

"To research each annuitant, to be sure, I'll need the entire time," Becca said.

Edie fought down her rage at Becca's insistence. "Can you do that from a library or use a local Wi-Fi? Somewhere where the IPS address is random, hard to track?"

Becca shrugged. "Shouldn't be a problem. Like you said. They don't know that they should be looking for us yet."

"Think, Firebaugh," Edie muttered. "I'll put in for sick time for all of us and email Tiny saying we've all come down with a twenty-four-hour bug."

"Don't put in the sick time until we've returned to work," Becca warned. "Otherwise, it will look pre-meditated. We don't know who is canceling the payments. They'd have access to the claims systems, but they don't necessarily have to be working in claims now."

"It could be anybody," Edie agreed.

Edie felt better having Becca leave work first. Watching Becca gather her things, and walking back with her to the six floor gave Edie more time to rationalize what she felt into sound logic. Easton Frost was involved in these deaths. The truth had a certain resonance, a constant tone and pitch, the sound of purity even if the volume was low. Like the small voice Father Tim called the Holy Spirit that allowed itself to be drowned by the distracting noise pollution of white lies and acceptable denials. Only in the silent moments of prayer, calm reflection, and meditation that allowed the brainwaves between planes of consciousness to emerge could one hear the truth, the actual alignment of vibrations that synced into one solid hum.

The emptiness of Home Office, mainly due to lunch hour, provided the tranquility to search for that voice, but distraction and accented, punctuated miscues drew her mind away from it: the clicking of shoes in the hallway leading to and from the elevator corridors, the grind and jilt of the elevator car, the ding of arriving at the six floor.

That dreadful misalignment abounded, invaded her body, her systems, breathing, her heartbeat, the adrenaline unmercifully cycling and recycling through her, perspiration that chilled at the precise nanosecond it left her pores. This coupled with the silence, the solitude of white noise, the slowing of time's persistence, was Edie's physical identification of Hell, a wretched negative space, a vacuum of indecision and inactivity, her flight-or-fight mechanisms waging victoriously over peace and calm and surrender. That urgent, reptilian need to seize control, to grasp at action, any action, any movement to assure her that she still held dominance over indifference, insignificance, and acquiescence. *It's Satan's final war for the soul, fought on the plains of corporate culture*, Edie heard that small voice say. The last of the parlor tricks where he was able to reverse the roles of loving surrender into the very action of sin, where inactivity and paralysis caused the greatest harm as though he were bent on proving after centuries the admonitions of writer and artist William Blake were wrong, that the unity of perfect truth could only be found in ignoring the feeble notion that anyone could do anything to change the outcome, tempting people to take back control when the last vestige of achievement was absolute nothingness.

Edie felt someone brush her elbow. "Are you okay?" came Becca's distant whisper.

Edie blinked the dryness from her eyes. "Yeah," she said, grogginess scraping her vocal chords.

"Where did you go?" Becca asked.

The volumes and rhythms of the present blew out the fog in Edie's mind.

"You're quiet," Becca said. "It's scarring me."

"Sorry, I just got lost in thought," Edie said.

"You went somewhere deep," Becca muttered. "It's like you wiped off all expression. Like you had hypnotized yourself."

"Frost goes to my church," Edie said.

They rounded the corner that led to their desks. Edie followed closely behind Becca until they arrived at her cubicle. Becca wasted no time grabbing her purse and a couple other personal items. Then she turned back to Edie.

"Okay, he goes to your church," Becca said. Checking her computer backpack to make sure she had everything, she darted her eyes back to Edie's.

"He once got up and gave a lay homily about his encounter with God and the vision of Heaven he received," Edie muttered. She was forgetting to blink again.

"You're still trying to justify believing he's involved," Becca said. "We have to stick to what we can prove. Right now, you can't prove anything you're feeling."

Edie grimaced and clinched her teeth. "You need to help me prove what I already know in my heart."

"Well, I'm heading out right now to find a coffee shop so I can start looking up what happened to these people," Becca said. "But whatever I find is going to be whatever I find. It's impossible to tie that to him. Either he's in the middle of it or he isn't."

"There has to be some way to trap him, some way to get him to admit his guilt," Edie said.

"That's for you to come up with," Becca said. "I'm just looking for the data. It's not for me to interpret."

"I know that, Becca," Edie snapped. Shaking her head, she took a deep breath and wrung her fingers together. "I'm sorry. My nerves are shot. I didn't mean to yell at you."

Becca shrugged. "It's okay. This is really terrifying. But if it makes you feel any better, nobody else could handle this like you."

Edie tried to smile but couldn't make the muscles in her face cooperate. "Thanks, Becca."

"It's almost like you've been training for something this heavy for a couple of years. Pretend you're an Olympic athlete. Most of those people spend years training for something that takes fifteen seconds to do."

That enabled the smile to break free. "Thanks, Becca."

"Seriously, Edie." Becca patted her shoulder. "You're doing the right thing. Just don't let the anger take over. Think of all the terminations you've delivered, and all those successful termination review boards. You were calm and concise, and you had all the evidence before you came to the table."

Edie nodded. "People weren't dying then, and other people weren't in danger."

"We will stop them regardless whether it's your church buddy or not," Becca said. "Stay focused."

Edie knocked a crescendo from timid to formidable on Tiny's office door then listened for the ruffling, scooting, and grunting that told her Tiny was buried inside.

"Just come in," came a muffled growl. "I hate having to get up to answer the door."

Edie opened the door and wedged herself between the stacks of dead and processed trees until she could see Tiny leaning back from her desk in that lopsided position.

"Edie Firebaugh," Tiny announced. "You look like you know something you didn't this morning."

Edie sat down and stiffened her position, running through her muscle memory all her preparations for review boards and discussions with John Taylor. "It's been a very long day."

"How did the annuities training go?" Tiny asked. "I have to admit I didn't peg Becca as the trainer type."

Edie smirked and laughed the edge off her nervousness. "She's not. At all. But she's the best at decoding all the sales jargon and deciphering the technical pieces of product development."

"How'd the other two manage?" Tiny asked.

"They powered through it," Edie said. "It's not really in their skill sets. Mona has been our executioner, and Austin consoles the dead."

Tiny humphed. "I'm sure all that pomp and circumstance is still necessary in the multiline channel. I can still see those district managers hiring mourners and throwing wakes for their terminated agents."

"All while secretly licking their lips over steepled fingertips, thinking of policy reassignment manipulation," Edie added.

Tiny grinned with a cocked eyebrow. "You enjoyed killing them, didn't you?"

Edie looked down and shook her head.

"It's okay to tell me, Edie," Tiny said. "I know I would have enjoyed it. Especially the morons who thought they could get away with it."

"It did provide hours of free entertainment."

Tiny clapped her hands. "What I wouldn't give to have been there when you handed that idiot Capote his walking papers."

"That was pretty rewarding," Edie admitted. "So was knifing Collins in Duluth."

"I never met him," Tiny said.

"He wasn't around for very long."

Tiny waved her hand, signaling she wanted to change the subject. "So back to Becca. She hates training, getting up in front of people, making presentations, but she does it anyway. For you."

"Yes."

Tiny smirked again and rubbed her jaw. "That's a good reflection. Your team is pretty loyal then."

"We're all very close. That happens when you're either hated or kept locked up as a dirty secret."

"Having to dye your hair probably helped with team building, too," Tiny added.

"It provided an 'us against the world' edge," Edie said. "And relocating us from Colorado Springs also solidified our relationships."

"They'll follow you anywhere now, won't they?" Tiny didn't wait for an answer. "So the question becomes who will *you* follow."

Edie froze. Tiny was giving her every indication that she already knew about the file Becca had pried apart. This signaled a bluff. As good as executives and directors were at corporate politics, they still routinely lost their savings at card tables during company trips to Vegas. Good was never really good enough. *To Tiny's credit though,* Edie thought. *She has been establishing trust with me. She's more open right now than she ever has been.* Edie realized she hadn't been exposed to quitting time Tiny.

"Do you know where Easton Frost is?" Edie asked.

Tiny furrowed her brow. "Why would I know where that putz is? Couldn't you just send him an email and see if his out of office notification comes back?"

"Just wondering if you'd seen him around."

"Wanting to stare at him over lunch again?"

Edie rolled her eyes. "That's absolutely the last thing I want right now. Do you know who processes the payments for the special annuities?"

Tiny squinted in thought but kept her eyes fixed on Edie. "I assume it's someone down in processing. We could find out easily enough."

"Without attracting attention?"

"You mean without alerting Maggie?"

"Among others."

"What did you find in that file I sent you?" Tiny asked.

"I'm not sure yet. Becca's still analyzing it," Edie said.

"Where are Mona and Austin? I haven't seen them all day."

"They left early. Both were complaining about feeling sick," Edie said.

"So they made it through the training and something made them sick?"

"Probably just a stomach bug."

Tiny grunted and snorted back a drip from her sinuses. "Did I ever tell you why our company in particular came to despise STOLI and IOLI?"

"Is that the where a stranger or investor buys a life policy from an insured or original owner?" Edie asked. She wasn't prepared for a long, winding story about yesteryear, but she needed more time and expression to determine Tiny's angle.

"You got it." Tiny leaned further back in her chair and folded her hands over her belly. "Now, granted, there are reputable viatical settlement companies out there, the ones who buy for more than cash value but less than death benefit for people who are terminally ill and need the cash. It's big business. It's unfortunate that more companies aren't trying to develop better critical illness policies, but where's the money in helping someone keep their life insurance in force until the death benefit claim is paid?"

Edie knitted her eyebrows together.

Tiny chuckled. "Don't tell me you're still too naïve to appreciate the underbelly of our business. Surely, you heard about that huge class action against those New York based life companies not paying death benefits dating back to the eighties."

Edie nodded but kept silent.

"I'm talking more about those shyster companies out there that buy life policies off people only to convince them to invest the proceeds into other Ponzi schemes, like land development with forged deeds, that kind of thing," Tiny continued.

"Okay. I'm with you."

"I had just moved over from sales support. I'd been working in licensing and commissions for the multiline channel. After a brief time in marketing with Maggie..."

"Maggie Waller was in marketing?" Edie asked.

"She was really good at it, too," Tiny said with a grin. "Could have been the Chief Marketing Officer if she'd stuck with it. Coulda had Dela Torre's gig. But that's, well, actually I think the stories are kind of connected."

"Really?"

Tiny had settled into full narrative mode. Her tells dissipated into recalling the details of a time long past. Her eyes blinked less and rested their gaze just above Edie and to her right, which signaled memory and honesty. "So we're outside smoking one day in like late March I think it was."

"You and Maggie?"

"Yeah, coming back from lunch. And this guy jumps out of his car. He was parked right out front in the visitor lot. Nice enough guy. He was really upset, totally freaking out. He was probably mid-thirties. Wearing a coat and tie, you know from when IBM set the standard for how men had to dress."

"IBM?"

"Good lord, I forget how young you are, or how old I am," Tiny said. "Never mind. Anyway. So this guy comes up to us, looks like he's about to cry or puke. And he's starts begging us for help. Says he's just come back from Vegas. Has this story of selling his life policy to a loan shark out there one night while he was drunk with his friends. Needed more gambling money. He starts bawling, talking about his wife and kids and how he thinks he's going to get killed. And wanting our help to get his policy canceled so he can go back to the shark, some guy he said was a part of the Russian mafia, and work out another payment or another kind of collateral."

The blood drained from Edie's face. The story was becoming the tell. Tiny was actually telling Edie her tell, not displaying it. "Maggie stayed stone-cold. You know the first thing she asked him? She actually told him she wouldn't help him one bit until he came clean."

"Had he cheated on his wife in Vegas?" Edie guessed.

Tiny snapped her fingers. "You got it."

"Did he? Did he cheat on her?"

"He said he didn't. He swore up and down and to God and his mother's grave, even though she wasn't dead yet." Tiny humphed and coughed again. "I don't know. I believed him. I can hear the truth well enough. It just sounds different. Even when it's just your voice in your head. The truth has a confidence in it. You sound like you have nothing to lose when you tell it. You know you're not going to lose your soul from telling the truth. Deep down everybody believes that, so the truth sounds different."

"I was just thinking the same thing not ten minutes ago," Edie said.

Tiny nodded as though she had read Edie's mind. "Maggie can't hear the difference. She doesn't have the ear for it. It's all numbers with her. That's her way of finding truth. You know how there are some people who like to talk? Others have to be face-to-face with people to really feel like they know them? Maggie's all math and numbers. She's a purist. Doesn't trust any other form of communication. Kind of like your Becca."

"So she didn't believe him," Edie said. "The man who needed your help?"

"I had to tell her it was okay to help him."

"So what did you do?"

Swiveling her chair away from Edie, Tiny peered out the sliver of window she hadn't plastered with paperwork. "I knew there was nothing we could do. To this day, I don't know how the man had his policy with him in Vegas. Unless he had the plan for selling it, and then buying it back if he ever got down to help him get back up. Some people and their self-destructive tendencies, I guess. Anyway, the loan shark had all the proper transfer of ownership paperwork." She shook her head and turned back to face Edie.

"It's still hard not to believe it was pre-determined, pre-meditated. Like the guy wanted to die, but didn't have the guts to kill himself or was afraid the policy wouldn't pay if he did. Maybe he got conned into thinking the shark would honor a deal on a portion of the death benefit cash. That makes the most sense. Sounds like a fine plan until you realize you're going to die soon, you just don't know when or how painful it's going to be. Talk about your ultimate Hitchcock suspense thriller."

"You couldn't do anything for him, I take it."

"Not one thing," Tiny agreed. "He was no longer the owner. Couldn't make any changes to the policy or cancel it. He couldn't force us to refund him the money on his last premium payment, and it was an annual premium policy for a hundred thousand face amount."

"That's all?"

"That wasn't bad in the eighties," Tiny said. "Anyway, three days later, he winds up dead. The cops found him in an uptown alley."

"And the death benefit claim?"

"Came in five days later once the county coroner's office issued the death certificate."

"Was there an investigation?" Edie asked.

"The policy had been sold six times since the man had sold it to the loan shark. The paper trail left the country, owned in Russia when it was all done," Tiny explained. "Back then, we weren't friendly with the Russians so there wasn't much they would provide. We paid the claim to the legal owner. I don't think the cops ever closed the case. Never found the killer. Probably just some hired gun picked up locally."

"So the man was killed because he sold his life insurance policy?" Edie asked.

"He effectively put a hit on himself," Tiny said. "That's the real danger in STOLI and IOLI. Agents helps customers come up with a value on their lives for income replacement and to support the families they leave behind. Strangers don't value your life. They'd just as soon have you dead for way less than your wife and kids."

"Then what happened?"

Tiny shrugged. "The company cooperated with law enforcement of course. The wife tried to sue the company, but that got dismissed. We all went on with our lives. Maggie moved over to finance, quit smoking on that side of the building, eventually quit smoking all together. I got promoted to compliance. And I still sneak a smoke every couple of days or so. We all gotta die of something, right?"

Edie looked down at her hands, which wouldn't stop trembling.

"So you haven't really digested the actuarial data on the specialty annuities yet?" Tiny asked. "And half your team came down with the stomach bug after the training session."

Edie nodded. "I should have a report on the commissions and the experience first thing tomorrow."

"Ever wonder why insurance types love gambling so much?" Tiny asked.

Edie couldn't follow her stream on conscious but humored her. "I know agents love to gamble."

"We deal in risk management all day long," Tiny said. "We are the worst at convincing ourselves we're in control. Gambling gives us release."

"So you were close with Maggie back then?" Edie said, finding nothing else to offer the current subject.

"We still are close," Tiny said. "We've learned not to show it in the office."

"So you trust her? I know that's not my place to ask," Edie said quickly.

Tiny learned forward far enough for her glasses to spill down her nose. "Absolutely."

"So if she knew something egregious was going on, she would act on it?"

"She single-handedly led the charge to cut off the excessive compensation to the life wholesalers last year," Tiny said. "She's not winning any popularity contests. Just come out with it, Edie. What are you holding back?"

Edie squared her jaw and lifted her face. "You mentioned her wanting to protect her deferred compensation the other day."

"Wait until you get to our age," Tiny growled. "Wait until you've seen the market tank and push back your retirement five to seven years to give it time to recover. I was just playing devil's advocate on the old what's-in-it-for-me attack."

"Okay," Edie said and rose from her seat. "Like I said, I should have a good handle on the specialty annuity data first thing tomorrow."

Tiny Campbell stood from her seat and rested her fists on her desk. "Edie, I know we haven't worked together for a long time. And I'm not accustomed to being so direct." She huffed. "Actually, I know that must sound absurd coming from me. But I get a strong sense that you know something bothersome if not terrible."

Edie's eyes watered with frustration. She looked down and back up, then shut her eyes to force away the accumulation. Her ability to remain silent stunned her.

Tiny squinted at her and rose to cross her arms. "Go home, Firebaugh. We all lead and we all follow. You need to decide who you're going to follow."

Chapter Twenty Two

By dawn, Edie hadn't been able to wear her mind down for sleep. She'd nearly achieved what she considered a conscious out of body experience close to three in the morning, something akin to shock, surging with adrenaline, overloaded to the point where she didn't feel as though her body were her own. Displaced, out of balance, she remembered feeling her breath come into her lungs, hearing the blood flow in the dread quiet of witching hours, feverishly waiting for the small voice that never came.

Her phone had rung several times, but she'd refused to answer it. She'd picked up a prepaid phone from a mall kiosk after work and texted Austin and Mona, warning them not to respond back but advising they get similar unattached, off-grid phones. Then silence and replaying voicemails.

"Edie, it's Austin. I'm fine. I'm still around. Found a decent hotel for the night. Planning on going to another one tomorrow."

"Edie. Mona. Did you and Becca make it out alive? Did Tiny catch you? Did she make you tell her anything? Anyway, I'm shacked up and fine. Hope you're not being a bonehead and staying home. I went and got my dog so don't go checking on me. Don't worry. I wasn't followed. Call me back."

"Hey, Edie. It's Becca. I'm having trouble finding out more on these people. Call me."

She'd texted Becca back first and had her call the new, anonymous cell phone.

"So what are you finding?"

"The tragic accidental deaths as ruled by coroners' offices are easy to locate. Just Googling police blotters from online hometown newspapers."

"How are they dying?"

"Hit and runs, falling down stairs, slipping on ice, falling into cold rivers."

The shiver of recall now coursed through her, but Edie couldn't decide if it were an emotional reaction or just her bare feet touching the tile in her shower. Still replaying the conversation with Becca in her mind, she hoped that the warming jets would return her to her own skin.

"How many?"

"I've found fifty-three. All over the country."

"Enough to take to Tiny and Maggie?"

"Is that your plan?"

"I had a conversation with Tiny late in the day."

"You stayed at work until the end of the day?"

"Thought I had to cover for you and Austin and Mona. Tiny knows something. Told me this story from thirty years ago about a guy who unintentionally sold his life policy to the Russian mob who then killed him once they had time to make someone else the beneficiary. Trying to win my trust."

"Do you trust her?"

"As opposed to Taylor?"

"Does it have to be either/or?"

"I'm not sure. I don't know if they will go to the authorities or just use it to push their agenda in home office?"

"Who are *they*?"

"Tiny and Maggie..."

"Maggie knows, too?"

"Apparently, they're really close. They just keep their distance at work."

"Any way to find out who's processing the payments and the death certificates?"

"I asked Tiny. Said we could find out without someone alerting the person."

"So she really does know something."

"I don't think she knows there are over a hundred," Edie has said.

"We have to keep death certificates, but I assume they are attached to the individual policy records and not stored collectively."

"You never know. We're due some luck. Or a sign from God."

"You still think your buddy is involved?"

"What if it was all a set up?" Edie had asked. "What if all those YouTube hero videos of him saving that woman and that kid were practice? What if the guy or guys who were trying to kidnap them were hired by Frost or his friends? Like they were just seeing what they could get away with, trying to see how inept local law enforcement actually is?"

"Most of these deaths occurred outside city limits, where counties would have jurisdiction," Becca said.

"County coroners instead of city officials."

"Exactly. No one to chase them, no one to follow up. Counties are going broke all over the country with decreased tax revenue from the economic downturn. It's the perfect time to stage accidents."

The shower was ineffective in reuniting her mind and body. Edie had tried several things throughout the night to feel inside herself: lying on her bed with her head hanging off the mattress until her eyes felt like they would explode from the pressure, eating a can of disgusting, lukewarm hominy she'd impulsively purchased at the 24-hour grocer down the street at 12:45am, sitting on the floor in a corner of her living room between the couch and love seat for a different visual perspective, sticking her head in the freezer while the microwave counted down five minutes. She was her own ghost, trapped for eternity in the senseless routine of getting ready for work when the sun finally rose.

It reminded her of an obscure Nicole Kidman movie where the ending's twist became that Kidman and her children were the spirits, in soulless denial of their own deaths. That the others occupying their house were the actual living.

Brushing her teeth, blow-drying and straightening her hair, putting on her makeup, everything appeared insignificant and trivial until she realized there were ten dozen people who were forever unable to complete such mundane tasks.

He was in on it.

So was Taylor.

They'd hired some nameless, faceless criminals to carry out the carnage.

They knew from the beginning that they were going to kill people. They'd planned on it, planned around it, knew who they could use on the inside.

"What if there had been someone else who'd survived Tiny and Maggie?" Edie heard herself ask out loud. Someone dedicated to Taylor. Someone who appeared to spin off the corporate track from marketing and sales support to compliance or finance then became buried in policy processing or claims. Maybe that's how Tiny could find out so quickly without causing a stir.

With only a vague memory of driving to work, fighting traffic, remembering to stop at red lights, check for pedestrians at turns, the next time Edie felt herself become aware, she'd arrived at work, badged in at the front desk, ridden the elevator, logged into her computer, sent Frost an email asking to schedule another lunch, received his out of office notification, and knocked on Tiny's door again.

Tiny looked expectant.

Edie took a seat and stared at her boss for an uncomfortable moment. "Who is she?" The words sounded foreign. Like she was asking a boyfriend about another lover.

"Who is who?" Tiny asked.

"Who is the woman who once worked under Taylor then got promoted to you and is now working in processing or claims?"

A grin slithered across Tiny's face. "Now you're getting it, Firebaugh."

"How much do you know?" Edie growled.

Tiny rose from her seat and popped her neck with a heavy sigh. "I appreciate how hard it must be for you to give up what you've found. It would scare the dinner right out of me, and no telling which end it would take out."

"What do you know?" Edie asked again, raising her voice.

Tiny paused and met her determined, unflinching stare. "I know enough to know it's horrifically bad."

"People are dead." Edie swallowed hard, but the lump kept coming.

"We're an insurance company," Tiny said at length. "We deal with dead people all the time. You'll have to be more specific."

"Okay, then." Edie leaned forward and cleared space on Tiny's desk for her elbows. "No one lives past their second annuity payment in specialty market annuities."

Tiny stumbled back. Her deformed chair caught her weight and groaned. "How many?"

"One hundred and twenty-one so far."

"Becca could see that from the raw data file?"

"That was the easy part."

Tiny grabbed some errant papers and fanned herself. Her coughing became a hack which devolved into choking. "That's why you all fled yesterday." She reached for a bottle of water at the edge of her desk and, after fighting with its cap, guzzled.

"I don't know where my team is, and I told them I can't know," Edie continued. "There's too much money in commissions and override to Taylor, not to mention what the company is retaining from no death benefit proceeds on the policies. They'll kill us all, Delores. Even you. Even Maggie. Frost has earned twelve million. Not two a year for three years. And Taylor has six million on his own."

"And you had the guts to come back to work instead of running to the police?" Tiny asked.

"Everything I have is circumstantial," she explained. "It's enough to make us disappear but not enough to convict or even indict."

Tiny's coughing and hacking had brought on tears. Veins encircled her eyeballs and heaved from her forehead. "You were asking me about someone."

"I'm making a profile," Edie said. "Someone who can live in obscurity, who is fueled by it. Someone close to Taylor, or who was once close to Taylor. Someone he sent you that you couldn't get rid of."

"One of his women?" Tiny asked with a nod of understanding.

"She's still emotionally attached to him, maybe even still in love with him," Edie said. "Sociopathic enough to maintain a normal lifestyle. Married, with kids. She clocks in, does her boring eight-hour operations jobs, has to stay late a couple of nights every two weeks for month-end close of business or first of the month reporting. Gets her fix from Taylor. Processes the death certificates to stop the annuity payments. Doesn't ask about it. Doesn't care. Someone getting juice on the side but knows how to hide it. It's not her shiny new car, it's her husband's. He's the one with the great job, not me. He's why we live in Edina, not me. He's the one who brings in the money to keep our kids in private school. His company sends us on extravagant vacations."

"That's extremely specific," Tiny replied.

"I've seen it in the Colorado Springs regional office," Edie said. "When the executives would visit, all the women would shun one of their coworkers for a couple of weeks, especially after she'd come to work with new jewelry or a new outfit, new shoes, new hairstyle, an unmentioned boob job. That's what finally made me think there was something to the rumors. Three kids, same husband, simple man who loves her so much he has no clue."

The air had left Tiny. She was nearing hyperventilation.

"So you need to tell me who this Debbie Doestaylor is."

"Marissa Tolbert," Tiny said. "It's probably Marissa Tolbert." No color remained in her cheeks. Most has fled down her neck except for minute lines along her eyelids.

Edie felt the urge to kill, a nanosecond flashpoint where her rage met its zenith. Had it been prolonged, had it been tinged with a layer of vengeance, Edie would have been mortified. The feeling could have tattooed her; the birthmark found on every person's soul would have grown. *That is the difference between justice and vengeance,* Edie thought. *Vengeance left no paper trail, no reports to file, nothing for notarization.*

Her mind and body realigned in that moment. Edie Firebaugh had returned to herself. "What's her story?" she asked.

Tiny sat down. "There isn't a story. That's what makes me think it's her," she replied. "She's been here for about ten years. Has a couple of kids. Two boys if I remember right. For all I know now, she has another."

"So no story?" Edie asked. "No accidental pregnancy that forced the promotion to you or Maggie..."

"No, nothing. She was probably the seventh or eighth he'd sent over to us. She worked in compliance for about six months after a year and a half as his administrator. Had absolutely no qualifications for marketing or sales support," Tiny said. "But even then, she didn't act like the others. She wasn't secretive. She wasn't guilty. She was the cleanest he'd sent until your team."

Edie wasn't convinced. "Do you still know her? Ever see her around?"

"I see her every once in a while, coming from the cafeteria or in the parking garage," Tiny said. "She always looks me in the eye, but never smiles, never waves, never really acknowledges me."

"What makes you think it's her if she acted so normal?"

Tiny raised her hand to count on her fingers. "She works in policy processing. She's a supervisor down there now, so she has access to most, if not all, lines of business."

"Okay."

"But that's what weird, Edie," Tiny said. "She's nothing special. She's a nobody. She would completely escape notice."

"Can you pull up her file from HR?"

Tiny swiveled around to her computer. "Shouldn't be too difficult. I'll at least be able to pull her performance reviews from when she was in our department." She opened an internet browser and accessed the human capital website. Flying through the log in screens, she'd ran a date range report within seconds.

Edie rose from her seat and scooted around the desk for a better view. Tiny's monitor displayed a list of names, all underlined as links. Edie pointed to the woman's name, and Tiny clicked on it.

Up came the profile and picture for Marissa Tolbert.

"She's unremarkable," Edie said. "Just like the executives' women in Colorado Springs."

Tiny chuckled with relief. "Why does there have to be a history, Firebaugh? This isn't TV. It's the girl next door. Could be just money keeping her secret. She doesn't have to still sleep with Taylor."

Too focused on the screen, Edie didn't question Tiny's defense of the woman. "She just looks like everybody else."

Marissa Tolbert's picture was full color but unastonishing. She had shoulder-length dark brown hair, minimal makeup, a regular Minnesota gene pool face and stone washed complexion. Her eyes were just as brown. From her face, she didn't appear shapely but also wasn't over or underweight. *She's just there,* Edie thought. *She's just present, available.*

"Maybe I'm wrong on the lover part," Edie muttered.

Tiny shot her a sideward glance. "Just don't get swallowed up in the mystery."

"It's hard not to vilify her," Edie said. "People are dying. This isn't like terminating some dufus agent." She held her head in her hands again, but the sensation felt foreign. "I watch too many of those deep cable Discovery and Bravo sub-channels. Like old reruns of *48 hours* and *To Catch a Predator*. But now they have new series on love triangles and plots to kill the husband or wife for the money. They're never gorgeous or hideous, like cartoon villains or succubae. They always look like people you've forgotten in your high school yearbook. It's always a let down. We're trained to look for the archetype. That's the cold dead shocker of those shows. It could be happening to your neighbors, the elongated raspy death rattle from the key bowl era."

Short of breath, Tiny chuckled again and then grabbed her chest. "I feel like I've got a lot of trapped gas in my ribcage. That or horrible acid reflux."

Edie returned to her seat. "You're right. This is all still circumstantial. We can't prove she's working with Taylor. We can't prove Frost is knocking these people off."

"Got any ideas?" Tiny asked.

"That's why I decided to bring it to you," Edie said, shaking her head. "You're the boss. You need to help me figure it out."

"What do we need?"

"We need a report that can establish her connection," Edie said. "Something from the internet servers or VPN that shows her accessing the specialty annuity policy records and whatever the system is for processing claims or changing payments from living benefits to death benefits."

"It's called NetSweep," Tiny replied. "It's the repository for death certificates. But just because she's processing the stops on the annuity payments doesn't make her guilty."

"We don't have to show guilt," Edie said. "We just have to show she's the one who processes them. Or if it's really not her because my profile is off, we need to find out who *is* doing the processing."

Tiny nodded. "Then we can turn that over to the authorities and they can work a deal with her once they find out more, like if she's getting a cut from Taylor or Frost. They could seize her accounts in their investigation and scare her with jail time unless she gives them up."

"You got it," Edie said. "But we need to think about how much time we have before people start getting suspicious. I need cover for my team. Who else knows Maggie sent you the file?"

"No one," Tiny said. "She pulled it herself. She has access to all the actuarial systems."

"So it wouldn't look funny her retrieving that file? Has she had access from the start?"

"Unless someone was looking for it..." Tiny said, ignoring Edie's dig.

"Or put a warning system on the file being accessed."

"That's good, Firebaugh, but would Taylor be that sophisticated?"

"We can't assume he isn't," Edie said. "It would put us in more danger."

"Okay, so how much time do we have?"

"It's been about twenty-four hours now," Edie said. "You need to get to Maggie and disappear. Both of you. It's Thursday.

So just leave work early and get away for the weekend. Maybe take Monday off."

"Okay, I'll call her..."

"No, when I leave, walk over and take her out of the building," Edie said.

"What are you going to do?"

"I need access to that NetSweep so I can get to those death certificates on the rest of the dead annuitants."

Tiny shook her head. "If they're looking, they'll be able to track your access point on the VPN. Trace back your IP address to your computer if not your location."

"I have Becca using coffee shop wireless in the 'burbs as close to police stations as she can get. She's only staying for an hour at a time then moving," Edie explained. "They'll be able to tell it's her computer, but not her location."

"No, I'll have Maggie pull some favors. That will be faster," Tiny said. "What are you going to do then?"

"I'll have Mona tail this Marissa lady. That will be good for her and Austin to do together. They'll be together and in a car so they can get away easily if they need to."

"Will they be safe?" Tiny asked.

Edie huffed. "Mona always has weapons on her."

"You're kidding? Guns? How does she get through security?"

"Not guns, knives," Edie replied. "I don't know how she gets through security, but she does. It's been a don't ask/don't tell policy between us. She actually pulled her knife on one of the agents in Duluth when he drugged her with that date rape stuff."

"Unreal, Firebaugh. But don't risk it," Tiny warned. "The access report is all we'll need."

"Taylor never saw us coming, never knew what we're actually made of," Edie said as though she hadn't heard Tiny's admonition.

"So you just hang out with your whole team." Tiny said, raising her voice.

Edie blinked away a stare. "No, I need to smoke Frost out." Lightning crashed through her mind. "I need to stop by my desk, get some things plugged in, laptops and cell phones. Do you have one of those old video cameras they issued for video conferencing a while back?"

Tiny rifled through her desk. "Somewhere around here," she muttered.

"Is it one of those thin, square ones? Something I can hide that shows my desk area?" Edie asked.

"Yeah, I think so."

Edie rose again. "Bring it to me when you find it. In the meantime, I'm going to milk Frost's ego with everything I have, the lonely woman, desperation, helplessness. He'll come running."

"You sure?"

"He's a sucker for it," Edie said. "I'm the one who said no over and over again. I'm the one the tricks and charms don't work on. Besides, he wants me to start going to church with him. I'll at least get him to meet me at church. He won't hurt me there."

She spelunked her way through the stalagmites of wasted trees, but turned back to Tiny before she lost total sight of her. "By the way, you mentioned that we would have been able to find out more on Frost if we had done more YouTube research."

Tiny cocked her head to the side from staring at her computer. "You should Google the newspapers in Oklahoma around the time he was in college and playing football."

"Why?"

"He and a couple of his buddies led their conference in personal fouls two years in a row. Also, there were several reports of university and association rule violations. He was suspended a few times. A couple of accusations from coeds that were withdrawn for lack of evidence."

"That doesn't help me," Edie admitted. "In fact, it does more to cloud my objectivity."

"Have Austin look into then," Tiny muttered. "There's already a lot of smoke and shade around your Superboy. It doesn't mean he's capable of murder."

Chapter Twenty Three

The hum of white noise silence was omnipresent when Edie returned home that afternoon, but her identity had returned to normal alignment. She had repossessed her skin, her face, her eyes. The adrenaline still popped up to remind her of the urgency, only now the doses were lower, manageable. Purpose had reconnected with wit.

Reminded of the sentiment that old people seemed to die when they lost their sense of purpose, Edie bolted up her townhome's split level entry and unpacked her work bag. The sun's shadows were growing longer, but she wasn't hungry. She'd committed her checklist to memory and needed to execute on it before thinking of herself.

Before she'd left the office, she'd docked Austin's laptop into her own work station and opened a Skype session, connecting the camera Tiny had given her. The point of view covered the expanse of Edie's work area. The intent was to connect to the session from her own company-issued laptop. Tiny was waiting back at the office to accept the video call request. Edie prayed this would work as impromptu surveillance to determine if anyone were tracking their access points to the home office reporting infrastructures and come along to see if she were there.

Once she had opened the window on her computer, she called Tiny from her company-issued smartphone and had her activate the call request on the docked laptop. Tiny's backside appeared on her screen as she scrunched over Edie's work station.

"Can you see me?" Tiny grunted. "I see up your nose, Edie. Move your camera down."

"It doesn't matter what I look like," Edie replied. "But thanks for reminding me not to face my camera. Move over so I can see what the camera covers."

Tiny moved out of the way, which opened up the view Edie had envisioned. Anyone who turned the corner at her office's cubicle wall would be identified. Better still if they were trying to locate the team's smart phones and the other two laptops, open and activated on their air cards inside the filing cabinet just under the camera.

"Looks great," Edie said.

"Did you get that Google stuff done yet?" Tiny asked.

"Austin's working on it."

"Okay, then I'm gone," Tiny said. "Me and my friend are heading up to my family cabin near the Iron Range. Won't be in tomorrow, maybe gone on Monday as well."

"Got it."

"Oh, Edie. I sent you the activity logs into the NetSweep repository. It's her. Her IT ID syncs with every processed certificate for those annuities. And it's linked to uploading them into the system."

Edie took a deep breath and accepted the next surge of fight-or-flight. "Any way to tell if she has access to install alerts on other users looking into the system?"

"My friend is on it," Tiny said. "Pulled those favors with her IT buddies. Didn't tell her to disable them though. Thought that would be the ultimate alert. She'll let me know when they tell her. Good things those little nerds work 24/7."

Edie shared Tiny's chuckle.

"Actually, they're big, hairy nerds," Tiny said. "Shouldn't stereotype anybody, right, Firebaugh?"

"Right. Thanks, Tiny."

Tiny nodded and turned from Edie. "Be safe, kid. Tell your friends the same. Oh, also, just in case I don't get to say it later: Good work on this, Edie. You're, well, you're a good person." Tiny's tone became course and pinched. "Most people are okay, at best. Morally average, just above the cut off for getting into Heaven. You're different. Sorry to have been so rough on you at first, but, you know, it comes with dealing with sinners for so many years."

"Thanks, boss," Edie said.

"Don't be a hero, Firebaugh. Call the cops if you so much as hear a walleye fart," Tiny said. "Same goes for Mona. I know she gets itchy and twitchy. That kind of thing is hard to wash off. Trust me, she doesn't need the armpit of sorrow at the company's art festival aural mapping of her body."

"Delores, you're spiraling off," Edie said with a smile. "Get out of there."

Tiny vanished from the screen with a few ghostly, off camera knocks and bumps. She'd said all she needed to say.

Edie pointed her camera to the wall beside her kitchen table and picked up her company phone to text Mona, Austin, and Becca updates. As she waited for their responses, she emailed Frost that she had reconsidered and would like to go to church with him this Sunday, asking if they could meet where he parked near the basement's fellowship hall entrance.

Her prepaid phone rang. It was Mona.

"Hello?"

"Hey, boss. It's me. Where are you?"

"Back home," Edie said.

"You're not hiding out like you told us? Some leader you are."

"I'm using myself as bait." Edie explained her meeting with Tiny and what they'd set up.

So you're waiting to see if he'll meet you at church?" Mona asked. "That's crazy. What's to stop him from coming to your house?"

"Nothing." Edie could hear a door slam and then another one open. Then the start of a car and Mona cursing under her breath.

"I'm heading home to pick up some clean clothes," Mona said. "Then I'm coming to your house. Looks like you got yourself a new roommate."

"No, Mona..."

"Stop it, Edie. You said Tiny told you not to be a hero, so I'm coming over there to make sure you don't do something ridiculous."

"She also told me to make sure you don't pull the same thing."

"What do you think I'm going to do?" Mona asked.

"As long as we agree to call the police if anything happens."

"You got it." There was a small pause and a huff. "I guess it should be an alcohol-free weekend then? To be on the safe side."

"Can you handle it?" Edie asked.

"Yes, but I don't like it. You better have Netflix or On-Demand. We're going to start a new series to fight off the boredom. This ain't no slumber party. We're not talking about boys or doing each other's hair. Understood? We're going to be locked in a vacancy. Together. For protection."

"Okay, Mona," Edie said. "Just call me when you get to your place and when you leave."

Edie had missed a call from Austin while talking with Mona, so she dialed her back. "Austin?"

"Hey, Edie. You're not going to believe what I found on Google," she said, a bit winded.

"Where are you?" Edie asked.

"Leaving a coffee shop," she replied. "Listen, I think I should come over. You need to see the pictures of Frost's roommate and one of his other bad boy friends from the football glory days."

"Okay," Edie said. "I just got off with Mona and she's coming over, too." It took even more time to apprise Austin, mainly due to what Edie thought of as the adverbs of the update: How did Tiny sound? Then what did she say? How did she look when you told her that?

"So what's up with the pictures you found?" Edie finally earned the right to ask.

"They're both a couple of Texan, cattle fed, human growth hormone experiments gone wrong," Austin said. "They're pretty scary. Like those guys who 'roid up but don't do all the cosmetic stuff for body builder competition. Neanderthal brow ridge and acne heads the size of dimes. I swear one had man boobs bigger than my head, except it's all muscle."

"Okay, that's too much information," Edie said. "What about the other stuff, the rule infractions?"

"Sorry, Edie, but there are a lot of disgusting shirtless pics of these beasts," Austin said. "As far as the rule breaking, substance abuse on these two. Not illegal but performance-enhancing drugs."

"On Frost?" Edie asked. "Makes sense. He does look deflated now."

"Didn't find anything for him on 'roids. But I did find curfew violations, accusations of getting paid by boosters for no-show jobs and four different accusations from coeds. All determined circumstantial."

"What do you mean?" Edie asked.

"It's college," Austin explained. "No one was sober, so no one can really prove if he actually exposed himself."

"Exposed himself?"

"Parts of himself," Austin replied. "But like I said there's no Clinton Lewinsky stain, no smudge of DNA."

"Gross," Edie said. Bile seared the back of her throat.

"No kidding," Austin said. "Of course, with these local papers the accused becomes the victim and the victim remains nameless but drops out of school."

"And there were four different stories?"

"That I could find, yes," Austin said.

"Okay. I need to check in with Becca," Edie said. "Call me when you get home and when you're leaving."

Edie dialed a new number. "Becca? It's me, Edie," she said

"Where are you?"

"At home. How are things coming?"

"I'm at a standstill until I get access to that payment processing system," Becca said.

It took five statements for Edie to inform Becca fully on her discussion and plan with Tiny.

"So Maggie will send you the file from the repository on the death certificates when she gets them?" Becca asked.

"That's the way I understand it."

"Do you trust them?" Becca asked.

Her unassuming monotony made Edie shudder. Becca operated in the binary, she reminded herself. She didn't see shades within the abstract. Trust was either given or taken.

Accept or rejected. Earned or withdrawn. "I trust that Tiny trusts Maggie enough to bring her along."

"Okay," Becca said. "I'm only asking because you know it's hard for me to read people. I'm not trying to question your judgment. I just needed to know what yours is."

"Don't worry about it, Becca," Edie said.

"So now you've set up a Skype camera in your office to show anybody prying around? What do you really think will happen?"

"Probably nothing, but Austin Googled Frost and his friends. Remember when Tiny mentioned that? She found out they were pretty rough in college," Edie replied.

"More circumstantial stuff, Edie."

Edie sighed and rubbed the bridge of her nose. "I know, Becca. But it gives more definition to the picture. It fills him in, gives me an idea of what he's capable of. Four allegations of sexual offenses if not sexual assault? What does that tell you about how he regards women?"

"I understand you have a need to make him guilty," Becca said. "But if he's really that dangerous, why are you trying to meet him? Do you really think he'll confess?"

"Don't you want to catch him?" Edie asked. Her tone and volume surprised her. "I mean we're so good at catching other idiots. And they're just doing white collar, wimpy stuff."

"Edie," Becca said sternly. "I want to killing the stop."

"So you believe, at least, that these people are getting killed."

"They are dying before most experience indicates they should, based on the standard thousand life comparison," Becca said. "All dying from accidents, which for their age groups is even more rare. I found one who was working under his car and it shifted into neutral and ran over him, crushing his head."

"Okay, Becca," Edie said. "You probably ran the numbers from death by avoidable accidents by geographic territory just to make sure he wasn't a redneck moron."

"I did, Edie. Just like you'd expect me to."

"And?"

"He lived in Indiana."

Edie huffed. "Look, yes, I want them to stop faking these accidents to kill people. But they should also be punished for it, right? The punishment for frauding garaging addresses for auto policies is termination of your agent contract."

"I'm not arguing with you," Becca said. "I'm just trying to help you see that you are taking unnecessary risks asking him to meet you at church, turning on all our smart phones and laptops, setting all these traps."

Edie shook her head and rolled her eyes. "Well, Austin and Mona are coming over to spend the weekend. They're tired of running from hotel to hotel..."

"I am, too."

"That's why I want you to come over and stay with us."

Becca became quiet. "Oh. Are you sure?"

"We're all safer together."

"Not if you're setting all these traps."

"Come on, Becca. I know you've seen all those ridiculous seventies horror movies. They always split up the girls and kill them off one at a time," Edie said. Laughter tickled the back of the throat.

"Yes, but there's also a moral bent to those movies," Becca said. "The good girls don't get killed."

"Rules some chauvinist came up with," Edie said. "The realism is in scattering the prey to pick them off. The fantasy is killing off the experienced girls first. Look, just come over. You're spending the weekend at my house with the rest of us. That's final."

"I'm not comfortable with that," Becca said.

"You're not comfortable with anything, Becca."

"I was comfortable working on the seventy deaths left to review to catalog causes of death, moving from coffee shop to coffee shop and checking in and out of hotels."

"But if they are tracking IP addresses and access to NetSweep, they might find you," Edie said.

"Your sense of risk is way out of whack, Edie. You think you're only putting yourself at risk..."

"That's what good supervisors do, Becca. Take on the risk that their subordinates shouldn't bear. That's why Tiny took the certificate report away from us and had Maggie retrieve it."

"But you're drawing attention to yourself and asking us to surround you, shield you," Becca said.

Edie lost her words.

"Are you still there?" Becca asked.

"Yes," Edie said. "I'm here."

"Are you mad?"

"No, well, yes, at myself," Edie admitted. "I wasn't thinking about it that way. I wasn't intentionally shielding myself. Mona invited herself over, rather forcefully. And griped about it. Austin, well, you know, if I hadn't invited her, she would have been hurt."

"Sounds right."

"Then I got swept up in it," she said.

"Look, I'm sure it feels exciting. Getting to catch this bad guy," Becca said. "If I know you, you've been playing the scene of some dark figure walking past the camera in your office and getting the big reveal, like you're filming a ghost on that show where the tough guys scream and wet their pants every time a breeze blows through the haunted warehouse. But I don't think it's going to feel that way if it really happens."

Edie's ears and throat were burning hot. "You're right. I have been."

"It's going to scar you, Edie," Becca warned. "It's going to cause post-traumatic stress, keep you up at night, disrupt your sense of reaction and your emotional well-being. If the killer is who you think he is, you've had lunch with him, gone to church with him, done charity work with him."

"He's been a creep the whole time," Edie said. "I think I can handle it."

"We're not talking about someone who overstays his welcome, or hits on you, or has annoying ticks, or just plain makes your skin slither off your body," Becca shouted.

"I know, Becca."

"We're taking about someone who is capable of ending a person's life, for money. There is no leverage. You have no relationship with him that will matter. He'll try to kill you, too."

"Okay, Becca. Okay. Can we talk about this when you get here?"

Becca grew silent. "Yeah, okay. Let me get some new clothes and I'll be over."

"You have the address?"

"Text it to me."

"Call me when you leave your place," Edie said. "It's already getting dark."

"It's always dark here," Becca muttered and hung up.

Edie had positioned her laptop at the center of her kitchen table. The four recovering blondes sat around it, poking through the Chinese takeout Austin had picked up. The usual giggly hilarity of adding the phrase "between the sheets" to the end of their cookies' fortunes rattled away empty and heavy like chunks of dry ice thrown into tap water.

Whenever one of them quit thinking about Edie's office, another was there to remind her with a nod, a look, a sigh, clearing the throat, a grimace. Edie had remembered to mute her laptop's built-in microphone, but superstition had settled among them, within them.

Austin and Mona had argued over the second bedroom. Becca claimed the futon in the split-level's basement as soon as she'd made her entrance. Mona, losing the heated debate given Austin's four bags compared to her two, opted for the recliner in the living room, facing the TV.

After dinner, Becca helped with the dishes. Mona glued herself to the recliner and activated Edie's Netflix account into her smart flat screen. Austin passed around her prepaid phone, showing pictures of Frost's hideous college buddies. They all agreed that had these two kept their builds, they could have easily been the kidnappers in the YouTube videos but admitted it was hard to make out their forms in the grainy shots as they were completely covered in black.

Mona dictated some drama series about zombies, but no one really watched.

Edie settled on the end of her couch where she could see any change on her computer screen.

Becca excused herself and headed downstairs, carrying a massive book written by some Robert Jordan. Mona mentioned knowing who it was.

Into the fourth undead episode, Edie brought herself from a long reverie where one evaluated life on a subconscious level. Daydreams without flight, whimsy or awareness. Those from once returned left one feeling wiser, older, exhausted. Strings of non-linear memories bouncing from childhood to work to her family to relationships in a logic unknown to the waking mind. Stretching, she scanned the room. Austin had nodded off. Mona's expression was locked in sensory overloaded, impersonating the limping, rotting flesh on TV. Edie could hear Becca downstairs turning another page.

Edie glanced to her laptop. She'd disabled her screensaver so her office, empty, looked back at her. The image of the lone computer standing guard, vigilant, made her think of the small candles that burn for three days to celebrate or mourn someone's passing. One hundred and twenty-one people.

A dark figured appeared on the screen. Black-on-black, breathing in the silence, standing next to her cubicle wall. Terror possessed her. Her throat seized. Her heart lunged forward. Every follicle in her scalp went rigid and electrified.

She willed her nerve to reach for a throw pillow and toss it at Mona, keeping her eyes fixed on the screen. Just as she threw the pillow, the being lumbered forward for an extreme close-up and peeled back its hood.

Chapter Twenty Four

"It's him!" Edie hissed. "Austin, grab your phone! Get that picture back up on Frost's friends."

The four huddled over the laptop in shadow drenched darkness. The TV played with light, casting a green-to-blue-to-white glow. The couch and recliner grew and shrank by this silent cadence.

Becca covered her eyes. Austin ran fingers over her phone. Mona stared directly back at the intruder's visage. Edie's eyes couldn't be pried away from her own camera, needing to make sure the lens hadn't by demonic force turned to face them. They all fought for their next breaths, sucking in each other's expirations. The arrhythmic jilt of shuddered and relentless hyperventilation created a disjointed chant within the quiet depths of cramped blackness. The calmness was horrifying as though their energies were being slurped into a vacuum, the void feeding a tornado or a thunderstorm that brought listless, drifting snowfall rather than sheets of torrential rain.

Austin put her phone and the image of Frost's college roommate next to the laptop.

"Hold still," Mona growled. "I can't make out anything."

"It's pretty impossible right now," Austin whispered.

Becca, with her hands still over her eyes, huffed. "Please tell me you've been recording the session to your hard drive?"

Edie nodded.

"Is this live?" Mona asked. "Is he there right now?"

Again, Edie nodded. But she couldn't feel her neck muscles. Once more, she was out of her body. Hovering two feet above them with a binary vision of staring at the white-tipped monolith in her office and peering over the tops of her team's heads.

Mona wrestled Austin's phone away, then with a steady hand brought it up to the screen. The man had turned away from the camera and was leaning over Edie's laptop.

"What's he doing?" Austin asked.

"He's there to steal our computers and phones," Becca said. The others sharply turned toward her to see a sliver between her fingers over her eyes.

"I locked Austin's computer to my docking station with the company-issued bicycle lock," Edie said.

A sharp, high knocking erupted over his shoulder. Then a few scratches. Now, a grunt and the tense cracking and snapping of plastic.

"He's tearing it off the dock," Mona said.

"How much slack is on the USB cable to the camera?" Becca asked.

The camera then leapt from its perch above Edie's locking file cabinet and clattered to the floor, startling the hornless minotaur.

"We're busted," Austin exhaled.

Mona and Edie were paralyzed before the screen. A slithering sound in the obsidian, rattling the camera into the man's gloved hands along its cord. His moon wide face exploded back into view in a disgusting close-up of his eyes and then up his nose.

"Nice," Mona muttered.

Then the screen went grey blank. The session program signaled its termination.

The four bolted into action.

"Retrieve the recording file and replay it," Becca barked.

"How..."

Becca shoved her way in front of the laptop. "I'll do it."

Austin and Mona pawed each other for control of Austin's phone. "Are we sure it's Frost's buddy?"

"I don't know, you were shaking like one of those speaking-in-tongues imbeciles," Mona grunted.

"You had the picture up longer than I did, Ice Queen."

"Where are the rest of our phones and computers?" Becca asked Edie.

"In that cabinet."

"He'll break that open, too." Becca's fingers stabbed at the keyboard and built-in mouse until she'd located the recording. It opened into a new window with playback controls.

"Fast forward to the very end," Mona shouted.

"No kidding, Mona," Becca snapped back. "It will take a little bit to load."

"Stop fighting over that phone," Edie said. "Just get the picture ready for the first time he pulls back his hood. We have to scan both for any unique features."

"Other than nose hairs that just won't quit?" Mona asked.

"Cool it, Mona," Edie warned.

"You need to call company security," Austin said. "Tell them that your office has been broken into."

"What if they have someone on the inside?" Mona said. "What if the security guard let the guy in?"

"When does Wayne's shift start?" Edie asked.

"Who?"

"The old guy who sits at the security desk in the front lobby," Becca said.

"You two know his name?" Mona asked.

"Earliest I've gotten to work is 5:30 in the morning and he wasn't there yet," Becca said.

"I've seen him at 6:00," Edie said.

"So call him at 6:30," Austin said.

"That's in three and a half hours," Becca replied.

She'd arrived at the point in the footage where the Neanderthal had scraped back his hoodie from his high ridged brow and expansive forehead.

"Okay, there he is," Edie said. "Where's the phone?" Austin handed it to her. "Alright, take a good look, ladies. Tell me if you see anything that matches."

Mona pointed to the screen. "There's a shadowy bump on the edge of his eyebrow and in the picture of shirtless Roido the Hutt shot it looks more like a mole."

"I see it," Austin said.

"Look for scars or something," Becca said.

"There!" Edie hissed. "There's a nick on his nose. Right nostril, and a claw scar on his upper lip. Like he got into a fight with a cat."

"Same here on the college picture," Austin said.

"Then it's the same guy," Edie said in a hushed tone. Her ankle buckled beneath her and her knees gave. Grabbing the chair next to her, she slid into it.

"It's a good indication," Becca said. "But we still don't..."

"Enough!" Edie said and slammed her hand down on the table. The laptop bounced against Becca. "It's him. It's always been him. I swear if I hear the word circumstantial again, I'm going to explode."

Becca looked down and pushed herself away from the table. "I'm sorry, Edie."

Edie cupped her ears in her hands and fought down fiery, acidic tears. "It's him and it's Taylor, and it's his friends from college on the YouTube videos. And now he's sent one to my office to steal our stuff. And when they trace the Skype session and the IP address, they'll have my address and come here."

"Has Tiny gotten back to you on the certificate report from Maggie?" Becca asked.

With great effort, Edie raised her head and looked up to her. "What?"

"Stay focused," Becca said. "There's still time. The computers lock whenever they are undocked. It will take time for them to hack through the encryption. They'll need to take it to someone who can override your sign on through administrative privileges. We have until sunrise at minimum before they know where we are."

Mona and Austin joined Edie at the table.

"I haven't checked my email," Edie said. "I don't know if Tiny sent me anything. My phone's on the counter there. Hand it to me, Becca."

Becca grabbed the phone and slid it to Edie.

"They already have our computers and phones. They knew where they needed to look based on the VPN, so they already have the inside connection," Edie said as she scrolled through her emails.

"Then we don't really have that kind of time," Mona said.

"Call the cops and have them do hourly drive-bys," Austin suggested. "Explain that you think you're being stalked. They pretty much have to when you call in and request it. Otherwise it could be a huge lawsuit against the city."

"How do you know that?" Mona asked.

Austin shot her a weary look. "Trust me. I've had my share of morons standing in the parking lot or front yard, blasting Peter Gabriel from a boom box."

"Why is all the sappy sweet stuff in movies always creepy and terrifying in real life?" Mona asked.

"Because men write those scripts and then a casting director gets a really good looking male lead," Austin explained. "In real life, well, you know what they look like."

"So you're suggesting we stay here?" Becca asked.

"We're safer than scattering and running all over the metro," Mona said. "They can hunt us down and run us off the road out there."

"Yeah, they seem pretty good at making murders look like accidents," Austin said. "Hard to stage an accident with four women dying in the same townhome."

Edie tossed her phone across the table to Becca. "Food poisoning, mostly botulism."

"Seventy times?" Becca asked.

"What are you talking about?" Austin asked.

"The death certificates on the rest of the victims say cause of death is food poisoning, according to Tiny and Maggie," Edie explained.

"Well that's one way to kill us all in one place," Mona said. "Force-feed us rotting chicken."

"What do we do, boss?" Becca asked. "It's your call."

"We stay here," Edie said. She rose from the table and popped her neck. "My trap worked. I didn't think it would, but it did. We spread shot out a lot of activity on the server then moved all the gadgets to one location. They came and stole them and found out we were recording it."

"So you're going to call the cops, right?" Austin asked.

"Right now," Edie said. She crossed into the kitchen and grabbed her landline phone. "Then after Wayne gets into work, I'll report the break in to him."

"What do we do until then?" Mona asked.

"It's Frost's move. We have nothing but time to prepare for it," Edie replied. "But it's his to make. Whether he gets back to me about meeting him at church, or they try to break into my house. I know they're coming."

"If you were recording on your end of the video conference, was it being recorded on the other end?" Austin asked.

Edie shook her head. "Even if it was, I had my camera pointed to the wall."

"But who accepted the conference request from your office?" she asked.

Edie covered her mouth. "Tiny set it up on that side."

"So when they find out where we are, they'll find out that she helped you," Becca said. "You need to warn her that they broke in."

Mona grabbed Edie's hand as she was reaching for her company phone. "Call her on your prepaid."

"She won't recognize it, and if I leave her a message she might not get it in time," Edie said. "She talked about her plan on camera about heading up to her lake cabin in the Iron Range."

"Maybe that was a diversion," Austin suggested.

"I know she's smart enough for that, but we can't take the risk," Edie said.

"There's no telling if she'll even have cell phone reception out there," Becca said.

"I know but I was going to email her, too. Those usually go through fine," Edie said.

"But if they're watching..."

"Mona, we don't know if Tiny has another cell phone," Edie said. "She certainly hasn't contacted me from a different number." She pulled her wrist free from Mona and dialed Tiny's number.

A growl erupted after five rings. "Who is this? Is this Edie?"

Edie could hear hacking and snorting and then another voice mumbling close by. "Tiny, yes, it's Edie."

"Dear God, are you okay?"

"Yes, we're all fine."

"Wake up, Mags. It's Edie." A pause, then, "Okay, okay. We're both up."

"Don't tell me where you are," Edie said.

"We're not where I said we'd be if you're worried," Tiny said.

"A man we think matches the photos we found of Frost's college roommate just broke into my office and ripped the laptop out of the docking station," Edie said. "We think he got the other computers and phones, too."

"Did you call the police?" Tiny barked.

"No, we have the recording from the video conference though."

"Judas Priest, Edie, call the cops!" Tiny bellowed. "The company building has been broken into and now they have your computers. What were you waiting on? When did this happen?"

Edie snapped to get Becca's attention. "Call the police. Use my landline."

"Tell her we also want the local cops to do drive-bys," Austin said.

"I heard her," Tiny replied.

"We were going to tell Wayne as soon as he came to work this morning," Edie said. "We thought we could trust him. We also thought that the night security guard might have let the guy in so we didn't want to call over to him."

"Give me the phone," came Maggie's tight voice.

"Why? What do you want to say?"

"Just give me the phone, Dee."

Muffles and murmurs filled Edie's ear.

"Edie, it's Maggie."

"Who's Dee?" Edie asked. "Is there someone else there?"

Another awkward pause. "I call Delores Dee outside of work, Firebaugh."

"Sorry."

"Listen, your little theory about Marissa won't hold up. We sent you the file on her processing the stop payments, but she's not in with Taylor."

"Okay. It was just a profile in my head," Edie said.

"Clear your head, Firebaugh. You and your team are playing this way too loosely not calling the cops, and setting up this little ruse. You need to get out of the realm of fantasy or you're going to get hurt. You and your people."

Edie swallowed down the swelling lump of humiliation. "Understood."

"Geez, it might be too late," Maggie continued. "What did you think? That your boyfriend would confess to you on your way to church? You Catholics and confession. It doesn't work that way when the guy's going around killing policyholders."

"Okay, Mags. I got it!" Edie yelled.

Austin and Mona threw shock at her with their eyes. Becca slowly hung up the phone with the police.

"I don't need a lecture based on short-term hindsight, Waller," Edie continued. "Either you've got something useful to tell me, or you can put your buddy back on the phone. Right now, I'm not a subordinate. I'm just one woman trying to keep myself and my friends from the bad guys. So knock it off!"

"Okay, Edie. Calm down. It's Tiny."

"Listen, sister, I was only calling to warn you that if you hit record on the video conference before you left the office, they'd have a good idea of where you two were."

"We're not where I said," Tiny retorted.

"Fine. Tell your pal that if you two were so concerned about our well-being you wouldn't have hoodwinked us into your little power play with Taylor in the first place, and you would have called the police as soon as you knew these people were dying, and you sure wouldn't have let me set that trap and go back home without better advice."

"I said calm down, Edie," Tiny said. "We're all terrified. It's going to be okay."

Austin, Mona, and Becca held silent Os with their faces but kept their eyes locked on Edie.

"Well, you can write me up on Monday if I haven't tendered my resignation by then," Edie said. "Because nobody signs on for this kind of detail. There's not a corporate ladder or jungle gym to climb from this point. You and your little friend have had it in for Taylor for decades and she's going to have to explain to the grand jury just how she turned a blind eye to this actuarial data before I forced her hand and yours. So enough with the berating. I'm going to save the day and you two can crawl over to Canada as far as I'm concerned." Edie hung up the phone and tossed it across the table.

Becca dared to speak first. "So the cops are heading down to the office now and patrolling here. I take it we're on our own."

Edie pressed her hands flat on the table to keep her fingers from vibrating. "We were always on our own. We've been on our own since we relocated." With the right kind of eyes, eyes Edie didn't know she had, she could now see how that statement settled over her team; their shoulders slumping, their heavy, dark circled eyes puffing, their chins shaking back and forth.

"Did you just quit?" Austin asked.

"I don't know," Edie said with a relieved chuckle.

"Do you think Frost and his people will find Tiny and Maggie?" Becca asked.

"Who knows?" Edie pulled herself up from the table. "We need to figure out shifts for keeping watch."

"Do you think other people know about Maggie and Tiny?" Mona asked.

Edie scooted between them and opened her refrigerator, looking for a bottle of water. "Know what?"

"Know that they cohabitate," Mona said.

Edie guzzled her water and turned to her team. "Now, Mona. That's all circumstantial, now isn't it?"

"So what now?" Austin asked.

"Who can stay awake for a couple more hours while the rest of us sleep?" Edie asked.

Mona leaned forward. "I've got more zombie shows to watch. I can see headlights from the recliner."

"Fine. I can see them from my window, too," Edie said. "Austin should be able to see them from hers. Looks like

Becca's the one who has to trust you most." The last slivers of energy were leaving her body, slipping out through her breath and her toes. "Wake me if something happens."

"Wait," Becca said, stopping Edie in the hallway. "Don't we need to figure out how much time we have before they come for us?"

"Or even if they'll come," Mona said.

Edie turned back to them and leaned against the wall. "My gut tells me Frost will send his guys to Tiny's if they know where to look. Then they'll stake out our places. He knows where to find me. But he can't assume we're all together yet. So if they don't find those two, they'll stake out your apartments and townhomes for a while. Long enough to figure you're not there."

"They're probably heading to our places now to see if we'll leave for work in the morning," Mona said.

"It's anybody's guess," Edie said. "I don't see Frost as someone who needs to go back to the crime scene for the thrill, but I can see him going into the office to see if anyone shows up."

"Then what?" Austin asked.

"We're here until the cops tell us otherwise," Edie said.

"Do you think we should contact a detective to tell him what we've found out?" Becca asked.

"Why not?" Edie said. "We don't owe this company anything. And if we don't, more people could die. Write it up. Gather all the evidence we have and put it in a thumb drive."

"Do you need help?" Austin asked Becca.

Becca shook her head. "No, I'll be faster working on my own. I won't be able to sleep until I have it ready."

Edie shuffled into her bedroom, shut the door, and had plunged into an abyss before she'd fully settled into her bed.

Chapter Twenty Five

Sleep was a vacuum of space and time. Sounds elongated, like the clock in Edie's bathroom she hadn't known to tick until the silence. She felt/remembered waking up every twenty minutes or so. But deep slumber somehow prevailed.

She felt alone. Even though the warring pressure inside her home and out hadn't changed from someone opening the front door, the sliding door to the deck, or the basement door to the garage. Her house was a cave with its own silkworm ecology that hadn't been disrupted for centuries, and she was the intruder who violated a calm not intended for people. A blip in timeless geology, like the humming of a gnat flying past the ear, so small it carried no Doppler effect. There and gone, no warning vibration.

Then movement sometime after the sun came up.

Someone was scrounging her cabinets for breakfast. The coffee pot's clank, the clap of its lid. A filter's ruffle. Then quiet. Back to sleep.

The sun warmer now. The toilet flushing and shuffling feet and the facet. Then back to sleep.

Suddenly, a cold arm that had wiggled out from under the cover. Naked, chilled, numb then pins and needles and fogged in eyes.

She pulled herself to a sitting position and rubbed her face. She couldn't feel the others, her team. It reminded her of Sundays, when she'd sloughed off the week prior, when she was left to herself, by herself, for herself, wondering what her self was. Wondering whether it'd be nice enough to walk around Lake Nokomis after church.

She looked down, trying to remember changing into a t-shirt and plaid pajama bottoms. She had no memory of it, only yelling at her boss's friend and corporate buddy, and the surveillance video with that hideous, murderous face.

The matted carpet was frigid on her feet. The door protested as she opened it. The guest bedroom was open. Turning into the kitchen, she saw Austin sitting at her table, cradling a coffee mug with a throw blanket over her shoulders. Austin, without makeup and bedhead, was as off-setting as she was refreshing to see.

"Morning," Edie whispered.

Austin smiled and waved then pointed into the living room. "Mona's still out."

Edie nodded and glanced at the microwave clock. 8:45 am. "When did she crash?"

"A couple hours ago."

"Is she a light sleeper?" Edie asked.

"What do you think?"

Rolling her eyes, Edie touched the coffee pot, still warm, then opened the cabinet for a mug. "When did you wake up?"

Austin shrugged. "Thirty minutes ago?"

"How's Becca?"

"Asleep, too. She finished putting the case on a thumb drive. It's on the counter."

Edie poured her coffee and scanned her kitchen for the drive. "That one? With the company logo on it?"

"It's the only one she had," Austin replied.

"When did she finish?"

"She said about 5:15. She stayed awake until 6:30. Called that Wayne in security. He already knew about the break in. Said the police were all over the office. There was no sign of forced entry and they were checking the badge reader log."

"So he had access?" Edie asked.

"Frost could have gotten him a job anywhere," Austin said.

"Or they could have stolen a badge or made one if they have someone in IT."

"Have you heard from Frost?" Austin asked.

"I haven't checked my phone." Edie reached for it. "Anything from Tiny or Maggie?"

"They'd check with you over any of us," Austin said.

Edie yawned. "Maggie could have called Becca." She'd tossed her phone across the table earlier. Now, it was on her circular, wooden cutting board, plugged into nearest wall socket. Punching in her passcode, she checked her call log and messages first. Nothing. Then moved over to her email. Scanning over the daily reports, warnings from IT, the official statement informing all employees of the break in, and the hurried compliance reminder about keeping ID badges and passwords secure, she hunted for any email from an actual person.

Hey Edie,

Just got back into town from a sales trip. Closed a few more accounts. Sure, I'd love to meet you at church. Have to ask why you changed your mind? Thought you were pretty much through with me, but I promise not to make it weird. Just friends and just for appearances.

Easton

Then another sent twenty minutes later.

Edie,

Your office was broken into? Are you here today? I just came to turn in my paperwork with new business processing. I tried to stop by your desk, but it's all taped off with yellow police tape. Are you okay?

Easton

Edie read them softly to Austin.

"He's playing dumb," Edie said.

"He sounds too casual. Too humble," Austin agreed. "Are you going to email him back?"

"No." She joined Austin at the table. Mona gurgled through a snore and scrunched further into the recliner. "Better to give him the wrong idea. See what he does when I ignore him all weekend."

Morning melted, dripping into daytime TV then a battery of game shows before an officer arrived from the Burnsville Police Department to take their statements and the thumb drive.

Thick necked and pink from the frigid air, the officer agreed to come in after Edie greeted him at the door. As disgusted and sorrowful as she was at seeing his califlowered ears, she couldn't take her eyes off them, especially when he peeled off his sunglasses. Adjusting his gun holster and radio receiver clipped to a strap on his shoulder, he took a seat at the kitchen table and opened a portfolio.

"You ladies look pretty spooked," he said as he glanced from Edie to Becca. He spent longer regarding Mona and subtly shook his head and whistled. "Did you all stay here last night?"

"Yes, Officer…" Edie said.

"Olsen, Officer Todd Olsen," he said and thrust out a hand. "I'm sorry. I forgot to say who I was at the door."

"That's okay," Becca said.

He nodded and cleared his throat. "So why am I here?"

"We have reason to believe that the break in at Edie's office downtown is connected to something we uncovered a couple of days ago," Becca continued.

"You all work at the same place?" Officer Olsen asked and waved his pen around to each of them.

"Yes, we're a part of a special investigation team," Edie said. "We investigate agent fraud. Mainly writing bad business or misrepresenting the insured."

"And you think that the B&E you called in is connected to something else?" he asked Becca.

"Yes, our company sells annuities to other businesses to fund their huge giveaways," Becca explained. "Like the million-dollar type giveaways."

"Like Monopoly at McDonalds?" the officer asked.

"Yes, like that, but they aren't customers of ours," Becca said.

"Okay," he said. "I interrupted you. Please continue, ma'am."

"Well, these aren't lump sum payments to the winners," Becca said. "They agree to accept fifty thousand a year for twenty years on the million dollar prize, for example."

"Kind of like the lottery?" Olsen asked.

"Like that from a funding standpoint," Edie replied.

"With you so far," the officer said. He looked up from his notes and smiled at Edie and Becca. Then he cast down his eyes and shook his head. "I gotta say. You all look really, really scared. I can almost smell it on you."

"So far every winner of these promotional awards dies after they've received two of the annual payments on the award money," Becca said. "There are a hundred and twenty-one who our company has processed the death certificates on."

Officer Olsen put down his pen and looked from Becca to Edie. "I'm sorry, ma'am, but did you say that there are a hundred and twenty-one people who have turned up dead after winning the payouts? That can't just be in Minnesota."

"No, it's all over the country," Edie said. "All of them that we've found have been ruled accidents, car wrecks, falls, drowning after drinking..."

"Almost seventy have died from food poisoning," Becca interjected.

"Food poisoning," he repeated to clarify.

Becca looked to Edie and then nodded.

"And you ladies think someone is going around killing these people and making it look accidental?" Officer Olsen asked.

Edie leaned forward. "There is only one agent who writes this business. There is only one person who has access to process the death certificates and the stop payments on the annuities. And there is no death benefit going to a family member or anyone else after the award winner dies."

"Who's the agent?" he asked.

"His name is Easton Frost," Edie said.

"Does he process the stop payments?"

"No, a lady in the company named Marissa Tolbert does," Becca said. "She works in claims. In this thumb drive is the report that shows her log in and access records for processing them." She turned from Edie and set her laptop on the table. "Also, this is a screen shot of the man's face when he broke into Edie's office." She spun her laptop around for the officer to see. Waiting for him to finish studying the picture, she glanced back to Edie. "And here is a picture of a college roommate of Easton Frost's when they played football together in Oklahoma."

Olsen rubbed his chin and clicked his pen several times. "You think it's the same man."

"We can't be sure, but they bear several of the same facial features," Edie said.

"Yes, they seem to," the officer agreed. "So let me see if I got this. You think there is a scheme inside your company where a couple of people are writing these annuities, then killing off the winners to pocket the money for themselves? How much money is involved?"

"The agent, Frost, has received over twelve million in commissions. His boss, John Taylor, has received six million in override commissions. The company has retained hundreds of millions in withheld annual payments," Becca said.

"Millions?" he asked.

Becca took the thumb drive from him and plugged it into her laptop. She spent the next ten minutes going over the numbers and explaining the reports to him. Austin made her entrance. Officer Olsen introduced himself to her and then faced Becca. Austin joined Mona in the living room and followed her channel surfing.

Once Becca had finished with her explanation, Olsen rubbed his face and popped his neck. "You seem pretty convinced."

"I deal in the law of large numbers," Becca said.

"I'm taking this seriously," Olsen said. "I understand you're very concerned. I'm just asking questions so I know better what to look for."

"We called your department about the break in," Edie said. "Your people must have called the Minneapolis police, right?"

"That's right, ma'am," he said.

"They are at the office right now going over everything. Can't you call and have them bring Marissa Tolbert in for questioning?" Edie asked.

"In connection with the break in?" the officer asked.

"In connection with what we're showing you," Becca said.

Olsen leaned back in his chair and drummed the table with his fingers. He looked from Edie to Becca. When that became uncomfortable, he darted his eyes from Austin to Mona. "Dispatch, this is 51NinerI," he said into the receiver on his shoulder.

"Go ahead."

"Need to call the Minneapolis PD and find out the officers assigned to the break in on Washington Avenue."

"Stand by."

He turned back to Edie and Becca. "I'm going to need a physical description."

Edie grabbed his portfolio and pen and started writing down what Marissa Tolbert looked like. "Also," she muttered. "It's best if you have someone in HR go get her and bring her to you. No reason to scare her into lawyering up by having the cop working the scene barge into her office."

Olsen looked over Edie's writing and then looked up at Edie with a smirk. "You're pretty good at this, aren't you?"

"I've been involved in six wrongful termination suits, and I haven't lost one for the company," Edie said. "And we didn't settle on any of them either."

"51NinerI."

Olsen jostled his head to respond to the call. "Go ahead, dispatch."

"I have the number for Officer Harkainen at the scene."

"Go ahead."

The dispatch rattled off a phone number starting with the 612 area code.

Edie nodded to Becca then rose to join Mona and Austin in the living room.

"Is there a place where I can make a call?" Officer Olsen asked as he stood up.

"There's the bathroom downstairs," Edie said. "That's the most private."

"Okay, thank you, ma'am. Is it okay if I show myself down there?"

"Of course," Edie said.

As soon as he'd shut the door to the bathroom, the four huddled on the couch and loveseat.

"You think he's actually going to get that woman leaned on?" Austin asked.

"That's the idea," Edie said.

"She might be able to identify the suspect from the break in," Becca said.

"She'll request an attorney as soon as she sees a cop sitting in the HR offices," Mona said.

Edie shrugged. "If they're smart, they'll take her in for questioning. They can hold her for twenty-four hours without charging her. Hopefully, she has a good lawyer who will meet her at the station this evening if that happens."

"So even if she does finger this guy or even Frost, they're both still out there," Mona said.

"It gets things started," Becca argued. "They could get warrants to search their homes and cars. They'll pull their registered vehicles. They'll have descriptions out on them."

"Becca's right," Austin said.

"This sucks," Mona said.

Edie slapped her knee. "Why? Because we have to turn it over? We can't run it anymore."

"Exactly," Mona growled.

"You need to quit living in a fantasy world, Mona," Austin said. "They're breaking actual law. Not agent appointment agreements."

Mona shook her head. "They won't find them. These guys are too good. They won't be able to do anything to protect us, either."

The scraping of the basement bathroom door against the threshold sent them hurling to their original positions on the couches. Without looking at each other, they waited for Olsen to return to the living room.

He took a deep breath and nodded to them from the top of the stairs. "Thank you, Ms. Firebaugh," he said. "I got a hold of the lead officer downtown. He's established contact with your HR already given that this may be an employee who broke in. He's asked them to locate Marissa Tolbert. She's at work today. She badged in this morning. Badged out around 11:30 am but badged back in at 12:45 pm. Must have taken a lunch. They are sending a rep down to get her and bring her back to the HR department where the officer will be waiting."

"Thanks, Officer Olsen." Edie rose and shook his hand.

"You're welcome. Thanks for the leads and reporting this to us."

"Don't forget the thumb drive," Becca said. She hurried to the table and removed it from her laptop. Handing it to Edie, she gave her a relieved smile.

Olsen took the drive from Edie. "Is there anything else you can tell me?"

"We'd like for you to keep doing drive-bys," Edie said.

"Absolutely," Olsen agreed.

"Can you check in with Delores Campbell and Maggie Waller?" Edie asked. "They are our bosses. And they are hiding out, too."

"So you think you're all in danger for knowing about this scheme?" he asked.

"Eighteen million is enough to kill all of us over," Mona said.

"And that's just the beginning of what we've uncovered," Becca said.

Olsen nodded. "Any of you know this Frost personally?"

Edie set her jaw and turned to face the officer squarely. "He goes to my church. I've gone to lunch with him a couple of times. He wanted me to start going to church with him."

Olsen slumped his shoulders. "I see."

"What do you see?" Edie asked.

"Is there anything else I need to know about you two?"

"Me and Frost?" Edie's face flushed with blood.

"Here we go," Mona muttered.

"There is nothing," Edie began. "Everyone thinks I should like him, or try to date him, or say yes to him about going to church. All until now. Everyone thinks I'm a freak for not being interested in him. You know, he saves endangered puppies while curing grandma cancer, and rescuing refugees from the Middle East and giving them a chance in America."

Olsen's eyes widened with every sentence Edie growled. "Are you involved romantically or in any other way with Easton Frost?"

"No, officer," Edie said. "I'm not. I'm concerned that he may be a murderer and profiting from people's deaths. Didn't the Unibomber's brother turn him in? So even if I was involved with him, does it change what he's suspected of doing?"

Officer Olsen threw up his hands and took a step back, nearly toppling down the stairs to her front door. "Ms. Firebaugh, I have to ask. I need to know what I'm walking into."

"Do you ask men the same question when they turn in women?" Edie barked.

Olsen nervously chuckled. "Actually, yes. I do. It doesn't happen as often, but I do."

Edie took a deep breath and looked down. "Oh."

"Can you get me the addresses and numbers for this Delores and Maggie?" he asked after an uncomfortable silence.

Becca relieved Edie of her post and gave him their cell numbers.

Arms crossed over her chest, Edie sulked in her kitchen. Too embarrassed to look back at Olsen, she stared at her feet.

"Okay, ladies, don't answer the door for anyone, and call us if anything else happens," Olsen said. "Ms. Firebaugh, I'll be in touch as things develop."

"Thanks, Officer Olsen," Becca said, shaking his hand. Within ten eternal seconds, she'd shown him to the door.

"You okay, Edie?" Becca asked from the landing.

"Fine, Becca."

"He was cute," Austin said.

"Don't start, Austin!" Edie snapped.

"I'm done trying to set you up," Austin replied. "We all know you pick losers like Frost. Did Officer Olsen leave a card?"

Edie stepped out of the kitchen and glanced from Becca to Mona to Austin, who was looking over Becca's laptop and where Olsen had been sitting for any traces of contact.

"I pick losers?" Edie asked.

"Yes, demon-possessed, murder-for-money losers," Austin said. "We all saw it coming, but you refused to see the warning signs."

Mona and Becca howled shrilly. Austin joined their much needed guffaws. Edie selected a choice finger and extended it to each of them.

Mid-afternoon found everyone rested and awake. After the officer had left, only Becca and Mona needed to get ready for the day. The initial decision on business causal for Austin and Edie devolved into jeans and hooded sweatshirts. Edie expected Mona to bring out a snuggie before dinner. Her outfit for the day hadn't strayed much from what she'd chosen to sleep in; comfy pants and a t-shirt either heralding or poking fun at a science fiction world.

Edie hadn't received any more emails from Frost. A passive debate floated over her mind on whether to call Tiny and Maggie, but Edie dismissed the notion just as easily. Regardless of what would happen to them or Frost, the Marissa lady or even John Taylor, she remained unsure of her future with the company.

It became the topic over Mona's insistence to bounce between the NatGeo and Discovery channels. Between storage unit auctions, repossessed cars, barns full of antiques and people digging up rocks and chopping down trees, Edie was lost and slightly annoyed by the deluge of jowly, hairy men with missing teeth and thick accents explaining things as experts in their fields.

Naturally, Austin initiated the conversation. "So Edie, I've been meaning to ask you. Do you still consider us employed?"

Grateful for the chance to unglue herself from meaningless TV nonsense, Edie smirked and shrugged. "I never resigned. Did either of you?"

"God no," Mona muttered over a mouthful of sea salt and vinegar potato chips. "They can keep on paying me until they get wise."

"I haven't," Austin said.

"Hey, Becca, you alive down there?" Edie asked, sending her voice into her basement and toward the anti-society of folklore tomes and futons buried under throw pillows.

"Yep, still here," came the muffled response.

"You quit the company yet?"

"Nope."

Edie grinned and shook her head.

Austin cocked an eyebrow. "Think they'll fire us?"

"On what grounds?" Mona asked. "We'd take the company to the cleaners on wrongful termination suits, especially with all the evidence we have of our final investigation. What have we done wrong?"

Edie pinched her bottom lip. Her eyes were drying out for lack of blinking. "I can't see myself working for them anymore."

"I agree," Austin sighed.

"We were just the next crop of young and naïve," Edie continued. "Taylor and Siemens were well-experienced at making me, and therefore all of us, feel special, unique. We're just human capital."

"Do you really believe there was a conveyor belt of young ladies washing out of sales and marketing and funneled into compliance before we moved out?" Mona asked. "That's really far-fetched."

"Is it?" Edie asked. "Things don't change in the insurance world. I dare you to name a more conservative industry other than guns and energy. Besides, I'm sure we could get Becca to create some equation that shows the likelihood of the anomaly coming into the factory after so many others before us."

"We're the anomaly?" Austin asked.

Edie held up her hand to enumerate her logic. "We're the cleanest crew they've ever found. We don't play politics because our accomplishments stand on their own. We aren't beholden to anyone. No one else is clamoring to leave Colorado Springs to move to the frozen tundra. No one considers it more than a lateral move. They underestimated how close we were when we arrived, and how much closer we became once we started terminating agents."

Mona rose and scanned the floor for her handbag. "I haven't smoked in a day. Can I go out on your deck, or do you want me to stand on your front steps?"

Austin and Edie stood up, too, Edie stretching her back and popping her neck. "We can go out on the deck."

"You going to smoke, too?" Mona asked.

Edie cocked her eyebrow. "Why not?"

The brittle snow ice mélange growled and cackled under their house slippers and sneakers. Mona handed Austin her pack and lighter who then handed them to Edie. A rancid, tan cloud accumulated between them and the sub-freezing late day sun.

"I pushed them too hard on the Laurent termination. Especially after Collins and Capote," Edie said to break the daydream laced silence. "I was upset from finding out Taylor had no concrete idea about where we were heading. When and where we'd get promoted. So I thought I could force his hand by a blitzkrieg of district manager terminations, and the threat of shutting down the northern districts."

"Is that why they sent us to compliance so suddenly?" Austin asked.

"You got it," Edie said, exhaling above them. "It was a reaction, muscle memory to a tried-and-true approach."

"Do you think Tiny and Maggie are together?" Austin asked.

"I hope they are staying safe, wherever they are," Edie replied.

Austin took a drag from her cigarette and shook her head. "No, I meant *together* together."

Mona chuckled then coughed.

Edie scrunched up her face. "I don't care if they are. What difference does it make?"

"It doesn't," Austin admitted. "But it would make sense about them being reluctant to attack Taylor head-on. Look for subversive tactics to whittle away at his power."

"Maggie did cut the wholesaler pay to the direct producer channel," Mona said. "Took the hatchet to it from what Becca says."

"That hurt sales," Edie agreed. "Our terminations improved retention and profitability, but the multiline channel has been drowning under higher sales expectations and 60% or less results on goal for the last ten years."

"What about the broker channel?" Austin asked.

"It's a faucet," Edie said. "You want more production you increase commissions or make the product dirt cheap. It works for increased annual sales, but there's nothing long-term about it."

"You think that's why Taylor cooked up this specialty annuity scheme?" Mona asked. "To pad the sales results?"

Edie crunched her cigarette butt into the snowpack. "No, my sense is that it was part of an exit strategy. Six million in cash over a couple years versus an unfunded deferred comp plan and stock options sounds better, especially if he assigned the funds into a separate business, an LLC or something."

"You think he knew they were getting closer to him?" Austin asked.

Edie sighed and stuck her hands in her pockets. "He's old. The world might not make sense to him anymore. Sales have been in a huge slump, profitability was in jeopardy. We were the Hail Mary from a lot of angles. I think he developed a way to cash out and it grew into something desperate once he found how easy it was to kill off the annuitants."

"Figures," Mona said and stomped out her smoke.

"I think the older some people get and the further in their careers they go, they start to underestimate new people's potential and talent," Edie said. "They've grown jaded. They question their instincts and discount real opportunities as a defense mechanism."

"Sounds like Taylor underestimated us," Austin said. "And Siemons overlooked us."

"So who's to say Taylor didn't do the same with Frost?" Edie asked. "He discovers Frost in specialty life insurance. Tests him on his morals. You know, couple of trips to Vegas, couple of strippers, couple of call girls. Maybe some drugs. Over time, finds out his asking price."

Mona huddled next to Edie and nodded. "Everyone has a price. Austin, you going to make love to that thing or can we get back inside?"

Austin thumped her cigarette over the deck's wooden ledge. "Sorry. I wasn't paying attention to it."

"Let's get back inside," Edie suggested.

"We still going no-alcohol?" Mona asked as they returned single file to the living room.

"What did you have in mind?" Edie asked.

"Wine," Mona barked. "I have wine in mind. Several bottles, red. Wine, wine, and then some more wine."

Edie couldn't miss Austin's agreeing, pleading eyes. "I can stay dry with Becca if you two want to cut loose."

"I think we still need to stay here though," Austin said, tentative apology at the edge of her words.

"No question," Mona agreed. "But what do you really think is going to happen, Edie? Do you think Frost is stupid enough to come here and take you to church? He's better off slipping into Canada with his buddies and then booking a flight to a non-extradition country."

"That's the smartest play," Edie said. "I think we need to stay here and ride it out. Who knows what the cops will to tell us?"

"You think they got to that Tolbert?" Austin asked.

"I hope so," Edie said. "That will blow the whole operation up."

"So we're cool to get some wine?" Mona asked.

Edie nodded. "Go together. There's a BlueMax three blocks down on the left at 42."

Austin stepped out of her slippers and jogged down the hall for her shoes in the guest bedroom. "So we just turn out of the circle. Then where?"

"Turn left on Portland, just out here," Edie said. "It's basically three lefts. Left out of here, left on Portland, left on 42, and it's an old brown building with a bright blue awning. It's on the left."

"Easy enough," Mona said while pulling on her black coat. "We'll call if we get turned around or something happens."

"Look out for anyone following you," Becca said from the basement.

Mona rolled her eyes. "What exactly are we supposed to look for?"

"Vans without windows and trucks," Becca said nonchalantly.

"You want anything, Becca?" Austin asked.

"No, but Saturday night's my turn and Edie's," Becca said. "You two have to be good then."

Edie was thrilled to cook for her team. The dish was simple, its prep work minimal. Setting out four plates gave dinner a stamp of normalcy, and she found herself wishing she'd invited her friends over for fun rather than now feeding them out of necessity.

Mona and Austin had returned before Edie had finished the pineapple salsa. They'd unloaded the six bottles of red wine, discussed the order of their selections, and poured themselves each a glass when Edie was popping the butter, sugar, cinnamon, and lime juice mixture into the microwave. It served as a last minute sauce on the Hawaiian chicken dish, a single breast, served over long rice, and garnished with a slice of lime. The pineapple salsa, consisting of diced red and green bell peppers, fresh cilantro and, of course, the pineapple chunks, was the only side.

Red wine wasn't the best pairing, but Edie's and Becca's iced tea was suitable. Recent scarring from lunchables, Ramen noodles, bagels, and Pop Tarts exacerbated their need for a tangible, planned dinner. Their plates and glasses were half gone before anyone spoke.

"This is amazing, Edie," Austin mumbled.

"No kidding. Have you always known how to cook?" Mona asked. "I can't believe you never told us. I could eat this once a week for the rest of my life."

"I know a few dishes," Edie admitted.

"You should have invited Frost over for one," Mona said. "That's how we could have caught him."

Becca rolled her eyes, but her smile was more vibrant than Edie could remember seeing.

Silently, Edie thanked God for the sense of balance, stability, and calm. The notion that such overwhelming peace could come from eating astounded her.

Mona finished her first glass of wine and asked Austin for a refill. Austin downed hers to catch up before pouring more for both of them.

"So what else is on the menu?" Becca asked.

"I'm glad you asked," Edie said. "I have this secret desert for special occasions, but usually they're not so special because I wind up making it just for myself. I think someone once told me it was Bananas Foster, but it's just battered and fried banana slices tossed in cinnamon and sugar and served with vanilla ice cream."

Austin dropped her fork. "You're going to make that? Tonight?"

"I planned on it," Edie said. "What do you think?"

"I think it's about time we had a victory meal!" Mona shouted. "We don't celebrate enough. Even when we hit happy hours, it's just to decompress from dealing with idiots all day."

Edie grinned and clapped her hands. "You're so right, Mona. I'm sorry I haven't been a better host. I've been in a fog since I told you guys to hide out. It's freeing to be done with it."

Austin and Mona sipped in silence.

Becca pushed the remains of her food around her plate. "I think Maggie and Tiny will retire soon. We could probably get another promotion within six months."

"Could we get back to terminating corrupt agents?" Mona asked. "Get out of the broker channel. Maybe go back to the multiline. Even get back to another state or regional office?"

"Weren't you saying Tigard or Kansas City at one point, Edie?" Austin asked.

Cocking an eyebrow, Edie gathered her plate and rose from the table. "You saying it's in your blood now? You have the stink in your nose?"

"Terminating?" Mona asked. "Definitely."

"Being hatchetwomen doesn't leave you soulless?" Edie asked.

"Not one bit," Mona replied. "It gives me the biggest sense of purpose I think I could get from a job. I feel like I was born for it."

Edie reached for Austin's plate. "What about you, Austin?"

"Only if I could start handing out termination letters, presenting the company's case at the review board meetings, initiating the investigations," Austin said. "I'm sick of being the emotional support. These guys have it coming ninety-nine percent of the time."

"You want more of Mona's role?" Becca asked.

"What about you, Becca?" Edie asked as she scooped up her data head's plate.

"Just keep me offstage, no limelight, no attention. Just let me gather the evidence for you guys to discuss and debate."

"I think we can handle that," Edie said.

"So where do we go next?" Mona asked. "I'm not staying in Minneapolis. That's certain."

"Tigard or Kansas City," Edie said.

"Where's Tigard?" Austin asked.

"I think it's outside Portland," Edie said.

"Yes, Portland, Oregon," Becca said.

"That's got to be better than here," Mona said.

Edie's cell phone vibrated on the kitchen counter. She set the plates in the sink, wiped off her hands, and looked at the number on the screen. She didn't recognize it. "Hello?"

"Ms. Firebaugh?"

"Yes, who is this?"

"This is Officer Olsen. We spoke earlier today."

"Yes, Officer. What's going on?"

All clatter died. Becca tiptoed to the sink to clear away the plates and pans. Austin gently set down her wineglass. Mona rose from the table and stepped closer to Edie.

"I wanted to give you an update. A lot has happened since you gave me that thumb drive and I took your statements," he said.

"Okay. What can you tell me?" Edie replied.

"Minneapolis PD has taken Marissa Tolbert into custody for questioning."

"She tell you anything yet?"

"I don't have direct contact with her, but that's really not the most important thing I need to tell you. You might want to sit down," Olsen said.

Edie's back stiffened, and she snapped her fingers to get everyone's attention. "Okay, I'm sitting down," she lied. "What happened?"

"Well, I don't want to scare you, because I think everything will be fine, but the Anoka PD arrested two men for a home invasion at Delores Campbell's residence," he said.

"Are they okay?" Edie hissed. The blood vanished from her head. She steadied herself on the back of Austin's chair. Her look sent shockwaves through her team.

"Is she still talking to the cop?" Mona asked.

Austin nodded. "What's he saying?" she asked Becca.

Edie waved her hand to quiet them down.

"Yes, Delores Campbell and Maggie Waller are fine," Olsen was saying. "They're both shaken up. It was entirely by chance that the patrolman on duty was doing his drive-by when the two men were kicking in the front door."

Edie covered her mouth. "Oh my God."

"You okay, Ms. Firebaugh?"

"I'm fine, Officer," she said. "It's just insanely terrifying."

"Yes, I know you're probably really scared."

"Who were the guys who broke in?"

"I've only been given a verbal description from the arresting officer. He contacted me through our mutual connection at Minneapolis PD. But what he described matched up with the guy who you caught on camera breaking into your office. The suspect's name is Ben Overland."

"What about the other guy?" Edie asked. "Was it Frost?"

"No, ma'am. Man's name is Jake Edny. Just as big as Ben Overland," Olsen said. "Does that name mean anything to you?"

"No, hold on a sec." Edie held the phone away from her face. "Hey, does Jake Edny mean anything to any of you?"

Austin, Mona, and Becca shook their heads.

"Nothing here," Edie replied.

"Okay."

"So Frost is still out there?" Edie asked. "Has Marissa told you guys anything?"

"Edie, you already asked me that, and I can't tell you," Olsen said with a heavy sigh. "In the meantime, if your Easton Frost is involved, chances are he's felt the heat rising. Come morning, he's a Canadian booking a flight to Central America."

"Can't you guys list him as a person of interest? Work with Canada, get him on a no-fly list?" Her hands were shuddering so violently she couldn't keep the phone next to her ear. With maximum effort, she was able to put him on speaker.

"We've alerted all authorities, put out an APB on him..."

"What about Taylor?" Edie demanded.

"Who?"

"Taylor. John Taylor, my old boss, the one who was getting six million in override commission from the annuities Frost sold," she growled.

"No one has been able to get a hold of him. Edina PD went to his home, but no one was there," the officer explained.

"So what now?" Edie asked. "What's next?"

"We'll continue to do drive-bys and keep up a steady presence at your house, Ms. Firebaugh. You need to stay safe. Keep your team with you. It's really unlikely that Frost will try to contact you, but be smart. I'll let you know more when I can about Marissa."

Chapter Twenty Six

*T*here will never be time for celebration, Edie thought as the night fizzled out. *Not for what we do.*

Mona had emptied the two open wine bottles into the sink while Edie gave the update. Becca had convinced her to call Tiny and Maggie. Tiny hadn't been grudgingly concerned about Edie's outburst from the last time they spoke. Nor had she sounded frazzled about her home invasion.

Edie had known more about the developing investigation than her boss. Tiny hadn't known Taylor's whereabouts or that the police had taken Tolbert in for questioning.

The two were now en route to the cabin Tiny had mentioned when they were setting up the video surveillance in Edie's office. They'd been at Tiny's since Thursday night. Edie had added that nugget to her evergrowing list of lessons in underestimation and the power of denial. While fundamentally, the logic of risk management, the very basis of their line of work, dictated for them to go into hiding, the emotion of denial had convinced Tiny and Maggie otherwise.

Edie had made a near parallel decision herself.

The final analysis placed more suspicion on Tiny and Maggie knowing about the specialty markets scheme and its impact to the company's shaken financial position. Edie's core told her they'd known for months but had somehow found a way to prove otherwise until her team was promoted and reassigned. The four recovering blondes were pawns of ever-changing color. Tactical grunts for transactional, translucent agendas. The only way to elevate themselves to the levels of leadership, to strategy over short-term utilization was to leverage their successes into other companies.

Edie felt hollow as she stagger/limped to her bedroom. She heard Austin follow her resignation into the night soon after she'd changed into her pajamas and brushed her teeth. Becca remained locked in her imagination over the fantasy novel she'd glued herself onto. In the recliner, Mona drooled over late-night syndication and redneck reality shows.

Sleep forced itself onto Edie. Her racing thoughts were overridden by a sudden reboot of consciousness where the deep, dreaded black screen prevailed.

Dawn.

Past dawn but cloudy. Grey-pink light oozing from her windows.

Thunderous, panic driven pounding at the front door.

Edie shot up, her eyes sending lightning bolts into the back of her head.

Four long-range thuds on the floor sprinting toward her bedroom door.

On her feet, Edie bent forward fighting for balance and succumbing to the power of her own adrenaline.

Her door flew open.

Mona. "Someone's at the door." Hiss whispered.

A wrecking ball collision shook the house. Once.

Edie shoved Mona out of her way and crossed the hallway passed Austin's door.

Twice. Glasses clanked in the kitchen sink. Silverware rattled.

Three times and a frigid explosion caved in her front door just as Edie reached the top of her split-level's steps. There he stood, huffing clouds of breath, swirling around his head, the only white about him. He was coated in black, his hair blending into his overcoat, shimmering down to his gloves, pants, boots.

He lunged.

Impossibly, Edie was falling toward him. Her heel had given way to the step's edge as she'd tried to backpedal.

He was on her, over her, swallowing her in humid heat and rage.

Her throat seized before she felt his fingers wrap around the back of her neck, palms and thumbs driving into her voice box. No chance for screams, no time not to.

Someone screamed though.

His head slammed backward. Again. Again. And he was off her sliding down the steps, piling up on the landing.

Edie propped herself up on her elbows for a better view. Air refused to come into her body. Something flew over her and crashed into his sprawled form. The brawl was black-on-black, a slender shadow riding the enveloping consuming darkness. Then a muted punch. Hissed, hyper breathing coated with spittle and a stiffening grunt. Another muted punch and a snipping sound like cutting fat from a chicken breast with butcher scissors.

A conjoined scream, hideously harmonious in the high and low ranges. Mona reared her head back. It was Mona. The slender shadow was Mona. She'd stabbed him. Twice. And now was fighting to twist her blade into his gut.

"Stop! Stop!" he bellowed. "It's done. You've killed me!"

Mona leaped backward, dragging her knife out of him, and buckled onto the stairs between Edie and Easton.

His eyes lost luster as he clutched his belly. His breathing grew shorter with each intake. "I knew if I came here one of you would kill me," he spat. His eyes locked onto Edie's. "There's no way I'm going to jail."

Edie pulled herself up on the railing and grabbed Mona by her armpit. "Get away from him!"

"Let me finish," Mona growled. "I want to cut up his face."

"No!" Austin shouted and joined the grappling to yank Mona back.

"The cops are on the way!" came Becca's voice from the basement bathroom.

"Have them send an ambulance," Edie barked. "We need to keep him alive. He can't get off this easily."

His lips shriveled back over his teeth, Frost's grin grew exponentially until his eyes dimmed and locked onto vacancy.

Epilogue

"**O**kay, Edie, check the volume on your headphones. Tell me if I need to adjust it."

The office was faux comfortable. Tissue boxes were within reach from the large, plushy chair and the love seat used for couples' therapy. The décor was a non-threatening, non-committal brown. The quietness was calming, the walls thick.

Edie had spent her first session discussing the attack, and the second session reviewing an outline of the incident with her new counselor. Now, she was beginning EMRD. She placed the headphones over her ears, and picked up the vibrating paddles. "It's loud enough, but the paddles are opposite the tone," she said.

Her counselor leaned forward. "Switch the paddles. Good. Now are they in sync with the sounds moving from one ear to the other?"

Edie nodded.

"How's the tempo?"

"It's good. It's medium."

"Okay, close your eyes. Now, describe the scene. Where are you? What are you feeling? Don't just think about it. Tell me what's happening so I can guide you through the memory."

The sun was setting over the expanse of Overland Park, painting its business buildings in orange and pink. Edie had been commuting from Oregon to Kansas, getting the split teams established with their new members. She'd finished interviewing candidates from Portfolio Underwriting at the company's regional office in Kansas City, and was on her way now to meet up with Austin and Mona at the bar connected to their hotel. They'd been staying there for the first few weeks of their relocation, Austin finishing things up in Kansas before moving out to Oregon to join Becca.

The non-disclosure she and her original team had signed afforded her sessions beyond the company's EAP allowance. Each had received a substantial raise, a full relocation package with a limited two-year service agreement, stock options, and a lump sum spot bonus that was equivalent to eighteen months' salary. Edie had also received a promotion two rungs up the proverbial ladder in terms of title while having essentially the same job description.

Her EMRD therapy sessions with her counselor in Overland Park left echoes in her brainwaves. The semi-unconscious state ushered in reflections and memories akin to sub-sonar naval experiments that drove dead dolphins and whales to land's end.

John Taylor had been indicted.

Marissa Tolbert had made a deal for her cooperation, most likely a commuted sentence and probation.

Edny and Overland were in jail, denied bail, and awaiting trial.

Easton Frost was in a separate Minnesota state facility, recovering from the stab wounds Mona had inflicted during their altercation. He would be tried separately from his minions.

Tiny had retired after a sputtering whimper of a goodbye party the company had strongly suggested Edie and her team attend. According to Becca, Maggie Waller intended to stay with the company for a few more years to protect her beloved deferred compensation arrangement. Mona and Austin had been fueling the rumor that Maggie and Tiny planned to wed once Maggie decided to retire.

Overland Park was a vast expanse of traffic lights, suburban sprawl, and perfectly gridded streets. Finding the hotel bar was as easy as a series of 90 degree turns and absently following her navigation system's advice.

Edie pulled her rented 4Runner into the parking lot without difficulty. Kansas was remarkably warmer than Minnesota, and she decided to take her time, nursing her disposal eCigarette before entering the bar.

Easton Frost. *I was right about him the whole time*, she told herself again. What kind of name is that anyway? The memory of his lay homily resurfaced, but she knew she'd never get closure on whether that testament was fabricated. The vision of him ascending to heaven after spending the rest of his life incarcerated was beyond her ability. She was thankful she wasn't assigned to the judgment of his soul. Heaven is bigger than Minnesota, bigger than the United States, bigger than the planet. She could spend eternity there and never run into him. God would oblige the request. She'd earned that much.

Mona waved her over to the table centered immediately in front of the open-mic karaoke machine. Austin smiled and called out to Edie when she saw her. The bar was a factory stamp of any other attached to a hotel, complete with drifters, businessmen with tan lines where their wedding rings should have been, and middle-aged women who pretended not to notice.

Edie's eyes had dimmed from her once overactive attention to visual detail. The world was blurry, laced with a translucence that filtered out most everything as insignificant. Her counselor had told her that would change over time.

She took her seat with her back to the stage. "How's the wrist?" she asked Mona.

Mona glanced down at the cast on her right forearm and shrugged. "The swelling and bruising on my thumb and index finger have gone done enough for me to bend them again. But I kind of miss it, the dull ache. It reminds me of what I did."

Austin furrowed her brow. "How did you get those again?"

"From forcing the blade deeper, and then trying to twist it inside his gut," Mona said with a snarl of satisfaction.

"How's your foot?"

Mona looked down and rolled her eyes. "First the torn ligaments in the left foot. Now, the deep bruise and broken toes on the right. I'm getting used to wearing a boot."

"So you're over that bucket list item?" Edie asked. "Stabbing someone?"

"It's pretty addictive," Mona said. "I can see how people get hooked on getting more tattoos once they start."

A woman Edie hadn't noticed earlier finished her rendition of Mazzy Star's *Fade Into You*, and returned the microphone to its stand to the eruption of few applause.

Austin gave her a couple of sympathy claps. "So how did your interviews go?"

"Yeah, find us a new data head yet?" Mona asked before taking a long pull from her beer.

"I've narrowed it down to two," Edie said. "Do I have to go to the bar to get a drink?"

Austin shook her head. "No, the guy will come around in second."

"Who are the two?" Mona asked.

"Best you don't know yet," Edie replied. "They're all still wondering what we're going to be doing."

"I get that," Austin said. "They seem to be in deep denial about their agents. Especially the new business underwriters."

"Where have we seen that before?" Mona asked.

"How's Becca doing?"

"Tigard suits her," Edie said. "I think she likes the weather. It's a good excuse to stay inside most of the time. I think I've found the right marketing specialist to offer the position to there. Straight from policy assignments, like you, Mona."

"Awesome," Mona said. "She anything like me?"

"No, he's not," Edie said. "I don't think he carries weapons on his body." She let that realization hover over them for a moment.

A man took the stage and cleared his throat into the microphone before sitting on the bar stool in front of the karaoke monitor. Another song started up.

"So when do you think you'll make your job offer to the new Becca?" Austin asked.

"Shhh," Mona growled. "Shut up for a second." Her eyes were fixed on the new singer.

The intensity of her stare made Edie scoot her seat for a better view. Taller than most, even while sitting, he sported thin spectacles, a light blue button up shirt and charcoal slacks.

"Sheets of empty canvas, untouched sheets of clay," he sang in a chesty baritone.

"What song is that?" Austin mouthed to Edie.

Edie shrugged.

Mona snapped her fingers then winced and rubbed her wrist.

Austin and Edie leaned back in their seats and exchanged a cautionary look.

"Now the air I tasted and breathed has taken a turn," the man continued.

The three remained silent for the rest of the song. When he finished, choosing to skip the falsetto do-dos in the finale, he looked down and welcomed no clapping. Setting the microphone next to the monitor, he rose and shoved his hands in his pockets.

Edie hadn't noticed Mona leave their table and approach the singer. Mona offered him her left hand and appeared to be explaining her right wrist. Edie got up, motioned Austin to follow her, and headed to the bar for a drink.